Crown Of Roses

The Faeven Saga
Book 1

Hillary Raymer

To Rose,
Enjoy the story!

♡

Hillary Raymer

To all the girls who dream, I see you.

Trigger Warnings

- Sexually Explicit Scenes
- Violence
- Trauma
- Mental Abuse
- Sexual Themes Throughout
- Torture
- Blood
- Death Threats
- Poisoning
- Emotional Abuse

"O'er the mountain and through the mist
Is the wild, the magic, and unseen
And none will 'er be as bright
Nor the sun, nor starlight
As the once now and forever faerie queen."

~ *Tiernan Velless, High King of the Summer Court*

Chapter One

The clang of swords echoing in the early morning air sent a rush of crackling energy down Maeve Carrick's spine. The skin on her arms pebbled despite the warmth of the sun piercing through the layer of lazy clouds coming in from off the coast of the Gaelsong Sea. All of Kells was asleep, save for those who had no fear in the face of death.

She looked into the dark eyes of her opponent. The space between them was nothing more than some sandy patches of ground and dead grass, a distance easily covered in less time than it took to breathe. Her heart thrummed inside the tight walls of her corset-bound chest as she tossed her sword from hand to hand, silently daring him to make the first move.

Casimir Vawda stood opposite of her, a fierce warrior with a face she long ago committed to memory. Like the dimple that appeared in his left cheek on the rare occasion he flashed one of those smiles, a grin illuminated by the remnants of stolen youth. He stood across from her, outfitted in the colors of Kells. Deep navy leathers, and pants the color of smoke. His hood was pushed back and a faint sheen of sweat beaded across his brow.

He shoved his disheveled crop of chestnut brown hair from his face and Maeve smiled.

"You're moving slowly this morning, Cas," she called out to him over the shouts of others on the training field around them. She gave her sword a little twirl and the blade glinted in the sunlight. "Were you up too late last night?"

He was on her in an instant.

When their swords met, it was a thunderous song, and she knew the melody by heart. She had trained alongside him since the day she was strong enough to wield a weapon. His movements and attacks were nearly an extension of her own. She matched his strength and duplicated his caliber. This wasn't just any soldier. This was Casimir. She *knew* him.

Arms crossed overhead, he pressed the weight of his weapon and his body against her. "What I do in my free time is none of your concern."

Maeve laughed. They both knew they had no free time.

She shoved back against him and dropped low, ready to twist away, and pop up behind him. But Casimir expected that, because even though she knew all of his tells, he knew hers as well. He kicked her sword from her hand and it clattered to the ground, just out of reach. Grit and grass slid beneath her, and the solid earth smacked her backside. Her head snapped once, and stars of twinkling black and silver danced in front of her eyes. Pain speared from her lower spine up to the base of her neck. She tried to roll out of the way, but Casimir was on top of her, the coolness of his blade pressed neatly against her neck.

She was pinned.

Casimir stared down her, his body pressed firmly on top of her, the weight of him making it difficult to breathe.

"What were you saying again?" he taunted, but the corner of his mouth lifted.

Maeve seized her opportunity. Distraction was often key. "I

was saying that whatever you were doing last night, must have looked incredibly similar to the position you're in now."

His mouth dropped open and he lifted off of her. It could've been the heat from battle, but she swore the warrior's face flushed to a deep shade of pink.

It was all the time she needed.

She dragged her knees up and kicked him squarely in the chest. She didn't miss the fog of admiration in his eyes before he ricocheted backward, and she scrambled over to grab her fallen sword. Armed once again, she barely had time to turn around before Casimir recovered. She sucked in a breath and charged him, leaping upon his back, and this time her blade threatened the flesh of his neck. With her free hand, she gripped his hair and tugged his head back.

"Such a brat," he muttered.

"Shut up," she snapped, refusing to be distracted by the tease in his voice. "Drop your weapon."

"You're not stronger than me, Maeve." He smirked. "You're a warrior. A fighter. But you have a weakness."

"No, I don't," she muttered.

"Oh, but you do." He knew exactly which button to push. "Fight harder, Maeve. Push yourself. Because if you don't, if your mother sees how quickly I can defeat you, she'll send you back to the cage."

Ice flooded Maeve's veins. She froze, paralyzed by the memories constantly haunting her dreams.

"Think about it, Maeve."

She loosened her hold and stumbled back, away from him. But he snared her by the elbow, pulling her closer.

"All that time you spent in a cage..." His gaze darkened and the phony humor vanished. "All alone, while you wondered if you'd fall to your death off a seaside cliff."

She shook her head and a stolen breath shuddered from her

chest. A curtain of dull strawberry blonde tumbled forward to hide the panic. Her throat closed and her knees quaked until her bones turned to mush, and only Casimir was left to hold her up. Images slammed into her. Blinded her. Left her dizzy and sick. Memories from her childhood. Every one of them filled with crippling anxiety.

A frozen metal cage, with a small child curled up inside, dangled precariously on a tree limb over a treacherous cliff. Sea spray from an angry ocean thrashed her, chilled her to the bone. A sinking sun, a starless and moonless night. Empty and all-encompassing darkness, with nothing but the roar of the sea to keep her company.

She'd been five years old the first time.

The cage was her punishment for being cursed.

"Focus, Maeve." Casimir's voice dragged her back to the training ground and he pushed her away from him. "Fight your fear."

Fight your fear.

They paced each other in a slow circle of caution. Each step was the prelude to a dance. The intimacy was there, the knowledge of one's partner, as well as the slow, simmering burn of anticipation. Maeve lunged for him.

The energy was a spike, a jump in adrenaline, fueled by fury. Every hit was met with intensity, every punch was thrown with accuracy. The rip of fabric against steel echoed in her ears, pain reverberated through her while he matched her every strike, hand to hand. Their swords crossed again, and this time she shoved him back with all she had left. She glanced down at her shoulder. The thin linen shirt she wore was torn open, and crimson slowly stained the white fabric.

"You asshole." Maeve glared up at him. "You cut me."

His brows lifted but he offered her nothing more than a casual shrug. "So, do something about it."

She flipped her sword high into the air, caught it hilt first. With that as her stronghold, she swung hard, and the nauseating crack of knuckle and metal against bone echoed in her ears. Her stomach heaved. Casimir's head snapped to the side with the blow. Blood sputtered from his mouth, scarlet and sticky. Splatters of it clung to Maeve's cheeks and chin, even her shirt, but she didn't want to think about it, because he'd recover.

He always recovered. That was the thing about warriors whose souls were owned; they couldn't die. They could suffer, but they could never die. Casimir had sold his soul to her mother years ago, and she never dared to ask why. It was the one subject he refused to speak on. Ever.

She respected him enough to let it slide.

"Shit, Maeve." He spat, wiping the back of his hand slowly across his mouth. His rich brown skin came away smeared with red. Piercing eyes met hers.

They didn't reveal anger. Or vengeance.

She didn't allow herself to consider what emotion was reflected back at her, and instead she rushed him again. Weapon poised for contact, she aimed for his throat. He was quicker than she expected, and their swords drew at the same time. Chest heaving, she stared up at him with her blade flattened against his flesh. But she didn't dare move, because the edge of his sword was pressed firmly to the base of her neck. They were in a draw. Evenly matched.

A steady, abrupt clapping sound pierced the air around them.

Maeve glanced over to see Roth, the queen's advisor. At least, she assumed that's what he was, she couldn't be sure of his exact title. All she knew was whenever he looked at her, it caused her skin to crawl. He wasn't scary, exactly, just...unnerving. What unsettled her the most, however, was the unearthly pallor of his skin. It was a chalky gray, like it had once been alabaster, then covered with ash. His eyes were too light for his face, and his fingers were blackened all the way to the palm of his hands—like he'd been burned.

Roth stood motionless and the other soldiers ceased their training, all of them stopping to hear what he had to say.

"The queen requests your presence." His voice was gravelly, as though he wasn't accustomed to speaking.

"Who, me?" Casimir continued to hold his sword to Maeve's neck. His gaze flicked over to Roth. "Or the princess?"

Roth's creepy gaze narrowed. "Her Highness."

"I thought you meant to address her as such." Casimir pulled his sword away. "Well, my lady, it looks like we will have to fight another day."

She lowered her weapon and Casimir snatched her wrist. He hauled her close, so the tips of their noses nearly touched. He smiled down at her, and that rare dimple of his made an appearance. "And for the record, that's *exactly* what I was doing last night."

He released her just as quickly, chuckling as heat bled into her cheeks. Then he bowed. "After you, Your Highness."

Maeve stood in the long hall just outside the throne room. The floors were onyx and the walls a pale gray, illuminated only by the brilliance of sconces. Massive double doors of ebony wood remained closed before her, their detailed carvings a reminder of her kingdom. The castle was situated at the edge of the Cliffs of Morrigan, though it stood more like a fortress than a palace, with its sweeping balustrade and rugged exterior. Kells overlooked the Gaelsong Sea to the east, and a winding stone path called the Ridge led down to the city's center situated at the base of the cliffside.

The throne room was a place where she was scarcely allowed. When she wasn't on the training field, she spent most of her time in the library, devouring books and tomes on the world outside her city. She was a voracious reader, consuming anything from myths and fairytales, to histories and literature. Reading kept her mind off other things, but more importantly, it kept her away from her mother. Away from the harsh reality that her blood curse had stolen everything. Her crown. Her kingdom. Her future.

The slight burning sensation in her left arm caused her blood to tingle. Already, the wound was healing. She was cursed with fae blood, an affliction that gave her pointy ears and filled her with dark and vile powers. Her mother told her it was punishment from the Mother Goddess for being born out of wedlock. She'd never met her father, and as far as Maeve knew, he was a useless man who snaked his way into her mother's bed, then left her at first light. As she got older, she tried to research blood curses to see if she could find someway to break it, or at least understand why the Mother Goddess would see fit to curse an infant. There was very little information on the subject, and most of it was damning. Blood curses were eternally binding and incredibly difficult to break. While unnatural fae magic ran through her veins, it sometimes proved rather useful, like healing wounds. Her body healed itself and while the heat from the curing wasn't comfortable, it wasn't too terrible either. She would never dare tell her mother as much.

As soon as the thought of her mother entered her mind, the double doors to the throne room burst open.

The queen stood before her, regal in a gown the color of blood and covered in a fine layer of black lace. A silk cape of midnight was draped across her fair shoulders, pinned in place with an oval stone that seemed to pulse with life. The virdis lepatite was the source of Carman's magic. It was one of the reasons her mother hated the fae so much. Their power was exceptional, it simply *was*, whereas hers came from a direct source, and she was ever reliant upon it. The virdis lepatite kept Maeve's wrists bound in cuffs, kept everyone around her safe from the fae magic coursing through her.

"Your Majesty." Maeve lowered herself into a proper curtsey.

Her mother didn't move. She didn't breathe. It was rare for them to be in the company of one another anymore. Carman saw only a blemish upon their bloodline. Maeve was flawed. Imperfect. But she was also the only heir to Kells.

"I see you've been training again." Carman's dark gaze flitted over her, lingered on the dirt covering her leggings and the bloodstain on her shoulder. Her thin lips curled in disgust.

Maeve pressed her lips together and rolled the snide comment off her back. "Apologies, Mother. When you requested my presence, I assumed you meant immediately."

"And I assumed you'd be smart enough to make yourself presentable." Carman waved a slender hand through the air. "No matter."

There was a beat of silence, long enough for shame to carve its way into Maeve's heart. Carman's guards stood at attention behind her, blocking Maeve from the throne room. She'd been banished from there for as long as she could remember. She had no idea what it looked like, and couldn't recall a day when she'd caught more than a glimpse of its interior. Her mother always met her here, in the doorway, like she was some sort of commoner.

Carman clasped her hands together. "I wanted to ensure you haven't forgotten about my guests tonight. Distinguished business owners and other important patrons from the city will be arriving within the hour."

Maeve clenched her jaw tight. Guests only meant one thing; a contract negotiation followed by dinner and dancing. Nothing Maeve had ever been privy to, because her mother liked to pretend as though she ceased to exist. Whenever nobility arrived to pay their respects or ask for assistance, she was told to make herself scarce. It didn't matter if everyone knew she was alive, if rumors circulated of how and why she was cursed. None of it mattered when she was blatantly ignored.

"I expect you will be on your best behavior." Carman arched one pointed brow.

"Of course, Mother." Maeve dipped her head.

"Good. That will be all." Carman's words were clipped and she spun away, allowing the large wooden doors to slam shut in Maeve's face.

She waited for a moment, processing the rejection, and accepting her fate. The pain in Maeve's shoulder had gone numb. She barely even felt it anymore. The barbs from her mother were often the same. Painful at first, sharp even, but she'd grown used to them over the years—all twenty-four of them—and was accustomed to locking such feelings away because her mother made one thing perfectly clear.

Maeve would never be worthy of the crown.

Chapter Two

Maeve wasted no time after her mother's dismissal.

She returned to her room, one of the last actual bedrooms before the servant's quarters. It was smaller, and not as decadent, but it had everything she needed, most importantly her own bathroom. Not that she was shy or timid about her body, but she couldn't imagine having to share a cramped suite with five other women.

After showering and scrubbing away the grime and sweat from her body and hair, Maeve inspected the wound on her shoulder. Or at least, what was left of it. The burning had subsided and though the skin was still slightly pink, there was no mark. No proof she'd even been cut.

She tugged on a pair of leggings that were as snug as they were useful with all of their convenient pockets. She grabbed another linen shirt and though she knew it would be unbearable with the heat, she laced herself into a corset, just in case. Carman reenforced the boning with magic, so the corset acted more like armor as opposed to something only meant to give the appearance of a skinny waist and ample breasts. Her hair was still damp and hung nearly to the middle of her back in a mess of curls. She finished dressing then slid one hand under her pillow, and her entire body reverberated when her fingers clasped around the hilt of her dagger.

Maeve held the weight of it in her hands. Its power caused her skin to tingle. It was iridescent and reflected all the colors of the world: the sun and sky, the mountains and seas, and the rose of dawn. She'd found it by chance one day when she was seventeen, after wandering into the Moors just west of Kells. It had been a sweltering day, with temperatures climbing so high, she thought she would melt. Humidity clung to her skin and left her hair a tangle of frizz. She'd ventured into the Moors in search of shade and cooler air to escape the heat, and what she'd discovered instead had been a lake.

Its surface was smooth, a reflective mirror to the world of overgrowth, trees, and wildflowers surrounding it. The water was crystal clear, a separate world all its own. She'd peeled off every piece of sweaty clothing, dropped them in a pile on a rock, and waded in. She didn't know how long she'd stayed, soaking in waters that moved around her bare skin like cool silk. Floating on her back, her eyes drifted closed as faint threads of sunlight sprinkled in through the overhang of dense trees. She wasn't a strong swimmer, thanks to her endless torment of the cage, but she could float and hold her breath. Basic yet necessary survivor skills. It was only when she was getting ready to leave, that she noticed a glint beneath the surface—a shifting of colors. She sucked in a deep breath and reached toward the shimmering object. Her fingers sorted through pebbles and silt, when her hands grasped something warm despite the cold stillness of the lake.

The dagger glimmered with ethereal beauty. Maeve kept it close to her ever since, strapped to her thigh.

She tucked the blade into her sheath and slipped out the

west gate of the castle, toward Kells. She had no entourage, no guards to follow her around and keep a close watch. For the most part, she was able to move freely. Since no one outside of the castle walls recognized her as the princess, she was perfectly capable of blending in and taking care of herself.

The Ridge deposited Maeve into the heart of the vibrant, bustling city. Shops yawned open, and their brightly colored awnings stretched out onto the cobblestone pathway in greeting. Music flowed from a local cafe, and the market was already teeming with vendors setting up their tables and offering a wide variety of wares. There were stalls of the finest fabrics, fresh fruit and vegetables, handmade pottery and arts, as well as freshly baked bread and treats. The fountain in the center of Kells gurgled to life while children ran around it in circles, their laughter echoing up to the rooftops.

A little girl spun round and round with outstretched arms, her face tilted up to the sun, and she nearly collided head first into Maeve.

Maeve caught her by the shoulders and smiled. "Careful, little one."

The girl grinned up at her with a sugar-dusted face. "Sorry, miss." Then she pulled a flower from the bundle of stems clasped tightly in her small grip, and held it up to Maeve. "Here. This is for you."

Maeve knelt down and accepted the flower. It was a blue wildflower, usually found along the coast. She stuck the blossom behind one ear and smiled as the girl ran off to join her friends.

She was considering heading down one of the side streets and following the delicious scent of something tart and lemony, when the cool fingers of trepidation slid down her spine. She recognized the sensation instantly.

She was being followed.

Maeve drifted through the maze of people and tents, careful to look oblivious, and ducked into a side alley right as a thick layer of clouds floated in from off the coast. On instinct, she pressed her back firmly against the brick wall and waited. Not even a minute later, a shadowy figure darted down the same alley, and Maeve launched forward, forcing her forearm to the windpipe of her stalker.

Summer blue eyes blinked at her in surprise and a slow smile spread across her would-be assailant's face. "You're getting better, Your Highness."

Maeve stepped back and released her hold. She rolled her eyes to the heavens where clouds started to drift in, hiding the warmth of the sun. "You could've just asked to come with me, Saoirse."

"And where's the fun in that? It's a far better idea to keep you on your guard." Saoirse winked and tossed her braid over her shoulder. Silvery blonde hair the color of moonlight twisted back into a smooth plait, and tucked behind one ear was a magenta orchid. She always wore a flower in her hair. She told Maeve once that flowers helped to disguise the stench of blood. Two daggers were strapped to her thighs, and a sword was at her waist. She was lethal. Savage. Trained to be unstoppable, and she was one of Casimir's most elite warriors.

She was also Maeve's best friend.

"Why were you in such a rush to get out of the castle anyway?" Saoirse asked, drawing Maeve's attention back from her wandering thoughts.

"The queen has guests arriving soon. "

It was all that needed to be said.

Saoirse nodded stiffly. She was well aware of Maeve's blood curse. She heard the way Carman spoke to Maeve, how she treated her, how she more or less exiled her to the city of Kells whenever her reputation was on the line.

"Come on." Saoirse linked her arm through Maeve's. "Let's go find whatever smells so delicious."

Together they strolled through the market square, passing numerous vendors and shop owners selling an abundance of goods. The center of Kells had come alive with townspeople moving through the stalls, bartering prices, and trading merchandise. They passed a bookshop filled with cozy nooks, stuffed with oversized chairs and comfortable pillows, and shelves upon shelves of reading material. There were jewelry-makers, blacksmiths, leatherworkers, and any number of store-fronts crammed into the old brick buildings, lending Kells an air of serenity and charm.

Off one of the side alleys, Maeve caught a glimpse of a large red tent with a wooden sign propped up on the cobblestone that read "fortunes". Curiosity piqued in the back of her mind, but Saoirse was already dragging her toward the cart where an elderly couple always sold the best lemon sugar scones.

Maeve took a bite of her scone, and the tart lemons collided on her tongue with gooey white chocolate and crumbling pastry. It was decadent. She bit off another piece and nodded toward the red tent. "Do you believe in fate?"

Saoirse, who was usually the epitome of a femme fatale, licked the lemon sugar drizzle running down the edge of her scone. "Of course. It's hard not to, but I also think everyone is given a chance to change their fate. Nothing is permanent."

Maybe not even a blood curse...

Saoirse had a point. The hands of fate wove a delicate tapestry, and each thread was a soul with a destiny all its own. But how often had she prayed to the night skies for the removal of her curse without a response? Perhaps it was a course she would have to change by herself, without the help of gods and goddesses.

Maeve glanced over at Saoirse who was finishing off the last of her scone. "What do you think is written in the stars for you?"

"For me?" Saoirse arched her brow, as though she'd never considered her own future. She looked out past the city, toward the Gaelsong Port. "Honestly? I believe my fate is tied to keeping you alive."

MAEVE GRABBED Saoirse's hand and tugged her toward the swaying red tent. "Let's go, I want to hear my fortune."

"What?" Saoirse eyed the tent where chimes jingled in the cooling breeze. Her hand instinctively went to one of the daggers on her jeweled band. "Are you serious?"

"Yeah, come on. Just for fun, I promise."

But the moment Maeve stepped inside the moody tent, her blood started to hum.

The air was perfumed, incensed with a scent of cedarwood and orange blossom that was so dense, it caused her eyes to water. Strands of glossy black beads dangled like a curtain, and ivory skulls were perched on stakes. In the middle of the tent stood a round table draped in a black cloth and a clear crystal ball was propped up on a block of wood. Overhead a bronze lantern spun slowly, causing flickers of gold to flash along the tent walls like shadows. Goosebumps prickled Maeve's flesh, and a strange sensation seized her gut, but she brushed off the feeling, thinking it had more to do with the heady scent hanging in the air, and less to do with her own intuition.

Saoirse scowled. "This is a terrible idea."

A second later there was a startling pop and a puff of smoke.

Maeve jumped and Saoirse glued herself to her side.

"Hello!" An old woman moved out from behind a sheer

layer of fabric draped from the ceiling and gestured them forward. "Come in, come in my dear hearts."

The woman ambled forward, and the stack of bracelets stretching up her arms jingled in song. Her back curved with age, she had long, spindly fingers, and her yellowed nails were sharpened to a point. Stringy gray hair fell down to nearly her waist, and when she smiled, tar and some other unknown substances clung to her teeth. She bowed regally. "I am Madam Dansha."

"You can't be serious," Saoirse muttered.

Maeve jabbed her lightly with her elbow.

Madam Dansha's beady gaze zeroed in on Maeve. "You... you are the one who wants your fortune told."

Saoirse crossed her arms, unimpressed. "Lucky guess."

"Sit, sit," Madam Dansha crooned.

Maeve ignored the complaints of her friend, and slid into the chair across the table from the fortune teller.

Madam Dansha stared at her without blinking, and her peculiar manner set Maeve's nerves on edge. She cleared away the crystal ball, and instead pulled a handful of runes from her robe. She shuffled the sparkling black stones in her palm, and mumbled to herself in a language Maeve couldn't quite understand.

"A curiosity, you are," Madam Dansha whispered and placed the relics on the table in the shape of a crescent moon. "Rune of Willow to symbolize a journey and survival. Rune of Apple for the force of life. Rune of Yew...endurance, and the eternal life. And Rune of Reed, well, the Rune of Reed is a symbol of divine might."

Maeve leaned forward in her seat. "What does all this mean?"

"Your hand, please." Madam Dansha extended her weathered hand.

"Maeve," Saoirse warned.

"It's fine." She brushed off Saoirse's warning. This was just an old woman with a knack for oddities. None of it was serious business. All of it was for amusement and fueling the constant wonders of futures, forecasts, and lucky charms.

Maeve reached out and allowed Madam Dansha to take her hand.

She flipped it over, palm up, and began tracing a wide circle around the inside of Maeve's hand with one of her pointy nails. "Your soul has lived a thousand lives. But the one you keep now will define the rest of them. Your future, however, is...unclear."

Maeve frowned. "What do you mean, unclear? That's the whole reason I walked into this tent."

Madam Dansha looked up. Her eyes had seemingly darkened to black in the dull light. "Your fate is not yet decided."

"But do you see anything? Anything at all?"

Anything that will make me worthy of my mother's crown?

Madam Dansha's lips pinched together, and her skin took on a grayish tone. "I see much pain, and the trauma of your past returning to you in time."

Maeve's hand jerked in the old crow's grasp. That hardly seemed like an ideal fortune. She hadn't been expecting to hear sunshine and rainbows, but part of her had been hoping for *something.*

"I see your tears. Your shadows. Both life and death. A path of destruction, and one of creation." Madam Dansha's sharp fingernail dug into Maeve's skin. "All of them leading back to you."

"Well, thanks." Maeve shifted, uneasy with the weight of the words. Her corset was suddenly too tight, too snug around her small waist and wide hips.

"Wait," the old woman hissed. "There's more. There is more to you than meets the eye."

"I don't think I want to hear it." She yanked her hand from Madam Dansha's increasingly tight grip, and the woman's dagger of a nail ripped across her palm. Crimson seeped out from the cut, stark against her light flesh. It could have been coincidence, but the ground beneath Maeve's feet trembled, and a gust of cold air caused the tent to ripple. The old woman breathed in, deeply. She sniffed the air, smelled the scent of Maeve's blood, then snarled.

"Your blood—"

"That's enough." Saoirse hauled Maeve back just as Madam Dansha leapt across the table. But Maeve was quicker. She'd drawn her blade from her thigh and the old woman collapsed upon the dagger. Her eyes widened and a faint gasp escaped from between her papery lips. Yet instead of toppling over in a bloody mess, she simply turned to ash. Her body evaporated as though it was nothing more than sand and earth.

Maeve sucked in a breath and stole a glance at Saoirse. Her friend's face paled significantly. The lantern above the table swung violently, then shattered into a dozen pieces. Outside the tent, instead of children's laughter, screams filled the air. A strong hand grabbed her arm and tugged her backward. She whipped around, ready to fight, and came face to face with Casimir.

"Alright, ladies." He glanced at the pile of ash, blinked once, then dragged Maeve out of the tent. "Time to go."

Chapter Three

Maeve rushed out of the tent with Saoirse and Casimir, and ran straight into chaos.

Tendrils of smoke curled up into a dismal sky, wails of terror filled the air, and the distinctive stench of decay filled her nose. It was so thick, she nearly gagged. Shops and buildings cracked from the earth's tremors, and their exterior walls crumbled, all while citizens rushed to put out a glaring amount of fires. Children were crying, women were screaming, and everywhere she looked, the people of Kells were alight with panic.

"What's happening?" Maeve demanded. "Who did this?"

"Follow me and I'll show you." Casimir took off toward the Ridge. They climbed the partially collapsed stone steps, and once they'd reached higher ground, he pointed down to the city's center below. "Look. Just there."

Maeve sucked in a breath and clamped one hand over her mouth. Where townspeople were running away, soldiers were running toward what could only be described as a gaping chasm. It was as though the ground had simply split open, the realm itself broken, and a scourge plagued the land. Black ooze bled across the cobblestone streets, slowly devouring anything in its path. Leaching everything of color and life. From its center, creatures of the night spilled forth from the chasm in waves, and Maeve watched in horror as Kells came under attack.

But these weren't enemies. They were *monsters*.

A dense shadow engulfed two humans, and when they screamed, it sounded like their souls were being ripped from their bodies. The shadow shifted, moving to its next victim, and all that remained were bones. There were monsters with empty pits for eyes, whose mangled bodies were littered with scales and spines. Beasts rose up out of the gaping hole, snarling and growling, with claws sharp enough to tear a human body to shreds. Demons prowled around the fountain, feasting on the flesh of the fallen, their mouths stained red with the blood of death.

Hot bile rose up in the back of Maeve's throat, but she couldn't bring herself to look away from the scene of horror unraveling below. Anger churned her stomach, and her blood curse throbbed, burning for release. She longed for that power, wanted nothing more than to explode from the inside with fury, and bring its wrath upon all the creatures who stood in her way. It seethed, prowled inside of her like a monster of its own. But if she dared ask to have her cuffs removed, there was no telling what sort of uncontrollable power would erupt from within her. All she knew was something had to be done. She had to stop this attack. Her beautiful city, with its life and vibrancy, was dying.

She spun on her heel, ready to sprint back into the throes of war, when Casimir caught her around the waist with one arm.

"What do you think you're doing?" He held her back from charging into the fray.

"I'm going to help." Maeve struggled against his hold and attempted to twist out of his arms. "Those are my people."

"And you are their *heir*." Casimir jerked his head at Saoirse. "Take her back to the castle."

"What? No!" Maeve kicked and ducked out of Saoirse's reach.

Casimir scowled, his sword drawn. "It's not safe for you here, Maeve."

"And I refuse to stand by and hide away in a castle while Kells suffers." Maeve pulled her blade from its sheath. She plucked a throwing star from her belt with her other hand. "You know damn good and well you need me down there. I'm going to help, whether you like it or not." She straightened and set her jaw. "I'll fight both of you if I must."

Casimir shared a look with Saoirse, who shrugged. "Sun and sky." He rubbed a hand over his face. "You are so damned stubborn."

"I'll take that as a compliment."

Maeve's boots pounded against the deteriorating stone path as she rushed back to the line of battle. She came upon her first opponent, a creature of night. Its bony limbs moved like smoke and shadows. Glowing orbs pulsed in place of its eyes, and it loosed a guttural growl as tapered fingers like birch bark reached for her throat. She spun from its grasp, and its shifting head reared back in fury. The monster dislocated its jaw and stretched its mouth wide, as though it intended to swallow her whole. Spirals of shadows descended upon her. She vaulted upward and brought her dagger down in an arc, slicing through the bark-like arms.

Its howl was cut short as the shadowy creature turned to dust.

Just then, a flash of moonlight streaked before her.

Saoirse.

Her silver braid whipped over one shoulder as she slid across the stone pavement on her knees. In the next breath, Saoirse swung her sword, taking down two creatures at once. She didn't even wait to see if she hit her target. She never missed her mark. Instead, she called out to Maeve from over her shoulder. "Aim for the neck!"

Maeve dropped low and dodged a blow from another shifting demon. She popped up and slashed her dagger across its chest. It froze, turned to ash, and dissolved completely. The corner of Saoirse's mouth curved upward. "Or just keep doing that."

A beast ambled toward her with a hissing snarl, and it towered over her in height. Two massive curved horns protruded from its head and its furrowed brow was so disjointed, it jutted out over a pair of yellow eyes. Barbs bulged from its spine, from the knees and elbows, and Maeve swore it smiled when it looked upon her. With arms as long as its body and razor-sharp talons for hands, it was capable of scouring the flesh of its victims, so the muscles snapped and bones cracked.

An earth-shattering growl split through the sky. She leapt up and plunged her dagger into its chest. Just like the other monsters she killed, it disintegrated to ash.

A whimpering cry sounded from behind her. Maeve spun around to see a small child cowering beneath the wrath of one of the shadow monsters. She couldn't be any older than three, and the creature had already unlocked its jaw, ready to devour her. Maeve took off, sprinting toward the child, her legs firing on a mission to protect the innocent. The little girl's scream chilled her blood, and right as the shadows unfurled, Maeve vaulted into the air, dragging her blade down a spine of smoke.

The smell of wet leaves and decay hung heavy in the air. Maeve scooped the child up, holding her close.

"It's okay, sweetheart. It's okay." Maeve brushed back the

girl's brown hair with one hand. Tears mingled with dirt on her round cheeks and large, dark brown eyes stared up at her. Small arms wrapped tightly around her neck and the child buried her face in Maeve's chest. "You're safe with me."

But no sooner had she spoken, another horned beast emerged, its talon-like hands swiping out to rip her apart.

Maeve staggered back and readied herself for the inevitable. She crouched low to the ground, bundling the girl into her chest, leaving her back exposed to the beast. But the strike never came.

She looked up and found Casimir. His sword moved through the air like lightning. With each strike, another beast met its death at the tip of his blade. Maeve stayed low and held on tight to the trembling body in her arms. "What are these things?"

"They're fae," Casimir grunted from beside her as he took on two more creatures. There was a slash across his chest and the fabric of his vest stuck to his skin.

"Fae?" Saoirse's voice came from behind them, protecting Maeve's other side. But Saoirse's disbelief was quickly replaced with focus as she launched two daggers at once. Jumping over the body as it crumpled to the ground, she yanked her blades out of its chest. Straddling the beast, she crossed her daggers high above her head, and brought them down together, slashing the monster's throat. "These are unlike any fae I've ever seen."

Without warning, the creatures Casimir declared to be fae vanished, as though they never existed. There were a few wails of hope, a few shouts of victory, but the terror they inflicted upon Kells came into view once the fog of battle cleared. Shops and homes were reduced to soot and piles of stone. The sky was dark from fire and smoke, and the world around them smelled of death. The metallic tang of blood lingered with the scent of the sea, and the stench made Maeve's gut clench. She would find a way to rid Kells of this vile attack, of this nightmare of a memory.

The streets were a river of blood. Of despair. Of tragedy.

In the distance, she could hear Casimir shouting orders to the other soldiers. To search everywhere for the source, to see if any more of the fae terrorized the streets, to setup a barricade around the chasm which still seemed to *throb* with something Maeve couldn't place.

A sob broke free from the child in her arms and she glanced down. The girl's eyes were wide with fright as she absorbed the chaos and destruction around her.

"No, no." Maeve held her head to her chest and shielded her from the damage. She eased herself into a sitting position, and cradled the girl in her lap. With her head and back propped up against the remains of a wall, Maeve began to sing softly in an effort to soothe.

"Beyond the shores, o'er the sea,
There's a land where magic blooms and grows.
But n'er will be, the power of the thee,
Until comes back, the one whom she chose."

A prickling sensation crept down Maeve's spine and she tilted her head up just enough to see Casimir looking down upon her. "What?"

His gaze was penetrating, but he shrugged and sheathed his sword. "I didn't know you could sing."

She wasn't sure if he meant it as a compliment or not and was considering responding with a sarcastic remark, when a woman's voice cut through the air around them.

"Cara!" A woman tore down the cobblestone street, her skirts hoisted in both hands. "Has anyone seen my daughter? She's only three! Cara!"

"Mama!" The name burst from the girl, and Maeve

watched as the child scrambled out of her lap, and jumped into the arms of her mother. "Mama! Mama!"

The woman held the little girl fiercely, then her gaze fell to Maeve. "Thank you." Tears sprang to her grief-stricken eyes. "Thank you so much."

Maeve offered a small smile. "It was the least I could do."

Rumbling thunder rolled in from off the coast of the Gaelsong Sea, and the clouds overhead shifted and stirred into the makings of a spring storm. Humidity clung to her skin, and the air was heavy and damp. The first few droplets of rain splattered against her arms and she tilted her chin up to catch some in her mouth. Sprinkles of rain cooled her heated skin and soothed her parched throat. She blinked as one drop, then two, stuck to her lashes and slid down her cheeks like tears. Slowly, the light mist turned to a steady downpour.

At least the rainfall would wash away the blood, the stains of assault.

"Come on, Maeve." A strong hand locked onto her elbow and hoisted her to her feet. She found herself looking up into Casimir's hooded face, his eyes cold. Furious. "We need to get back and brief the queen on what happened here tonight."

He didn't mean that, of course. It was just his way. To make Maeve feel as though she was valued, like her opinion mattered. He would be the one informing her mother of what they witnessed tonight. Not her.

"What are we going to do about that?" She nodded to the chasm, to where the realm still looked as though it had been split in half. A scorch of black death had torn through the center of the city, destroying all that was green and living. Decay and rot marked its path. It pulsed with life. With death. With magic.

"I don't know." He jerked his head toward the castle and

they started up the Ridge. "But if we don't stop it soon, it's only a matter of time before it consumes all of Kells."

Saoirse fell into step beside them. "What do you mean?"

Casimir glanced over at both of them, his dark eyes unreadable. "It's spreading."

"So," Saoirse drawled and pretended to file her fingernails with the edge of one of her blades. She was perched on Maeve's bed with one leg crossed over the other. "Are we going to talk about what happened?"

Maeve twisted her hair back behind her, then secured the curls in place with a couple pins. She had just finished washing the grime and filth of battle from her hands and face, when Saoirse knocked on the door. "Which part? The part where some old crow pretended to be a fortune teller, predicted horrible things about my fate, then tried to attack us? Or the part where the realm *broke open* and our city nearly fell?"

Saoirse cocked one brow straight up. "All of it?"

"Okay." Maeve blew out a breath, dropped onto her bed, and crossed her legs beneath her. "Let's talk about all of it. What do we know?"

Saoirse laughed but it was harsh. It grated against the walls of Maeve's bedroom. "Practically nothing. We don't know where the chasm came from or how it formed. We also don't know why. And Captain Vawda is certain all of those creatures are fae because let's face it, what else could they possibly be?"

Maeve smiled thinly at the use of Casimir's proper title. She was the only one allowed to call him by his given name.

"Madam Dansha, or whatever it was..." Maeve started but Saoirse cut in.

"Definitely fae. You saw how she turned to ash with one

strike, and speaking of one-hit wonders—" she glanced pointedly at the dagger strapped to Maeve's thigh, "that's one hell of a blade you've got there. It cut straight through them. Like they were nothing."

Maeve's hand drifted to the smooth leather hilt, to where the blade that glittered like rainbows was tucked safely away, but always within arm's reach. Saoirse had seen her train with the dagger, but neither of them had seen it perform in battle the way it did tonight. "Yours didn't?"

"No." Saoirse eyed the one in her hand. Black leather wrapped the hilt, and where one side of the blade was the color of onyx, the other resembled diamond dust. She flipped it into the air, caught it by the tip, then rolled her eyes to the ceiling. "It wasn't as easy as it was for you. We were having to strike multiple times just to slow them down. Only the hit to the throat proved fatal." She sheathed her blade to her waistband. "All of which reinforces the Captain's theory of those monsters being fae."

"A valid point." Maeve wanted to agree, but in truth, she'd never seen a fae. She'd read stories of their deceit and the mystery surrounding their very existence—how they were made of the breath of life and the soul of death. She always assumed they looked...like her. With pointy ears, much like her own. Though hers were from a curse, but she supposed it made no difference. What she witnessed tonight, however, was horrifying. She didn't know the fae could be so terrorizing, she didn't know they could care so little for human life, and she certainly had not been prepared for their frightening appearance. It made her despise them even more. But if this sort of magic was what cursed her blood...

Saoirse pushed up from the bed and stalked over to Maeve's vanity. She admired herself in the mirror, then smoothed a balm on her pale pink lips, before meeting Maeve's gaze in the reflection. "About the chasm. Captain Vawda said it's growing."

It wasn't a question, but Maeve confirmed the underlying inquiry. "Yes. He's right. Whatever it is, it's alive. I can feel it in my blood." She shivered, remembering the way the chasm pulsed with magic, how it seemed like something she should recognize. "It will continue to spread until it engulfs all of Kells. It could venture even further, taking over neighboring kingdoms within Veterra if we don't stop it."

"Could you sense it somehow?" Saoirse adjusted the flower in her hair. She had already replaced the magenta orchid with a startling blue rose.

"I could, yes." Maeve absently reached up to where she'd tucked the flower the little girl had given her earlier, before the attack. It was gone. "There was this scent, did you smell it? Orange blossom and cedarwood?"

Saoirse shook her head.

"Well, I did. As soon as we walked into the fortune teller's tent, this sensation settled over me. The air was dense, almost crackling with a kind of energy." Maeve unhooked her belt of throwing stars and laid it across the bed. "As soon as she took my hand, I could feel it. The darkness. And you know...like calls to like."

Saoirse whipped around and her eyes frosted over. "You do not possess the blood of dark fae. What you saw tonight, will never be you."

"How do you know?" Maeve countered. She shoved up from the bed and her boots clicked noisily against the wooden floor. "I've been cursed since the day I was born, before that, likely. I can feel the darkness inside me, the bloodthirsty fury. Most people aren't cursed with goodness and light, Saoirse."

A sensation washed over her. It left her skin cold and her hands clammy. She remembered the rage she'd felt toward

Casimir during training. How easy it had been to slide into a void of emptiness. And all he'd done was use her memories against her.

"Most people aren't you, Maeve." Her friend's expression softened. "Your blood might be cursed, but your heart is too pure." She draped an arm around Maeve's shoulders. "You are the sun. Radiant and glowing. So bright, not even a thousand moonbeams could eclipse you."

"You have a poet's soul, you know?" Maeve leaned into the offered embrace. "Despite the outward appearance of a hardcore killing machine."

"Please." Saoirse sniffed and turned up her nose in disgust. "Don't ever insult me again."

A rough knock sounded against Maeve's bedroom door, but before she could move to answer, the heavy wood swung open and revealed her mother, flanked by two soldiers.

Carman's lips were pinched, her fingers clasped tightly before her. She wore a gown of liquid silver which seemed to melt over her thin figure. Chains fell from her waist and the shoulders of the dress were studded with tiny spikes. Her black hair was pulled into an intricate updo, but wisps had fallen from their tightly bound place, which only ever meant one thing—she was furious.

Saoirse dropped onto one knee while Maeve hesitated between a kneel and a curtsey, and ended up doing some foolish mashup of both.

"You." Carman's piercing gaze zeroed in on Saoirse, then flicked fleetingly to Maeve. "Both of you. To the throne room. At once."

Chapter Four

Maeve couldn't believe her mother's words, but she and Saoirse followed behind Carman to the throne room. Two soldiers walked just in front of the queen, and two more seemingly appeared from thin air and kept pace with them from the back. Maeve remembered when she was a little girl, how the soldiers of Kells always reminded her of breathing statues. Their movements were always precise and measured. Stiff. They never spoke, simply followed commands.

The double doors to the throne room opened and Maeve smelled the sea before she saw it. It was more than she expected; open to the air, to the balustrade overlooking the Cliffs of Morrigan and the Gaelsong Sea. Bronze squares of polished stone gleamed beneath her boots, each one hungry for light, for reflection. Pillars of slate rose up on either side of her, and darkened alcoves lurked between all of them. Some were illuminated with soft light, displaying statues of human-like creatures carved from ivory, their faces etched with perfect detail, their bodies frozen in time. They almost looked real.

At the end of the room sat Carman's throne. It was simpler than Maeve imagined, positioned upon a small dais, with three silver spears reaching up to the domed ceiling. Beyond it, was an entire world Maeve would never get to see.

More important than any of the mystique of the throne room, was the number of people currently within its confines. At least twenty soldiers—including Casimir and Saoirse—stood off to the side of the throne, and then there were a cluster of people she didn't recognize. She could only assume they were the city officials and guests from earlier in the evening. Maeve sidled up beside Saoirse, while her mother took her place upon the dais, taking control of the space with nothing more than a harsh inhale of air. The tips of Carman's nails tapped ruthlessly against the hardwood arm of the throne. It was enough to make Maeve's skin crawl. "As I'm sure you're all aware, Kells came under attack tonight."

Obviously.

Maeve kept her mouth clamped shut. Those sorts of thoughts would only get her in trouble, but she couldn't help the rush of animosity. While Carman was enjoying a night of fun and fancy, of feasting and drinking, blissfully unaware of all that went on around her, the city of Kells suffered. Her *people* suffered. She hadn't even made an appearance. She hadn't shown her face, not when her kingdom needed her most.

"I sincerely doubt this will be the last time such an attack occurs," Carman continued, her demeanor ever cool, ever calm. "This *chasm* which has erupted at the center of the city is not a tear in the realm. It is called The Scathing. And it is a product of the dark fae."

Carman's cold gaze lingered on Maeve.

What was her mother trying to imply? That the Mother Goddess saw fit to curse her with the blood of *dark fae?* Her mind spun in a flurry of unanswered questions. A hushed gasp and trepidatious whispers echoed up into the cavernous hall. There were grunts of disgust and murmurs of hatred. Maeve recoiled into her skin, when sudden tingles of awareness prickled along her neck.

She shuddered against it. She was being watched. Again. Her gaze immediately sought out Casimir in the crowd, but he was staring straight ahead at Carman, and failed to look her way at all. She stole a glance at Saoirse next, but her best friend appeared to be mumbling a list of obscenities under her breath.

Then the world shimmered. Barely. It was the faintest shift. No more than a breath. Yet she seemed to be the only one who took notice.

"But the dark fae were vanquished to the Sluagh after the Evernight War." The man who spoke was one of Carman's advisors. Lord Whorton was a rotund man with ruddy cheeks and an exceptionally large wart that protruded from beneath his left eye.

"It's true, Your Majesty. They weren't supposed to exist anymore." Saoirse moved through the crowd, and Maeve found herself jostled to the front, right along with her. "Could they have come back somehow?"

"It certainly appears that way." Casimir folded his arms, daring anyone to cross him.

"Back from the Sluagh?" Roth barked. "What utter nonsense."

Maeve hated to admit it, but Roth was right. It was impossible for any soul to return from the Sluagh. It was not an eternal paradise, like Maghmell. Nor was it Ether, the home of the Wild Hunt, a realm of the in-between for those whose fates were not yet determined. No, the Sluagh was a punishment. A binding for the vilest and most evil of souls for all eternity. A relentless purgatory.

Dark fae.

The words repeated in Maeve's mind, coated her with a foulness she didn't understand.

"I have reason to believe the dark fae have returned, and there is no telling if or when they will strike again." Carman pushed up from her throne and everyone standing before her edged backward. A ripple of fear caught on the wind and drifted through the space. "But, we must be prepared. Captain?" She turned to face Casimir, and he snapped to attention. "How many casualties did Kells suffer tonight?"

"Thirty-two civilian deaths. Four soldier deaths. Seventeen injuries." His jaw was set, the rest of his face barely visible beneath the hood of his cloak.

Carman's brows deepened into a scowl. "I want extra guards posted around the city center with The Scathing completely blocked off from the public view. They do not need to constantly be reminded of the unfortunate atrocities of tonight."

Lord Whorton angled himself closer to the dais, but Roth stepped forward, blocking him from advancing any further. "And what of the rest of the city, Your Majesty?"

Her head whipped toward him and her black gaze glittered like onyx. "What of it?"

He shifted his overtly round belly, and when he squinted, his wart jiggled. "We have it on good authority there were dark fae lingering within the city walls. Some of them had been living among us for quite some time, setting up shops, working alongside our people, glamouring themselves as though they were one of us."

Disgust fell from his words, and Maeve's thoughts circled back to Madam Dansha. To the fortune teller who'd fallen to ash at the strike of her blade. To the dark fae who'd been living inside Kells, who'd been masquerading as a human, using glamour to disguise their true form. Maeve shuddered in spite of herself. She hated the fae, hated how she'd been cursed with their toxic blood magic, and hated how they'd destroyed her city. Her home.

"Those dark fae are not a priority for Kells at the moment." Her throat worked furiously, as though she was trying to swallow down the rest of her words. "The ones who dared to live inside our kingdom had done so peacefully up until tonight, and we will deal with them when the time comes. But right now, The Scathing is our largest threat."

"Because it's alive," Maeve muttered under her breath.

Every set of eyes in the room cut to her. Silence descended upon the marble walls and even the wind died. Tension hung in the air. Thick and hot.

"What?" Carman stalked over, her dress slinking and moving around her like a waterfall of liquid silver. Fury was etched into the pale crevices of her skin, but she maintained an eerie sense of calm. She spoke again, her penetrating gaze focused on Maeve. "What did you say?"

Maeve steeled her will. She would not cower. She would not bend. Not beneath her mother's harsh accusations. Not beneath the promise of her birthright. With her shoulders rolled back, and fully aware of everyone watching her, she nudged her way through the crowd until she faced her mother head on. A few gazes dipped to the silver cuffs branding her wrists, but she refused to hide them. "The Scathing," she repeated, "is alive. I saw it moving."

Breathing. Pulsing. Thriving.

None of which she would mention out loud for fear of her life.

"Maeve speaks the truth, Your Majesty," Casimir confirmed, coming to her rescue, and Carman's anger ebbed. The wrath subsided. Her features smoothed. "The Scathing is alive and it is moving, gradually stealing over the ground, and leaving a path of rot and decay in its wake. It will destroy all of Kells, and other kingdoms within Veterra, unless we can find a way to destroy it first."

MURMURS and collective gasps echoed through the expansive chamber. The Scathing was a plague upon the lands. A scourge. A sickness from an unknown source. It had to be stopped.

"But how?" Saoirse asked. She tossed her braid of moonlight-colored hair over one shoulder, and more than one of the men in the room eyed her with interest. Some of their gazes lingered longer than they ought. "How can we fight an enemy when we know nothing of its origin or how to defeat it?"

Maeve's blood pulsed in her veins, a low thrum, and the world around her shimmered again. It was as though a veil of gossamer had been draped across her vision. But then Maeve blinked and it vanished completely. Her balance wavered, and she lost her footing, stumbling into Saoirse

"You okay?" she whispered.

Maeve nodded, ready to answer, but the words died on her tongue. Her throat wouldn't work. Her chest was tight, and she couldn't catch her breath.

"We know there are certain materials that can prove fatal to any fae, dark or otherwise." Casimir's clear voice cut through the quiet, cut through the rise of panic bubbling up inside of her. Though she couldn't see his eyes beneath the shadow of his hood, she knew he watched her. She knew he spoke of the dagger strapped to her thigh. "Perhaps these same materials—"

"The Scathing is not a fae." A male voice slid into the night air and it coated Maeve's skin like ice. The hairs along the back of her neck prickled. Then a figure, a man she hadn't seen earlier, emerged from the shadows.

His hair was teal, the color of the Gaelsong Sea, where the water was darkest. Where the sunlight never touched. It was short, messy, and swept over one eye. He wore a black shirt that gaped open at the neck, revealing jagged scars across his tanned chest. His gray pants were loose, his boots worn and scuffed, but he edged forward with swagger. The kind of movement belonging to a man who knew his worth. Except...he was *not* a man.

Every mortal soul within the room instinctively recoiled.

He was *fae*.

His ears were longer and smoothed to a point. His face was painfully handsome and chiseled to perfection, crafted by the hands of a god. He was nothing like the dark fae she'd seen wreaking havoc upon Kells. In fact, he was the complete opposite. He was beautiful. And she hated him on instinct.

"Who are you?" The words were forced out of Lord Whorton's clenched jaw, and the fae inclined his head.

"An old friend."

Casimir made to start forward, ready to tear his body limb from limb for such disobedient speech, but Carman heeled him with a snap of her fingers.

"His name is Rowan." She addressed everyone as a whole, but not once did she acknowledge the fae in question. A true affirmation to her hatred of his race. "He's been an asset to me for a number of years."

Maeve didn't believe that for a minute. There was no way her mother would dare keep a fae as an "asset". A pet, maybe. A servant, more like. And given the scars littering his chest, it looked very much like he'd been tortured a time or two.

"As I was saying," Rowan drawled and shoved his hands in

his pockets, strolling closer toward the dais. "The Scathing is not a fae, and therefore cannot be *killed* like a fae."

Maeve watched as Casimir seethed beneath the composed indifference of Rowan's disposition. He tossed his hood back and his molten eyes locked onto the offending fae. "And how do you know?"

"I just do." Rowan's chilled voice sank deep into her skin, and it was so cold, she felt it in her bones. "It will take more than some fancy metal or charmed stones to destroy The Scathing." When he spoke, his lavender eyes landed on her.

Maeve sucked in a breath and Saoirse casually bumped into her. "What sort of sorcery is that?" she muttered. "It's unfair for a creature so capable of brutality to be so devastatingly gorgeous."

Yeah. Gorgeous and brutal. Was there ever a worse—or better—combination?

"Tell us what you know," Roth demanded.

Rowan's smile was cruel. Wicked. But just as quickly as Maeve was blinded by its vicious gleam, it vanished. "I know how to decimate The Scathing...and the dark fae, should the threat persist."

Saoirse lifted her voice. "How? How do we rid Kells of The Scathing and defend the rest of Veterra?"

Rowan strolled as he spoke, effortlessly and insolent, because he alone held all the answers. "Before the Evernight War, the goddess Danua descended upon Faeven."

Faeven, the realm of the fae. It was an island all its own, a world of magic and wonder, and made up of the Four Courts. Spring, Summer, Autumn, and Winter. The only way to get there was to cross the Eirelan Pass, a body of water connecting the Gaelsong Sea to the Lismore Marin. And last she checked, no one had been successful in years.

"She bestowed a gift, the *anam ó Danua*," Rowan continued, weaving a story of fascination in Maeve's mind. Yet there was something about the words, an old familiarity which caused her heart to skip a beat. "A blessing of creation. It granted its keeper a great many things. New beginnings. Infinite power—"

"What, like magic?" Roth barked out. "Our queen is the most powerful sorceress in the realm. In all of the human lands. There is no being alive who is stronger."

Rowan chuckled, and its low rumble echoed through the great throne room, out into the darkened skies beyond. "The *anam ó Danua* is unrivaled. It is the one true source. The lifeblood of fae magic."

"What is this *anam ó Danua*?" Casimir cut the distance between himself and Rowan. Though they were toe to toe, the fae had at least three inches on him. "What does it mean?"

The question was meant for Rowan, and Maeve should've kept her mouth shut. She should've known speaking out of turn would draw the wrong sort of attention, would bring the wrath of her mother upon her, as well as any number of harsh consequences. But she couldn't help herself. She understood the meaning, she recognized it as Old Laic, an ancient language thought to have been gifted by the gods and goddesses of time to only those they deemed worthy. "It means the soul of Danua."

Maeve didn't move. She didn't flinch under the furious stare from her mother, or when Casimir's mouth fell open, as though he'd been slapped by her words. Not even when Rowan's pretty eyes sifted over her, and then through her, reading her soul like a book.

"I didn't know you could speak Old Laic," Saoirse whispered.

Maeve glanced up at her best friend. "Neither did I." Another flaw brought on by her blood curse, no doubt.

"She's correct." Rowan lifted his arm in a casual gesture to Maeve. "The *anam ó Danua* is the soul of the goddess Danua, passed down through the maternal fae bloodline only."

Carman stepped off the dais and her deep red lips curved with interest. "Where do we find this soul of Danua?"

"That's the problem." Rowan towered over the queen but when she moved closer, his entire body stiffened. It was then Maeve knew without a doubt that the scars on his chest were from Carman. "The last known female carrying the blessing vanished during the Evernight War. No one has seen her since."

It was a good thing she was cursed and not blessed. She wouldn't want any gift, ever, if it meant she was somehow tied to the vile fae responsible for wrecking Kells. A curse kept anger in her heart, a blessing would only bloom hate, and hate was too difficult of an emotion to navigate. It clouded the senses, fogged the mind. It was responsible for mistakes, mistrust, and failure. But anger...anger was her fuel. It gave her reason to thrive.

"So, we have to find the soul of a goddess, which isn't a thing but an actual *being*, and one that hasn't been seen in more than fifty years?" Casimir crossed his arms and a sort of smugness settled over his bloodied and bruised features from their earlier brawl, and then the fight in the city. "And how do you expect us to do that?"

"Easy." Rowan grinned but it wasn't kind. It was malicious, and it made Maeve's skin crawl. "We venture to Faeven and find her."

Chapter Five

Maeve caught herself before she laughed. Instead she made a kind of choking noise, and Saoirse clapped her soundly on the back.

There was no way this fae could be serious. Was he suggesting they just waltz into Faeven, hunt down a faerie who could maybe, possibly, be from the bloodline of a goddess, then bring her back to Kells, and expect her to save the world? It sounded absolutely ridiculous. More so, it sounded like a death wish.

But Carman seemed to consider his absurd proposal. Her lips pursed like she'd bitten into a sour lemon. She spared Rowan a glance and her chin lifted, even though he stood far above her head. "If I send one of my most highly trained warriors to Faeven, what are the chances of recovering this *lifeblood of magic*, as you call it?"

Rowan bowed regally. "That's where I come in."

"You?" Roth snarled and his hands coiled into meaty fists. "Why should we trust a filthy fae?"

"Because I know how to find her." Rowan didn't even flinch

at the insult. "Before you ask me how I know, may I remind you, I'm fae."

Faeries couldn't lie, at least, not directly. They could deviate from the truth. They could embellish and speak in riddles, but they could not tell an outright lie. As far as Maeve was concerned, that hardly seemed like reason enough to trust Rowan. Everything about him oozed deceit and chaos. His gorgeous looks were simply a disguise, a way to conceal predator from prey. He was the wolf in sheep's clothing. The monster under the bed. The villain of the story.

And Maeve didn't trust a single word he said.

A few soldiers exchanged uncomfortable glances and there was an energy moving throughout the room, a crackling spark of hope born from desperation. No one wanted to place their faith in Rowan, but as of now, he was their only option. The only one with the means to put an end to the Scathing.

"Very well." Carman raised her voice so it echoed up through the arching walls above. "We will assemble a team of our most lethal warriors to go with you into Faeven."

"Bear in mind, Your Majesty," Casimir interjected with a curt nod. "The more people who travel with us, the greater our chances of not returning alive."

True, it was far easier to hide a party of three or four, versus a group of twenty.

"Indeed." Carman spread her arms wide and the chains hanging from her gown clanked softly like chimes. "Captain Vawda, you will lead a team. I'll send Saoirse Kearney as well, since she's one of the most highly trained warriors we have in our company. The faerie, of course. And one more..."

Maeve held her breath.

"Many have said there is no nobler way to die, then to forfeit one's life in favor of the crown." Carman smiled, and the chill of death ran its icy finger down Maeve's spine. "I shall make such a sacrifice, and appoint my heir to venture to Faeven with you."

Shock and awe swallowed up the gasps of curiosity, but it was Maeve who couldn't move. Who couldn't breathe. Carman, the Queen of Kells, her *mother*, was acknowledging her. In public. Where rumors, and whispers, and questions would ultimately break free from the throne room and spread like wildfire through the city of Kells and beyond. Her stomach twisted into a knot of uncertainty and dread fell like a weight on her chest. She wanted this. Of course she wanted this. She'd been waiting years for her mother to see her value, her worth. She'd done everything within her power to please Carman, to make her proud, to elicit an emotion, a response, anything. Now, all of it was finally within her reach.

Her mother stretched her arm out, her pointy nails motioning for her to step closer. To come into view. Carman's smile softened. Slightly. "My daughter, Maeve Carrick, Princess of Kells."

Maeve froze. She couldn't get her legs to move. They were in quicksand, sinking deeper and deeper, until it was covering her entire body. The cool breeze coming in from off the Cliffs of Morrigan vanished, leaving her with stagnant air that made it impossible to breathe. Someone behind her muttered her name, and shoved her from her stupor. Maeve stumbled into the clearing of people surrounding her mother.

Carman's scowl was fleeting but unavoidable.

Maeve glanced around the circle. Casimir stood to her right, with Saoirse beside him.

"Well, isn't this cozy?"

Maeve lurched into Casimir at the sound of the velvety voice that coated her skin. She looked over to see Rowan, with his hands tucked into the pockets of his pants, and the curve of a smirk on his face. She hadn't even heard him approach.

Casimir swiftly maneuvered Maeve so she was on the opposite side of him, next to Saoirse. His glower only deepened when Rowan chuckled at his expense.

"The four of you will travel to Faeven to search out this *anam ó Danua* and bring it to me, so that I may rid the human lands of The Scathing." Outside, waves crashed against the cliffs, and the roar of the ocean filled the cavernous ceilings. Carman lifted her voice to match its wrath. "This journey is not for the faint of heart. You will face creatures of darkness and death. You will struggle, you will suffer, and there is a good chance not all of you will return."

Rowan made a scoffing noise and rolled back onto his heels.

"Get some rest." Carman whirled away from them and returned to her throne on the dais. "You leave in two days' time."

REST WOULD BE IMPOSSIBLE.

Maeve didn't even wait for the throne room to clear; she shoved and shouldered her way out of the grand space and into the hall. Soldiers milled about, awaiting orders, and she ducked past them to the open-air corridor where it was easier to cling to the shadows. She didn't know if her mother's newest announcement meant she would have guards tracking her every movement, because the last thing she wanted was soldiers following her around like trained watch dogs. She enjoyed her freedom and she planned to keep it that way for as long as possible.

Once she knew she wasn't being followed, she darted up a set of gunmetal marble steps, careful to stay on the tips of her toes to avoid the clicking sound of her boots. A large wooden door with a brass handle stood before her. She heaved it open and slipped into the one place she knew no one would bother looking.

The library.

It was overwhelming in the best way possible. The walls reached up to a massive domed ceiling where windows show-cased the night sky full of stars and the remnants of smoke. Paintings hung along the back wall and all of them portrayed images of death, destruction, and darkness. They were riveting —so lifelike, Maeve often wondered if they weren't somehow captured in time. The library was illuminated with iron chandeliers that dripped down from the ceiling like skeletal hands, and golden lights filled the space with warmth, despite the cold nature of the library. Shelves upon shelves of books filled the walls from floor to ceiling, though most of them were untouched, their bindings and pages covered in a thick, grimy layer of dust.

She often slipped away here as a child, usually after returning from time in the cage where she was left alone with her nightmares. Or sometimes after being on the training field with Casimir, being too bloodied and broken to lift a sword. This had been her safe space growing up, the one place she could learn, the place she could come when nowhere else seemed to want her. She went to the library for stories, to get lost in adventures within unknown worlds. As she got older, she came for other things like lessons in war-fighting and stealth, how to outmaneuver and understand an enemy, and more recently, the art of seduction.

Though she had to admit, the latter had proven to be rather useless.

But now, Maeve came to refresh her knowledge. She needed to understand Faeven on a deeper level, she needed to know what she was up against. She found herself in a familiar section full of texts bound in worn leather and embossed with silver lettering. She skimmed through the shelves, searching out ancient books of myth, lore, and legend. Long ago, those stories were nothing more than fairytales to her. Now, however, she realized there was perhaps some truth to them after all. Minutes dragged by into hours while she poured over information. Most of which had been passed down over generations through song, story, and the written word. She read about the history of Old Laic, a fae language, which had all but disappeared over the course of hundreds of years. It was rarely used, and even now, there were only phrases left. As far as she could tell, it had died out from conversation long ago.

Which she supposed was a good thing. At least that meant she'd be able to understand the fae, if and when they came face to face.

The mere thought of coming across another one of those faceless creatures that crawled out of the Scathing caused Maeve's skin to pebble with goosebumps. Sure, the ones who ravaged Kells were hideous, but Rowan, despite his devastatingly good looks, was equally as terrifying. At least, the books piled around her and propped open in her lap claimed as much to be true.

According to legend, some fae resided in Faeven and belonged to the Four Courts or other faerie realms; many of which seemed to exist only through time, and magic, and other powerful means. Other fae, however, like the ones who attacked Kells, were the banished ones. The dangerous ones. She flipped through the gossamer pages of the book in her lap, and trailed her finger along the inked words. Faeries were capable of great magic, and were graced with speed and beauty. But not all fae were created equal. Some possessed little magic, while others, the Archfae, were the most powerful. They were also the most lethal. They lacked human emotion and found the existence of mortals to be a curious wonder.

Nowhere in the book did it say what sorts of magic the fae were capable of, and Maeve found she wasn't entirely sure she wanted to know.

She stifled a yawn, continuing to close one book and open the next, determined to learn as much as possible before the journey to Faeven. The books she held grew heavier and the words on the page blurred together. She blinked, cracked her neck, and forced herself to keep reading. Her muscles ached from the fighting in Kells and exhaustion was creeping in, threatening to drag her under into the bliss of sleep. She turned the next page.

The Evernight War was brought on by the dark fae. They attacked their own and they swarmed and overran the cities of Faeven. When the war was finally over, a devastating plague spread across the realm. The Four Courts fell, too weak from their own civil war to fight against the assault, and slowly they succumbed to the threat. Until the goddess Danua came down from Maghmell and purged the land of darkness.

Maeve almost felt bad for the fae.

Almost.

She settled back against one of the shelves on the floor and the last thing she filled her mind with was a story of a magical being made of moonlight, starlight, and eternal night.

She wasn't sure how long she'd been cramped on the floor of the library, sound asleep, when a prickling sort of awareness stirred within her. The kind that caused her senses to awaken, and a knot of trepidation to form in the pit of her gut. She knew it before she opened her eyes.

She wasn't alone.

Maeve bolted upright and slammed right into Roth's gnarled chest. He captured her with one arm and she tried to scream, but he covered her mouth with a white cloth. The pungent smell attacked her, filled her lungs, and caused her vision to swim. She swung her legs and kicked, but it was like dragging a fan through the dirt. She was losing feeling, her body weakening against a numbness she recognized.

Fear twisted through her like a knife.

The world went fuzzy, then sideways, and before it faded to black completely, she saw her mother's smiling face.

Chapter Six

Maeve's head was aching. The pain throbbed at her temples and the base of her neck. Her body was stiff, sore, and cramped from laying in one position for far too long. The metal of her cuffs was cold against her skin. Like ice.

She licked her lips. They were dry and cracked, and tasted of salt and the sea. The flavor lingered in the air and when she took a breath and her lungs filled with the tang of sea spray. Damp clothes clung to her already chilled skin. In the distance, a rushing sound filled her ears; the crash of waves as they rolled over rocks and back out to sea. She imagined she was swaying in time with their crests. A slow, methodic rocking, similar to how a new mother might soothe a babe in her arms. It was a lulling motion, and she thought perhaps she was already on a ship sailing to Faeven. Until she heard the distinctive creak of branches.

Terror jolted her awake. Raw and pure. Her heart jackhammered inside the tight wall of her chest and her eyes flew open. She was in the cage.

Built from mangled wrought iron, it was big enough to house a bird of prey. The wooden planks beneath her were warped and battered from years of strong winds, pelting rains, and suffocating summers. It hung precariously between two branches of an old oak tree, whose limbs had long since stretched out over the Cliffs of Morrigan. Below the cage, the Gaelsong Sea churned in anger. Its mighty turquoise waters lashed the cliffside and roared over rocks that jutted up in sharp points.

Maeve swallowed her scream and scrambled to the back of the cage. The branches groaned in agony against her sudden movement, dangling her closer to the foaming mouth of the ocean.

Tears burned Maeve's eyes, but she blamed them on the sting of the breeze. Her fingers tightened around the cold, rusted bars, turning her knuckles white. She knew it was pathetic, but no one could see her, and no one would care. Her mother sent her here often as a child, usually as some sort of necessary discipline, and every night for weeks Maeve would dream of the vengeful sea and its desperation to drown her. Casimir taught her a great many things, and he'd taught her to overcome many of her fears. She wasn't afraid of death. She didn't dread the dark, or the unknown. Though she had an aversion to the creatures that brought their wrath upon Kells, not even their nightmarish figures would be enough to stop her.

But the ocean?

She was *terrified* of the ocean.

It was the one fear she could not conquer.

A prickle of unease crept along her shoulders and down her spine. The world shimmered, just slightly, and her blood hummed a low, haunting melody. She angled herself so she could peer out of the bars. Someone was there, lurking in the shadows of the forest.

49

"Show yourself!" Her voice echoed into the growth of trees and mangled vines. "I know you're out there."

Her eyes skimmed the bushes and branches. Nothing moved. Nothing breathed. There was no birdsong, no whisper of the wind, and even the ocean's chilling call seemed to soften. The sun was already high, but a thick wall of clouds blanketed the sky in shades of gray, and the air was dense with the threat of rain. Low-lying clouds crawled along the cliffside and floated through the brush of brambles and stone. She strained against the haze of fog to see what loitered past the rocky ground, to the sparse woods beyond. Basked in shadows, a figure emerged from behind the aged oak tree.

"Good afternoon." Rowan stepped into her view and the bank of silver mist seemed to part for him. His cloak of midnight moved and flowed of its own accord. His shirt still gaped open, revealing his scarred chest. But it was different this time. Some of them looked fresh. Some of them looked sticky.

Her grip tightened on the bars of the cage, until her fingers dug into her palm. "What are you doing here?"

He strolled toward the edge of the cliffs, his lavender eyes alight with amusement. "I believe the real question is, what are *you* doing here?"

Maeve bristled against his mocking tone. "It's just a punishment." Though she didn't know what for this time.

"A punishment? For what?" Rowan moved closer, and his bemused expression took in the curved, bird-like cage with its tarnished metal and feeble planks. "Have you done something naughty?"

"No, " she snapped, annoyed with how easily he scraped under her skin. "And even if I did," she fired back, "it wouldn't be any concern of yours."

Rowan chuckled. He shoved his hands into the pockets of

his loose pants and kicked a few random rocks off the cliffside. They fell for an eternity before being swallowed by the frothing sea.

Maeve shuddered.

"Humans are such curious creatures." His gaze swept over her, lingering on her hips before settling on her mouth. "They claim to feel all these emotions. Fear. Grief. Love. Yet their hatred of one another is stronger than any of those."

"I don't hate my mother." She ground the words out.

He blinked. "I never said you did."

Maeve opened her mouth, then snapped it shut. She would have to be extremely careful with whatever she said to him. The fae were notorious for taking things out of context, for being exceptionally literal, for twisting words, and weaving them into contracts that could last an eternity.

She shifted. "My mother doesn't hate me, either."

"Doesn't she though?" Rowan murmured and his words wrapped around her like the kiss of night. "Why else would she lock you into a cage, if not to instill fear? A fear so deep, you risk never overcoming it? Why would she volunteer you to go to the fae realm, where you are more than likely to meet your death?"

Maeve had hoped certain death wasn't a real possibility once they arrived in Faeven, but now she was beginning to realize it was more likely than not. Again, though, she would face it when it looked her in the eyes. When she failed to answer him, Rowan's arms shot out and he grabbed the bars of the cage, covering both of her hands with his own. Maeve flinched, but he held the cage steady, and she couldn't look away from him. She could barely breathe. His eyes, pools of pale purple, were flecked with silver stars. Waves of teal hair fell over one side of his face and rippled in the sea breeze like a wave. His fingers were warm over hers, and when she finally caught her breath, she inhaled the scent of dusk. Of night jasmine, wooded moss, mountain sage.

She jerked her hands free from his hold.

"Why have I never seen you in the palace before?" Her pointed gaze focused on his chest, where fresh slashes ripped his shirt. To where the flesh had been torn open by something sharp and jagged. "You're obviously indebted to my mother."

It was a low blow, but he took it without even blinking. "I wouldn't go so far as to say indebted...held captive against my will is more like it."

She didn't like to consider the thought that her mother made a habit of keeping faeries as slaves. "A pet, then?"

He eased back onto the edge of the cliff, releasing the cage, and Maeve held her breath when bits of rock and debris tumbled down the side. His hands spread wide, displaying his cuffs with purpose. "Pet. Slave. It's all the same when your power is taken from you."

The insult jabbed her in the ribs and she bristled against the harsh scrape of truth. "I am not a pet. Or a slave."

"Perhaps not." The corner of Rowan's mouth ticked upward. "Maybe you're something else, Princess. Something more. Maybe the reason your mother binds you in cuffs, diminishes your beauty, and keeps you from the greatness you are destined to become, is because she sees you as something greater. Like a weapon."

Something about the way he spoke to her struck a nerve. The way he thought he *knew* her. It set Maeve's nerves on fire. "These cuffs are meant to protect everyone else."

"From what?"

"From me."

His brows shot up and a laugh burst from him. "From *you*?"

"You know nothing about me." She grit her teeth and slammed the metal bound to her wrists against the bars of the cage. "Nothing good comes from being cursed, Rowan. Not ever. I'm the bastard daughter of a sorceress. Do you really think the Mother Goddess would look kindly upon me? These cuffs protect everyone around me from the monster lurking just beneath the surface."

"Is that what you think I am? A monster?" Rowan grinned, a savage sort of smile.

"Yes. All fae are monsters." She slid to the other side of the cage and the branches overhead moaned against her sudden movement. She gripped the bars with one hand, while the other slid to her thigh on instinct. Except her sheath was empty. Her blade was gone.

Apprehension coated her skin like ice. Tiny droplets of rain pattered down from the broody sky. They clung to her lashes and slid down the back of her neck. She cringed, and raked one hand through the mess of wet curls stuck to her face.

"Do you know what this is, Princess?" Rowan's voice carried over to her from the safety of the cliffs.

"Stop calling me that." She glared at him, until she caught sight of what he held in his hand—her dagger.

He flipped its razor-sharp edge back and forth between his fingers with ease. Never missing. Never hesitating. The iridescent blade sparkled like a thousand rainbows caught by the first glimpse of dawn. "I can't imagine how someone like you could be in possession of something like this."

Maeve was sure he meant it as an insult, but she didn't care. It was her dagger. She was the one who found it buried beneath the silt and sand at the bottom of the hidden lake in the Moors. She was the one whose lungs had almost burst from lack of oxygen to retrieve it. And she would get it back.

He flipped the dagger again, a trick meant to intimidate, and Maeve leapt across the cage. But the wooden floorboards were too slick, and she misjudged the distance. Her arm shot out through the bars, and the tips of her fingers grazed the hilt as it maneuvered around his knuckles. The momentum of her body caused the cage to rock, and it swung violently between the two branches, tossing her to the opposite side. Her head smacked into the bars, and a blaze of stars streaked in front of her eyes. A horrible cracking sound filled her ears as one of the branches snapped, and the cage tilted backwards.

Maeve screamed.

But then Rowan was there, holding the cage steady on the weight of the longest branch, keeping it from toppling off the Cliffs of Morrigan, and taking Maeve with it. If the last branch broke, there would be no saving her.

"This is an Aurastone." His voice was a lullaby, a balm to the terror that wrecked her and left her shaken. "A rare blade of exceptional power and magic." Again, his lavender eyes lingered on her mouth before sliding back up to hold her gaze. "Where did you get it?"

She shivered against the velvet of his words, and though her pulse jumped, she wasn't foolish enough to tell a faerie the truth. "That's none of your business."

He answered in a low chuckle, but then went eerily still. Maeve opened her mouth to speak, but he pressed one finger to his lips, and silenced her with the slightest shake of his head. He looked through the tree line, to the uneven path leading back to the castle at the top of the cliffs, before returning his attention to her.

"Do not lose this, Princess. Ever." Rowan handed the Aurastone to her, and she snatched it from his grasp, quickly tucking it back into the safety of the sheath strapped to her thigh. He pulled his cape around him and walked backward, never taking his eyes off her, until he was swallowed by the mist settling in from off the sea.

Voices sounded from the path. Some she knew, some she didn't. But within a few minutes, she caught sight of her mother, flanked by guards, with Casimir following from behind.

It was only after Rowan left her, did she realize the birdsong returned, the wind whispered over the cliffs, and the sea once again began to roar.

THE RAIN STOPPED and all Maeve could hear was the muffled sound of approaching footfalls and the creaking of the branch over her head, as the cage swayed slowly. Back and forth. Barely hanging on.

"Oh good, you're awake." Carman wore a gown of slate and layers of black lace clung to the fabric like spider webs. The virdis lepatite glowed at the base of her throat, a murky, dark green color. She waved her fingers through the air dismissively. "Take her down."

Maeve held her breath as two of the guards reached out for the cage and yanked it back to solid ground. There was never a guarantee they wouldn't drop her. The last remaining branch creaked in protest, its old arm bent and exhausted from years of misuse. One guard held the cage in place, balanced between the ledge and the frothing ocean below, while another unhinged the lock. The bars swung open, and Maeve toppled out onto the damp ground.

Wet blades of grass slid between her fingers and moss cushioned her cheek like a pillow. She clenched her jaw shut to keep her teeth from chattering and shoved up from the ground, but not before silently saying a prayer to any god or goddess who would listen to her. She thanked them for sparing her from the wrath of the ocean. Maeve stood and scrambled away from the cliffside, but her muscles screamed in agony from being cramped for so long and her legs rioted against her. The toe of her boot stuck in the soggy earth and sent her stumbling face-first. She flung her arms out and braced for impact, but it never came.

A strong hand clamped around her upper arm and hauled her to her feet.

"Easy," Casimir murmured.

She looked up into his face. His hood was pulled low, so his eyes were hidden from view, but she knew he watched her. His hand slid from her arm to the small of her back where he kept her upright from the tug of exhaustion and the bite of hunger. The press of his palm on her back, and the unintended heat from his body, was almost enough to make her melt. But if he'd taught her one thing, it was to never show weakness, and to always keep her mask of strength in place. So, she pulled herself away from him and stood on her own. She rolled her shoulders back, ignored the ache in her head, and curtseyed before her mother.

Carman swept through the fog swirling at their feet. Her raven hair was piled high on her head, circled into place with her silver crown. Her eyes were lined with kohl and her lips were painted a deep berry shade, making her look every inch the powerful sorceress.

"Maeve. Darling." She smiled and Maeve fought the urge to seek approval beneath the emptiness in her eyes. "I'm sure you're wondering why I volunteered you to go to Faeven with the others."

"Actually." Maeve lifted her chin and kept her expression

schooled into one of feigned confidence. "I was wondering why Roth put me back in the cage."

"Because I told him to do so." Carman's explanation was simple. Caustic. "It was necessary, you see. Faeven is a realm of danger. Of peril. Nothing there is as it seems. You must be prepared for anything, including death."

Maeve's brow furrowed. "I don't understand what any of that has to do with the cage."

Carman's lips pursed. "Fear will be your enemy, Maeve. You must fear *nothing*, or you will die."

"But I'm not afraid of death. I'm not afraid of the dark fae, or any fae." Maeve took one small step and the guards positioned by her mother's side reached for their weapons, as if she was a threat. It unleashed a fury within her. So deep, so treacherous, she swore her blood boiled. "I'm not afraid of anything."

"Maeve," Casimir warned, but it came too late.

The whites of Carman's eyes turned black and the virdis lepatite crackled with such fierce energy, it caused the hairs on Maeve's arms to stand on end. "You aren't afraid of *anything?*" her mother hissed. "Is that so?"

An unexpected force slammed into Maeve and stole the air from her lungs, knocking her off her feet. A rock collided with her elbow and sent spasms through her arm. Thrown to the ground, she grappled for any kind of purchase. Small stones and clumps of mud slid through her fingers as she was dragged across the cliffside. Her head smacked a hard surface and pain exploded behind her eyes in a wash of blackened stars and dizzying lights.

Casimir lunged for her.

"Stand down!" Carman bellowed, and her power held him in place.

Without warning, she threw her hands out in front of her, and her nails protruded like talons. Suffocating power ripped into Maeve, and her body jerked and kicked in protest. The cuffs on her wrists were like fire against her skin, and she struggled to fight against the terrifying grip of power coursing through her. Carman raised her arms and Maeve was hoisted into the air, moving closer and closer to the edge of the cliff. The slick hand of fear held her in its grasp. Her heart plummeted to her gut, where it roiled with panic. Carman's power lifted her higher, until she dangled like a limp doll, useless, above the crush of waves below.

"Mother!" Gusts of wind slapped her face, and the sting of sea spray burned her eyes. Unbidden tears slid down her cheeks and she choked on her words. "Mother, *please*."

Carman smiled again, a bit more cruelly this time, and her eyes finally cleared. "I thought you said you weren't afraid of anything."

"This is different!" She swung her legs out. The tips of her boots just barely scraped the moss-covered ledge. "The ocean is not an enemy! It's nature, it's beyond our control!"

Her mother's mouth twisted into a sneer until it looked like blood ran from her lips. "Nothing is beyond my control."

The force holding Maeve in place suddenly plummeted down the rocky coast. A scream ripped from some hollow place inside her, and she realized in the startling flash before her imminent death, that Rowan had been right.

Her mother hated her.

Maeve plunged into the frigid sea.

Salt water filled her mouth. Choked her. Drowned her. Waves lashed her, sent her tumbling in the watery depths, and left her disoriented. She didn't know where the surface started and the ocean began. Her lungs seized and burned. Her blood was fire and fury, and the curse that pumped through her veins yearned for release, but it wouldn't come. It wasn't strong enough to break through the bonds of her cuffs. She wasn't strong enough to save herself. This was how she was going to die...at the hands of her mother.

Then she was torn from the might of the sea and her body dumped upon the sodden earth. She coughed, her stomach clenched, and she vomited seawater and bile. Each breath was a gasp, a greedy gulp of oxygen. On her hands and knees, she crawled through the muck, over the slick mossy rocks, and away from the cliffs. Her fingers wrapped around the rough stone and she hung onto it, held it like a lifeline.

"Maeve." Casimir's voice sounded different. Strange.

"Don't touch her." Carman stalked closer to Maeve and towered above her. Cold, onyx eyes glared down at her. Heartless. "You will go to Faeven. And you will prove yourself worthy of my crown. Do you understand?"

Maeve tried to swallow but her throat was raw, scalded by salt and brine. She didn't understand. She didn't know what her mother wanted from her. Not anymore.

"You will bring back the *anam ó Danua*. You will bring it to me so I can rid this world of the vile darkness threatening us." Carman leaned closer and the scent of bitter violets clouded Maeve's senses. "And if you can't, if you *fail*, then do not bother coming back at all."

Carman stood and Maeve sank onto the stone that supported her. "I...I won't let you down."

"We'll see about that." Carman lifted one hand and her frigid gaze cut to Casimir. "Leave her. She knows the way back."

Maeve laid there as seconds drifted by into minutes, and the rain began to fall once more. She tipped her head back and let the rainwater slide over her battered body. Cold droplets slid down her arms and neck, over her cheeks and chest. She opened her mouth and laid there until the fresh drops cleansed her of the gritty salt, and until her mouth no longer tasted of the sea.

Maeve stole a breath. And then another. She would go to Faeven. She would find the soul of a goddess. She would save Kells from The Scathing. She would rid the world of darkness. And then, she would kill her mother.

Chapter Seven

By the time Maeve dragged herself back to her quarters within the castle, she discovered her room had been emptied. Not that she had a lot of personal belongings anyway, but every trace of her was gone. The space was bare, save for the plain bedding and pile of freshly folded towels. Her mother fully expected her not to return. Which was fine, she mused to herself. It would make her homecoming all the sweeter.

Strewn across her stiff mattress was a clean pair of woven leggings, a blouse, a corset, and a pack filled with a few essentials for traveling. There was a fur-lined overcoat, a rough-hewn blanket, some rations, and a few pins for her hair. The corner of Maeve's mouth twitched. Saoirse must have packed for her. She headed into the bathroom, and carefully placed her dagger —the Aurastone—on the stone counter, then peeled off her ocean-soaked clothing. Her thighs were raw from chaffing against her wet pants, and her hair stunk of saltwater.

She switched on the overhead spout and lukewarm water sputtered, then shot out at full blast. The burst of water was harsh against her skin, and she winced when it pelted the tender flesh of her legs. The amenities at this end of the castle were not so luxurious. Maeve had never taken a bath before, though she'd heard stories of its wonder. Things like bubbles and milk, lavish scents, and water so hot it would turn her skin pink. She decided then, once she returned from Faeven with the *anam ó Danua*, that her reward would be a proper bath.

Water poured over her, rinsed her of the sea, and took with it a few harbored tears. It was better to release her emotion now, to give into the fact that her mother wanted her dead, then to think of such things while coming under attack. She supposed she'd always known Carman didn't care for her. Inside the castle walls, there was no such thing as love and affection. She'd never been shown kindness. Or empathy. Or support. Carman was always cold, callous, and unwavering in her irritation. Maeve tried to think back on a time when it wasn't always like that, a time when maybe she meant something to her mother. But there was an emptiness whenever she reached for those memories, a vast expanse of nothing. She didn't know if it was her blood curse that caused her mother to despise her so much, or if it was merely the fact that she'd been born.

Maeve squandered away the thoughts. Thinking and reflecting on them now would prove useless to her.

She scrubbed her face, washed away the last of her distress, and switched the water off. There would be no more time for her to wallow in her own pity. She was beyond such things. Perhaps she always knew her mother resented her. Despised her. But she'd been so desperate, so starved for attention, that she'd been blind to believing any of it was true.

Maeve grabbed the frayed towel slung over the hook on the wall and gingerly dried herself clean. She needed to be focused. To be ready. To be prepared for anything.

"Maeve!" The door to the bathroom burst open and Casimir walked in.

She yelped and clutched the towel to her naked body.

"Shit." He whipped away from her so quickly, he almost collided with the door. "I didn't look, I swear."

Yeah. Right. He'd most definitely gotten an eyeful. "You didn't knock either."

"I know, I'm sorry. I just...I don't know what I was thinking." Casimir turned back toward her and a scowl marred his brow. "No, that's a lie. I know exactly what I was thinking. I was so fucking worried—"

"Still naked."

"Right. Shit." He averted his gaze once more and held up his hand to the side of his face.

Maeve was by no means ashamed of her body, or too modest, but it did give her a kind of satisfaction watching him squirm.

"I had to make sure you were okay," he muttered lamely.

She wrapped her towel around her and knotted it in the front. "Could've fooled me." She moved past him toward her bed but he caught her by the arm.

"What's that supposed to mean?" His dark eyes were unreadable.

"It means, you were more than content to let me die." Carefully, she pried his fingers from her forearm. "You were going to let her kill me, Casimir. All she had to do was reprimand you like a misbehaving pup, and you obeyed. You stood by and did *nothing*."

He released her. "I had no choice, Maeve."

"We all have a choice." He stepped in her direction, and she held up one hand. "Stay where you are, and no peeking."

Casimir closed his eyes, but his brows were furrowed. "You know my choices are not equal to yours."

Maybe not, but at the very least he could've tried. Maybe begged for her life, or bartered with Carman, or simply just asked. He was the Captain of the Guard. He was her favorite soldier. Because he would die for her. Because his loyalty was to her above all else. Because he was bound to her.

She pulled on the leggings and slipped the blouse over her head. "I understand our choices may not ever be the same. Forgive me if I thought some part of you might not want to see me dead."

"I would never wish death upon you." His voice was strained, and when she glanced over at him, his eyes were focused on her. The way he watched her, the way his gaze harbored his emotions, she knew he meant it. She'd known him her entire life, trusted him with every fiber of her being, and yet when she was on the brink of death, he'd done nothing. He allowed it to happen, like she was of no value. No meaning.

"You know, if the roles had been reversed, I would've died trying to save you." She snatched her corset off the bed and slid it around her waist. Frustration and something like sorrow caused her hands to tremble, and she couldn't get the metal hooks into place. "I wouldn't even have to think about it. I just would've done it. I would've done anything within my power to keep you alive. But you—"

He closed the distance between them in one stride. His capable hands captured the hooks of her corset and he expertly fastened them into place, hesitating only when he neared her breasts. His jaw clenched and when his knuckles lightly brushed across her rounded flesh, she sucked in a breath.

"Are you alive?" he asked. His hands fall away from her, but he didn't step back.

"Yes." Maeve jerked her head up and glared at him.

"Then you can thank me later." Casimir flashed a smile. A real one, a rare one, and she caught sight of the dimple in his left cheek. Then he broke away from her and headed for the door. "We leave in an hour. Don't take too long fixing your hair, Maeve. I only packed you a few pins in case you lose some on the way."

Her entire body froze.

Casimir had packed her bag for her? And he cared enough to pack extra pins for her? "Um, thanks."

"You're welcome." He opened her bedroom door and hazy light filtered in from the open hall. He glanced back over his shoulder at her. "Oh, and one more thing."

She wasn't sure she wanted to know. "What's that?"

Casimir smirked. "I definitely peeked."

Maeve's mouth fell open, but the door was already closing behind him. She laced up her boots, tucked her dagger into the sheath on her thigh, and slung her pack over her shoulder. She snatched her belt of throwing stars from the bed and buckled it around her waist, then walked out of her room for what she could only assume would be the last time. There was no looking back, no turning back. The walk to the castle gates was less eventful than she expected. She passed plenty of guards, and none of them even spared her a glance. Apparently, no one cared if she was the heir of Kells. It meant she wouldn't have her movements tracked, or be watched every hour of the day. She rounded the corner and passed the throne room, kept her spine in place when she heard her mother's voice echoing within the grand walls.

She headed through the courtyard to the gates, where Casimir was readying the horses and securing their packs for the journey. She wasn't even sure if Faeven was accessible by horse, but she figured they'd find out soon enough. Rowan stood against one of the stone archways, one ankle crossed over the other, watching her walk in his direction. Her gaze instantly dropped to his chest. He wore another tattered shirt, but this one disguised his scars. As far as she could tell, he didn't appear to be bleeding anymore. But it made her curious as to who inflicted those awful wounds. Not that she should care. At all.

But she would bet anything it was Carman's doing.

"Maeve!"

She barely had time to react before Saoirse threw herself at her. She wrapped Maeve into her arms and squeezed. Maeve dropped her pack and welcomed her best friend's strong embrace. Saoirse pulled away, but held onto both of her arms. Her eyes scanned Maeve's body, searching for cuts or bruises. They were healing thanks to her blood curse, and mostly hidden beneath her blouse, but she was grateful for her friend's concern.

"Are you alright?" She slid her hands to Maeve's shoulders, then cupped her cheeks. "Casimir told me your mother put you back in the cage. I couldn't find you anywhere. I didn't think she'd...it never even occurred to me she would—"

"It's okay." The lie came easily, like a blade slicing through skin. "It was nothing."

"Don't tell me it was nothing." Saoirse glanced over to where Casimir stood, staring to the west, beyond Kells, to the Moors. "I can see it all over your face, Maeve. What happened?"

She didn't want to relive it. She didn't want to tell Saoirse how utterly terrified she'd been when Carman used her power against her, when she suspended Maeve in the air, then sent her plunging into the sea. She didn't want to explain the fear. The panic. The realization that Carman wished to see her dead.

"I'll tell you about it later." But she secretly hoped her friend would forget.

"I'm not going to let you off that easily," Saoirse warned.

"I know." Maeve placed her hands on top of Saoirse's.

"Trust me, I know. But we have more important things to deal with right now."

Like venturing to a foreign realm, through unfamiliar lands, in search of someone who may not even be there.

"Alright, listen up." Casimir motioned for them to come closer. The warm breeze whistled through the towering trees lining the path away from the castle. He pulled his hood down. "We're going to head west out of Kells toward the Moors, and that's less than a day's trek. From there, we'll cut north through the Fieann Forest."

"You make it sound so easy," Rowan mused, and his black cape moved around him like the shadows of night.

Casimir cut him down with a hard glare. "Because it is."

Rowan shrugged and shoved his hands into the pockets of his pants.

"From there, we'll reach the Shores." Casimir glanced up at the sky, then back to their group. "Now, the Shores is neutral territory, and they aren't ruled by human or fae. So, this is where we'll make our crossing."

"How do we cross into Faeven?" Saoirse asked. "Our realms are separated by a sea of magic. I've heard rumors of people who have tried to enter into Faeven, but none of them have been successful."

Rowan lifted one finger into the air. "That's where I come in."

Maeve crossed her arms, already annoyed by his haughty expression. "And why should we trust anything that comes out of your mouth?"

Rowan's mouth curved into a vicious smile. He rolled up the sleeves of his worn shirt and Maeve caught sight of the cuffs bound to his wrists. They were plain silver, but eerily similar to her own. "What other choice do you have?"

"The faerie is right." Casimir silenced any objection with a look. "We have no other choice, and we will need his assistance to help negotiate a crossing."

"Negotiate?" The idea of negotiating anything with the fae left Maeve unsettled. Owing a debt to a faerie was never a good thing. Ever. "What do you mean, negotiate?"

"Everything comes with a price, Princess." Rowan sidled closer but Maeve held her ground.

"How do we negotiate a crossing?" Saoirse drew his attention to her. "What sort of things should we be prepared for?"

"Anything." Rowan lifted both of his hands. "Everything."

Maeve couldn't stand his flippancy. It infuriated her, left her seething, and made her want to...*stab* something.

"Enough of your riddles, Rowan." She spun around and closed the distance between him, ignoring the way his eyes briefly flashed with amusement before sobering. "Tell us what to expect, otherwise I will ensure that you're the first one to die."

"Ouch." He clamped a hand over his heart then stole a glance at Casimir, who looked like he was about to combust in rage. "Is she always this feisty?"

Casimir dipped his head and when he spoke, his voice was low and deep with tempered fury. "Don't ever speak ill of Princess Maeve in my presence."

"Enough!" Saoirse's voice was thunderous. Her beauty was rattled with a tinge of exasperation. "We'll all be dead before we make it out of the Moors with this constant bullshit."

Maeve swallowed her shame. Arguing and bickering like children wasn't going to get them anywhere, and it definitely wouldn't save their lives. "You're right. If we don't work together, we won't come out of this alive. Our kingdom will fall. Our *realms* will fall."

Casimir kicked the ground with his boot and gravel skittered across the path. "And you expect us to trust a fae without even questioning him?"

"No." On this Maeve was firm. "I expect us to do whatever is required to survive."

There was a slow murmur of agreement.

"As I was saying," Rowan stated, but some of his arrogance diminished. "Crossing into Faeven will fall to me. It is not something easily accomplished by mortals. Sometimes, if conditions are favorable, the Dorai will ferry willing travelers."

"The Dorai?" A line of worry cut across Saoirse's forehead. "What are the Dorai? I've never heard of them."

"I'll explain more on the way." Rowan's lavender gaze lifted to the haze of clouds above. "But if we don't set off soon, we won't make it to the Moors before dark."

He was right, though no one wanted to admit it. But instead of arguing, the group mounted their horses in amicable silence and set off down the Ridge toward Kells. There was no farewell party, no bidding of goodbye, and no backward glances. Only the quiet acknowledgment that there was a fairly good chance not all of them would come back alive.

THEY RODE in silence for what seemed like an eternity, until the walls of Kells and the call of the Gaelsong Sea were behind them. Until The Scathing nothing more than an indistinct murmur of death. The Moors rose in the distance, their dense overhang of vine-covered trees and lush greenery offered a tempting reprieve from the sun. Sparkling streams glittered along either side of the worn dirt path, like ribbons of pale blue silk. Flowers of purple and red bloomed over hollowed-out logs, and furry little woodland creatures scampered across fallen branches and under berry bushes.

The Moors possessed an eerie sort of beauty. Traveling through it was like walking through the pages of a fairytale. A land of enchantment, hidden away from the rest of the world.

Maeve knew if they continued in this direction, they would eventually pass the lake where she found the Aurastone. She hoped Casimir didn't stop, she hoped he didn't even see it. The lake was a secret, something just for her. Her own sort of treasure.

Rowan rode up alongside her and kept pace.

She knew he was watching her, but she didn't dare look over at him. Any conversation with him would only annoy her. She didn't like how easily he'd been able to disarm her. She didn't like how he acted as though he knew everything about her, or how he carefully crafted his words. But more than all those things, looking at him caused her blood to hum, because the beauty of him was damn near painful.

"I know why you refuse to look at me." Rowan's low baritone rolled over her and Maeve tried not to shiver.

She gripped the reins tight in her hands, kept her gaze on Saoirse and Casimir in front of her. "And does my aversion inflate your ego?"

"On the contrary, it infuriates me."

Maeve looked up at him sharply. "I don't know what you're talking about."

He wasn't smiling. But he wasn't scowling either. He looked...displeased. "You won't look at me because you see too much of yourself in a creature you've been bred to hate."

Maeve blew an errant curl out of her face. "I don't hate you," she muttered. The words were out of her mouth before she could stop them.

"Such a pretty little liar." Rowan steered his horse a bit closer, so close, their legs nearly touched. "The only thing stronger than your hate for me is your fear of the ocean."

Her nails bit into the leather of the reins. Oh, but he was maddening. "It must be difficult for you." She bit the words out.

His dark brows rose with interest. "What's that?"

"To be unable to lie." She offered him a smug smile, grateful to recall reading the rules of the fae so many times. They could deceive, or twist their words in such a way that fact was lost in confusion, but they would never be able to tell an untruth.

Rowan's face registered surprise first, and she wished she hadn't been looking at him because then he smiled, and she nearly toppled off her horse. His laughter rang out, rich and musical, and she couldn't help the way her mouth fell open at the sound of it.

"Not everything you read in your books is true. A lot of it is made up, stories the fae told humans as a means to placate them, so they'd leave us alone." He reached out and gently squeezed her thigh. "I assure you, I am perfectly capable of deceit."

Maeve clamped her mouth closed to keep from gaping. She expected him to pull away or laugh at her expense. Maybe even chuckle and shake his head at her foolishness. But what she didn't expect was for him to rub his thumb along her upper thigh.

Twice.

The humming of her blood grew louder and there was another sensation, something she didn't recognize.

"Mind yourself, Princess." His gaze followed the road to where Casimir led their group. They were leaving the Moors, the last of the brush and beauty falling behind them. The Fieann Forest was up ahead. "These woods are not safe."

Then he urged his horse forward and matched pace with Casimir.

The memory of his touch through the thin fabric of her

leggings was still fresh when Saoirse fell back and glanced over at her, a bright and searing smile on her face.

Maeve leaned to the left, away from the creepy grin on her friend's face. "Why are you looking at me like that?"

Saoirse wiggled her eyebrows. "Rowan seems to have taken an interest in you."

That was the most absurd thing Maeve ever heard. She shook her head in protest. "No. I think he sees me as a conquest. Something he wants but can't have. Something he'd like to use, then discard."

Saoirse rubbed her lips together and adjusted the blossom tucked behind her ear. Today it was a pale pink dahlia. "I'd let him use and discard me any day of the week."

A flush bled into Maeve's cheeks. She wasn't a prude, but unfortunately, she was still pure. Men of worth were scarce in Kells, either too focused on training or already married, and she found most of them were intimidated by her. Or maybe it was because Casimir was always lurking in the background and scaring them away like a protective older brother.

"Saoirse," Maeve chided. "He's our enemy."

"I don't discriminate when it comes to the beauty of males." She tossed her braid of moonlight over one shoulder. "Besides, he's fae. He's had *years* of practice. I bet he's great in bed."

Maeve laughed. No, choked. But when she finally caught her breath, the world shimmered. The sky darkened. And her blood ran cold.

"Movement to the left!" Rowan called out.

"What is it?" Casimir stalled his horse. "What do you see?"

"Dark fae," Rowan muttered, his gaze trained on the trees of the Fieann Forest.

"Where?" Saoirse hopped off her horse, one hand on her sword and at the ready.

"In the shadows." Rowan's face was stone.

Maeve stared into the woods where shadows crawled and silence reigned. She hadn't realized they'd reached the forest so quickly. She hadn't noticed there were no more birds, or animals, or any breath of life at all. Just a deep and sinister stillness. She couldn't see anything, but she *knew*. She could feel it in her bones, in the darkest part of her soul.

Like calls to like.

She shook the memory away. "We won't be able to outrun them, will we?" she whispered.

"Not them. *It.*" Rowan slid off his horse and unsheathed his sword. "And no, we won't."

Maeve followed suit and pulled her sword as well. It was nothing spectacular, as she was far more proficient at handling a dagger, but it would have to be enough. Casimir joined her, with Saoirse on her opposite side. Casimir nodded once. "Stay with Maeve."

She glared up at him. "I can handle myself."

"I know you can." His hand fell to her shoulder, and squeezed lightly. "But until we know what this thing is, I don't want anyone getting separated. So, Maeve, you will stay with Saoirse, and keep to the back." He issued orders like a man of worth, one who'd gone into battle plenty of times. The kind of man who had war in his blood and an invincible soul. "Fae, you're coming with me."

Rowan smirked. "Wouldn't have it any other way."

The last thing Maeve heard was Rowan saying, "Oh fuck," before a wall of cold slammed into her and she was overcome by the sensation of a thousand lost souls.

Chapter Eight

Darkness pummeled Maeve. She blinked, but she couldn't see. There was nothing. Nothing but cold. Dread cloaked her shoulders, hung around her neck. Something pulled her, tugged her. She was surrounded by emptiness. Unease crept over her, ran its slithering fingers along her skin. She clutched her sword with one hand, and her head swiveled in every direction, toward the harsh whispers that scraped across her cheek and past her ears like an old friend. There were so many words, but none she could understand.

"It's a Hagla!" Rowan yelled.

The velvet of his voice reached for her and she threw her arms out blindly. Desperate to grab ahold of something, anything but the draining darkness. She remembered reading about Haglas in one of the books in the library. There wasn't much to be said about the creature of shadow and gloom. It preyed on emotion and misery; it brought a person's worst fears to life. A mortal could be lost in their own nightmares forever, trapped until madness took hold of their mind, leaving them to die of delirium.

Something warm brushed over her hand. Squeezed. "Keep moving!" Saoirse's voice urged from beside her.

Her feet were cemented to the ground, gripped by the spongy earth. Then she saw it. The wall of impenetrable black, more fearsome than the darkest night.

"Don't let go!" Saoirse yelled as she was ripped from her side.

Maeve reached for her, for something, but her fingers clutched empty air. Blinded and terrified her blade would strike her best friend, she lowered her weapon.

"Saoirse!" She screamed and the pungent stench of decay filled her mouth. Her knees slammed into the ground, fists coiled into the damp terrain. Her sword was ripped from her grip. Hot bile scalded the back of her throat, and she gagged, coughed, struggled to get back on her feet. Pain lanced through her, stole into her mind, and she squeezed her eyes shut against the agony, against the assault. She gasped and her lungs filled, burned with air tainted by aged oak and sea salt. The howl of the wind faded away, only to be replaced by the deafening roar of an angry ocean, and the distinctive creak of frayed rope grinding against a weakened tree branch.

No.

She'd already lived this nightmare once before; she couldn't suffer through it again. She wouldn't survive. Peeling one eye open, panic sank deep within her, dug its claws into her bones, and spread through her body like a plague. Every muscle seized with fear and her joints locked up. She couldn't move, she couldn't escape. Her heart hammered wildly, and her chest rose and fell like rapid fire. Shadows sneered from the corner of her mind, threatened to leave her in oblivion. Terror stole into her, snatching the air from her lungs like a thief, leaving her breathless. Stricken.

She was back in the cage.

She took a breath and was left hollow. Her heart pounded, galloped like a thousand wild horses racing across the shore. She scrubbed her damp palms against the smooth fabric of her pants and inched herself backwards, away from the rusted bars of the cage. The wind returned, lit with fury this time, and whipped her hair against her face. The sting was a harsh slap, the replica of Carman's hand across her cheek. Iron creaked and the cage rocked. Maeve grabbed a bar on either side of her and pressed her back to the frozen metal, dragged her knees to her chest. Another gust of wind tossed the cage further over the ledge in a violent lashing. Her stomach heaved into a tangle of unforgiving knots and the branch anchoring her above the crashing sea groaned in agony.

A smothering blanket of gray loomed on the horizon. Streaks of lightning shattered across the sky, and in one thunderous crack, the heavens broke open. Chills prickled along Maeve's flesh and the tiny hairs at the back of her neck stood on end. Shots of icy water pelted her hands, her face, her body. Heavy rain hammered against her, and soaked her through until her body convulsed and shuddered. But there was nowhere to go. Nowhere to hide.

A storm ravaged around her, blew in hard from the seething coast.

The cage wouldn't survive.

She wouldn't survive.

It was all of her fears come to life, worse than she ever remembered. The anger of the ocean. The irrational fear of drowning, despite knowing how to swim. The numbing, gripping anxiety of heights, of losing control, of never being enough. Tears streamed down her face, hot and fast, a harsh contrast to the frigid temperature.

Lightning struck close, and the shocking jolt of it snapped the oak's branch in half. She watched in terror as her lifeline broke away from the tree. The cage lurched and Maeve tumbled with it. Metal slammed into her stomach first, then her back. Her head snapped against the lock, sending spasms of pain screaming through her temples and down her spine. She clawed at the baseboard of the cage and tendrils of wood curled beneath her nails. Shards of oak splintered her skin as she tumbled out of the cage toward the jagged cliffs of the sea.

Maeve screamed.

A blinding slash cut through her vision, like the colors of twilight set on fire. Something snagged her by the elbow; a branch of some fallen tree, or a claw of a wild animal. She didn't know, she didn't care. Reaching out, she clutched it, and swung her feet wildly to keep the sea of death at bay. Then she was moving up. Up and away. The rocks that jutted up like vicious teeth from the ocean's ravenous mouth slipped away, receding into a damp forest floor.

But she was done. Her body, her bones, her mind...all of it was gone. The Hagla stole her energy and fear rendered her useless. Maeve collapsed into the vaguely familiar scent of night jasmine and moss, and then there was nothing.

MAEVE WAS ROCKING. A gentle, swaying motion kept her calm and steady. She sighed onto the cushion behind her head, then inhaled slowly. Deeply. There was a scent too; citrus and fresh earth. It soothed her. But the beating of her own heart didn't guarantee her safety, so she peeled her eyes open, only to be blinded by the brilliant blue of the sky. Lazy white clouds stretched overhead and sunlight warmed her body. A shadow loomed on the outskirts of her vision.

She blinked and Casimir came into focus. She was looking up at the underside of his chin, the outline of his jaw. An odd view. It was then she realized she was on a horse, his horse, presumably. She was nestled against him and her legs were swept over his lap. In the distance, she heard muffled voices. They were hushed, like whispers. One was Saoirse. The other was Rowan. She would recognize them anywhere.

"Captain." Saoirse's call drifted over to them. "The clearing is up ahead."

Casimir shifted her in his arms, curled her closer to him. Kept her protected. "We'll stop there to prepare for the crossing."

She squeezed her eyes shut. It was easier to keep them closed than to look up at him, knowing she was reclining in his arms.

A low rumble sounded from inside the hard wall of his chest. "I know you're pretending."

Damn.

Her eyes fluttered open. A grin stretched across his face, and he carefully eased her into a sitting position. Her gaze skimmed their surroundings. Saoirse rode alongside Rowan, and Maeve's horse was nowhere to be seen. They were hardly a day into their journey, and possible death already hung heavily in the air. How would they manage? There was no telling how long it would take to reach Faeven, or how much time would pass until they found the *anam ó Danua*—if they even found it at all. The possibilities of all of them staying alive for the duration seemed fleeting. Defeated, Maeve let her head roll back onto Casimir's shoulder.

"How are you feeling?" His words were soft. Kind.

"I don't really know." Her voice cracked and she pressed

her fingers to her forehead, let a breath escape her when there was no sudden pain. Her throat, however, was parched. "Exhausted, I think. And a little thirsty."

"I bet you are." He pulled a flask of water from his pack and handed it to her. She guzzled a few mouthfuls. "You slept for a day."

Maeve choked on the water, then forced herself to cough when her lungs seized. Casimir patted her roughly on the back. His face was illuminated with the remnants of amusement, but something else was layered just beneath the surface of his features. A ghost of another emotion. Relief? Regret? She couldn't be sure.

"A full day?" Maeve asked.

"Just about." Casimir smiled once more but then it vanished, replaced by a scowl. She understood why a moment later.

Rowan circled his horse around them and came up on their right. "I see sleeping beauty is finally awake."

Maeve rolled her eyes to the piercing blue sky and Casimir's grip on the reins stiffened. "We're here," he announced, to no one in particular.

A few paces ahead, the trees fell back like they were parting in ceremony, giving way to a wide expanse of sparkling sea and crystalline sand. Gentle waves of glittering emerald came up to greet the shoreline. Tiny shells, white sand, and shards of sea glass lined the curved beach. The breeze was cool, but the sun was warm, its rays already heating Maeve's skin. She peered out at the horizon, where the air seemed to waver and breathe as though it was alive. As though it was sustained by magic. The expanse of stunning water stretching before them was Eirelan Pass.

Casimir helped her slide off the horse and once she was on the ground, she made her way to the beach. Swirling shells and rainbow-hued sea glass crunched lightly beneath her boots. She knelt down and scooped up a handful. The sand sifted between her fingers like sugar. Halfway buried underneath the sand, she spied a piece of sea glass the color of wild summer roses. Its edges were smooth and rounded, having been tumbled by the waves, and when she picked it up and held it to the sun, it glittered pink, then red, then gold.

Maeve slipped the piece of sea glass into her pocket.

"There's nothing I love quite as much as the feel of the sun on my skin." Rowan's rich voice caused Maeve's spine to tingle, despite the warmth.

"And why is that?" She bent down to scoop up a shell, swiftly checking to make sure her dagger was still secured in her sheath. Not that she was worried, but he was still a fae. The shell in her hand was a swirly mix of brown and cream, and it spiraled to a point.

"No particular reason."

Her head whipped in his direction. The way he said it was wrong. It should have been a casual turn of phrase, but instead it seemed to harbor a deeper, darker meaning. She found it curious when he wouldn't meet her eyes. His gaze was trained on where the blue of the sky met the turquoise of the sea.

She stole a glance over her shoulder. Casimir was seated on a piece of driftwood, sharpening his sword. His black hood was shoved back. He glowered in her direction, though she imagined it was aimed at Rowan, not her. Saoirse was sprawled in the sand like a sun goddess. She twirled a flower lazily between her fingers and hummed something reminiscent of a sea shanty.

"What happened?" Maeve asked Rowan, knowing he would at least give her some variant of the truth. "After I was attacked?"

She couldn't be certain, but she swore his body tensed. "You were rescued. And that's about it."

He plucked the shell from her hand and tossed it to where wisps of sea grass crawled toward the swaying trees. She opened her mouth to protest until she saw what slithered out of it; a long gray insect with hundreds of legs and speckled with tiny red dots. It was a centipede of sorts, and highly poisonous. She stumbled backward but Rowan's hand shot out, bracing the small of her back. Maeve tried to push away from him. "I'm not fragile. I'm—"

"You're weak." His eyes flashed and he tucked his hands into his pockets. "Your weakness will be the end of you."

She didn't need a protector or a guardian. Not if she was ever going to be queen. Not if she intended on becoming her mother's match. She marched right back up to Rowan, and as much as she would've loved to look him dead in the eye, she stood a whole foot shorter than him. She rose up on her toes and the corner of his lip twitched.

"Is that a threat?" she hissed.

"That's a promise," he purred.

Maeve reared back, ready to punch him in his pretty little face, when a pair of arms hoisted her up and away from him.

"Easy, tiger." Saoirse set her back down, away from striking range, but stood by, just in case.

"Your weakness is not determined by whether you can throw a punch or fight with a weapon. And it isn't determined by fear. It's here." Rowan pointed to his heart. "Maybe once you figure that out, then you won't be such a liability to the rest of us."

Maeve's fists clenched until her nails bit into the skin of her palms. "You bastard."

He bowed regally. "At your service, my lady."

Maeve launched herself at him. Her fingers curved like claws but caught only air, because Saoirse snatched her by the waist and hauled her back.

"Leave him, Maeve. We only need him until we find this damn soul of a goddess." Saoirse's grip around her waist remained firm, but she sent a cool death stare to Rowan. He chuckled. "After that, I promise I'll let you kill him."

"Fine." Maeve heaved a breath. She didn't have weakness in her heart, at least not like he said. She was a warrior. She read and studied, she armed herself with both knowledge and sword. She didn't fear death. Instead, she merely prepared for its inevitable arrival. The only way she could possibly be a liability was because of her curse. Possessing fae blood could very well be a problem once she crossed in Faeven, mostly because she had no idea if the cuffs her mother bound to her would hold true. If the spell was strong enough to keep the monster inside her away.

A thought formed in the back of her mind. A tiny glimmer of light. The makings of a spark. She was going to Faeven. Surely there were fae within the realm more powerful than her mother. If she could find one, perhaps she could find a way to rid herself of the curse. She might have to make a bargain, though it was bound to be dangerous, but nothing could be worse than being cursed with the blood of faeries.

Unfortunately, she might have to ask a particular fae for help.

Rowan sat upon a cluster of rocks, his arms stretched out behind him, his legs crossed, his face tilted up to the sun. He looked like a god, with the way his biceps were perfectly sculpted and with thighs seemingly made of steel. Sweat dampened his shirt so it clung to him, to his abdomen, and the ripple of muscles there caused a flush of arousal to stain her cheeks.

It made her stomach turn.

Maeve turned away from him and faced Saoirse. "I should go thank Casimir. I forgot to do it earlier."

Saoirse fiddled with the new, vibrant orange flower tucked

behind one ear. The dahlia had been lost during the Hagla's attack. "Thank him for what?"

"For saving me."

"Maeve." Her friend dipped her head low, so their conversation was only shared with each other. The beautiful planes of Saoirse's face were solemn. "Casimir came out of the forest without you."

She blanked. "What? Was it you?"

Saoirse jerked her head in the direction of the rocks. "It was Rowan, the fae you just tried to kill."

Chapter Nine

Twice now, it seemed Casimir had left Maeve to die.

Twice now, it seemed Rowan had saved her life.

Maeve mustered up what was left of her diminished dignity and trudged through the sand, careful to avoid any more of those swirly shells. She stood near Rowan, not too close, but near enough she could feel his gaze roving over her. She owed him a life debt. Not so much for the centipede, but for her survival against the Hagla.

Small waves lapped against the shore, the pretty water constantly grasping for more of the warmed sand, like lovers desperate for a kiss. She watched as her shadow, stretched out before her, was joined by another. Restlessness coasted over her and skated down her spine. It was annoying, the way he managed to slide beneath her skin. She shifted her weight from one foot to the other, then clasped her hands together and stared down at the silver cuffs on her wrist. The only barrier from herself and the dark power lurking inside her.

Perhaps she was not so different from Rowan after all.

Maeve wrapped her arms around herself to ward off the chilling thought.

"Don't tell me you're getting nervous now," he mused and nudged a rock with his boot.

"I'm not nervous." Her voice lost most of its biting edge. But it was true. She wasn't nervous. Not really. Just unsettled. "I've never been past the Moors before. I've never seen the world outside the borders of Kells." She shrugged, and drew circles in the damp sand with the toe of her boot. Books offered her a glimpse into cultures and worlds other than her own, and she'd admired the few maps her mother had in the library, but the rest was left up to her imagination. "I don't know what to expect."

"There are Four Courts in Faeven. You've read about them in those books of yours." Rowan ran a hand through his hair, left it mussed in different directions. "Spring, Summer, Autumn, and Winter. But after the Evernight War, a plague settled across our realm. For forty years the terror reigned, and spread, and destroyed. It devoured our lands. Poisoned our streams. Obliterated our people. Until finally, Danua herself came down from Maghmell and purged away the eternal night. She poured her soul into the earth. Together, we were able to rid Faeven of darkness. Of evil. Of violence."

He looked down at Maeve. Dark lashes framed his lavender eyes. "But the Courts are not as they once were, and it may be difficult to determine friend from foe."

The histories she'd studied growing up told stories of regal fae and Courts anointed by seasons, arrogance, greatness, and immortality. She'd read about the plague, the darkness that nearly incapacitated the Four Courts. If not for the goddess Danua stepping in to save them, Faeven would've fallen forever.

"Tell me." He faced her then and his cape of shadows

swirled, but never touched the ground. "What do you know of Faeven?"

She tried to remember all the books she'd read over the years, all the pages she'd pored through before Roth had rendered her unconscious and left her in the cage. "I know all fae have magic, but it isn't equal among the race. Some fae are far superior."

Rowan ran his thumb along the small cleft in his chin. "The Archfae are among the most powerful of the faeries. Every fae within the realm of Faeven swears his or her allegiance to an Archfae of their choosing. The Four Courts are not decided by the magic one possesses, instead, it's a matter of loyalty."

Interesting. "And the Archfae are...?"

"Few of them are High Kings and High Queens respectively. With some princesses and princes thrown into the mix." He shifted, his gaze on the horizon separating them from another world. "Other Archfae serve their High King or High Queen, and none of them are to be crossed."

"So many rules," Maeve muttered, and Rowan laughed.

"You'll learn quickly enough."

"Which one is yours?"

The question seemed candid enough but Rowan blinked. "What?"

"Which Court?" she clarified. "Which Court was yours before you ended up in Kells?"

Shadows haunted his beautiful eyes. "My Court is Spring."

"You must be excited to return home."

Rowan stretched out his arms, examined the cuffs bound to his wrists, the ones that looked so similar to hers. "That's an understatement. I imagine your mother is expecting my return after this little adventure. I'm afraid I have every intention of disappointing her."

You and me both, she thought.

"How did she capture you?" The question spilled out before she could stop it. "My mother, how was she able to hold you captive?"

He absently rubbed one hand over his chest, over the cavern of scars there. "Nightshade."

"Nightshade?" Maeve bent down at the edge of the shoreline and ran her fingers through the cool water. Her reflection gazed back at her—Gray-green eyes, a perky, button of a nose, and full lips. She glanced back over at Rowan and stood up. "Isn't that poisonous?"

"It can be, yes."

Seconds of thick, humid silence passed between them while she struggled to find the words to say next.

"Saoirse told me what you did." Maeve was the worst at apologizing. It was even more difficult when she owed someone gratitude as well. "Back in the forest. She said you—"

Without warning, Rowan was flush against her. One arm snaked around her waist and hauled her against his chest, held her so close, she could feel the erratic beating of his heart. He pressed one finger to her lips and silenced her.

"Don't." His voice was rough. Strangled.

Maeve frowned. "But—"

He jerked his head sharply. "Never thank me, Maeve."

He'd used her name. Her actual name.

"Why...why not?" She was trying hard to ignore the way his fingers were lightly tapping against her waist, how his other hand had slid from her lips, to her cheek, to her neck.

"Think about it."

He leaned in so close, she could see the stars dancing in his eyes. The scent of orange blossom and cedarwood pulsed in the air around them. A bold rhythm. A dark melody. One Maeve somehow knew, one she recognized in the deepest, loneliest part of her soul. Her fingers tingled, the cuffs against her skin burned, and her blood sang, a crescendo to the symphony of magic inside her.

Maeve tried to focus, but her mind was a muddled mess, and his fingers were so distracting. There had to be a reason he wanted nothing to do with her appreciation. Because... because...His palm slid higher now, and his fingertips followed the hard line of her corset, right to the sensitive area just beneath her breast.

"Oh." The word fell from her on a sigh, and then understanding slammed into her, jarring her out of the moment. "I'd owe you a debt, wouldn't I?"

"Perhaps." His teeth grazed his bottom lip, and Maeve found herself wondering what he might taste like, if he would be rich and decadent like her favorite icing, or tempting and poisonous like forbidden fruit? "Are you afraid?"

His breath was cool across her cheek.

"Of Faeven? No." She wasn't afraid of anything, not even him. Part of her longed to reach up and brush a fallen lock of silky teal hair from his face. "Should I be?"

"No. As long as you remember to always keep your guard up." He bent down, closer, until their mouths were barely a breath apart. If she rose up on her toes, she'd kiss him, and she knew with every fiber of her being, with every part of her cursed soul, she'd enjoy it. "And trust no one."

Maeve swayed into him. "What about you?"

"Especially not me." Rowan winked, then released her so quickly she almost fell face first into the sand.

Maeve thrust her arms out and caught her balance. Embarrassment bled into her cheeks while she grappled with her own composure. *Sun and sky.* She'd wanted to kiss him, she'd wanted to kiss a *fae.* It had to be a trick, a play against her mind to use her emotions against her. And she'd almost fallen for it. She'd been seconds away from wrapping her arms around his neck and pulling his mouth to hers, and she would've brought down the moon for a taste of him.

She shoved her hair back from her face, inhaled deeply, and squeezed her eyes shut. She would have to be more careful. It would be careless to make a mistake like that again. She knew nothing of Rowan, nothing of his history, of his loyalty, or anything of his plans. For all she knew, he would get them into Faeven and then leave them to fend for themselves. Which, she had to admit, seemed rather plausible.

Maeve sucked in one more calming breath, inhaled the warm air and soft sea breeze, then opened her eyes.

Determination fueled her. She would not be so easily blinded again.

"Oh, look." Rowan glanced back at her, then pointed out over the rocks. "Here comes our ride."

Maeve climbed over some of the rocks for a better view. She peered out at the horizon, where the air seemed to waver and breathe, as though it was alive. Sustained by magic.

She saw the banners first, streamers of burnt orange emblazoned with the image of a glittering black creature she'd never seen before. It possessed three heads, each one with the golden beak of an eagle, and skinny, curved horns. The heads shared a body, like a dragon with a long tail and sharp talons. Glossy black scales covered it, and the wings were feathered, dark orange like the first start of a flame. The boat was long and narrow, made of a rich, polished wood, with a curved hull and scalloped railing. A canopy of goldenrod stretched across the open decks, a shield from the blinding sunlight. Despite having no sails, the boat propelled effortlessly across the sea, straight toward the shore.

The air surrounding her throbbed, dense and heavy. It pulsed with magic, calling to her, whispering her name.

"Wow." Saoirse perched herself on a nearby rock, and wisps of silver hair floated around her face. "That's the fanciest boat I've ever seen."

"It's fae." Distaste dripped from Casimir's words.

"Of course it's fae." Rowan cut him down with one look. "What else would it be?"

Casimir yanked his hood over his head and grabbed his pack from the sand. "I'd been hoping for something a little more subtle."

Saoirse adjusted the sword at her waist and slung her pack over one shoulder. "What? A bright orange banner with a three-headed beast doesn't scream low-key to you?"

Maeve choked on a laugh.

"Hilarious." Casimir stalked across the sand, kicking up bits of sea glass and shells in his wake.

"Sarcasm suits you, Saoirse." Rowan cocked a sideways grin and crossed his arms, apparently impressed with the warrior's jest. "You should do it more often."

"I can think of other things I'd like to do more often," Saoirse murmured and Maeve swallowed down another laugh. That one burned.

"Later, Saoirse." Maeve bumped shoulders with her friend. "There'll be plenty of time for that later."

The boat docked near the crescent-shaped shore, with no rope or line. The moment Maeve saw the fae who captained it, her magic swam and coursed through her in a wave of hysteria. She swallowed down her apprehension, scrubbed her damp palms against the smooth fabric of her leggings. When he stepped into the sunlight, she clamped her mouth shut to keep from gasping.

He was glorious.

Rich auburn hair the color of crisp autumn leaves fell in a sharp angle across one side of his face. Tiny gold hoops were pierced all the way up one of his ears, and both were longer than any human ear, distinguished and pointed. A clear mark of a fae. His eyes were emerald green with bursts of gold fanning out from the center. The cleft in his chin was marred by a jagged scar and he towered over all of them, beating even Rowan in height. The brown leather collar of his coat was flipped up and its hem hit well past his knees. The shirt he wore beneath it was partially buttoned and a compass hung around his neck; the chain, a mix of knotted silk and beads. His pants were tapered, tucked into excessively shiny boots, and a belt of bronze and a sash of burgundy were slung around his waist. His sword rested casually by his side, just within reach. Plank after plank unfolded from the boat's port side, and seamlessly connected the empty deck to the shoreline. Each step he took, each click of his boot against the grainy wood, boasted confidence.

When he smiled, it was slow. Intentional. Dangerous.

Maeve's blood roared, so loud, she swore he could hear it. She shrank inside of herself, but there was nowhere to hide.

"Well, well." The fae was standing on the bridge to his ship one minute, and the next, he was right in front of them. His speed set her heart racing. She'd forgotten. Forgotten he was immortal. Forgotten fae were notoriously fast, quicker than any mortal. "What have we here?"

She fully expected him to watch them, to begin circling them like predator to prey. But his gaze was locked on Rowan. A familiarity filled the space surrounding them. Whether or not they were on good terms with each other was another story completely.

"Hello, Aran." Rowan inclined his head, just barely.

"Rowan." The fae named Aran glowered, and he closed the

distance between them until their faces were mere inches apart. "The last time I saw you, the sky was black, we were covered in blood, and you were running away from death."

Okay, so not on good terms.

Rowan lifted his arms and displayed the cuffs branding his wrist. "As you can see, not much has changed."

Aran's scowl vanished and was replaced with a vicious smile. "Got yourself into some trouble now, have you?"

"No more than you," Rowan quietly fired back.

Casimir cut between them. He kept one hand firmly planted on the sword at his side, but his gaze was trained on the new fae. "Aran, is it?"

The faerie in question raised an auburn brow.

"Casimir Vawda, Captain of the Guard to the kingdom of Kells." He gestured to Maeve and Saoirse. "We seek entry into Faeven."

Aran pressed his lips together and his dark green gaze lingered on Saoirse. Then Maeve. She swallowed the growing knot of panic in the back of her throat. He tossed Rowan a pitying glance. "You really must have fallen out of grace with Parisa, if you're hanging out with a bunch of mortals."

"Like I said—" Rowan began, but Maeve was growing impatient with the indirect conversation and the ambiguous jests.

The longer they stood about debating on crossing into Faeven, the more time The Scathing had to spread into Kells. It would take over the cute little shops, suck the life out of the one place she cared about, and destroy everything in its path. Annoyed, and despite her better judgment, Maeve barged right up to Aran and pointed her finger in his chest. "Are you going to take us into Faeven or not?"

"Stand down, Maeve," Casimir muttered.

Maeve whirled on him. Her chest burned with a fierce sort of anguish, and she clenched her fists. "Excuse me?"

Saoirse blew out a low whistle and she snared Rowan's arm to pull him to safety. The fae's mouth gaped open.

"You forget your place, Captain. I am *not* one of your soldiers." Maeve glared at the man she'd known since childhood. The man who knew her better than she knew herself. The man who taught her how to fight, how to survive, how to live up to the expectation of valor. She looked up to him, she relished in the fact that he treated her as an equal, and she was never ungrateful when he gave her extra training because he knew she would need it. He knew her life would be a fight. A struggle. Her very existence would be an endeavor. Except he'd forgotten one thing. "I may have been ignored and humiliated by my mother for the first twenty-four years of my life, but I'm still the fucking princess."

"Apologies." Casimir ducked his head. "You take over then, Your Highness."

"Ouch." Aran's brows shot up in interest. "I like her."

"Don't get any ideas," Rowan warned, then sent a wink her direction. "She's feisty."

Aran bowed. Excessively. "I'm afraid it's not very safe for mortals in Faeven right now." A strange look passed over his face. A silent debate. "Then again, it isn't very safe for fae either."

"It doesn't matter if it's dangerous." Maeve dismissed his warning. There was more at stake. "We'll be crossing either way."

Aran considered her for a moment. He crossed his arms, and his gaze flicked to Rowan, then back again. "Payment will be required."

"Obviously." Maeve rolled her eyes to where the sun sank lower in the sky and colored the clouds shades of pink and gold.

"Careful, Maeve." Saoirse reached out and gently took hold of her wrist. "Don't make any promises you don't intend to keep."

Maeve nodded. She understood. She knew what was at risk, what was being asked of her. The books in the library weren't always filled with the wonder and magic of Faeven. They recounted the horrors as well. Stories of humans being carried away to Faeven to become play things of the fae. On more than one occasion the fae had taken interest in a mortal sexually, and sometimes those humans were content to live out the remainder of their days as a kept soul, but for others, it was against their own will. Their minds had been swept of memories, and they'd been stolen away as slaves to do whatever bidding the fae demanded of them.

Whatever she said, she had to remember. Her words would be taken literally.

Maeve's shoulders rolled back and she looked up at Aran. She kept her mask of indifference in place, just as Casimir had suggested. "What are your terms?"

Aran's gaze wandered over to Saoirse and Casimir placed himself between them. This time he pulled his blade from the sheath at his waist, flashed the slightest glimpse. It was silver, but shone red in the fading sunlight. "None of the females in our party are variables. Nor are they bargaining chips. Nor are they at your disposal."

"Darn," Aran snarled, but then his brows rose in interest. Once more, he cast a hasty look toward Rowan, whose face remained impassive. "A princess *and* a captain. This must be a very important visit indeed."

Casimir stepped up and Maeve was half-tempted to smack him. "We'd appreciate your discretion as well."

Aran's bemused expression deepened into a scowl and he

set his sights on Maeve. His unsettling gaze burned into her. "Your price keeps going up."

"Name it," she fired back, unwilling to waste anymore time.

"Fine. I'll cross you into Faeven as you ask. On one condition."

Her heart slowed to a near stop.

"That I'm able to call in any favor," he lifted a finger and loosed a disgruntled sigh when Casimir made to protest, "none of the sexual kind, from any member of your party when the time comes." His mouth twitched and he pinned Casimir with a pointed finger. "You ruin all the fun."

"Deal." Maeve offered her hand and when Aran accepted, when the warmth of his palm pressed into hers, an image crashed into her. It was so strong, it stole her breath. A vision of autumn woods, of crimson and gold, of harvest skies, and the cold feel of death.

A ribbon of scarlet appeared between them, shimmering and pulsing with magic. It extended from Aran's hand to her own, and imprinted upon her skin. The glowing thread wrapped around her forefinger like a vine, before settling into the shape of a leaf.

Maeve jerked backward. "What in the seven hells is *that?*"

Aran watched her carefully. "It's called a Strand. It's the bond that ties two beings together when they enter into a contract."

He held out his hand, letting her see the same incandescent thread on his finger. "When the contract is fulfilled, the Strand will vanish." Then he swept his arm back gallantly, allowing her entry onto his boat. "Welcome aboard the Amshir."

As much as she didn't want to love it, the Amshir was splendid. The hull of the vessel was long and tapered, and had been meticulously hand-carved both at the bow and stern so the glossy wood curled toward the water, much like a vine or fern would unfurl for the rain. A canopy stretched overhead, a shield from the elements, and there was a small room toward the back of the ship which she assumed was the main quarters. It looked like it sat shallow, so she wasn't sure if there was a below deck, and while the craftsmanship was stunning, it was nothing like the ships that set sail out of Gaelsong Port. Those boasted masts and foremasts, shrouds and chains. Quarterdecks for command. Gun ports constructed for cannons and weapons. Mighty sails to catch the breeze and carry their crew home. Those ships were designed for conquest and war, to control and overtake.

But this...

This was more for lounging, a casual pleasure yacht, nothing more. The Amshir pulled away from the Shores and Maeve stayed near the back, watching the only world she'd ever known disappear into the distance.

"Captain!" Saoirse's voice called to Casimir from the starboard side. "Captain, you've got to come see this, there's a whole wine cellar in here!"

Maeve smiled. Leave it to Saoirse to find the wine, like they were sailing on a relaxing adventure, instead of venturing into the unknown. Alone, she leaned out over the railing and gazed up at the sky streaked with gold, fuchsia, and coral. Dusk would be on them in no time, the air would cool, and the stars would come out to dance.

She felt him before she heard him.

"What do you want, Rowan?" she asked, refusing to take her eyes off the twilight sky for fear of missing any of its beauty.

"Nothing." He propped his elbows up on the railing beside her. "Just admiring the view."

Maeve sighed, dreamy and content. "It's gorgeous, isn't it?"

"Stunning."

But when she looked over at him, he was looking at her. A flush crept up Maeve's neck and bled into her cheeks.

"Stop doing that," she muttered, frustrated with herself for enjoying his attention.

He leaned in closer, braced his chin on the crook of his elbow. "Doing what?"

"Looking at me like I'm something you want to devour."

"Maybe I do."

Maeve shoved away from the railing but he snatched her by the arm and twirled her into him. A low hum started in the back of his throat, and the soft breeze carried the haunting melody past her cheek, and down her neck.

"You're a fascinating creature," he murmured.

She twisted out of his hold. "Last time I checked, you said I was a liability."

"So I did." He stood where the dying rays of the sun stretched across the deck of the Amshir. Shadows of his cloak moved around them and he angled his head in study. "A sweet, tempting liability."

Maeve turned around and crossed her arms over the railing, refusing to be distracted by his pretty words and handsome face. "Tell me more about the Dorai," she said, in an effort to keep him away.

"Alright."

He came to stand beside her, close, but not too close, and stared up at the sky like he'd never seen it before. In that moment, she realized maybe he hadn't. If he'd been locked in the dungeon in Kells, the sky would certainly be a treat. There was no telling the last time he'd been able to gaze upon the inky blues and golds of a twilight sky. Maeve inhaled again, took the scent of him into her lungs. Only their even breathing and the brush of the waves along the Amshir broke the silence while she waited for him to speak.

"A long time ago, before the Evernight War, there was peace between the Four Courts. But even when tranquility lingers upon a land, there will still be those who love nothing more than to cause hate and discontent." Rowan's voice rose and fell like the tide. Lulling. Calming. He gestured to the expanse beyond the darkening night and cresting sea. "There were fae among us who thought they could be spiteful and vengeful without consequence. Fae who were treasonous to their Court and considered themselves above punishment. But what you must understand, is the High Kings and Queens do not take the decision of banishment lightly. Some choose to enforce it, depending upon the crime, while others do not."

Maeve looked over at him, at the way the shadows seemed to dance around him like an old friend. "What sorts of crimes?"

His jaw clenched and he blew an errant strand of hair out of his face. It left him on a sigh. "The worst you can imagine. Rape, among the most notable."

Her hand flew to her mouth. "Aran...did he—"

"No." Rowan cut her off before she could even finish the thought. "He would never. His crime...was of another kind. One he committed during the Evernight War, during the spread of the darkness."

"What did he do?" Her voice was low, scarcely a whisper in the night.

He angled his body toward her, and she found she enjoyed the scent of him. The way it mixed with the salt of the sea. "That's not my story to tell, Princess."

"Of course." She fidgeted with the belt of throwing stars wrapped around her waist, knowing he was watching her every move.

"You have the most mesmerizing eyes." Rowan studied her, like he was committing her to memory. "They remind me of the

Lismore Marin when the waters are calm. Sometimes green. Sometimes gray. Always moody, and full of magic."

The corner of her mouth lifted at the compliment. No one had ever remarked on her appearance before, or even paid her any kind of affection. She knew she should be wary, but it was kind of wonderful to know someone thought she was pretty. He reached out, slowly as to not startle her, and his thumb grazed her cheekbone. Maeve swallowed. But her throat was dry, like she'd spent one thousand days in the desert.

"And those lips..." His gaze lingered on her mouth. "So pink, like fresh spring roses."

Rowan leaned in. Closer.

"Are you going to kiss me?" Maeve's voice escaped her on a harsh murmur.

He pressed his forehead to hers and his eyes were the most dazzling shade of violet. Full of hunger and desire. "No."

Chapter Ten

But then Rowan's hand moved from her cheek to her throat, and Maeve's blood ran cold. She snatched his wrist held him back, away from her. The press of the Aurastone was safely tucked away and strapped to her thigh, just within reach.

Lust shaded his eyes a rich purple and the stars twinkled. He rubbed his lips together, then looked to where she held his wrist.

"Do you think I would hurt you?" he asked, his voice thick like honey.

Maeve searched his face. He already warned her not to trust him, and she knew in her heart he spoke true. "Yes. Even if it's not intentional."

"You might be right." He stepped back and the distance between them filled with a rush of cool air. Ribbons of navy blue and indigo blanketed the sky, and there were so many stars, it looked like they were falling straight into the sea. "Get some rest, Princess. We've got a big day tomorrow."

Right. Rest. Something she should be looking forward to,

though it would be impossible to fall asleep. Mostly because she was expected to sleep on a magical fae boat and she had no idea where they were sailing to, but also because Rowan left her longing for his touch. Any touch, really. She'd gone without affection, without tenderness and kindness for so long, she didn't even know what it felt like to be desired. Rowan though, he made her wonder. The beauty of his body made her mind fill with images from all the books she'd read on the nature of sex. Though she imagined anything involving him would far surpass the pictures she'd memorized to keep her warm at night. She bet Saoirse was right, he was probably fabulous in bed.

Unbidden scenes of him moving over top of her, of his mouth searing her skin, and of his hands roving over her body caused a swell of heat to rise at her core.

Rowan's gaze darkened and his jaw clenched. She turned away from him then, trying to ignore the way shame and humiliation sank their claws into her skin. "Goodnight, Rowan."

"Night, Princess."

A wave of guilt surged inside her but she tampered it down with reason. It didn't matter if she was sexually attracted to him. So what if she wanted to kiss him? It was *just* a kiss, nothing else. It made no difference if she was a mortal and he was a faerie, it was attraction, plain and simple. Carnal and innate. Besides, she read books. She knew all about bedroom intimacies and activities. Even though she'd never actually partaken in any, the colored images were *quite* vivid. It was natural, only human. Except, well, Rowan was not a human. But he was most *definitely* male.

And incredibly too tempting.

There was no doubt in her mind that his hands would move over her with ease, that he'd bring her right to the edge of pleasure before waiting to watch her shatter. Just thinking about all the things he could do to her made her breasts ache. Other areas ached as well, but there was nothing to be done about it now. Unless, of course, she made it safely to her room. Then maybe...

Distracted by her own needs, she rounded a corner and plowed headfirst into the hard wall of a chest.

"Oh!" She instantly went to smooth her hair and use it as a shield to protect her face, like Casimir would be able to see the flush of arousal coloring her cheeks. "Hey, Cas."

"Hey, yourself." His dark brown gaze looked beyond her and a line formed across his brow. "What are you doing out here alone?"

Alone? Rowan was right behind her. Surely he—

Maeve turned around. The impenetrable darkness was illuminated only by swooping glass leaves dangling from metal hooks that cast the ship in a fiery glow. Rowan was nowhere to be found. And yet...

And yet she could feel his eyes upon her in the shifting night. She wondered if he knew she kept her thighs clenched, if the heat pooling at the center of her was almost unbearable.

"I was just looking at the stars." The lie tasted foul in her mouth, like sour grapes. But she drank in the night sky anyway, imagining what gods and goddesses roamed the heavens, wondered if they watched her do unthinkable things when it was just her, alone in her bed. "Just looking and thinking."

"About?" Casimir pressed.

"About if what we're doing is really worth it."

Golden light and shadows reflected off his face, displaying his prominent frown. "You think saving Kells isn't worth the fight?"

"No. I'd do anything for Kells." And she would. For her city, for her home. For the people she loved.

Casimir leaned out over the railing. "Then what's the problem?"

Maeve spread her arms wide, exasperated. The heat burning inside her slowly cooled. "We'll be in Faeven soon, Cas. In *Faeven*. A land I've only ever read about in fairytales. We have no idea what to expect and no clue what we'll face. We don't even know if we'll even find the *anam ó Danua*. What if we fail?"

"We won't." He was so certain. So confident.

Maeve peered up at him and tried to read his somber expression. But shadows and light played tricks on the eyes, so she questioned him instead. "How can you be so sure?"

He didn't look at her. Instead he continued to keep his eyes on the inky night, where the sky and the sea bled into one another. "Because I've been to Faeven before."

"What?" Maeve reared back. "When?"

"Before the Evernight War."

Maeve knew he was without a soul. His very existence was shackled to Carman. After all, it hadn't taken her long to realize he never aged. In all her twenty-four years, his appearance had changed in just as many days. She supposed she had never taken the time to calculate his true age. She didn't know he'd been alive during the Evernight War. Or that he'd been to Faeven.

"It was a while ago. Another life, really." He turned, leaned into the railing and let his head tip back to face the sky. His deep brown skin glowed like the polished amber in the moonlight. "Parts of Faeven are dangerous. But other areas are enough to make you want to live there forever, to never want to leave."

"Will you tell me about them?" She used to love his tales of adventures growing up. She remembered after a long day of training, they'd walk down the Ridge to one of the docks along the Gaelsong Port to cool their skin and sometimes their tempers. There, he would tell her stories of his battles fought, his wars won, and everything in between. Faeven, oddly enough, he never mentioned.

"Sure." Casimir settled into himself, just as he'd done so many years ago. Resting his elbows on the railing, he crossed one ankle over the other and let the weight of the world fall away. "I've only ever been to the Spring Court. It's beautiful. Lush and green. Everything is blooming. Flowers. Plants. The days are warm and the nights are cool. There's a river that runs through Suvarese, the Crown City. When the sunlight hits it, it shines in hundreds of colors. Sometimes it will rain for what seems like forever, anything from a downpour to a sprinkle. When this mist rolls in from off of the Lismore Marin...I've never seen anything like it."

"Sounds magical." Maeve imagined such a place was magnificent. A rainbow-hued river? She would love to wander in a world where it was constantly springtime. The mere thought of it made her heart sigh. "How long were you there?"

"Long enough." His voice was strange. There was a stiffness to his tone. Words he'd locked away, never to speak of again.

She tried a different angle. "Why were you there?"

"That's a long story." He shook his head and glanced down at her with a sympathetic smile. "From a long time ago. Before..."

"Before what?" she prodded.

"Just before." He pushed up from the railing, morphing out of the role of obliging protector and back into the frame of fierce warrior. "I'm speaking with Aran tomorrow. In the morning. You should be there, too."

It wasn't a command, exactly. But it was definitely a pushy request. "What, like a meeting?"

"You could say that." Casimir adjusted his black hood and flipped it up over his head. "He has a particular talent for map-making."

"Map-making?" Maeve thought of all the maps she'd seen hanging on the walls of the library, and the ones tied up with red ribbon for purchase from quaint little gift shops in Kells. She knew the layout of Veterra by heart. She knew where the borders of each kingdom blurred, where the capitals were situated, but a map of Faeven would be a treasure. "What sort of maps?"

"I don't know how to describe it, exactly. You'll have to see them for yourself." His tone shifted and his shoulders bunched, an imperceptible movement to almost anyone. Except Maeve. He was hiding something. "I saw some of his work earlier when I asked him about where he plans on dropping us off."

"And what did he say about that?" Irritation was beginning to claw its way to the surface of Maeve's calm exterior. She didn't care to be excluded from important conversations. She didn't like how Casimir was taking charge of every situation, not when they'd spent the better part of her life making those decisions together.

Another barely noticeable shift in his demeanor. "He's going to drop us off in Niahvess. It's positioned on the sea for an easy escape if necessary, and the Archfae there are fairly neutral when it comes to humans."

"What's Niahvess?" Maeve found she enjoyed the way it rolled off her tongue, like some exotic locale.

"It's the Crown City of the Summer Court."

"Is it safe?"

"More or less."

Not really a reassuring answer, but she'd take it. She pieced together everything she knew so far. They were being transported to the Summer Court by Aran, who was a Dorai. His reasons for being a Dorai were still a mystery to her, but she had a feeling she would find out at some point during their travels. Niahvess was the Crown City of Summer, and the safest place for them to enter Faeven.

Everything else was just a guess. An unknown. A lingering omen of their fates.

Casimir gestured toward the arched doors that opened up into a glinting hall of crimson walls and dark wood flooring. "You should get some rest."

"Why does everyone keep telling me that," she muttered.

"What?"

"Nothing." She waved her hand in dismissal of the thought. "Night, Cas."

"Goodnight." Casimir opened the door for her and she wandered down the autumn-hued halls.

Aran's vessel was resplendent. Golden scrollwork of leaves crawled along the ceiling and colored lanterns of deep amber and crimson glowed overhead. But the lighting wasn't a bulb or the flicker of a flame. It was something else entirely. Faerie fire. Carved door knobs shaped like twisted branches invited her to peer into every room, and running windows of stained glass depicted scenes from what she could only assume was the Autumn Court. There was a mountain range set against the backdrop of a harvest moon, and a valley of trees whose bark was as white as snow, but whose leaves were lit up like fire. And then there was a palace...

She was half-tempted to reach up and run her finger along the beautiful edges of the glass palace walls, but the door right next to her burst open, and Saoirse popped her head out.

"Maeve, there you are!" Her hushed whisper was obnoxiously loud and she gestured for Maeve to follow her into the room. "This one has a big bed, so I figured we could share."

Maeve smiled and followed behind her. The room was small, but cozy, and draped in decadent hues of aubergine, marigold, and sapphire. Jewel-toned pillows were piled on top of an ebony bed, making it glitter like a crown. A gilded mirror hung on one wall and a wardrobe was positioned on the other. It was a room fitting for a princess.

The sort of room Maeve had never been given.

Saoirse stretched out like a languid cat, then curled her legs back up. A yawn stifled her words. "I know it's late, but the bathroom is fantastic if you want to freshen up before bed."

Maeve unhooked her corset and took off her boots. She pulled the pins from her hair and set them on the glossy nightstand next to the bed. "Perfect. I'll try not to wake you when I'm done."

But Saoirse was already waving her off, her eyelids too heavy, much like Maeve's heart.

She stepped into the bathroom and wasted no time soaking in her luxurious surroundings. Shimmery gold marble with streaks of iridescent champagne lined the walls. It was another overhead faucet, just like the one back home, except the water which poured over her was hot, and fragrant, and came down with the kindness of a gentle rainfall instead of a bruising blast. She tipped her head back and let the water soak her hair, her body, and rinse away her worries. Maeve scrubbed her face and stared down at the silver cuffs bound to her wrists.

To protect us. To keep the monster away.

Carman's words played back in her mind and doubt burrowed its way into her heart. What if she was cursed with dark fae magic? What if she was a monster? What if part of the darkness looming inside her came from Carman herself?

She stood in the glass-enclosed stall until steam filled the room with the delectable scent of cinnamon and earthy florals. Until her skin was pink from the burning heat of the water. Until she remembered why she was going to Faeven in the first place.

To save Kells. To break her curse. To take her crown.

Chapter Eleven

I t wasn't the early beams of dawn that woke Maeve from a fitful slumber, it was the sensation of being watched. Maeve's eyes flew open to see Rowan's face inches from her own. His hand clamped over her mouth to silence her scream and on instinct, she reached for her dagger strapped to her thigh. The tips of her fingers barely grazed the hilt when he smiled, and put one finger to his lips. Then he nodded to where Saoirse slept on the other side of the bed, half naked, with a blade gripped firmly in her fist. Even in sleep, she was lethal.

"Come with me." Rowan's whisper floated over her, and tingles shivered from her shoulders to her toes. "There's something I want to show you."

Maeve propped herself up on her elbows. "Can I get dressed first?"

His eyes lit with interest and his gaze trailed down her body, skimmed over the threadbare cotton blouse she wore. Her skin went hot beneath the intensity of his stare. When he spoke, his voice was dry. "Yes."

Maeve climbed out of bed and let Rowan get away with

brushing his fingers along the tops of her thighs when she slid past him. She gathered up her clothing and disappeared into the bathroom, reappearing a few minutes later fresh-faced and fully clothed.

He stuck his bottom lip out in a pout. "I missed the show."

Her lips twitched. "Pity."

Rowan extended his hand, and with a cautious glance back at the sleeping Saoirse, Maeve accepted. He led her from the room to the starboard side of the ship. He gestured to the horizon, to the stunning sunrise, where the sky was awash with ruby and bronze. Teal waves were dipped in gold like a watercolor painting brought to life. It was breathtaking. She wanted to ingrain this moment in her mind, to never forget the beauty of the realm. The world shimmered in an explosion of radiance, and a burst of magic coated her skin. Orange blossom and cedarwood filled her senses, and made her feel *alive*.

She knew in her soul, down to her core, they'd entered Faeven.

"Sun and sky," Maeve breathed.

"Literally." Rowan smiled and Maeve drifted closer to him. "Where do you think that phrase originated?"

Her mouth fell open. She never considered the possibility that words she spoke, phrases of little consequence, could be centuries old. They stood there until the sun rose higher, rising up from the east, and drenching the sky in shades of blush and turquoise. Ribbons of warmth caressed her skin and wisps of snowy white clouds swirled across the horizon. She didn't know how much time had passed, but she knew she was terrified to look away or even blink, for fear of missing the dawn's glory. "It's beautiful."

"Mm." Rowan nodded his head, his eyes on her. "It is."

"You're doing it again."

He sidled up closer, until his hand covered hers on the railing and she was flush against him. "Doing what?"

"Looking at me like that again."

The tip of his nose brushed against hers. "Like what?"

"Like..." Like she was the sun and he wanted to worship her for all eternity.

"What do you think you're doing?" A male baritone sounded from behind Maeve and she whipped around, stumbling backward into Rowan's chest.

He steadied her and stepped away, putting some distance between them. She fully expected to see Casimir glowering down at her, but instead it was Aran who stood before them. But his scowl wasn't directed at her. Instead, he looked like he wanted to kill Rowan.

"Nothing," Rowan muttered, and he adjusted the collar of his shirt, displaying the band of scars across his chest. "Anymore."

"Good. You should know better than to sully things of beauty." Aran's voice was eerily calm and drenched in so much fury, Maeve shivered. "Especially when they don't belong to you."

What the hell? Was this fae actually implying she belonged to someone? Like property? She would die before she allowed such a transgression to pass. She found her spine then, and fisted her hands on her hips. "I don't *belong* to anyone."

Aran's emerald gaze flicked to her, and for a brief second, his stormy expression softened. "Of course." Then he shot a look of warning to Rowan and held it until Rowan finally looked away first.

What the fuck?

There was a past between these two. She suspected as much from their tense greeting yesterday afternoon, but now there was no mistaking it. They did not like each other. At all.

"Would you care to join me for breakfast, Your Highness?" Aran inclined his head. "The rest of your companions are already there."

The subtle inclination was understood. She was late, and her absence had not gone unnoticed. No doubt she would suffer an earful from Casimir, as well as Saoirse—though for vastly different reasons.

"Okay." Maeve rolled her shoulders back.

"This way."

She glanced back at Rowan one final time, and though he said nothing, he watched her walk away.

MAEVE TURNED BACK to follow Aran and wasn't quick enough to silence her gasp.

"It's okay." Aran spoke quietly. Not quite a whisper, but a low, subdued murmur. "You can stare. I assure you, I'm used to it."

Maeve's gaze roved over his back. He wore a sheer green shirt with tiny gold embroidered leaves, but it was not enough to disguise the scarring along his back. There were two identical gouges, one on each side, just below his shoulder blades. The skin was jagged and torn, the edges of flesh red and blackened, and pulled taut into the shape of deformed crescent moons.

"What..." She didn't even want to ask. But her curiosity was a secondary curse. "What happened to you?"

"I almost died."

She scoffed in return. "Obviously."

Aran whirled around then with one auburn brow arched high, and Maeve simply shrugged. "How?"

Scrutiny flowed from him. He wasn't sure what to think of

her, or her daring foolishness to use sarcasm when speaking with a fae. She could only hope he had a decent sense of humor. He took a slow, steadying breath. "My wings were cut off."

Maeve's hands flew to cover her mouth. She stared at him, wide-eyed. What an awful, torturous thing to have suffered. But then, "You had wings?"

The awe of his admission was more than she could handle.

A low chuckle escaped him. "You sound surprised."

"Just impressed."

He smiled then, and it warmed a cold place within her soul. "Yes. I had wings. And they were resplendent."

She stepped closer, enraptured by the notion. She knew some of the more powerful fae were capable of *fading*, a movement which had been likened to teleportation according to her books, however, she never heard of a single faerie with wings. "What did they look like?"

Aran studied her. "You ask a lot of questions."

"Keep your enemies close."

"What makes you think I'm your enemy?"

"All fae are the enemy."

He watched her. Carefully. "But why?"

Maeve opened her mouth, then snapped it shut. She didn't have an answer. As far as she knew, no faerie had ever personally affronted her. She'd been born to hate them, bred to hate them. And she'd never known anything else. She'd never questioned it, either.

"Fine." Maeve crossed arms, annoyed with him for outsmarting her. "All dark fae are the enemy."

"Agreed." Aran stepped aside and allowed her entrance to the stairwell first.

She climbed up the small spiral staircase and struggled to contain her surprise when she discovered where it led. Before her was an outdoor seating area on a patio, and one of the crimson banners swept across the space for shade. Casimir and Saoirse were seated at a large round table, surrounded by platters and trays steaming with bacon, chopped potatoes, grilled vegetables, and any breakfast food Maeve could imagine. There were bottomless mimosas, cranberry and orange juice, and a dark liquid that smelled faintly of hazelnuts and cinnamon.

"Coffee." Maeve caught the drool before it fell from the corner of her mouth. She looked up at Aran. "How?"

He winked. "I, too, prefer the finer things in life."

She filled up a plate, poured the largest cup of coffee she could find, and sat down at the table. Saoirse was busy drenching her pancakes in a gallon of syrup, while Casimir picked at the pile of eggs and peppers on his plate. From the corner of her eye, Maeve saw Rowan slip across the deck without being overly obvious. He grabbed a glass of straight champagne and lounged against the railing at the far side of the patio.

Aran seated himself beside Maeve, and she figured that was as close as she'd get to uncovering more about him.

"So, Aran." Maeve blew on her coffee and sipped. It was sweet and spicy and liquid perfection. "Where are you from?"

He added one lump of sugar to his coffee. "You know where I'm from."

Rowan edged forward, away from the railing.

"Yes, Faeven. I know." She propped her elbows on the table and looked at him from over the rim of her cup. "But did you have a Court...before?"

"Before I was exiled, you mean?"

She couldn't read him. The planes of his face were smooth and impassive. He didn't look at her, but he didn't look away from her either. There was no sternness or edge in his voice, but more of a vague transparency.

"Yes." She struggled to keep her voice from wavering.

Aran gave her the side eye. "My home is the Autumn Court."

"Was," Rowan interjected, downing the rest of his champagne.

Aran's face darkened with malice.

Rowan tipped the empty glass toward him. "Your home *was* the Autumn Court, before you—"

It happened so fast, Maeve didn't even have time to react. One minute, Aran was beside her and Rowan was smirking at them from across the patio. In the next, Aran had his hand around Rowan's throat. Fury radiated off of Aran and his eyes darkened to a deep forest green. Where Aran's hand touched, the veins beneath Rowan's skin turned black. Like he was dying.

Maeve pulled her dagger and Saoirse raised her sword. Casimir lurched across the patio, his blade at the ready.

"Aran." Casimir kept his tone cool and collected, but he maintained his aim. "Stand down."

"Careful, Aran." Rowan's voice sounded garbled, like he was speaking underwater. "Wouldn't want to show your hand too quickly."

"My mistakes are my own." Aran ground the words out, then released his hold on Rowan and let him drop to the hardwood.

The stench of near-death lingered in the air between them. Slowly, Rowan's skin cleared, and his veins, which once looked filled with ink, returned to normal.

With her dagger still clutched in her hands, Maeve rounded the table and held the tip of it to Aran's throat. "Why were you exiled?"

"Your constant questions are giving me a headache." Aran suffered her an eye roll and returned to his seat like nothing had happened, completely dismissing the dagger aimed to slay him, to kill him in seconds. He pressed his fingers to his temples and rolled his neck. "You're like an annoying little sister who never shuts up."

Maeve flinched, but she blew out a breath and didn't lower her weapon. "Well?" she demanded.

Aran's lip curled. "I'll make you a deal."

"Fine," Maeve said, at the same time Casimir shouted, "No!"

Casimir stormed up to her. His face was etched with vehemence but his eyes were pleading. "You don't know what they're capable of."

Aran took a drink of his coffee. "It won't be anything outlandish."

Maeve glanced over at Rowan, who'd recovered completely and didn't look at all like he'd been on the brink of death. She met his gaze and he nodded, once. She tucked her dagger back into her sheath, but didn't miss the way Aran's eyes remained trained on it the entire time.

She eased herself down beside him. "What are your terms?"

Casimir groaned. He looked torn between screaming at her and tossing her over the railing into the sea.

"Simple." He slathered butter onto a honey roll. "A truth for a truth."

"Meaning?"

"You ask me one thing, and I'll tell you the truth. But only if I get to do the same."

"And I can ask you anything?"

It seemed too...easy. Too much like a trap. Her insides were a tangled bundle of anxiety. This would be her chance, her opportunity to ask him *anything*. Anything about the Evernight War, about the plague, about the soul of a goddess.

"Anything," he confirmed and held out his hand. "Don't worry, there won't be another Strand since we're merely exchanging information, and not offering up favors."

Maeve hesitated only a second, then clasped his outstretched hand. "Deal."

They shook on it and again her mind was barraged with images she couldn't place. A kaleidoscope of autumn leaves swirling down from the sky. A lake as smooth as glass and water as pitch as night. Crumbling stone. And a set of beady, glassy eyes gazing at her from a shadowy brush.

She yanked her hand back and Aran's steady gaze remained trained on her.

"After you," he said mildly.

Hundreds of questions boggled her mind and consumed her thoughts. It was a chance circumstance, a means to find an answer without risking life and limb. Aran may have thought she was thoroughly invested in the reason he was exiled, but she didn't care that much, not really. It was merely a tactic to get him to talk.

Maeve pinned him with a hard stare. "Why are the dark fae attacking the human lands?"

He didn't even hesitate. "For the same reason they're attacking Faeven."

Maeve waited a beat. Then two. "Which is?"

"That's two questions." Aran's smile was calculated.

It took a full three seconds for her to understand the depth of how he'd tricked her. Rowan laughed out loud, setting her teeth on edge. She shot him a menacing glare, which made him laugh even harder.

"Sorry." He raised his hands in self-defense. "But the look on your face."

Even Casimir was amused. He'd at least been smart enough to try and disguise it by pulling his hood down over his head.

But his shoulders shook and she knew he was laughing at her, too. She slammed one fist down on the table. Embarrassment scalded her cheeks. It streaked down her neck and flooded her chest with heat.

"Bastard," she hissed.

"Tsk tsk," Aran admonished mockingly. "My turn."

The laughter stopped. Maeve's palms dampened and she hastily scrubbed them on the soft fabric of her leggings. Every nerve in her body was on alert. She knew better than to go back on her word to a fae. Anxiety wrapped its knobby arms around her, kept her rooted in place so she couldn't move.

Aran leaned forward. "Would you die for those you love?"

"Yes." The answer came automatically. She didn't even have to think about it. "A thousand times."

"I thought as much," Aran murmured, then stood abruptly. "Casimir, the map you requested is ready."

Casimir motioned for Maeve to follow. She stepped out from around the table behind him, but Rowan caught her by the hand.

"Be careful, Princess." He grazed his thumb across her knuckles. "Not all fae are so kind."

Her pride stung from the bite of humiliation. "You mean like you?" she fired back.

Rowan dragged her arm to his mouth and lightly pressed a kiss to the inside of her palm. "Exactly."

Chapter Twelve

The room Aran led them to was full of curious wonders. Warm sunlight spilled in through amber windows and cast the entire space in an ethereal glow. Glass spheres filled with sand floated along the ceiling, suspended from nothing. Rolls of textured paper stuck out of an onyx vase. One stick of crimson wax dripped steadily onto a piece of parchment. Books were stacked on nearly every surface, some covered in a fine layer of dust, others appearing to be so thoroughly read, the bindings were split and torn, the pages marked by slips of colored papers. Bottles of ink and jars of paint were cluttered together next to a bin of brushes and pencils, and a collection of scales for measurement poked out of a brass box. But what snared Maeve's attention were the walls. Maps of all different land masses and scales were pinned and plastered to every empty space. To see the world, the realms of mortal and immortal, sketched with such precision and care, was a wanderer's dream. Some were foreign and some were archaic, from before...

All of them were drawn by hand, each one painted and

outlined with the tedious tip of a paintbrush. The strokes of colored paints were detailed and precise.

Casimir hovered over the desk while Aran unrolled a crisp scroll, bound in black ribbon.

"You made all of these?" Maeve asked, and her voice sounded too loud in such a sacred space.

Aran looked up. "I did."

"Your cartography skills are fascinating." She pored over the contents spread along the desk, over the maps that resembled paintings, and whose landmarks moved like bewitching watercolors. "Where did you learn to draw these?"

Aran's lips pressed into a line.

"Right. Sorry." A distinctive heat flushed Maeve's cheeks. "Too many questions."

"It wasn't anything I learned." He unrolled the scroll in his hands. "It's a gift."

"Your magic, then." She inspected a collection of books stacked eight high. The spines were frayed and well-loved, and the cloth covers were embossed in gold. She nodded toward the desk. "These maps. They're your magic."

"A small part, but yes." He spread out an atlas of a mythical isle. Judging from the bold colors—vibrant orange and red, bright turquoise and yellow, deep green and blush, icy blue and gray—Maeve assumed it was a hand-painted map of Faeven. Or at least, the Four Courts. A blur of gold in a sea of blue caught her eye.

Maeve gasped. "That's us!"

Casimir bent over for a closer look. "Seven hells. She's right."

Moving across the map, through the sea, was the Amshir. It was impossible, beyond her mind to comprehend, but the painted vessel moved across the map. She swallowed the sudden knot of anxiety clenched in the back of her throat.

They were incredibly close to Faeven. Closer still to the Summer Court. It was only a matter of time until they docked.

The detailed atlas of Faeven made sense; it was Aran's home. But the other realms?

"How are they so precise?" Maeve asked. "Your maps?"

Aran's smile was small and it did not reach his eyes. "Sometimes, when one has already been alive for hundreds of years, it can be rather easy to grow bored of your surroundings. Especially once the sea becomes your home."

He reached up, ran a finger along the curved edge of a parchment pinned to the center of the far wall. There, the colors bled together into a forest—tree after tree of crimson, hunter green, burnished gold. Harvest colors. Autumn colors. Winding foot paths splintered off in different directions like the branches of a tree. Most intriguing, however, was the smear of black towards the edge of the map, where a palace had once been marked, now smudged by ash and soot.

"Cartography became a pastime of mine, and I found I desired to travel," Aran murmured, "when my home was no longer my home."

Stiff and awkward silence settled between the three of them. Maeve busied herself with the pile of books beside her. She slid one of them out and admired the cover of roses, and leaves, and a crescent moon. The embossed letters were smooth beneath her fingers, and though she didn't have time to decipher the words, she knew they were in Old Laic.

Aran cleared his throat and rolled up the map of Faeven, then tied the black ribbon around it. He handed it over to Casimir and turned his attention to her. "Since you're here, Maeve, I feel I must warn you away from Rowan."

Maeve scoffed and flipped open the book in her hands. "We're not dating or anything, if that's what you're worried about."

Casimir coughed, but it sounded more like a strangled choke.

Aran's face remained impassive, but humor danced in his eyes. "Uh, good. That's good. But you must know that in Faeven, nothing is as it seems."

"I figured as much." Maeve didn't even look at him. She was too mesmerized by the book of fairytales in her hands. Every letter, inked by hand. Every picture, painted by hand. The work was exquisite, so detailed, and so painstakingly beautiful. It was a work of art and she wondered if Aran had been the one to create it.

"Maeve." Aran's voice was firm. He closed the book in her hands, forcing her gaze to him. "Rowan is not what he seems."

She hugged the book to her chest. "He seems pretty intent on getting under my skin."

"Or getting in your pants," Casimir muttered.

A flush scalded Maeve's cheeks. "My sex life is none of your concern."

Aran pinched the bridge of his nose. "He can't be trusted."

"Funny, he said the same thing about you." Undercurrents of frustration flared to life inside her. Vexed, she clamped her jaw until her temples ached. What in the stars was this anyway? The sex talk? What and who she did, if anything or anyone, in her spare time was none of their damned business. "And if we're being brutally honest here, which I assume we are, he already told me not to trust him."

Aran shared a look with Casimir, who shrugged and held up his hands in innocence.

"Are we done here?" she demanded.

"He won't be the hero in your story, Maeve." Aran's tone was lower. Colder.

She stalked toward the carved doors of mahogany and yanked one open. She propped her ankle up against it and tossed one glance at both of them, over her shoulder. "I don't need a hero. I'm not a damsel in distress. I'm not a princess in need of saving. If it comes down to it, which I'm sure it probably will, I'll save myself."

Aran crossed his arms, muscles rippling. "We'll see about that."

"Indeed, we will," she snapped.

"Maeve?" When Aran said her name, he was right behind her. She hadn't even heard him approach. "You're forgetting something."

She spun around on one boot. "What now?"

He held out his hand and nodded to the tome clutched against her chest. "I believe that belongs to me."

Maeve held the book out, but was gripped with a desire to keep it. She wanted to pore over the colorful pages and translate the words she couldn't quite understand. She wanted to hear the fairytales from before, and the legends of after. Willing herself a smidge of humility, she looked up into Aran's eyes. And so what if she fluttered her lashes a little bit? A girl could try.

"Might I keep it?"

"You...you want this book?" His mouth was slightly parted, like he had more to say, but couldn't find the words.

"I do." Maeve nodded. "Very much."

"You realize," he spoke slowly. Carefully.

"I'll owe you something. Of course." Maeve searched the pocket of her leggings and pulled out the piece of sea glass she'd found at the beach right before Aran arrived. It was like holding a bundle of summer roses in her hand.

"This." She held it out to him. "You can have this. I found it along the Shores while we were waiting for you. Maybe it can be a piece of land you can carry with you. At least until you're allowed to return."

She placed the sea glass in his hand and closed his fingers around it.

Aran ran his thumb over its smooth surface, never taking his eyes off it. "You're very optimistic."

His gaze locked on hers and she smiled. "Usually."

There was a flicker across his features. A brief glimpse of an emotion Maeve didn't recognize, and then it was gone. She took that as her cue to leave.

With the book of colorful illustrations and ancient script locked in her grip, she strolled along the deck to the helm of the boat, where the warm wind kissed her skin and the gentle crash of waves cocooned her in silence. For a moment, she wanted nothing more than to be alone. This was the most time she'd spent among others in quite awhile. Back in Kells, when she wasn't on the training field with Casimir and Saoirse, she was alone. The piles of books in her room and the shelves of the castle's library had been her only company. She'd found solace in magical worlds not her own. The wicked, and wild, and wonderful.

Once Carman had learned of her blood curse, Maeve had been all but forgotten.

She could remember that day clearly. She'd been foolish enough to think she'd been given a gift from the goddess, a blessing. It had been neither of those things. At the tender age of five, she'd been playing outside like any ordinary child. The winter had been bitter that year. The skies were gray and bleak —already, Kells had been blanketed in six inches of snow—and the air smelled of more to come. But the fierce wind couldn't reach her within the high walls of the courtyard, so she'd taken to building a palace in the snow. Her governess was nearby, chatting with two of the maids and laughing, their noses red from the cold.

Maeve was sick of the winter. She longed for warm

summer days, for the heat of the sun against her skin. It was then her blood sang, beckoning her. The blossoming warmth spread through her. Frightened her. Thrilled her.

She slipped behind one of the barren oak trees and cupped her small hands together. Tiny pink blooms unfolded in her palms. The buds of fresh roses and baby green vines swirled together to form a crown. Their little petals fell like satin against her gloved fingers, beautiful and charming. Then her mother's cry of anger bounced off the courtyard walls and as quickly as the flowers formed, they turned to ash, and crumbled on the wind.

That night was her first night in the cage.

The first of many.

Maeve closed herself off from the harsh memory. She refused to let her mind drift down that path again. Instead, she gazed out to the sea, and a glimpse of jagged shapes caught her eye.

Land.

The clear definition of mountains came into view. Excitement exploded inside her. Her heart hammered and the rush of adrenaline left her vibrating with exhilaration. Or maybe she was going to throw up. It could go either way.

Saoirse stepped up next to her at the railing of the vessel and wrapped a protective arm around her shoulders. "Are you ready?"

Maeve nodded and handed her the book of fairytales to be tucked safely away into her pack. "Yes."

Even if she wasn't, she would be. There was no other choice. It was time for her own story to begin. One she hoped would be recorded in a beautiful book with leather bindings and shimmery words. One she hoped would be read and passed down through the ages of time.

Perhaps it would last an eternity, even if she did not.

MAEVE COULD HAVE MELTED into the beauty of summer. Into its delicious heat and brilliant warmth. Glimmering rays of sunshine spilled across lustrous mountaintops, down onto a city built atop curling canals nestled in a valley, dusting everything it touched in gold. A winding staircase of ivory stone rose up from the frothing waves and plateaued onto a veranda with ivy-wrapped pillars and a carved statue of an impossible size. It was a fae, of that she was sure, down on one bended knee. A mighty sword of granite was gripped between his palms, tip down, and his head was lowered. The helmet he wore left room for his pointed ears and a detailed cape was pinned to his shoulders with gilded wings. He was a guardian. A warrior. A protector.

Her blood sang and the song pitched, the melody of the magic coursing through her clearer now than she'd ever heard it before.

A shadow fell across her and she looked up to see Aran by her side. He smiled, but his eyes were focused on the city on the horizon. "What do you think of Niahvess, the Summer Court's Crown City?"

"It's..." She couldn't find the words.

Niahvess was unlike anything she'd ever experienced. Magic floated around her, kissed her skin, tickled her cheek. It was everywhere. Living. Breathing. Thriving. All of the books she'd read in the library back home, hidden under a blanket with a half-melted candle for light, were nothing compared to the reality of the fae realm. All the maps, all the drawings—none were as detailed or intricate. The terrain should've been treacherous, filled with poison and unknown dangers. All the rough sketches and blotted outlines were distant memories, hand-drawn lies about what to expect.

But she had to remember. She had to remember she was in Faeven.

With Aran's book clutched to her chest, one hand slid over the ornate railing of his ship, and her nails bit into the smooth, glossy wood. Maeve rolled her shoulders back, adjusted her corset, and ignored the way the stiff leather stuck to her skin. Her gaze lingered on the city in the valley, on the way the beauty seemed to shimmer like a mirage, like it wasn't even real. "It looks criminal."

"Positively." Aran looked down at her then, his delightful eyes warmed with approval, and he offered his arm as the planks unfurled from the side of the vessel, one by one, to take them to the verandah overlooking the city of Niahvess.

She accepted without hesitation.

Once they crossed the planks, Aran stepped onto the closest stone step, and waves of turquoise crashed near his feet. They docked by a pavilion, where a staircase of sandstone cascaded down into the depths of the sea. Maeve's foot hovered between the safety of the boat and the land of eternal summer, and when her boot touched down onto the slick stone, the world around her shuddered. Sighed.

Saoirse followed behind her and didn't look nearly as comfortable. Her sapphire gaze scanned the area, darting left then right and back again, waiting for some sign of life. She carried both hers and Maeve's packs on her back, and her hand was positioned on the hilt of her sword. Casimir stalked down the planks after her. His hood was pulled up, his face a mask of shadows, but he, too, had his hand wrapped around his weapon. Only Rowan, who was the last to stroll down the wooden steps, had any sort of lackadaisical air about him. In fact, he looked ready to take on the world, and when he caught sight of Maeve, the slightest uptick of his mouth was enough to make her heart palpitate.

Aran captured her hand and tucked it into his arm. "Walk with me, Maeve."

Casimir jolted forward, his hood slipping back with aggression, but Saoirse grabbed his collar and hauled him back. Maeve glanced at her friend, at one of the few people she trusted. Saoirse gave a slight nod, but her brilliant blue eyes were cold with a vow to fight to the death if necessary.

"I won't hurt you," Aran assured her, and he led her up a few of the steps toward the verandah, toward the towering statue of the warrior fae whose armor was adorned with the crest of a swirling sun rising between twin mountain peaks.

"I know why you're here." He looked down at her and when she met his eyes, she saw they were clear and kind. "What you seek, it will not be easy to find. It was torn from this world, and no one knows if it survived."

She swallowed down the sudden lump of panic in the back of her throat, and forced herself to take a steadying breath. To remain calm. Her gaze hooked onto the towering mountains, the rows of colorful buildings shoved together, forming a city full of life. "I will not leave without it. If I fail, my kingdom will fall, and I won't let the death of innocent souls smear my hands."

"You should know, there is one who has fallen from the grace of the goddess. She should be banished, like me. But she managed to remain in Faeven. She's found a way to control the dark fae. To bend them to her will." He paused and a pained look pulled his expression tight. "Creatures that only existed in nightmares, in legends of the past before even the Evernight War, now exist. And they're a very real danger."

"To you?" A chill raked over her, the warmth suddenly stolen by the memory of the Hagla in the Fieann Forest. The one who dragged her back to the memory of that wretched cage on those damned cliffs.

"To all of us." Aran patted her hand. "Neither human nor fae...nor you, are exempt from the wrath of dark fae. The only ones who are, are the soulless."

She glanced back down behind her to where his boat rocked gently upon the foaming waves. Casimir watched her, Saoirse watched him. And Rowan, his glare could cut her skin. He looked ready to take off Aran's head. She peered up at the fae in question. "Why are you telling me this?"

"Nothing is as it seems." Aran studied her and the wind picked up, slashed across them both. "Sometimes the mind taints what the heart knows to be true."

"So, you think I should trust you?"

He laughed and it was the most rapturous sound. Pure and joyous. "Of course not." He grinned and leaned in close, enough so that the glaring daggers Rowan shot their way pierced her neck and back. "Just something to consider as you make your way."

Then he swept into a low bow. "This is where I leave you, Maeve. Don't forget, I'll call upon one of you for a favor."

He left her on the stone steps and returned to his vessel, where his banner of charred orange and the strange black creature unfurled and whipped in the now merciless breeze. There was a chill in the air, cooler than before but not cold. The sun disappeared behind a blanket of clouds and the waves threw themselves upon the sandstone staircase. Even the warrior fae crafted from fine quartz and marble seemed to kneel to whatever storm was coming. The harbor of Niahvess was no longer as lovely or welcoming. Saoirse climbed the steps toward her, with Casimir and Rowan not far behind. But something was missing...Maeve couldn't shake the feeling she was forgetting something.

She rushed down the steps past them, toward Aran's boat.

Her boots slid along the damp stones and she threw her arms out, fighting with the air for balance.

"Wait!" The wind swallowed her call to him. "Aran! How will we find you once we're ready to return home?"

He gave another knowing, smirking smile, and her heart sank. "We only agreed I deliver you to Faeven, dear Maeve. Not return you to the Shores."

"Bastard," Saoirse hissed, and she dragged her silvery blonde braid over her shoulder.

Aran *had* told them not to trust him.

Casimir's scowl cut across his mouth.

Summer roiled. The sky overhead turned an angry shade of gray, and menacing clouds rolled in from the steep mountain peaks, where two of them rose like twin protectors. Mist blanketed the harbor and stole the sun. Goosebumps broke out along Maeve's flesh as the once gentle breeze now whipped around them, sprayed them with the salt of the sea. It clung to her lips, the briny tang of it all too reminiscent of the cage above the cliffs. Maeve shuddered, wrapped her arms tightly around herself, and shook off the vengeful memory. Drops of rain pelted down; the storm of summer was now upon them.

A blur of teal and black shot past her.

Suddenly Rowan was further down the stairwell. Waves crashed at his feet, soaked his cape of shadows. He stood firm, fists clenched by his sides while the wind tossed his hair across his face.

"You called him to us?" Accusation lit his tone and the world shimmered once more.

"Called who?" Casimir asked, his sword already drawn.

Maeve tossed a reckless glance over her shoulder. On the verandah, Saoirse's daggers were drawn, her hawklike gaze trained on the skies.

"Aran!" Fury infused Maeve. Scoured her. Carved her. But

the sea shoved her back. Its crashing waves lashed at her feet, forced her further up the stone steps. "You said we'd be safe! That the Summer Court was accepting of mortals!"

Aran's lips pressed into a thin smile of disappointment, a look she knew too well. It was the same one her mother always gave her whenever Maeve should have known the answer, or should have performed better, or should have killed without remorse. "I said they were tolerant."

Maeve rushed forward and yanked Rowan's arm, pulling him back to her. The rising, seething sea was now to their knees. His arm quickly slipped around her waist, and together they climbed back up the steps to the safety of the verandah.

"What's happening?" Maeve's heart thundered, and her blood roared as adrenaline caused her awareness to pulse. "What did he do?"

Rowan sighed, but drew no weapon. "Aran is a Dorai, remember? He's been banished from Faeven. They are not allowed to return, no matter the circumstances." He scrubbed a hand over his face and shoved his hair back from his eyes. "When Aran stepped onto the stone of the verandah, he summoned Niahvess's Archfae. The High King of Summer."

"Let me guess." Casimir admired the svelte edge of his sword and ran his tongue along his teeth. "This High King is on his way to us right now."

Rowan nodded.

Casimir groaned.

The wind barreled into her, and a wall of silver clouds stretched before her. "We can still bargain with any fae, right?"

"If we have something he wants," Saoirse muttered, rolling her wrists, ready for a fight.

"She's right." Rowan's lavender gaze flicked to Maeve. "There's not much a High King would want or need from a group of mortals."

"I can think of something." Casimir scoffed, and his stiff frame turned toward the mountain of mist.

Chills riddled Maeve's flesh and the fae magic in her blood rippled and sang. Called and beckoned. Longed to be free from the cold, hard metal binding her wrists. The surge of it was dizzying. Captivating. It left her lightheaded, so her entire body tingled until her toes were numb and she couldn't feel her fingers. Then, as quickly as it came, it was crushed, dampened back down, swallowed whole by the charms and spells of her mother's sorcery. A longing she didn't know she possessed tugged at her, whispered for her to listen.

Maeve brushed off the murmured pleas as the most terrifying being she'd ever seen strolled out of the storm.

He headed straight for her.

Chapter Thirteen

He was summer and death.

Terrifying and striking.

He walked with storms but ruled the sun.

His hair was dark like a night without stars. Haphazard, windblown pieces fell across his tanned face and a pair of startling blue eyes watched her from beneath a drawn brow. His ears were long, pointed, and exceptionally fae. A ruby glittered in his left lobe. He strolled toward her with his hands tucked in his pockets, the sleeves of his cobalt silk shirt cuffed to nearly his elbows. A swirling tattoo crawled up his neck; it looked to be made of gold dust. His pants were white in color, nearly cream, and a gold belt slung low at his waist. Sheathed on either side of him was a set of matching swords. But there was something about him, something about the way shadows danced around him and lightness kissed his skin, as though he was a prince of summer who owned the twilight hour.

Maeve's blood surged and the magic in her sang, a violent melody only she could hear. The burst of magic inside her collided with the charms of her cuffs, then crashed, leaving her breathless. Her knees quaked until she thought the ground would split open and swallow her down to the sea below.

"You okay?" Saoirse's whisper came from somewhere to her right.

She could only nod.

Three other fae flanked either side of him. Two males and one female. One of the males scowled. The other smirked. And the female looked bored out of her mind. But then the Archfae shifted, and out from behind him stepped the most beautiful female Maeve had ever seen.

She was nearly identical to the High King, yet opposite in every way.

Cloaked in pale, shimmery gold, her gown swept across her neck and pulled tight at the waist. Layers of silk and chiffon billowed toward the ground like a cloud, the hem dotted with sapphires and golden beads. Her sun-kissed skin was marked with floral tattoos from her hands to her bare shoulders, and the ink was the same soft, pearlescent gold. Rich, golden waves of hair fell to nearly her waist, and woven into the perfectly coiffed strands were ribbons of brilliant yellow and blue; the sun and the sky. A strap of five jeweled daggers was tied onto a satin sash at her hips, a hard edge to counter all of the softness she evoked. Though the planes of her face resembled the High King, they were gentler somehow. Smoother. Not so stern or harsh. But everything else was the same. The eyes. The mouth. The walk.

Sister. The word echoed in Maeve's mind and she knew it to be right. They were siblings.

The High King stopped before her, inches from her, and she was overwhelmed with the scent of him. Of sun-drenched palms, sandalwood, and a warm floral she couldn't place. Maeve held her breath while her fingers lightly played along the tips of her throwing stars banded around her waist. She'd fought worse things. She could fight a fae.

"What do you think, Ceridwen?" The High King lifted his hand and his knuckles grazed Maeve's cheek. She stiffened against the intimate touch.

The stunning female named Ceridwen spoke. "I think she's missing something."

"I think you're right." He twirled one finger around Maeve's hair and the strawberry blonde strands whipped and swirled into a beautiful twist over her shoulder. Flowers bloomed down the intricate braid, pretty pink roses, blossoms of aqua and green, all fastened by gold-tipped ferns. Maeve's heart stopped in her chest.

"Mortals." One of the males laughed and raked his bright, hot pink hair back from his face. "Always impressed by the smallest of things. Especially the women."

The bored-looking female jabbed him in the ribcage with her elbow. "Shut up, Merrick."

The Archfae leaned back, tilted his head as though admiring his work. Yet he still managed to look unimpressed. "I've seen better."

The insult shamed her, burned her cheeks with unexpected heat, and darkness roused inside her. She clung to the vicious strands of it and her magic exploded within her, a blinding burst of everything she'd kept hidden and bottled since childhood. Her blood curse raked over the surface of her skin, snaked past the charms of her mother's sorcery. For one brief, fleeting moment...she wanted it. Wanted the power. Wanted the fae magic, to rule it, to own it. But just as quickly as that traitorous thought stole into her mind, the cold metal cuffs on her wrists tightened and squeezed. Spells stole her breath, left her gasping, and aching. Tiny beads of sweat slid down her corset, and her blouse clung to her skin. Until a harsh, shuddering sigh escaped her and she trembled from the pain.

Saoirse was there, the warmth of her palm pressed firmly into Maeve's back to keep her upright. Focused. How could she not possess the blood of dark fae? That fracture inside her, that sudden, spiteful desire to use her magic for harm was a sure sign. It had to be. There was no other explanation.

But then the High King waltzed over to where Rowan was casually propped up against one of the verandah's pillars. The High King crossed his arms and Maeve looked away when his biceps bunched and strained against his shirt. "Where the fuck have you been?"

Rowan lifted one shoulder in feigned nonchalance. "Here and there. Mostly there."

The High King glanced at his sister, then again to Rowan. "You shouldn't have come back here. It's not safe."

"Yeah, well." Rowan's arms spread wide. "I was running out of options, and it sure as hell isn't safe where we came from either."

The High King snatched Rowan's arm and examined his wrist. The storm rolled in, hard and fast. It was fury unlike anything Maeve had ever seen. She was nearly crushed from the blow of wind. It whipped them, beat them, threatened to drown them in the sea as the waves rose higher up the sandstone staircase.

"What is the meaning of this? A slave?" the High King growled. "And the mortals think *we're* cruel and merciless? You think *we* are the monsters?"

His gaze ravaged each of them, accusing them all of a crime.

Maeve tugged on the cotton sleeves of her blouse, and pulled them tight to hide her own cuffs.

Fury radiated from the Archfae. "Who dared enslave a fae?"

"Wow," Merrick mused, smiling broadly. "Ballsy."

"Merrick. Seriously." The one female smacked him on the back of the head. "Shut the fuck up."

Casimir stiffened. "The cuffs were put in place to ensure he didn't use his magic against us."

"*Who?*" The High King demanded.

Casimir kept his gaze steady and didn't even flinch. "The cuffs were my idea."

"No!" Maeve darted forward, determined to protect him from the High King's wrath. There was no telling what the Archfae would do, and he would be more likely to kill a Captain of the Guard who was of no consequence, then a princess from the human lands of Veterra. She lifted her chin. "It was my mother who put Rowan in the cuffs."

Saoirse yanked Maeve close to her, and tried to haul her to safety, but it was too late. The High King was in Maeve's face, his bewitching eyes a hurricane of rage. He grabbed her by the throat, lifted her up until her feet dangled in the air, while his grip slowly crushed her windpipe.

"Put her down!" Saoirse's scream pitched over the shouts of the others. Casimir was yelling something, but Maeve couldn't understand his words. And Rowan kept saying the High King's name, over and over.

Tiernan.

"He's *your* slave?" The High King, Tiernan, kept his grip firm and dragged her face closer to him until she was barely a breath away. Wave after wave of disgust and magic slammed into her, and she frantically clawed at him. Her nails tore into his skin, desperate for release. She ripped a throwing star from her belt, arched her arm in one fell swoop, and slammed the tip of the star into his wrist. Blood spurted out from the wound and Tiernan hissed. The words were garbled, but she could've sworn someone laughed. He yanked the star from his flesh, and Maeve watched in horror as her throwing star turned to dust before disappearing into the wind. The pads of his fingers squeezed tighter, pinching off her air supply. Her lungs burned and dizziness swept in, while the sweet sensation of nothingness crawled up her back. Her vision swam and shifted, and the world tilted with her. Her hands closed around his but he was stone and she was sand. One useless against the other. Maeve's eyes fluttered closed.

"Answer me," he demanded.

Then she heard it.

"Did you do this?" His voice slipped into her mind, and she heard his words as clear as her own. They scraped along the inside of her head and tore through her thoughts. She convulsed against the pain but she couldn't answer. She couldn't breathe. She couldn't think.

"Is he your slave?" He asked again, and the harsh words dug into her flesh, leaving behind wounds she couldn't see.

"No." The word fell from her lips on a gasp. She swung her feet once more, and wanted to scream her denial, but her throat wouldn't open. She did not fear the god of death, but when he came to collect her, it would be on a battlefield, not at the hands of some infuriating fae lord. "Never."

She meant it. She would never enslave another. Not even a fae. Once she could catch her breath, she'd kill the bastard.

"Tiernan, leave her alone!" Rowan shifted so he was in Maeve's line of sight. His gaze darted to hers, desperate. "She was only a child."

Tiernan dropped Maeve on the ground. She collapsed upon the verandah, braced herself on her hands and knees, all while sucking in greedy gulps of air. Her body sagged backward in an effort to keep from toppling over. Suddenly, curls of delicious heat wrapped around her, comforted her. The glowing warmth eased the ache in her throat, bathed her in light, and filled her with the sweet lullaby of calm. She was a child of the sun. Golden rays caressed her skin, soothed her soul, slowed her mind. She relished in it, in the euphoria of summer.

She sought the source of the unexpected serenity, but Saoirse and Rowan were by her side in a second.

"Maeve." Worry filled Saoirse's eyes and she cupped Maeve's cheeks with both hands. "Are you alright? Are you hurt?"

Maeve shook her head. "My throat is a little sore, but I'm okay."

Saoirse's face quickly morphed from concerned friend to cold-blooded killer. "That fucking—"

"Easy there." Rowan grabbed her shoulder and held her back. "That's an Archfae, and your sword won't save you for long."

Saoirse's gaze snapped to him. "He attacked my princess. After The Scathing and the dark fae assaulted Kells, I swore I would defend my homeland against *all* fae who proved hostile against my kingdom. And that includes its heir."

"Dark fae have attacked the human lands as well?" Ceridwen, the High King's sister, glided forward, and the tension on the verandah melted away. "When?"

"Recently." Saoirse stood and adjusted her daggers, placing herself between Tiernan and Maeve. Her thumbs tapped restlessly against the hilts. "Our kingdom is under siege from The Scathing."

"And you think you'll find the key to defeating it here?" Tiernan asked dryly.

"Yes," Maeve snapped and clutched Rowan's forearm for support as she hauled herself into a standing position. Tiernan towered a good foot above her, and she glared up at him. "You think we won't?"

"That remains unseen." Tiernan took one step closer, ensuring there was no space between them. A method of intimidation. "I will allow you and your party to stay here for as long as needed to devise a plan, on the strict condition I am made aware of *every* thought, every movement, and every decision. Do we have a deal?"

He offered Maeve his hand.

"Maeve..." Casimir's voice was a warning in the background but she ignored it. They were in Faeven. They'd made it. And she was going to do whatever it took, no matter the cost, to save Kells.

"Fine." She extended her hand and this time, a Strand of binding sapphire glittered in the air between them. It wove around their fingers and glowed beneath their skin, before settling into the shape of a sun against her palm. Already she'd been in Faeven for less than twenty-four hours, and twice she'd been marked. She certainly didn't feel like she was off to a great start.

Tiernan spun around and stalked off. Ceridwen and the other three fae followed in his wake.

"Where are you going?" Casimir demanded.

"Home." Tiernan didn't bother to look back. "I have other things to do that don't involve standing around and negotiating with mortals."

For a moment, Maeve didn't move. None of them did. It was a moment of truth. A test. They could stay at the edge of the sea, just out of Faeven's luring reach, and fend for themselves. Or they could follow a High King further into his domain, into the depths of unknown territory, and hope they came out alive on the other side. Faith and luck had yet to prove they were reliable allies. But with the sun sinking further into the western sky, and bursts of deep orange, crimson, and magenta bleeding across streaks of gray clouds, Maeve was only certain of one thing.

She needed the *anam ó Danua* to save her people. And Tiernan, High King of the Summer Court, was the first step in finding her. It didn't matter if she could still feel his grip around her throat, or how he slipped into her mind, like her thoughts belonged solely to him. None of it mattered because she'd made it. She was in Faeven.

THEY ENTERED Niahvess's summer palace through a side courtyard just as the sun sank below the horizon, and the reds and pinks of the sky bled into twilight.

It was a breathtaking structure, built from white stone with open-air archways, sweeping terracotta roofs, and inlaid knot-work details. Pristine corridors were brushed with soft pinks and golds, and sandstone paths led to turquoise pools surrounded by lush ferns and other greenery. Palm trees reached up, their swaying figures nothing more than shadows against the early evening sky. The air was warm and thick, dense with the fragrance of intoxicating florals, and somewhere in the distance, music was playing, accompanied by the calming whisper of water.

Maeve was deposited at her living quarters first, and Saoirse wasn't too keen on the two of them being separated. But Ceridwen assured them no harm would come to them within the confines of the palace walls. Tiernan, on the other hand, made no such promises.

Though she had to admit, being surrounded by such a sumptuous bedchamber made it rather difficult to remember to remain on guard.

Double doors swung open to a balcony overlooking the city below that seemed to float above winding rivers. An inviting four-poster bed stood in the middle of the room, covered in silken sheets and piled with fluffy pillows. The white walls of the room curved upward to a domed glass ceiling where stars were just starting to dot the sky. The entire room was illuminated with the same glowing orbs like the lanterns from Aran's ship, except these were contained in lamps shaped like crashing waves. The door to the bathroom was cracked open, and a stream of golden light spilled through. Gauzy curtains the color of the sea floated in the summer breeze, and ruffled the loose strands of Maeve's braid, still plaited with flowers from Tiernan's magic.

She stalked over to the mirror and plucked all of them out. One by one she watched the blooms fall to the wooden floor. While part of her wanted to crush them into the ground with the heel of her boot, the other, more sensitive side of her knew she simply couldn't leave them. She scooped up the discarded flowers and placed them on the surface of the small vanity.

It was then she noticed the other door in her room. Made of sleek, gleaming wood, she trailed her fingers along the ornate roses carved into its surface and the swirls of tiny opals ingrained between each whorl.

She reached for the handle, but doubt caused her hand to hover. Maybe it was just a closet. Maybe it was another room. She twisted the knob, but it didn't budge.

Or maybe it was locked.

A sudden knock sounded on her bedroom door and Maeve spun around right as it opened. A woman walked in with a bundle of clothing in her arms and a bright smile on her face. Her dark hair was streaked with threads of gray and pulled back into a tidy bun. She wore an off-white dress with a green apron wrapped around her waist, and she hummed an unfamiliar tune. The lines along her face were deep with age, and when she smiled, it was full and genuine.

That was when Maeve realized it.

This woman wasn't fae. She was human.

"Hello, dear heart." The woman shuffled over to the bed and laid out the bundle of fine fabric in her arms. "I'm Mrs. Tidewell, but everyone calls me Deirdre. I've brought you a gown to change into before dinner."

Maeve stared at the woman. "You're mortal."

Deirdre's eyes crinkled at the corners when her smile widened. "Yes, love. I am."

"And you live...here?"

"I do, indeed. Live here, work here. It's all one and the same." She motioned for Maeve to come over by the bed. "Now come along, let's get you dressed."

"I don't understand." But Maeve obeyed. She'd heard of ladies who had women help them change their clothing, but she'd never been privileged to such an occasion. It wasn't that she was modest, exactly, but Deirdre seemed intent on making sure she obliged, much like a mother hen would corral her chicks. So, Maeve unhooked her corset, but kept her Aurastone within reach, just in case. She couldn't imagine doing this daily, least of all multiple times a day. "Why are you here? In the Summer Court, that is."

Deirdre helped lift her blouse over her head and folded it neatly. "Everyone has their own reason for being in Faeven, do they not?"

She couldn't argue that point. "I suppose." Maeve unbuckled her boots and peeled off her leggings. A shiver crept over her despite the balmy breeze.

"Here you are." Deirdre lifted a gorgeous gown of creamy chiffon. The bodice was tight and heavily decorated with pearls, a beautiful kind of armor. The flowing sleeves hung low off of her shoulders, and the skirt tumbled to her ankles. Slits on both sides crawled up to the middle of her thighs, and the shoes she was expected to wear were delicate, princess-like heels.

Maeve's mouth twisted to the side. "I'd prefer a pair of leggings."

Deirdre laughed, a rich and warm sound. "Nonsense. You're in Niahvess, child. In the presence of the High King of Summer, one does not wear pants."

"I bet the men get to wear pants," Maeve muttered.

"And are you a man?" the old woman countered.

"Well, no. But—"

"Then you wear a dress." She helped Maeve step into the gown. "Don't worry, most of them have pockets and places to stash valuables. What are these?"

Her keen gaze snagged on the cuffs bound to Maeve's wrists.

"They're bracelets. I wear them as a reminder to...make good choices," she finished lamely, and though Deirdre arched a staunch brow, she said nothing. But it was painfully obvious she didn't believe a word Maeve said.

"I'll see about getting a few more casual items made for you."

"I doubt I'll be here that long."

"Mmhmm." Deirdre didn't meet her eyes. She held out the pair of high heels. "We all say that, at one point or another."

Maeve bristled against the woman's cryptic words and fastened her Aurastone to her thigh.

Deirdre sighed and took a step back to admire her work, then gestured vaguely to the vanity. "Feel free to use what you'd like. Dinner is in twenty, don't be late." With that, she was gone, and Maeve was alone again.

She stared down at the vanity, at the intimidating amount of products meant to enhance one's natural beauty. She considered them of little worth, having never used them. She flipped her head upside down, raked her fingers through her curls, then tossed it back up. It was wild and messy, and mostly undone, but she decided it didn't really matter. The gown Deidre had given her would draw more attention than her face.

The pearly bodice cut low and pushed her breasts up to nearly her chin. The slits up the side revealed plenty of thigh, including the sheath where she stored her Aurastone. At least her cuffs were covered.

Maeve opened her bedroom door and walked directly into the hard wall of a broad chest.

Chapter Fourteen

Maeve stumbled back and stared up at the man—no, fae—before her.

She recognized him. Mostly. He'd been at the verandah when Tiernan rolled in with his thunderstorm. But he was the only one who hadn't spoken. His skin was a cool, jewel-toned umber. Dark and flawless. Silver beads pierced all the way up his pointed ears, the sides of his head were shaven, and his deep brown hair was divided into small twists. He wore an emerald shirt with a popped collar and a brown leather vest embroidered with the crest of a sun and twin mountains. Two swords were fastened to his waist, his pants were sleek, and the toes of his boots were covered in sharp studs. A scowl marred his painfully handsome face and his silver eyes watched her like a hawk. He looked downright ruthless.

She glanced down the empty hall.

"I suppose you're on guard duty?" she asked.

He didn't respond.

"Bet you must love that," she mumbled. "I'm Maeve Carrick. From Kells."

She waited, but the intimidating fae said nothing.

"Right." Annoyed, she rolled her eyes. "Let's get to dinner, then."

She headed to the right, without having a clue as to where she was going, but was grateful when he followed along. Yay, progress.

Maeve started walking down the bright hall, and she let her fingers glide against the smooth, marble stone of the walls. They were the softest shade of blush, with veins of gold and turquoise climbing throughout. The entire palace was mesmerizing. It was a wondrous maze of open-air corridors, secret passages, and moonlit escapes. She turned another corner, stole a glance over her shoulder to a door that was cracked open, and came to a halt.

The fae collided into her and grunted before trying to regain his bearing.

She peeked into the room and carefully nudged the door open a little more. Inside was a library, and not just any library, but a glorious room complete with lofty shelves filled with hundreds, if not thousands, of books. A ladder stretched up a to balcony where even more books were displayed. The ceiling was a mural of some kind, with elaborate paintings and dazzling colors that seemed to shift and move, much like Aran's maps. It was a decadent, beautiful tribute to the written word as far as the eye could see.

Her heart leapt to her throat and she stepped inside, only to be hauled back by her shoulder. The fae kept his grip firm and steered her toward the corridor.

"Can I just look around a little bit? It's a library. A *wonderful* library." Maeve looked up at him, but his features remained cold. "I'm sure no one will mind."

Nothing.

"Please?"

More silence.

"Fucking fae," Maeve muttered, and stormed down the corridor.

Eventually, they arrived at the dining hall. Except, it wasn't really a dining hall at all. It was nothing like the showy and pretentious room where her mother hosted lavish parties and extravagant dinners. This was instead a much smaller, more intimate outdoor space. There were a few tables set up on a balcony, and she realized they were close enough to the water to hear the call of the sea. A group of fae musicians were situated in the corner, playing a low and moody kind of music, and everyone else was already there.

Ceridwen was to Tiernan's left, and seated next to her was Rowan. Opposite of Rowan was Saoirse, and beside her was Casimir. The fae with the hot pink hair, Merrick, lounged against the railing, talking with the female from earlier. They all looked up as she walked out onto the balcony. She didn't miss the way their gazes lingered, or how she was drastically overdressed for the occasion. Even Saoirse's mouth fell open.

"How kind of you to join us," Tiernan drawled from his seat at the head of the table. Maeve tried to ignore the way his gaze swept over her, the way the corner of his mouth quirked with purpose. "Lir, what took so long?"

Ah, so the fae who escorted her had a name after all.

Lir grunted. "The princess was distracted by the library."

"Oh, sure. Now you want to talk." Sarcasm dripped from Maeve's tone and Tiernan's brows shot up. She supposed it would do her good to not piss off a fae, more notably one of notorious power, but she found herself agitated at her current situation. She was being treated like a child; being told what to wear, where to be, what time to be there. She was constantly being underestimated, even by Casimir. To top it all, she had a damn *babysitter*.

So, she didn't really care much if she infuriated a fae. She would earn, if not demand, their respect.

Tiernan stood and pulled out her chair for her. Slowly, she lowered herself into the only available seat at the table. The one directly next to him. All the males stood until she sat down.

"The library?" Amusement sparked in Tiernan's eyes and he leaned toward her. She had the decency to lean back. "I didn't know you could read."

Maeve's smile was pinched. "And I didn't know you were an arrogant prick." She spread her hands out before her. "Yet, here we are."

Someone coughed. Someone else snorted. And she was fairly certain at least one of them choked.

"I like you," Tiernan mused, drinking her in. Her skin crawled against his assessment. "But that smart little mouth of yours will get you in trouble."

"Perhaps." She summoned every ounce of boldness within her and turned away from the High King, refusing to acknowledge him or his comment. Instead she faced Saoirse, who was gratefully seated on her other side. She glanced over at her best friend. "Were you escorted here, too?"

Saoirse nodded. "We all were. Well, everyone except Rowan. He came in by himself." She pointed to the female fae, who looked to be far friendlier than Lir. "That's mine over there."

She was tall with killer thighs, and her muscled arms put Maeve's toned ones to shame. Bouncy, burgundy curls framed her heart-shaped face, and a smattering of freckles dusted her cheeks and nose. When she caught Maeve looking, she winked.

Maeve ducked her head. "Did she at least say anything to you?"

Saoirse touched the blue lily tucked behind her ear. "Her name is Brynn, and she likes my flower."

Maeve's brow furrowed as she took in her friend's attire. "You didn't have to wear a dress?"

Saoirse was in fitted black leather pants and wore a cropped blouse of gray satin. Studded chains fell from her shoulders and glossy black ribbons bound her hair into a silver braid. Saoirse touched one of the sharp studs with the tip of her finger. "I was a little more explicit in my demands."

"Are you calling me a pushover?"

"You know you are." Saoirse grinned then pecked her cheek with a kiss. "But really, that dress on you is something else. It makes your eyes sparkle brighter than all the stars in the sky."

Maeve matched her friend, smile for smile. "Poetic heart."

"Shameless flirt," Saoirse corrected. "To both men and women."

Within the next moment, the intense scent of orange blossom and cedarwood filled Maeve's lungs, and a spread of food appeared before them. There were platters of roasted meat and succulent vegetables, bowls of fresh fruits drizzled in a shiny glaze, and baskets overflowing with rolls and muffins. Carafes brimming with sparkling wine were topped with fizzing red berries, and glasses of water spiked with slices of lemons and plump raspberries were waiting to be enjoyed. Maeve's stomach growled in protest, but she refused to touch any of the food. This was not like on Aran's boat, the Amshir, where the food had been brought into the dining area by two servants. No, this dinner display simply *appeared*. Only Rowan, Ceridwen, and Tiernan started to eat.

"Let me guess." Tiernan lifted his glass of sparkling wine in a faux toast. "You don't like it."

Ceridwen scooped a spoonful of glazed berries onto her plate. "They think it's harmful."

Rowan laughed, then quickly coughed in a poor attempt to

cover it up when Maeve shot a glare in his direction. He sobered and straightened in his seat. "Are you serious?"

"Yes." The scent of buttery rolls and sugared fruit caused Maeve's mouth to water. "In all the books I've read about Faeven and faeries, the food here is dangerous to mortals. We can be drugged, tricked, confused, tormented. The Amshir was different. It wasn't made from magic."

"So, you intend to starve to death while you're here?" Brynn asked, watching them expectantly.

Maeve opened her mouth, then clamped it shut.

Tiernan propped his chin on his fist and feigned interest. "I'm afraid your education has failed you."

"Just because it's not enchanted doesn't mean it's not dangerous," Casimir countered.

Tiernan leaned back far enough so the chair rocked onto two legs, and he propped his feet up on the table. He kicked one ankle over the other, his boots terribly close to Maeve's empty plate. For a High King, he was incredibly callous and crude. She shifted away from him.

"Well then. I suppose we'll have to find out if the stories in your books are true or not." He propped his hands behind his head and his muscles flexed. Maeve tried not to stare. "After all, we can't have you starving while you're in Faeven. At least not on my watch."

He gave the barest incline of his head.

"Tiernan," Ceridwen warned.

Lir and Merrick appeared by Casimir and grabbed him. He struggled against them, but two versus one was an unfair fight. There was a satisfying crunch of knuckle bone meeting flesh, and unfortunately it was Casimir's head that rocked backward. Blood dribbled from his nose onto his lips. He coughed and spit until they forced his mouth open and shoved food down his throat.

"Stop!" Maeve screamed. She tried to jump up from her chair, to reach for her dagger, but her body was immobile. She was pinned against some invisible force, frozen by something she couldn't see to fight. Beside her, Saoirse thrashed in her seat, unable to break free. "Stop it, now!"

"Let him go!" Saoirse jerked left and right, her body stiff as she tried to wrench her arms free from whatever power held them down. "You're going to kill him!"

Casimir choked and his face distorted as they forced forkfuls of the food down his throat. The veins along his neck bulged, and his eyes were wild and watering.

Maeve tore her gaze from him to Ceridwen. "Please," she begged. "Please make him stop."

"Tiernan." Ceridwen's voice was as smooth as silk, as calm as the summer before a storm. "Enough."

Tiernan flicked his hand and they finally released Casimir. He slumped over the table, choking. His hands gripped the edge, knuckles white while he struggled to catch his breath. Rowan shoved a glass of the lemon-filled water toward him, and he chugged it down in five gulps. His eyes were bloodshot and his hands were trembling, whether from fear or fury, Maeve couldn't be sure.

"There, you see? Nothing wrong with the food." Tiernan dumped a slab of roasted meat onto Maeve's plate and stabbed the fork into its flesh. He slammed it down with such force, her plate rattled, and she jumped in her seat. "Now, we're going to eat. You're going to stop believing in all this fairytale bullshit you think you know about my world, and you're going to tell me why you're *really* here."

"Maybe she should utilize the library, then." Ceridwen offered a thin smile and sipped her sparkling wine. "You can't fault her for what she's read. It's all she knows."

"That's not a bad idea. I can give her some lessons." Rowan

tossed an apple in the air, caught it with one hand, then took a bite. "She's got all kinds of fanciful faerie misconceptions."

Maeve stuck up her middle finger and he winked.

"And as for you." Tiernan's voice deepened to such a low baritone, it caused tremors of terror to race down Maeve's spine. "You have something that belongs to me, and I want it back."

"I'm willing to negotiate." Rowan tossed a careless glance around the table. "Later."

"Fine." Tiernan kicked his feet off the table and sat up. "Now, why are you in Faeven? What are you looking for?"

"We want to find the *anam ó Danua* to rid Kells of The Scathing." Casimir's voice was raw and scratchy. He coughed once more, then idly examined the butter knife in his hand.

Stark silence filled the outdoor space, save for the continued melody of the musicians. Merrick and Brynn shifted on their feet, uneasy. Only Tiernan looked unperturbed by the mention of it. "The soul of the goddess Danua? You honestly think you can find her, and that she'll save your pitiful excuse for a kingdom?"

Maeve ground her teeth together.

Tiernan spared her a glance but his sister spoke first. "The soul was ripped from its previous owner. No one knows if it even continues to exist."

"Ceridwen is right." Tiernan picked up his glass. "The final bloodline for the soul is a mystery. If such a thing is even real."

"It is." Rowan dropped his half-eaten apple onto his plate.

"How do you know?" Casimir countered.

"I just do."

"That's kind of vague." Saoirse crossed her arms and a line marred her usually smooth forehead.

Rowan leaned back. "I'm a vague kind of guy."

"The hour is late and my patience is thin." Tiernan stood

and pointed at Rowan. "You, come with me so we can discuss your terms. As for the rest of you, I strongly suggest you return to your rooms. We will deal with your dilemma in the morning."

Maeve pushed up from her chair, her appetite suddenly lost, and Lir was by her side in a second. She leaned over and planted a kiss on Saoirse's cheek. "I'll see you in the morning."

"Yes." Saoirse wrapped her in an embrace, and when she pulled away, concern flashed in her sapphire eyes. "I wish our rooms were closer to each other."

Maeve's brows drew together. "Your room isn't down the same hall as mine?"

Saoirse shook her head. "No. Casimir and I are that way." She pointed in the opposite direction of Maeve's bedroom. "And I don't know where they put Rowan."

"What in the stars..."

"Don't worry." Saoirse squeezed her hand once, then let go. "Right now, we need to rest. Then we need to prepare."

"Agreed." Maeve looked up at Lir. "I'm ready."

He nodded once and led her back to her room, but instead of going directly there, he stopped in front of the door to the library. "The High King mentioned you should be allowed to choose some books to read from the library, so long as they *enhance* your education."

"Really?" A burst of excitement shot through her and she bounced on her toes. The library, he was going to let her peruse the library! She didn't want to think about how many hours she could spend in there, about how many sunrises and sunsets could drift across the sky before she resurfaced for air. Her fingers reached for the door handle. "May I?"

Lir nodded sharply.

Maeve heaved the door open and her breath caught in her chest. It was even more dazzling than before. She stepped inside.

The library smelled of books—of texts and ink, of flipped pages and midnight readings. Her heels softly clicked against the tile floor, where a mosaic sun spiraled out in every direction. Some shelves were covered in a fine layer of dust, and the books looked to be in pristine condition, as though they'd never been touched. Others were more well-read, with broken bindings, and peeling, leathery spines. Wonder lifted her heart, filled her soul, as she absorbed the glorious wealth of knowledge at her fingertips.

She wandered over to a section where the books were organized by color, and realized she had no idea how to find anything of worth. She turned back to Lir. "Do you have any suggestions?"

The permanent scowl on his face lifted and he blinked. "What?"

"To enhance my education?" She pointed to the vast walls and shelves brimming with books. "I don't even know where to begin."

"Oh." Lir scanned the room, then walked over to an area where thick, leather-bound tomes were ordered by dates. "Everything you need can be found here."

"Perfect."

Maeve smiled, then dove into a world she only thought she knew. She found books on the history of Faeven, of the gods and goddesses who once ruled the realm, of Maghmell and the Ether. She sifted through pages of illustrations and drawings, and sorted through a selection steeping in the different types of fae magic. She found myths on the human lands, legends of the dark fae, and an entire book devoted to familial bloodlines.

That one in particular snagged her attention as it mentioned the *anam ó Danua* more than once. She gathered a few books into her arms and stuffed one on the history of Old Laic into the stack. Her arms burned, but she didn't care.

Lir eyed the pile of books. "Let me help."

He took most of the books into his arms without waiting for a response, and the Old Laic history book fell to the ground. He was faster than she expected and swooped it up, dropping it carefully onto the small tower of books. He skimmed the title and his lips pursed. "What do you know of the old language?"

Needles of apprehension poked along her spine. She couldn't gauge his tone. She didn't know if he meant to mock her or if he was simply curious. So, she shifted her weight, and went with honesty. "Admittedly, not much. I know I can recognize it when I hear it. But it takes a lot of effort to understand the meaning. Reading it, however, is another beast entirely."

The faintest hint of a smile graced Lir's lips, then vanished. "It's like that for us, too."

Us. Them. The fae. Not her.

They returned to her bedroom and Lir stacked the pile of books on the floor near the bed. Then he walked out without another word and stood in the hall across from her door.

Maeve followed him. "Will you be posted here all night?"

Again, he didn't respond.

"Okay. Well, goodnight. Thanks for helping me with the books."

"It's not me you should be thanking, Your Highness." His gaze darted down each direction of the corridor and he kept his voice low. "And be wary to whom you extend your gratitude."

Right. The last thing she wanted was to be indebted to a fae for their help in carrying books or some other trivial task.

"Of course." She offered a small smile and slipped back into her bedroom. "I'll take that to heart."

She carefully undressed, and hung the delicate gown in the empty wardrobe. There were a few large drawers on the inside and she pulled them open to see if she could find something to sleep in that wasn't made of lace. Several fancy underthings, all of which she had no desire to wear, caught her eye, so she just tugged on her old white blouse since it fell to mid-thigh anyway. The Aurastone would go beneath her pillow, and she set her belt of throwing stars on the nightstand. Wonder overcame her when she realized her bathroom had a proper soaking tub. One day, she reminded herself. One day she would bask in warm, scented waters and smile while rose petals floated around her. But, today was not that day. Maeve scrubbed her face and brushed her teeth, then grabbed two books and took them to the balcony.

Balmy summer air slid over her skin and grazed her bare legs like a lover's caress. She took a long, deep breath, and her blood hummed in a warm, welcoming sensation. The blood curse made her comfortable here, she realized. It was as though the magic coursing through her recognized Faeven as home, and knew its creation stemmed from the land, the seas, the skies, and realm. Unnerved, she dropped her books onto a cushioned lounge chair that was positioned on the balcony just outside the glass door overlooking the Crown City of Niahvess. From her vantage point, she could see the dazzling display of lights and the shadowy outline of rooftops and palm trees. The soothing lullaby of gentle waves echoed in the distance and she knew that out there, in the eternal night where the stars dipped beyond the horizon, was the sea.

She settled onto the lounge chair and grabbed the first book on top of the stack. Its thin pages were like satin between her fingers, and with the bewitching thrum of a guitar playing from somewhere far away, Maeve settled in to read.

Her mind devoured the words as she read about beastly

winged creatures, glittering birds made of starlight, and solitary fae who lurked in dark forests to steal secrets, borrow memories, and collect dreams. She didn't notice when the tome felt heavy in her lap, or when her eyes fluttered closed for good.

When Maeve woke to the sounds of birdsong and the glow of dawn, she found herself still on the balcony curled into the chaise. The last book she'd been reading was closed, and the page was marked with a slip of paper. An azure blanket of downy fabric was draped over her, and her skin was kissed by morning dew.

Chapter Fifteen

Maeve jolted upright and almost toppled out of the chair.

Someone had been in her room during the night. Well, technically not in her room, she was on the balcony, after all. She'd left her door unlocked because Lir had been standing just outside of it. Surely if she'd been in any kind of grave danger, he would've done something...at least, she told herself as much.

The slip of paper tucked into Aran's book caught her eye.

She carefully pulled it out and her breath caught in the back of her throat.

SUMMER LOOKS GOOD ON YOU.

GOOSEBUMPS BROKE out over her flesh and the breeze flowing in from the sea tickled the hairs on her neck. She read the words again, studied the smooth lines of the script, and the way the ink blotted at the end of the sentence. It was a leisurely, casual note. Nothing written in haste. The knock on her bedroom door jarred her out of her stupor and she jumped up off the chaise.

"Come in!" she called, then grabbed the books and blanket, and dumped them hastily on the bed as Deirdre waltzed into the room.

"Morning, love. I've brought you another dress..." Deirdre's gaze shifted to the dumped books on the unused bed, then back to her. "Gracious, did you sleep outside all night?"

Maeve tugged on the hem of her blouse, which now seemed indecent, and embarrassment colored her cheeks. "I fell asleep reading."

The old woman's eyes crinkled when she smiled. "There are worse ways to fall asleep, I suppose."

She shuffled over to the bed and laid out another gown. This one was a shade of coral that cut low in the front and back. Tiny pearls lined the bodice and dotted the lace sleeves. "Now, I know it's a gown. I'm working on those leggings you require. And this one has pockets." She cut Maeve down with a look. "But don't you think for one minute I believe those silver cuffs on your wrists are bracelets. I don't know what they are, but if you're in any kind of trouble, you ought to come clean."

Maeve tucked her hands behind her back. Her cuffs protected everyone. They were a necessity to keep her power tucked away, until she could find someone who could tell herself otherwise. "I'm not in any trouble."

Deirdre's lips pursed and she grunted in disbelief. "Mmh-mm." She helped Maeve slide into the gown then applied a light cream to smooth her curls. "Breakfast is already being served on the balcony this morning."

Once Deirdre disappeared back into the hall, Maeve attached her sheath to her thigh. It wasn't as easily accessible beneath this gown as she would've liked, and she really needed to see about finding a proper sword. Hers had been lost in the Fieann Forest during the Hagla's attack. Plucking her belt of throwing stars from the nightstand, she wrapped it around her waist. It wasn't a pretty match, but she had no plans of being left unarmed.

A moment later she was out the door, and there was Lir again. Still waiting and still scowling.

"Good morning, Lir." She smiled up at him. He glowered down at her.

"Ah, so we're back to the silent treatment, I see." Maeve spun away from him and headed down the hall. "It's strange how you're acting like we don't even know each other."

If he sensed her sarcasm, she couldn't tell, but he cleared his throat as he followed her. "Your dress is nice."

A grin escaped her.

"Thanks." She shoved her hands into her pockets and did a little twirl. "It's got pockets."

The corner of his mouth curved and it was a small enough win for her. When they rounded the corner and the door to the library came into view, Maeve slowed. But Lir nudged her forward with his palm braced against the small of her back.

"Don't even think about it," he warned. "Breakfast first."

It took every effort for Maeve not to stomp off like a petulant child. "Fine."

The scent of breakfast coming from the verandah was entirely too tempting, and the thought of books was suddenly lost to the smell of honeyed rolls, maple-covered pastries, and fried bacon. She took a quick survey of the outdoor seating area. Saoirse was sitting at a table with Ceridwen, but Rowan and Casimir were nowhere to be seen. Merrick and Brynn sat down at a smaller table closer to the railing, and Maeve bit her cheek to keep from smiling when Lir joined them, stretching out his legs, clearly enjoying being temporarily off duty.

She wasn't *that* difficult of a charge.

"Morning, Maeve." Saoirse patted the empty seat beside her. "How'd you sleep?"

Dreamlessly, for the first time ever. Soundly, and without fear. Without nightmares.

"Pretty good." Admitting she slept outside on a chaise hardly seemed like the best course of action. "Where are Casimir and Rowan?"

Saoirse rolled her eyes and waved one hand through the air. "Casimir mentioned something about finding a place for us to train while we figure out what we're doing here." She grabbed a roll and spread a healthy slab of butter on top of it. "And I haven't seen Rowan since last night."

"Rowan and my brother are currently indisposed until this afternoon." When Ceridwen spoke, her voice was like a song. "They'll be along later. Care for some jam?"

She offered Maeve a plate of toast and a little pot of red jam. As much as she knew she shouldn't, Maeve liked her. "Indisposed? Doing what, exactly?"

She imagined it had something to do with Rowan's cuffs, and the mere thought of it caused tiny beads of sweat to prickle at the base of her neck. Even though they were cast in the shade, with the pink dawn rising behind the palace, Maeve was uncomfortably warm.

Ceridwen poured herself a mug of steaming coffee. "You have a lot of questions."

It wasn't a question. It was an implication.

"Yes, I do." Maeve slathered the berry jam onto a piece of toast. "Do you have any answers?"

"Some." Ceridwen added some cream to her coffee, then passed the pitcher to Maeve.

Blessed fae.

"The fae who sent The Scathing to Kells, her name is Parisa. She lives in Suvarese, the Crown City of the Spring Court." Ceridwen stirred her coffee. "You'll need to come up with a plan if you have any intentions of confronting her."

"Confronting her?" Maeve glanced up. "She attacked my kingdom without warning. She destroyed my city and sent a mass of dark fae to do her dirty work. They wrecked my home. They ruined innocent lives. No..." She shook her head. "Confrontation won't work."

"Like I said." Ceridwen was about to take a sip of her steaming coffee but then she paused, the cup halfway to her mouth. "You'll need a plan."

Maeve stabbed her fork into the berries on her plate, and the white porcelain stained red. "I already have a plan."

Lir sat up straighter. "You do?"

"Yes." Her gaze flicked to him fleetingly. "I'll just kill her."

Merrick tossed his head back and laughed. "That's not a plan." He blew an errant strand of pink hair out of his face. "That's a death trap."

"Merrick is right. That's just your revenge talking." Saoirse propped her elbow on the table and pointed with a forkful of biscuit. "I know you want retribution for Kells. Trust me, so do I. But this realm is unlike ours and we can't afford to go in blind. We need to know what to expect, what we'll be up against. Because you know as well as I do, that if we go in there without any kind of strategy, we'll all die."

"She speaks the truth." Brynn's gaze slid to Lir. "The land has changed...but I suppose there is *one* way to get in, if you intend on getting out."

"No." Ice dripped from Ceridwen's voice. "It's out of the question."

"What's out of the question?" Maeve asked.

"Her curiosity could work in her favor," Lir mused, framing his chin with his thumb and forefinger while he rocked back in his chair.

"Absolutely not." Ceridwen's ruby lips thinned. "He won't allow it."

"Okay, first of all," Saoirse cut in. "No one *allows* Maeve to do anything. She's not a child. Or property. Or...whatever else. She can do what she wants."

"It's too dangerous. Especially for a mortal." Ceridwen lifted her chin, putting an end to the discussion. "You are not prepared to enter the Spring Court. And any other method of entrance is strictly forbidden. My Court, my rules."

Saoirse crossed her arms, but Maeve made a mental note to find out about this forbidden other option. If it meant they could get into the Spring Court undetected, she would do whatever necessary to rid Parisa from the land. Her end goal was always to protect Kells, and if she ended up helping Faeven in the process, then so be it.

There was so much to ask, so much to process. She wanted to confront Brynn and Lir right now about any other options they could possibly have, and there was so much she wanted to know about the *anam ó Danua*, so much the books weren't telling her. Then there were the stories she'd read in Aran's book last night, in the one he'd written. Stories of macabre monsters and creatures who hoarded secrets the way one might collect pretty little teacups. There was so much to learn, so much to understand. She wanted to know everything, but time simply wouldn't allow for it. She had no way of receiving an update on Kells, no way of knowing how her city fared against The Scathing. Being so cut off from her realm left her unsettled, and caused a thread of anxiety to weave itself into her heart.

MAEVE TOOK a drink of her coffee when she realized Ceridwen was staring at her.

"People underestimate you, don't they?" she asked.

"All the time," Saoirse supplied for her, and Maeve sent a smile in her friend's direction.

"Yes. I find I'm usually treated like I can't defend myself, like I can't stand up for myself." Maeve looked down at the cup of steaming liquid before her. "It's a careless mistake."

"Maeve is a beast with her dagger." Saoirse adjusted the red rose pinned behind her ear, then leaned back and propped her hands behind her head. "Because she's pretty and bookish, foolish men often mistake her for a foolish girl. But her bravery knows no match, and knowledge is her strongest weapon."

"Sounds like my kind of girl," Brynn mumbled, and she adjusted the strap on her leather armor.

But Maeve didn't want to talk about herself. She wanted to talk about Ceridwen. And Tiernan. She directed her next question to the Archfae.

"Do you have any other siblings?"

Ceridwen's smile reached up to her sparkling eyes. "No, just Tiernan. My twin."

Maeve froze, Saoirse scooped up a spoonful of berries, then paused. "You're twins?"

"Yes." The Archfae sipped her coffee, and settled herself back in her chair. "Fraternal. Twins are quite rare among the fae. Fraternal are even more so."

Fraternal twins. *Fae* twins. Fascinating. "If he's the High King, what does that make you?"

"A High Princess."

Maeve balked. "That's it?"

"What? That's some bullshit." Saoirse's mouth fell open

and she snapped it shut at Ceridwen's shocked expression. "Sorry. What I meant to say was, that's some bullshit, *Your Highness.*"

Brynn snorted in laughter, and even Lir cracked a smile. Ceridwen's eyes, a mythical kind of twilight shade, and a perfect match to her brother's, sparkled like a thousand stars. "I agree, it's old-fashioned in its sentiment. But he was born first... by eight minutes."

"You were *this* close." Saoirse pinched her thumb and forefinger together. She downed a glass of lemon water then stood. "I'm going to go check on Casimir...make sure he hasn't mouthed off to anyone and gotten himself killed."

"That's my cue." Brynn jumped up, grabbed a muffin from the table, and took a hefty bite. She flicked a wave in their general direction. "See you later, Cer."

Ceridwen handed Maeve a plate of crispy bacon. "So, The Scathing has plagued your land."

Again, not a question. Just an assessment.

"Yes." Maeve didn't want to remember, but the images came rushing back in a flood of hysteria. The screams. The cloying stench of smoke that made her eyes water and the metallic tang of blood in the air. The dead, lifeless bodies of the innocent and of the soldiers in the streets. The lost little girl who cried in her arms, terrified and alone. "I have to stop it."

She couldn't leave her people. She refused to abandon Kells, no matter what her mother's motives.

"Mm." Ceridwen tilted her head and her long, golden locks spilled over her shoulder. She fiddled with the silk strap of her bright red gown, and as she did, gold bangles jingled along her wrists.

Maeve dropped her own hands into her lap, determined to not draw any unwanted attention to herself. Or her cuffs.

"You're here to find the *anam ó Danua* to help you defeat

it?" She dabbed her napkin at the corner of her mouth and set it down.

Maeve nodded. "Rowan said it was the only way."

"It is," Ceridwen agreed. "The soul of the goddess Danua is exceptionally powerful...if she still exists."

"What do you know of her?" Now was Maeve's chance to ask as many questions as she could. To glean as much information as possible, so they could figure out who, or what exactly, they were looking for. Then they could get back home. Back to the human lands.

"Let's see." Ceridwen tapped a nail to her chin. "The *anam ó Danua's* identity was originally kept secret for many years. Since it only passes down through the maternal line, a daughter must be born. The last Archfae to possess the gift was the High Queen of the Spring Court."

"Was?" Maeve's brow puckered and a wash of disquiet crashed into her. She knew, without asking, their task was about to become much more complicated. "Is she still alive?"

"I'm afraid not." Shadows crept into the High Princess's eyes.

"She was killed." Lir's deep voice sounded off the walls of the palace, but the crashing waves did nothing to drown out the anger when he spoke. "Murdered in cold blood."

Maeve whipped around in her chair to face him. "What? Who would do such a thing?"

"Her daughter."

Nausea roiled in Maeve's stomach. Lir's words should've stunned her, should have left her breathless with shock. But instead, they gripped her by the throat and squeezed. A cloak of guilt settled around her shoulders and threatened to smother her. Once she finally returned to Kells, wouldn't her plan accuse her of the same sort of crime?

"How...awful." The words were hollow to her own ears.

She too, would be just as awful. A hint of darkness swirled inside her, and churned below the surface of her skin.

"She was jealous." Ceridwen tapped her nails against the wooden table. "Brigid, The High Queen of the Spring Court, was the epitome of grace and beauty. Her magic was uniquely powerful as she had the ability to create visions, to make you think you were somewhere else entirely. She looked kindly upon everyone, no matter their race. Fae. Mortal. Monster."

Lir's silver eyes flashed like lightning. "She was everything her daughter is not."

Maeve peered over at him. "And she killed her for it?"

Ceridwen nodded. "She did. Doing so passed the gift of her mother's magic to her."

Maeve sorted through all she knew of faeries so far. Almost everything she'd read in her books was untrue; all of it was constantly being countered by the fae themselves. Their magic was passed through bloodlines, gifted to them thousands of years ago by the goddess Danua, back when the ancient ones of lore ruled the realms. When fae reproduced, their offspring were blessed with the same form of magic, either through maternal or paternal bloodlines, but with far less intensity. At least until the parent's death. Then the parent's power was passed to the eldest child. But if the High Queen of Spring was also the *anam ó Danua*, then the maternal lineage of the gift would've been passed down to her daughter.

"Wouldn't it make sense for the daughter to possess the soul of the goddess, then?" Maeve was on the precipice of understanding something new. She could feel it in her bones. In her soul—a shift in knowledge that would change everything.

"So you would think." Shadows danced across Ceridwen's sunlit features. "But the gods and goddesses don't approve when a fae slays a member of their own family. Especially the one who birthed them."

Lir stabbed a piece of bread with a knife, then lifted it up and examined it. "It's considered a terrible crime, an affront to the natural course of magic within the fae realm, and punishable by death."

She didn't want to think about what the gods and goddesses would do to her once she killed Carman. "And this daughter, she wasn't destroyed by the goddess?"

"No." Ceridwen's voice was cold, and Maeve swore the air around them cooled. Chilled. "Her father begged for her life in exchange for his own."

"What?" Maeve clamped a hand over her mouth. "And they let him?"

"It was a good trade, but not enough to make amends for the slaying of Brigid." Lir tore off a piece of the bread and popped it into his mouth. "Danua graced this realm once more, except this time she came with Aed."

Aed, the god of death, of the Ether. The realm of the in-between. Just speaking his name was enough to cause Maeve to freeze and fear to slide into her heart.

"Danua removed the soul, ensuring the blessing would cease to exist within Spring. And Aed ripped her magic from her." Ceridwen didn't seem too upset by this. "So now she is a fae with no magical abilities. She has to suffer an eternal life of nothingness."

"Unless she is slain," Lir countered.

Ceridwen's smile illuminated her face. "Unless she is slain."

A restless trickle of unease slithered down Maeve's spine. She shifted in her seat as this new information continued to shock her, to leave her reeling. She forced herself to take a breath. And then another. The food she'd eaten suddenly felt sour in her stomach. She had no idea the god Aed and the goddess Danua were capable of such power, of tearing magic from a being. It sounded absolutely terrifying, but what was worse is it meant the *anam ó Danua* was lost. If Danua retracted the blessing, there may not be any way to get it back, which meant Kells would not survive The Scathing. All of the kingdoms within the human lands would fall.

"This daughter." Maeve took a large drink of lemon water to cleanse her parched throat and swallowed down the disquiet bubbling against her calm exterior. "Is she who I think she is?"

"She is the same one you seek to destroy." Ceridwen sat back in her seat, sipped her coffee, and eyed Maeve from over the steaming rim. "Parisa, of the Spring Court."

Chapter Sixteen

As promised, after breakfast Lir stood watch while Maeve aimlessly browsed the mountains of books in the Summer Court's library. For the most part, she, Casimir, and Saoirse had been given free rein of the palace, so long as one of Tiernan's lackeys followed them around. It seemed silly, really. None of them were any match for a fae. Well, except for Casimir. He was soulless, and probably *was* the reason they still had babysitters and were deemed untrustworthy from the start. Because even though Maeve was quick with a blade, she posed no real threat to a faerie, much less an Archfae.

So she made Lir's job easy, and sat at a table with her collection of books. Some she'd already skimmed, others she read in their entirety, and then there was Aran's—the one she kept returning to every time.

His collection of fairytales, of stories detailing the curious types of solitary fae with obscure sorts of magic, continued to captivate her. In his book, there were no dark fae. Every being listed was by name only, and some of them did not even exist in Faeven. This had been her most recent, and most startling discovery. There were other worlds where faeries lived and thrived, other realms she didn't even realize existed. Perhaps the soul of the goddess Danua had been transferred somehow, moved to another realm, and graced another fae bloodline.

If that was the case, it would make her current situation much more of a burden.

They couldn't come to Faeven and not accomplish anything. If nothing else, she vowed to exact her revenge. Since Parisa just so happened to also be the last being in possession of the *anam ó Danua*, it made sense for them to go to the Spring Court. Best case scenario, they could unearth what happened to the goddess's soul once it was stripped from Parisa, and she would have her vengeance. Worst case scenario, they would all die.

Unless...unless they chose the route Ceridwen expressly forbade.

"Lir?" Maeve flipped through Aran's book, thoroughly not expecting an answer. "At breakfast, you and Brynn were discussing a way to get into the Spring Court undetected—and also be able to escape..."

She glanced up to find Lir's gaze focused on her. He stood with his large body propped up against a bookshelf and his arms crossed. The look on his face told her she was going to have to fight for every word.

"There is another way," Maeve paused for dramatic effect. "Isn't there?"

He gave a barely audible grunt. "It's not up for discussion."

"But—"

"But Ceridwen said no, and to me, that's a direct order from my High Princess." His jaw was set. "One I don't plan on disobeying."

"What if you give me a hint?" Maeve offered her best impression of a simpering smile.

Lir scowled in disgust. "Don't pull that shit on me, Your Highness. You're better than that."

Damn. Already he knew her so well. Maeve stared down at her books. She saw the words, but she wasn't reading them. She tried again. "Please?"

"No."

"Let me ask you this, then." Maeve stood and faced him. "What would you do if you were me? What would you do if the only way to save your kingdom, to save your people, was to go on some ludicrous trek through a realm of terror in the hopes you could find the key to saving all of them? Would you do it?" she asked, daring him to deny her. "Or would you do nothing?"

For the first time since she'd met him, Lir looked uncomfortable in his skin. Uncertainty warred with loyalty, and the two stretched across his forehead in a frown. He mumbled something under his breath.

"What?"

"The will o' wisp." The words were hardly a murmur from between his lips, but then he shifted and looked away, like he'd said nothing at all.

The will o' wisp.

Maeve dreamt about her, about a faerie made of moonlight, starlight, and eternal night. She was certain she'd read about one somewhere, most likely in Aran's book. She flipped through the pages, and a spark of excitement fired through her when she came across a brief mention of such a creature. The will ó wisp was an exceptionally rare fae, hardly ever seen, and hardly ever mentioned in any of her readings. A solitary fae to the extreme, the will ó wisp was a seer who wandered alone, was incredibly shrewd, and eagerly offered visions in exchange for cunning accords.

But Maeve had no need for prophecies or unjust bargains.

She shoved her messy waves back from her face. "I don't understand how the will ó wisp could possibly help."

Lir reached over the table and tapped the page with his finger. "Read."

"I *am* reading." She skimmed the inky script on the page. "It says here the will ó wisp's knowledge of the realm is steeped in longevity of the sight and the capacity of acquiring all manners of secrets, legends, and lore. So long as everything is spoken in truth."

"Exactly."

His short responses weren't entirely helpful, but Maeve was willing to take whatever she could get from him. She read the phrase again. Slowly.

So long as everything is spoken in truth.

"Does this mean the will ó wisp will tell me the truth if I ask it a question?"

Lir lifted one shoulder then let it fall, already done with the mostly one-sided conversation. Agitation fired through her. Maeve looked down at the page again, and when she turned it over, some blotchy words written in Old Laic were scrawled across the bottom. The language, she'd discovered, was incredibly difficult to decipher in written form. She squinted and tried to sound them out with no luck. She sounded like she was speaking gibberish.

"Lir, do you speak Old Laic?" she asked suddenly, curious if the stony fae would give her a little more insight into the world that was so unlike her own.

He simply watched her with his cold, silver eyes.

"Can you read it then?"

More silence. Maeve scowled. "I mean, if you want me to sit here and talk to myself for the next couple of hours then fine, I will. I get there are plenty of other things you could be doing with your time, and I know the last thing on your agenda was babysitting a mortal, but—"

"Okay!" He spoke so loudly, Maeve reared back, surprised by the outburst.

Lir dropped into the chair across from her and stretched out his legs. He braced his hands behind his head and kicked one ankle over the other. "He told us not to engage with you."

"He, who?" Maeve leaned forward. "The High King?"

"Yes."

"Why?"

"Because he doesn't trust you." The answer was simple and Lir shrugged, as though it was the most obvious thing.

"Oh. Well." Maeve thrummed her fingers along the open pages spread before her. "I suppose that makes sense. I mean, we don't really trust any of you either, so—"

Lir shook his head, and a ghost of a smile lifted the corners of his mouth. "What do you need, little bird?"

"Little bird?" Maeve's brow quirked.

He opened his hands in feigned innocence. "It's a kinder way of saying annoying chatterbox."

Embarrassed heat colored Maeve's cheeks.

"Thanks," she grumbled, reminding herself not to take it personally. She'd easily been called worse names by her own mother. She held out the page with the illegible handwriting along the bottom. "Can you read this to me?"

Lir took the page, and she noticed the way his eyes flashed, then shifted from something like shock to unease. "You want me to help you read Old Laic?"

"Yes." She didn't think it was too outlandish of a request. "Please."

Puzzlement flicked across his stern features and he handed the book back to her. "It's difficult to explain, even harder to teach. Old Laic is more innate, it's something I'm born with, something the gods and goddesses deemed me worthy of, something you'll never understand."

Affronted, Maeve splayed her hands on the table and leaned toward him. "I can understand it if you speak it."

"Oh, can you really?" His gaze glinted with humor and his tone was mocking, full of ridicule. He fiddled with one of the silver beads dangling from his pointed ears.

"Yes." She snatched the book back. "I can."

"Okay, let's see just how clever you are." He looked up to the ceiling, where the paintings moved with the stories they told, then back at her. *"Na biogh kyolan ta na cohsh."*

Maeve closed her eyes and heard the words in her head. She played them over and over, noting the sounds, the ebb and flow of Lir's pitch, and the inflection in his tone. "The little... the little bird sings. I know there's another part, just give me a second."

Her gaze flew open. "The little bird sings in the...cage."

Lir grinned, his face nearly unrecognizable behind the emotion. "Fascinating."

Maeve paled and dropped back down into the chair. There was no way Lir could've known about the giant cage, about all the times she'd cried and begged for her life while swinging back and forth in it like a songbird. He wouldn't understand the terror that gripped her, or the way the wind rattled the cage so fiercely, it caused her body to quake. He wouldn't realize such a seemingly harmless phrase would take her right back to the moment Carman decided to try and drown her.

Tiny drops of sweat slithered down Maeve's spine and the heavily beaded gown clung to her skin.

"Are you alright?" Lir leaned over the table, and a ripple of concern marred his brow. "You look like you're about to throw up."

Lir reached out and pressed the back of his hand to Maeve's forehead. Despite everything, she flinched.

The doors to the library burst open, and the shelves shuddered. Two piles of books toppled off a ledge, and a hanging glass orb shattered to the ground. Curling shadows unfurled to reveal Rowan, except he wasn't at all the same. It was the wonder of him, multiplied a thousand times over. Magic rolled off of him in thick, heady waves. It surrounded him, and encompassed her. His cloak of darkness stretched and swarmed around the edges of the library. He wore sleek black pants with shining boots and a pale blue shirt buttoned to the middle, revealing his mass of scars. A sword was positioned at his waist. His teal hair was brilliant, and shone like the purest of waves at the edge of the Gaelsong Sea. Lavender eyes, framed with thick lashes, locked onto her. He drank her in. Devoured her.

He sauntered forward. "Hello, Princess."

"Rowan." His name was a breath between her lips.

"You need to leave." Lir was on his feet in a second with both of his blades drawn. He edged toward Rowan with cautious, intentional steps, ready to strike. "I've been sworn to protect her, and I will do so by any means necessary."

Rowan's gaze flicked to Lir and the corner of his mouth ticked up. "Yeah. And you're clearly doing a fantastic job of it."

Lir looked over at Maeve and shrugged. "She wanted some language lessons and then got all..." He waved his sword in a circle. "Weird-looking."

"What did he say?" Rowan was calm, but his body reverberated with a kind of energy, a terrifying sort of magic Maeve couldn't name.

"It was nothing," Maeve answered quickly, before Lir could dig himself into an even deeper hole.

"Yeah," Lir agreed. "We just talked about birds and cages."

"You son of a—" Rowan growled and his shadows thickened and grew, shrouding the library in a kind of eternal darkness.

"Rowan, stop!" Maeve leapt up from the table and launched herself between them. She catapulted herself into his arms and he snatched her by the waist, hauling her against him. "He didn't know."

She had no idea what sort of magic Rowan was capable of, and she didn't want to find out. At least, not like this.

Rowan clutched Maeve to him like a possession and sneered down at Lir. "Get out."

Lir laughed, but it was harsh and barking. "And leave you in here alone with her? Yeah, right."

A cruel smile stretched across Rowan's mouth. He looked downright savage. "Do you want to *watch?*"

Lir jerked back and his jaw hardened. His gaze cut to Maeve. "Scream if you need me."

Rowan waited until Lir stalked out of the library and slammed both doors shut behind him. Then he grabbed Maeve's chin, tilted her face up to him, and lowered his head so his mouth grazed across the flesh of her neck. Hot and tempting. Her body coiled into him, soft and pliable, desperate for whatever he was willing to give to her.

"I'll make you scream. But it will not be his name." His tongue ran a steaming trail from the base of her throat to her earlobe. "It will be mine."

Before Maeve could blush, Rowan scooped her up off her feet and set her down on the table in front of him. He cupped her face with both hands, and his lavender gaze—wild and feral —absorbed and lingered over every inch of her.

"Are you hurt?" He ran his hands along her arms, down her

waist, to her thighs where he stopped, and the heat of his palms burned through her gown and into her skin.

Maeve shook her head. "No. Just brought back some unwanted memories, is all."

Rowan's thumbs drew lazy circles over the tops of her thighs. "I know someone who can help with that."

"You do?"

He nodded. "A memory keeper. A fae capable of taking away awful memories, of planting new ones in your mind."

"They can do that?" Her body tingled everywhere he touched, and a delicious heat spread through her, caused parts of her to ache. Caused her to want. To desire.

"Anything can be done. For a price." His gaze dropped to her mouth and he stroked her bottom lip with his thumb. "You're so beautiful."

"So are you." The words were out of her mouth before she could take them back, and Rowan blinked down at her in surprise. "Your cuffs are gone," she explained "It makes you... overwhelming. In the best way."

He grinned and it was enough to boost her confidence, so she carefully reached up and wrapped her arms around his neck. He stiffened and pressed his lips together in a firm line. But she tugged him closer. "Thank you for coming back for me."

He shook his head abruptly. "Don't give me your gratitude, Princess. It's not what you—"

"It is." She pressed one finger to his lips and silenced him. "You like pissing everyone off and they all think you're some kind of deceitful prick." His eyes widened and she jerked her head to the library doors, where Lir stood just outside. "But you..."

She ducked her head, unsure of how to continue. "You're the only one who's ever made me..."

His finger slid beneath her chin and tilted her face, so she looked up at him. "Made you what?"

She tugged on her bottom lip with her teeth. "Made me want."

"Now you're just trying to flatter me," Rowan murmured.

"Is it working?" She inched closer to him, as far as her gown would allow.

His hands slid under her bottom and he dragged her forward, then growled when the long length of her skirt kept her from being flush up against him. He reached down and grabbed the hem of the fabric. "This is a pretty little number."

"Yes." A sigh escaped her. "Apparently it's not appropriate for me to wear leggings."

"Absolutely not," Rowan agreed, and the corner of his mouth curved.

"But, it has pockets." Maeve arched back and displayed them proudly. She found she liked the way his greedy gaze engulfed her. The way he watched her like she was a treat, luscious and satisfying. His hands moved to the front, and he gathered the hem of her dress in his fists, raising the fabric inch by inch. But then she noticed his wrists, and the skin was raw and tender where his cuffs had once been.

"Rowan." She placed her hands on top of his and stilled his movements. "Did Tiernan remove your cuffs?"

"Yes." His face was a mask. Not offering anything, not hiding anything. Just blank.

She thought of her own cuffs, of the powerful blood curse pulsing beneath the metal bound to her skin. She imagined what it would be like without them, wondered if it would be freeing, welcoming, or terrifying. "Did it hurt?"

Rowan winced. "Yes."

"What did you give him in exchange for it?"

"So many questions." He bent down and planted a light kiss on her forehead.

"I'm sorry."

"Don't apologize to me." He eased her dress higher, so the beaded fabric pooled around her upper thighs. "It's a good quality to have, being curious and inquisitive."

"I suppose." So far it seemed to get her into too much trouble.

"May I ask you a question now?" Rowan tugged her to the edge of the table and Maeve's legs instinctively lifted and wrapped around his waist. She could feel him then, every hardened inch. His fingers toyed with her sheath before gliding higher.

"Yes." She prayed to the goddess she hadn't made a mistake. "But don't be cruel."

"Never." He let his palms trail up over her hips and along her ribs. "Can I kiss you?"

"Now?" He wanted to kiss her. Maeve's stomach flipped when he nodded and she shivered in his arms. "Here?"

He bent down so his forehead barely pressed against hers. His mouth was so close, she could almost taste it. "Say yes, Princess."

"Yes."

When he kissed her, it was a sweet press of the lips. Testing. Tasting. He was cautious. Careful. Deliberately taking his time. But she didn't want to be treated like she was a fragile piece of crystal, like she would shatter at any moment. She raked her fingers through his silky hair and held on. They fused together, and their tongues clashed, deepening the kiss. Bolts of heat exploded inside her, until every muscle quivered and hummed with electric energy. Her blood pulsed, and the magic in her veins ebbed and flowed like some intoxicating dance. Everywhere he touched set her skin aflame, until she realized needing him, wanting him, was like trying to catch wildfire. Reckless and impossible.

She let her hands wander over his chest, and when she touched the rugged, harsh edges and lines of his scars, he froze.

"It's okay." Her breathy whisper filled the thin space between them. It lingered in the air like an unanswered question. An unspoken request. The admission of trust.

Rowan hitched one arm around her waist and shoved all the books onto the floor. He eased her back, cradling her head with his hand, and she arched up to greet him, desperate for him. Liquid heat pooled between her legs and she locked her ankles tighter around him, urging him closer until she swallowed his groan of desire with her mouth. His free hand glided up and over her thigh, over the sheath holding her Aurastone, and higher still until the pads of his fingers hesitated. She squirmed beneath him and angled her hips up, but he refused to move, and kept his fingers pressed against the heated skin of her thigh. Teasing. Tormenting.

Maeve opened her mouth to speak, to say something, perhaps even beg, but then his mouth swept over hers. Back and forth. Testing. Tasting. He was velvet, dark and delicious, and all the things she shouldn't want. Every nerve inside of her sparked to life, fueled by his touch, by the smooth caress of his hand. Cautiously, she wove her arms around his neck, stifling the space between them. He stilled. Waited for her, to see what she would do next. She drew him closer to her, and when their mouths met again, she sucked on his bottom lip, letting her teeth scrape lightly across his flesh. He crashed into her, drowning her like the frenzied sea. His tongue slid out, traced the seam of her lips, and she opened for him. Her body spasmed against him, desperate for more, for everything he offered.

He cupped her ass through the fabric of her gown, and dragged her to the edge of the table.

Rowan nudged his knee in between her thighs, gathered her against him, swallowing her gasp with a groan. Heat burned through her and her skin caught fire. She sank into him, into his arms, and into his kiss. His mouth moved to her neck, where he licked and left a trail of heat with his tongue, and a surge of tension swelled at her center. Waves of arousal washed over her and she arched again, exposing her throat, and the way her densely beaded gown rubbed against her was a torment to her pebbled nipples. Every brush sent another rush of desire crashing into her. She squeezed her thighs together, squeezed his leg between hers, and that was when she felt the hard, full length of him press into her. She wanted to reach for him. To grab him and take him in her hand. Her skin was hot, and prickling with need.

"Please, Rowan." Maeve's head fell back and his hot tongue swirled along her neck, then he lightly blew against the trail. She shuddered against him.

"Please what?" he murmured.

"Please touch me." Her voice was a whimper, a pathetic plea to her own ears. But she didn't care. She was lost in an otherworldly haze, a mesmerizing fog of finally knowing what it was like to be touched, to be coveted, to no longer be alone.

Rowan nuzzled her neck. "Where?"

"Anywhere." She clenched her legs around him, dug her heels into his back. "Everywhere."

His confident hands slid over her thighs, then higher still. She writhed against him, panting. He swiped his thumb over the bundle of nerves at her core and she nearly bucked off the table. Rowan reared back. "You're not wearing any intimates."

Maeve's mouth twisted in distaste. "They were all lacy and

silky bits of fabric. Honestly there was hardly anything to them, and they looked terribly uncomfortable."

"Divine. Absolutely divine." He grinned, then plunged two fingers into her wet heat and Maeve yelped. Her entire body spasmed and clenched around the intrusion.

Rowan jerked back. He soaked in her expression. "Fuck." He withdrew his fingers and Maeve sucked in a gasp. "*Fuck*. You're pure."

"Yes, but I'm not a prude." She latched onto his shoulders, fearful he'd stop whatever kind of pleasuring he'd been about to pursue. "I know how it works. I've read books, and some of the pictures were fairly graphic. I'm fully aware of what goes where, and how reproduction happens when you—"

He quieted her incessant talking with a kiss. "I should've been gentler."

"Please don't stop." She was begging him. But for the first time she was experiencing something raw and wonderful, and it didn't involve daggers and swords. "I just, I just need..."

"What do you need, Princess?"

"You. I need you, Rowan."

"Let me make it all better for you." He laid her back against the table, and lifted her knees, spreading her wide before him. He pebbled her inner thighs with kisses so hot, they scorched and seared. But when he lowered his head, Maeve bolted upright.

"What are you doing?" She propped herself up on her elbows and sucked in a breath.

He looked up from between her legs, one dark brow arched. "I'm making it all better."

"With your *mouth*?"

Rowan didn't respond. Instead he bent down and at first, there was nothing. Maeve trembled, her entire body wrought with anticipation. Then there was everything. She melted against the press of his mouth. She soared against the flick of his tongue. He licked and sucked, and when his hot tongue delved deeper between the folds of her most sensitive skin, she nearly came undone. But his strong hands held her hips in place and kept her bared to him. He gripped her firm, holding her still against the table while she wiggled beneath the velvety caress of his tongue. Without warning, he drew her little bud into his mouth, then slid two fingers deep inside of her.

Maeve cried out, but he was relentless. He made a noise, a kind of rumble with his mouth, and she arched toward him, offering herself like a sacrifice. Over and over, he continued to stroke her with his fingers, delving deeper into her core until she was hot and slick with need. Another thrust, another suckle, and just like he said, she screamed his name. Layer by layer he unraveled her, and she writhed in his arms. Her nails bit into the hardwood of the table and when those two fingers inside of her curved, when his tongue lashed the tip of her release, she fell into oblivion.

Gasping, Maeve came up for air.

Rowan kissed her thigh, just below the sheath where she kept her dagger. Then he stretched her leg up and kissed behind her knee. Then her ankle. He scooped her into his arms and off the table, before carefully depositing her back onto solid ground. He gave her a flirty wink, and she nearly buckled when he licked his lips. Her gaze betrayed her and she glanced down to where he bulged against the fabric of his pants. She stepped toward him, but her legs were useless, her body was spent. A rapturous song exploded inside her, and she wanted nothing more than to throw her arms around his neck, and ask him to do it all over again.

"All better?" he whispered against her hair and kissed the top of her head.

Maeve could only nod. She'd forgotten words. Speech was overrated.

He adjusted her gown, and made sure it hung in all the correct places. He gathered up the books she'd been reading from off the floor and tucked them into her arms. Then he gave her a gentle pat on the rump and led her to the library doors.

Lir was there, as cold as a stone statue. His jaw was clenched so tightly, the veins of his neck bulged and vibrated with displeasure. He wouldn't even look at her.

Rowan moved his hand to Maeve's lower back and guided her down the hall. Her heels clicked quietly against the white stone, but the sound was too loud, and it grated against the arched walkway.

Rowan glanced over his shoulder to where Lir followed behind them. "Don't you have somewhere else to be?"

Lir kept one hand braced on the sword at his waist. "Nope."

"He's right where he's supposed to be." A low baritone coasted from somewhere behind her and fell around her like cold silk.

The summer air cooled, the way it would right before an impending storm, and chills raked over Maeve's skin. She spun around to see Tiernan, the High King of Summer. He leaned against one of the pillars with his arms crossed, the collar of his deep blue shirt popped, and the sleeves rolled to reveal more tattoos of swirling gold crawling up his tanned skin. Sunlight spilled over him, and his eyes were a threatening mix of fury and amusement.

The corner of his mouth lifted in a cocky, half-smile. "Did you find everything you were looking for in my library, Your Highness?"

Maeve held the books close to her chest to hide the flush of disgrace. His words scorned her and her cheeks flamed hot. She swallowed, but it was useless against her parched throat. "I did."

"*I bet you did.*" His voice scraped down the walls of her mind and she blanched against the violation. "*And did you enjoy it when he splayed you open like one of your books? When he pleasured you until you exploded with ecstasy?*"

Nausea roiled inside her, a tumultuous wave of mortification. He'd watched them somehow. Tiernan had seen everything. He witnessed her become a pathetically weakened female, a wanton object of her own sexuality. Her gut seized and her heart tumbled down into the acidic pit of her stomach. She took a heaving, staggered breath.

"*Oh, don't worry, Your Highness.*" He slinked into her thoughts again. "*I didn't see anything. Fae, however, have an exceptionally keen sense of smell.*"

"Pervert," she snapped and Rowan looked down sharply. "What is it?" His quiet voice was meant solely for her.

Tiernan strolled forward and the air pulsed around them, electrified by his magic, tainted by the torment he could inflict. "I never pegged the Princess of Kells to be such a little tart."

Rowan jerked like he'd been slapped and pulled Maeve into his side. "Watch your mouth."

Tiernan rolled his shoulders back, shoved his hands into his pockets, and his teeth skated along his bottom lip. "My Court, my rules." His ruthless gaze slid to Maeve and he edged even closer. He snared her by the chin. "Care to share? I've never been fond of seconds, but I might make an exception for you."

"Get the fuck away from her," Rowan growled.

"No," Tiernan drawled. "You get away from her." He stretched his arm out, barely flicked his wrist, and sent Rowan careening into one of the sloping walls, then pinned him there. His stormy, twilight eyes coasted over Maeve and her skin crawled. "For a mortal who hates the fae, you were certainly quick to give in to your most basic of needs."

Maeve locked her spine in place and refused to cower to the High King's crass remarks. He lifted her chin like he was inspecting her and she tore herself from his grasp. "Don't touch me."

His taunting smile dissolved. "I do what I want."

Pain exploded behind her eyes as his rich voice sank into her mind. *"He was warned not to touch what didn't belong to him, and he did it anyway."*

Maeve shook her head violently. The books tumbled from her arms to the stone floor and she gripped the sides of her temples with both hands. Her blood burned, and the darkness rose up, desperate to overtake and overwhelm.

"No." She spat the word out through gritted teeth. "I belong to no one."

A silky, rumbling laugh echoed in her mind. "Foolish girl," Tiernan muttered.

Piercing bolts of violet lightning struck her, ricocheted through her, and forced her onto her knees. She gasped from the agonizing shock of bone grinding against marble, and rocked back and forth on the ground. She squeezed her eyes shut against it and blindly reached for her Aurastone. Her fingers grazed the rigid leather of the sheath, but her vision blurred, and her thoughts muddled.

"You are so wonderfully weak. A useless mortal in every sense of the word." Then he bent down close to her—so close, she could smell the scent of him. Sun-drenched palm trees. Warm sandalwood. The scent of a flower she couldn't name. He overwhelmed her senses. Her lungs ached and she couldn't breathe.

"What do you say, mighty Princess of Kells?" His voice echoed in her mind and his words were like a balm to her

despair. She hated herself for wanting to hear him, for needing to hear him, because with every word he spoke, the unbearable pain throbbing within the walls of her mind eased. Just slightly. *"Would you let me kiss you like that? Until you quivered beneath my palms? Until I swallowed every delicious drop of you?"*

"Get out of my head!" Maeve screamed. A torrent of tears plagued her eyesight and she clutched her head once more.

"Leave her alone!" Rowan roared as he fought the invisible bonds anchoring him to the wall. "Leave her!"

"No." Tiernan stepped back and the agony receded. Maeve swiped hastily at the hot tears streaming down her face. He nodded once and Lir appeared beside her. He lifted her up off the ground by her arm, his grip firm, but gentle. Tiernan faced Rowan, then peeled him away from the wall. "It's time for *you* to leave her."

"Leave?" Maeve's voice was scratchy. It pitched with panic.

Tiernan adjusted the rolled sleeves of his silk shirt. "I believe Rowan's time with us has come to an end."

"What? Why?" She sprang forward but Lir held her back, and kept his grasp ironclad around her upper arms.

Tiernan's lip curled in disgust. "Rowan's allegiance is not to the Summer Court. He pledged his loyalty to Spring. Years ago."

"Enough," Rowan snarled. "She knows I'm loyal to Spring, I already told her as much. I can explain the rest of it myself."

Maeve staggered forward but Lir held firm, refusing to allow her to get any closer to Rowan. "Explain what?"

Darkness tore through the beautiful planes of Rowan's face. "Part of the deal I made with Tiernan was to return to my Court after he removed my cuffs."

"What? No!" Maeve angled and distorted her body. She tried to reach him, to convince him he was making a mistake.

But Lir gave her no leniency. "You're supposed to help us. You promised to help us find the *anam ó Danua*. You can't just leave!"

He looked down at his shiny boots and didn't meet her eye. "I'll return to help."

"With my permission," Tiernan interjected and Rowan cut him a look.

"Rowan, you can't be serious. We don't even know where to start looking!" Panic bubbled up in the back of her throat and tried to choke her. "The whole reason we're here is because you said you knew how to defeat The Scathing. You said you knew how to track the soul. And now you're abandoning us? *Here?*"

"I'm sorry, Princess." His apology was empty. Just like everything else he'd told her. Yet the sting was distinctly sharp. "My duty is to my Court. Always."

"Rowan!" Maeve screamed, though she couldn't tell if it was shock or anger that caused her tone to crack with despair. She blinked and he was gone, nothing more than a glimmer of sparkling dust.

White-hot fury ripped through her, and a sound so terrifying, so inhuman, tore from her throat. It was all the emotions she was never allowed to feel, to suffer, to absorb. Resentment. Anguish. Sorrow. Rejection. Loneliness. Her sobs were broken, a disturbing bout of hiccups, mumbled words, and ragged breaths. She screamed at nothing and everything. Emptied herself of wrath and trauma. But then there was warmth. The soft, comforting warmth of summer. It wrapped her in a cloak of calm, of serenity, and ease. She was lifted from the floor and carried, inhaling the delicate scent of ocean breezes, sweetened coconut, and endless sunshine.

At some point, she was aware of being carried back to her bedroom. And there she was left, as silent tears continued to slide down her cheeks. Rowan's betrayal was the deepest of wounds. Her one source of hope, her only lifeline to save Kells, to rid her land of the Scathing, had vanished before her eyes. But there had to be a way to find the *anam ó Danua* without him, and she would do it. No matter the cost. She would not continue to cry. She wouldn't grieve for her own humiliation. She wouldn't dwell upon the deception she'd endured. No, she would overcome. As she always did.

Because her kingdom was worth it. Because she was a warrior first. Because she was a princess second.

And she would not break.

Chapter Seventeen

In the stillness of predawn, Maeve's blood hummed. It was low at first, a gentle thrum, urging her to awaken. She ignored it. She didn't want to open her swollen eyes. She didn't want to remember Rowan had abandoned them in the Summer Court, or that he'd left her shouting his name and suffering from the sting of his betrayal. But tingles of awareness coasted up and down her spine, and the magic coursing through her veins throbbed with alarm. A warning. Her balcony doors had been open, and she'd grown accustomed to the warm summer breeze, yet now the air was cold like the touch of death upon her skin. The nauseating stench of rot permeated the air. Acidic breath. Her stomach heaved and she nearly gagged. Maeve slowly slid one hand under her pillow. Her palm encircled the hilt of her Aurastone.

In one swift movement, she flipped over and cut the air above her with her dagger. Her eyes flew open and she stared in horror.

Hovering above her was a grotesque creature the color of ash. Stringy, gray hair hung around its hideous face. Its eyes were white, the skin surrounding them had been blackened, and inky ooze slid from the corner of its mouth from where she'd cut it. It smiled, displaying a full set of razor-sharp teeth and spiders crawled out from the side of its mouth.

Maeve screamed and scrambled to a sitting position as its spindly arms reached for her. She slashed out with her blade again, satisfied when her dagger cut off both of its hands and they turned to dust. The dark fae screeched and its head jerked toward her, convoluted and unnatural. This beast was not as easy to kill as the ones in Kells.

She rolled off the bed, hit the ground, and jumped up.

A shadow darted from the edge of her vision and panic slicked Maeve's hands. There were two of them. Pounding sounded outside of her door, and a muffled voice called her name.

"Lir!" she screamed, refusing to take her eyes off both of her enemies. "Lir!"

The dark fae with both of its hands attached lunged for her, its disjointed mouth gaping open. Spiders crawled in and out of its mouth and eyes, and bile burned in the back of Maeve's throat. It lurched for her, its claws outstretched, ready to tear apart her flesh. She dropped low and kicked its legs out from under it.

The door to her chambers burst open and Lir exploded into the room, all wrath and fury. His silver eyes widened. "Fuck."

"Tell me about it." Maeve popped up off the ground, then struck hard and fast. The tip of her blade pierced the flesh of the dark fae at the base of its throat. Black blood that resembled tar oozed and bubbled from its neck. The creature howled, its white eyes going dark, before it turned to dust.

Lir slashed the other one clean through. His curved sword ripped its torso in half and black blood splattered all over the bed, speckling his face. He tore through the rest of the room and slammed the doors to the balcony shut. "Are you alright?"

"Yes, I think so. But there were spiders, and..." She shuddered, not wanting to remember. Those images would haunt her dreams for many moons to come.

"I know." He nodded to the dagger in her hand. "What sort of blade is that?"

"It's an Aurastone." She didn't offer any more of an explanation and if Lir knew what it was, he made no point in saying as much. "I think we should tell someone what happened."

Someone meaning Tiernan. But he was the last person Maeve wanted to see.

"I think—" A siren wailed through the early dawn hours, cutting through the calm of the night. Lir muttered a swear. "I think he already knows."

The siren continued to sound, shattering the silence. "What does that mean?"

"It means we're under attack." Lir glanced over at her. "You should stay here. Where it's safe."

Maeve gestured to the severed fae still leaking black goo onto her bed. "Are you serious?"

"Right." He wrapped a steadying arm around her waist and pulled her into him. "Hold on tight."

Maeve gripped the leather armor of his vest and the bedroom suite *faded* away. The world around her shifted and blurred, crushed her lungs, and spun her in a dizzying spell of darkness and smoke. Tears slid down her cheeks, and when her feet finally landed on solid ground, her knees softened, and if it wasn't for Lir keeping a firm grip on her arm, she would've collapsed.

She flung her arms out to regain her balance. "What the hell was that?"

"I'll explain later," he muttered.

"What the fuck is *she* doing here?"

Maeve knew that voice, the one that dripped with disdain. She looked up sharply and saw Tiernan glaring down at her. He was in full armor; cobalt leather with gold stitching protected every inch of him. There were other faeries surrounding him, many of whom she'd never seen within the walls of the Summer palace. They wore armor of the same colors, but each one reflected a personal style. Large shoulders studded with gold metal spikes. Leather vests etched with mountains and swirling suns. Cuffs bound with whorls. They were terrifying. Powerful. The dense scent of orange blossom and cedarwood overwhelmed Maeve, and she stared at the beauty of the fae before her. Brynn stood off to Tiernan's right and offered a small wave. Merrick cocked his sword over his shoulder and winked, his dimpled smile devious. But if they were here, then where were Saoirse and Casimir? Had they been attacked in their rooms as well?

"They're fine," Tiernan snarled, intruding upon her thoughts once more. Her fist clenched around the hilt of her Aurastone. His gaze flicked to it, a shadow of something flashed in his twilight eyes, and then it was gone. He pointed his sword at her and Maeve stumbled backward into the solid wall of Lir's chest. "She's in a fucking nightgown, Lir."

Maeve glanced down and warmth bled into her cheeks. Sure enough, her cotton nightshift skimmed her thighs and the ballooned sleeves barely kept her cuffs hidden from view. It wasn't much, but it was better than those sheer bundles of lace Deirdre had originally left out for her.

Lir stepped up beside her. "She was attacked in her quarters. Two dark fae."

Brynn looked stricken and even Merrick blinked in surprise.

"How'd they break past the wards?" Tiernan shook his

head. "Never mind, we can figure that out later. Brynn, take half the guard to the northern border. Merrick, take your forces and protect Niahvess, and our people. Lir and I, and the rest of the guard, will take the palace grounds."

Nobody questioned him. Nobody doubted him. She watched as every fae moved with purpose at lightning speed, rushing to their posts, and taking control of their commands, while dark clouds churned above them and the crackle of lightning splintered through the sky.

"And as for you," Tiernan warned. "Stay out of the way."

Maeve stalked toward him. "You son of a—"

Lir snatched her up by the waist and set her down behind him. "Not worth it, Your Highness. Quarrel with him another time."

She opened her mouth, ready to spout off a number of reasons as to why she shouldn't have to wait to punch Tiernan in the face, but then a shrill cry pierced the air. She looked up to the overcast sky, where the clouds moved like smoke, and the shadowy outline of a beast took form. It was monstrous, and it dove through the air like a bird of prey. The screech broke out again, drowning out the clang of swords and the cries of battle, and as it swooped closer to the palace, Maeve could discern the true shape of it. Long, curved horns were set atop three eagle-like heads, and they snapped and shrieked. Its body was overwhelmingly large, an armor of glittering dragon scales. Sharp talons plucked dark fae from the ground and tossed them into the sea like they were toys.

Maeve shrank back into her skin. She knew this beast. She'd seen it once before—on the flag of Aran's ship. She looked up at Lir. He had both swords drawn and his gaze was focused on the edge of the courtyard, beyond the outlying walls of the palace. The air seemed to vibrate and a cold wind blew in, so frozen, Maeve could see her breath billow up before her. She shivered, and the smell of rot slammed into her.

Her lungs seized and she coughed. The stench was the same as when the two dark fae had attacked her in her room. "Where are they?"

She knew they were coming.

"Just there." Lir nodded to where palms stood still in the breeze, to where a murky haze settled upon the horizon, to where a horde of dark fae prepared to assault the Summer Court.

THE DAWN WAS ECLIPSED by the rise of shadows and smoke.

Maeve barely had time to breathe before the dark fae were upon them. She crouched low and as the first one attacked, a creature with jutting fangs and fire for eyes, Maeve darted upward and tore her dagger through its midsection. It howled, then crumpled into a pile of dust.

Okay, she had to strike true with her Aurastone. Little cuts and slices weren't going to work if she wanted to destroy them on the first attempt. Every thrust and stab would have to count, every strike would need to be intentional. Her aim couldn't falter.

Another one ambled toward her at a full sprint. She dodged the first blow, ducking to the ground, but its gangly claws snagged and got caught in her hair. Maeve hissed as pain tore through her scalp. Her body jerked in the other direction, and she cut her dagger through the air, chopping off the dark fae's arms from the elbow down. The creature yowled as blackish blood poured from its missing members. The stench was unbearable; it smelled of decaying flesh, of charred magic. But being dismembered wasn't enough to keep the dark fae from attacking her. It opened its slimy mouth and licked its lips with a snake-like tongue. Maeve swallowed down the compulsion to vomit and closed the distance between them. She jumped high and plunged her dagger into its throat. A moment later it turned to ash, and the hacked-off arms tangled in her hair covered her shoulders with a thick layer of dust.

She cringed, but there was no time to wipe the lingering death from her, because the second she turned around, another one was coming right at her. All around the courtyard, the fae soldiers of Summer and the dark fae clashed in a battle of metal and magic. She cut and tore through dark fae, shredding their vile skin with the scorch of her dagger. The Aurastone burned brighter with each death, its radiance illuminated in a reflection of rainbows among the darkness. Sweat dripped down her neck and back; her nightshift clung to her damp and sticky skin. Her cursed blood seemed to boil as she sundered every creature she came across. Never before had she taken so many lives, even if they were vile. Even if they were an adversary. She tried not to think about the souls she was ruining with every pile of ash and dust. There were no lost souls when she struck with her Aurastone. They simply disintegrated, vanishing into oblivion. Not even the fires of the Sluagh would claim them.

The realization tore through her gut. She didn't want to keep a tally of those who died at her hand.

Nine.

Lir slashed through them in nearly double the time she could kill one. He moved with lethal grace, turning, dodging, and killing like a dancer in a ballroom. She supposed that was the advantage to being able to wield two swords at once, one for each hand. He could fight from a distance. He could cut two down and keep moving without looking back, without having to watch the remnants of life vanish from their eyes. But her dagger required more intention. She had to be up close to kill.

"Watch the sea wall!" Tiernan called out, his voice booming across the courtyard.

Maeve spun in the direction of the sea. A wall of white stone ran along the border to the verandah where Aran had dropped them off. Three dark fae fell on top of one of the Summer soldiers. Her broken scream struck Maeve in the heart, and she bolted in the direction of the fallen faerie. Her bare feet slid across the sticky surface of the stone and she grimaced, hating the way the metallic smell of blood permeated the air. She vaulted over one of the curving streams and drove her Aurastone into the spine of a dark fae. Black blood splattered her face and chest. She jerked the dagger upward and the cry that erupted from the creature sounded so terrifyingly human, Maeve nearly faltered. But then it was gone, turning to another useless pile of cinders.

Ten.

The Summer solider writhed beneath the assault. Her face was bleeding and contorted in pain as she struggled to regain her bearing. But Maeve had already eliminated one of the dark fae. Two versus two would be an easy win. She climbed up onto the white stone wall and a gust of wind slammed into her. Shudders tore through her but she pumped her legs and sprinted on top of the wall's smooth ledge. It didn't matter if the sea was on the other side, if there was nothing to catch her fall from the furious waves. She would save at least one life tonight. She would not simply end them.

"Get away from her!" Maeve shouted, her voice unrecognizable.

She jumped onto the back of one of the dark fae and forced the Aurastone into the base of its neck. Its shriek of agony was lost in the howl of the wind, and Maeve pulled her blade free. But the creature didn't turn to dust. Instead it reached back and sunk its claws deep into her shoulder. Hot pain ripped through her. The creature's talons shredded through her flesh like the tips had been heated over a forge and then serrated. The dark fae's claws sank deeper, tearing through muscle and tendons. Somewhere, a guttural, ear-splitting scream echoed in Maeve's head until her vision swam and her head thundered with a throbbing ache.

The sound came from her.

Something was wrong. She couldn't breathe, couldn't think. The pain spread from her shoulder down to her elbow, and across her chest. Each inhale was a struggle, and the pounding rush of adrenaline firing inside her dwindled so there was barely anything left. The racing beat of her heart slowed to a dull thump, and her body grew lax with exhaustion. It required too much work to even lift her head. The Aurastone slipped from her grip and she watched it fall. Slowly. Slowly. It clattered against the cobblestone and she could do nothing but stare, helpless. She couldn't fight. She couldn't move. Couldn't even scream again. The cuffs on her wrists fired hot, and the fae magic inside her pulsed to a fever pitch. Frenzied and frantic.

Poison.

In the recesses of Maeve's mind, she knew she was right. She'd read through volumes of books regarding all different kinds of substances that could be used against a body. She'd studied the signs and effects for weeks after she'd caught Carman slipping crushed darmodh root into her morning tea to encourage forgetfulness. Apparently, her mother wanted her to endure full-blown memory loss. That way, every time Maeve was sent to the cage, the terror was new. Fresh. It was revolting and malicious, but eventually Maeve learned to dump her tea and switch to coffee. The bitter brew tasted slightly of earth when darmodh root was added, whereas the tea disguised its flavor well.

Her stomach revolted, and she wanted to retch.

But instead, the dark fae heaved her forward in one swift motion and slammed her down upon the sea wall's ledge. An agonizing crack crippled her spine, and she sucked in a ragged, wheezing gasp of air. She imagined sand filling her lungs, so heavy, it was impossible to breathe. Limp and lifeless, she was splayed upon the wall, while the battle ensuing around her was nothing more than a mess of upside-down, blurry images all streaming together in an endless fog. It sounded like someone yelled her name. Something warm and sticky slid down her face and into her eyes, and blood filled her mouth. Her body was on fire. Burning. Her blood curse tried to tend to the numerous wounds, to keep her alive. How ironic the one thing she loathed should try and save her.

But the curse bound to Maeve could not cure poisoning.

There was more screaming. It was everywhere, filling the void of all sound, until there was nothing else. Her eyes grew heavy, weighted down by despair and the keen sense of knowing this was how she would die. The pause between her heartbeat was long and drawn out, a reminder death was watching. Waiting. She knew what would happen next. Her heart would slow and leave her in a haze, fogging her mind so she would forget to breathe. Eventually, drawing breath would become a struggle, until she quit altogether.

Her lungs ached, desperate for oxygen, a problem made worse by her snapped spine. *Thump...thump.* A hesitant pause, and longer than the last. *Thump...*

...*thump...*

Every second, Maeve slipped further into the void of the unknown. Her conscience was drowning, noises were garbled, and numbness stole through her so the pain ebbed away like the tide. It simply faded into nothingness. Just like her.

Chapter Eighteen

Fever wrecked Maeve's body.

It was more difficult than Maeve realized to discern reality from the shroud of memories haunting her mind. She drifted in and out of consciousness, slipping between a recollection of dreams and nightmares. At one point, she thought she may have awoken. But then she saw Saoirse, whose eyes were bloodshot, and whose pretty face was splotchy. But it was wrong, it was all wrong. Saoirse was crying.

Saoirse never cried. Ever.

The visions swirled and stormed as she was dragged under a blanket of darkness. Voices tried to lull her back. They were full of soft words, of endless promises, of hushed whispers. But haunting shadows crawled out from the corners, and their misty, death-like tendrils coiled around her like a snake ready to strike.

Then Casimir was there.

She blinked, but he blurred before her, like she was looking at him underwater. No part of him was clear. She could make out the color of his hair—rich, dark brown. He grabbed her hand, his warm brown flesh a harsh contrast to the pallid, sickly color of her own skin. She could see his mouth moving but there were no words coming out. And as quickly as he was there, she was gone.

In the far recesses of her lucid mind, Maeve knew her body was fighting the effects of the poison. She knew the vile substance had been siphoned from her system. Otherwise, she would already be dead. She was struggling, desperately fighting to survive. Every so often, a low thrum of music whispered past her, causing her blood to hum in response. A softly strumming guitar. The evocative melody tugged at her, urged her to return, and was accompanied by the deep rumble of an unfamiliar baritone.

Maeve reached for it. For the alluring song. She hauled herself through a thick fog of incoherency, past the fitful recollection of her youth. The ones swallowed by darkness, plagued by terror, and smothered until there was nothing left. Fingers outstretched, she groped for something to hold onto, anything to bring her out of this constant state of delirium. The music played again, except this time the notes sounded closer, just within her grasp. She grabbed hold and didn't let go. She ripped through the realms, helpless while she watched the fractured remains of all she ever knew be torn from inside her. She was gutted. A blade of fire sliced through her stomach, then spread her open like an animal ready for slaughter.

A gasp caught in the back of Maeve's throat and her eyes flew open. She thrashed, desperate to escape the pain, when a cool hand slipped over hers.

"Easy there, love." Deirdre's soothing voice coasted over her, and she gave her a gentle pat. "You're not alone, I'm here."

Maeve blinked, unable to look away from the woman who held a wet washcloth to her forehead and brushed her damp hair back from her face. She shuddered as the remnants of fever fled her body, leaving her chilled and drenched with the foul scent of her own sweat. Her muscles seized and ached, and pain came in swells of nauseous, bile-filled waves.

"W-water," Maeve croaked, her throat stuffed with grit and sand.

"Of course, dear." Deirdre bustled over to the vanity and grabbed a blue glass pitcher, then poured a small cup of water. She brought it back to the bedside, and slid one arm around Maeve's back, carefully easing her into a sitting position. "Slow sips."

Intense throbbing pulsed at Maeve's temples, but she forced herself to take in at least a few drops of water. The cold shock of it caused her stomach to flip, and dizziness slammed into her so hard and so fast, it stole her breath.

"Just a couple more sips," Deirdre crooned, "and you'll start to feel better."

Maeve might've believed her if at that very moment, Tiernan hadn't tore into her bedroom.

His dark sweep of hair seemed to steal the shreds of sunlight. He wore slate pants and a shirt the color of fresh berries. The top buttons were left open, revealing the golden swirls of tattoos that crawled along his neck. He was terrifyingly beautiful and Maeve's gut clenched. Or maybe it was the water. But then his stormy eyes narrowed at Deirdre. "You didn't tell me she was awake."

Deirdre patted Maeve's forehead with the washcloth. "Her eyes have only just opened, *moh Rí.*"

Old Laic again. King. My King. She never heard him addressed by the title, but at the moment, it was the last of her worries. Because her head felt like dozens of razor-sharp talons were raking down the inside of her brain. She winced and clutched the bed linens to keep herself from toppling over.

"Leave us," Tiernan demanded.

Deirdre crossed her arms. "With all due respect, my lord, she's still fighting symptoms of the poison and is not yet healthy enough for—"

But Tiernan's face shadowed, and a distinctive chill crept into the air.

"Now," he growled.

Deirdre scowled and huffed, clearly peeved by her High King's request. She sent him one cold glare before glancing back over her shoulder and making eye contact with Maeve. The look on her face was nothing short of pity, but she left the room, and shut the door soundly behind her.

Maeve sucked in a shallow, trembling breath. Her skin was slick with the stink of illness and fever. Her body was weak, having been ravaged by poison. She wouldn't be able to defend herself if she tried.

Tiernan stalked over to the bed and glowered down at her. His gaze flicked to the cuffs binding her wrists, and when he spoke, it was the rumbling sound of thunder. The threat of summer and the fury of its storms. "You've been keeping secrets from me."

Maeve shook her head but the violent movement was a mistake. The room spun around her in a flurry of colors. Her pulse jumped and her insides quaked.

Tiernan snatched her chin and forced her to look up at him. "What do you mean, no?"

"You—" Maeve heaved. She slapped his hand away, hurled herself toward the edge of the bed, and vomited.

"Fuck."

"I'm s-sorry." Tremors shook through her shoulders and down her spine. Hot tears of humiliation pricked at the corners of her eyes.

Tiernan's lip curled. With a flick of his wrist, the vomit vanished from the floor. But he looked utterly disgusted. Mortification stung Maeve's cheeks and a tear slid down her nose, to her chin. She smelled of putrid bog water and was soaked in her own sweat. The traces of foulness lingered in every crevice of her body. Her hair was matted to her neck and face. And this bastard wanted to interrogate her.

Tiernan's eyes widened. Amusement flickered, then vanished. "You have quite a lot to say."

"I don't like you," she snarled, hating the fact that he'd read her thoughts again.

"Wonderful." He stood back, took in the absolute wreck of her. "We're even on that score."

The Archfae turned on one boot and walked into the bathroom. The sound of rushing water filled her ears, and soon the sweet smell of plumeria and coconut filled the room. She breathed it in, relished in the tantalizing scent. It was vaguely familiar to her, but then Tiernan came back into the bedroom and reached for her.

Maeve jerked the sheets up around her for protection. "What are you doing?"

He sighed. A glint of aggravation. "I'm giving you a bath."

She reared back, away from him. "What? Why?"

"One, because you reek of blood and sickness. And two," he scooped her into his arms before she could protest, "I need you to answer my questions."

She swallowed, hating the way he held her the way one might cradle a lover. "What kind of questions?"

"Questions about these." Tiernan tapped one finger to the metal on her wrists and her heart sank. She didn't want to talk to him about her cuffs. She didn't want to talk to him about anything.

But when he set her down and her feet hit the marble floor, a delicious shiver settled deep into her bones. Steam filled the room, and the glorious scent was a luxury to her senses.

Bubbles frothed and foamed in the huge soaking tub. Then she glanced down and shame settled upon her shoulders. She wore her nightgown from the battle. It was caked in blood and grime. She dared a glance in the mirror, and the reflection gazing back at her looked nothing like the woman she remembered. Her pallor was lackluster. Her eyes, hollow and sunken. She looked positively dead.

Her gaze landed on the bath. The inlaid tile around the edge sparkled like the scales of a mermaid. It was wide, probably capable of holding three full-sized humans—though, she supposed, that would only be the equivalent of two faeries. She was worried if she blinked, it would vanish like a figment of her imagination. The beautiful tub filled with tempting wonder looked fit for a queen. But she didn't dare move. She couldn't.

"What's wrong?" Tiernan's words were short and bitter, like his temper.

"I..." She took a long, steadying breath, then met his eyes. "I've never had a bath before."

The fae looked upon her like she'd sprouted an extra head, completely traumatized by her words. She shocked the High King so severely, he was rendered speechless.

"I've *bathed*," she snapped, and irritation flared through her. How dare he think she had no sense of hygiene, the prick. "Always in showers. Never an actual tub."

A beat of strange silence passed between them.

"Let's remedy that, shall we?" He continued to watch her, and his gaze lingered in certain areas a bit too long.

She crossed her arms over her chest. A useless feat, considering her nightshirt was rail thin and tattered.

"Mortals and their modesty." Tiernan rolled his eyes to the gilded ceiling, then raised both hands in defense. "Don't worry. I won't look."

Maeve didn't believe him. The smirk on his face vanished

right before he turned around and faced away from her. She stripped out of the nightshirt and it pooled around her feet. Using her toe, she edged it to the opposite side of the floor, not wanting to touch the filth mottling the fabric. On a breath, she gripped the curved pearl railing, and stepped down into the tub. The hot, silky water soothed the ache in her body and she gasped.

Tiernan whipped back around. "What is it?"

Maeve froze. She stood in front of him, ankle deep in the sudsy water, completely naked. "Nothing. I just...nothing."

An emotion banked in his gaze and his eyes scalded everywhere they touched. Her shoulder, where the dark fae left its mark, still healing. Her breasts. Her stomach, and lower still, until every part of her was aflame from his fixation.

"Get. In. The. Tub," he snarled.

"Okay." Her voice came out in a harsh whisper, but even as she lowered herself fully into the hot, bubbly water, she couldn't control the rapture bursting inside of her. A bath. She was going to take a *bath*. Scented water moved like satin over her skin, and when Maeve finally sank down to her shoulders, a small moan of pleasure escaped her.

Tiernan stood completely still; it didn't look like he was breathing. "Better?"

Maeve could only nod because then he was rolling up the sleeves of his shirt and kneeling on the rug beside the tub. "What are you doing?"

The High King looked over at her, and he was so close, she realized she could finally see the true color of his eyes. They were pools of twilight, swirls of purple and blue, flecked with the gold of the sun.

The corner of Tiernan's mouth lifted. "I said I was going to give you a bath."

Maeve watched him, calculating his every move. He grabbed a white washcloth and loaded it with soap, then gently rubbed it over her arms. She glimpsed the sunburst tattoo on his neck, and the way the golden flares seemed to sprawl across his chest, below the buttons of his shirt. He dabbed the cloth against her shoulder, where her skin was pink and angry from the dark fae's touch. The wound was still tender, and she hissed when he pressed lightly to clean the area.

"How did you get your tattoos?" she asked, seizing the moment to distract herself from the pain radiating down her arm.

"Magic."

Ass. "Care to elaborate?"

"No." He moved her hair and lathered her back. "I'm the one asking the questions. Not you."

"Fine."

Tiernan cupped the back of her knee and lifted her leg from the tub. He washed her toes and ankle, working his way up her thigh. He repeated the movement with her other leg, methodically rubbing in deliberate circles, scrubbing away the grime and blood. Every nerve in her body was on fire, ignited by the awareness of his touch. And when his knuckles just barely grazed the sensitive area between her legs, Maeve almost jumped out of the tub.

He didn't even react. His expression was shuttered, his sharp features in line with not giving a damn. Instead, his hand moved the cloth along her abdomen, then up over both of her breasts, as though he made a habit of bathing women. "Tell me about the cuffs on your wrists."

Maeve tried to shift away, but the tub was slippery and she

was covered in soap, so Tiernan simply hooked her by the elbow and pulled her back to him.

"I will only ask nicely once." Behind his cool façade, the unspoken threat lingered. He would do whatever was necessary in order to get the truth from her. No matter the consequences. She didn't even want to think about the capabilities of his power, and based on what she'd seen last night on the verandah, she knew it was well beyond her best interest not to cross him. He was a destroyer of worlds. Capable and violent. Violet lightning had crackled around him, enhancing his power, and he'd torn through the dark fae like they were nothing more than puppets on a string. His magic was far greater than any she'd ever witnessed in her short life.

"I'm cursed with fae blood," she muttered, more to herself than to him.

"Come again?"

"Fae magic runs through my veins." She glared up at him and angled her chin to a level of defiance, daring him to doubt her. "It's a curse I've lived with since I was a child. One bestowed upon me by the Mother Goddess for being a bastard-born daughter."

"A curse," he murmured, considering. "What sort of magic?"

"I don't know." The lie was as smooth as silk when it flowed off of her tongue. Though she supposed it was more of a partial truth. She didn't know what kind of magic cursed her; she'd never been fully able to tap into her powers. She knew she could make things, like pretty little rose crowns, but that was all. Carman had placed the cuffs on her not long after the courtyard incident when she was five, and the extent of her magic remained a mystery ever since.

"I see." He dunked the cloth into the sudsy water, then wrung it out. "And why do you wear them?"

"To protect everyone else," she answered automatically. The response had been drilled into her for as long as she could remember.

"From?"

"From me."

The smug uptick of the corner of Tiernan's mouth was unmistakable. "Tilt your head back," he commanded.

Maeve hesitated, but worried that if she mouthed off with another smart comment, he'd shove her under the water and drown her. So she obeyed. Propping herself up with her arms slightly behind her, she leaned her head back into the bathwater, all the way to her scalp. Her back arched and the damned fae growled. Annoyance fired through her. What did he expect? She was a human. A mortal. And she was fairly well-endowed. It's not like her breasts were going to vanish overnight. If he didn't want them shoved up in his face, he shouldn't have told her to lean back.

But then he was shampooing her hair, and massaging out all the kinks and tangles from her messy curls. He worked some kind of oil into the wild strands, and it smelled faintly of blackberries and citrus. Beads of warm water slid down her neck and in between the valley of her breasts. She bit down on the urge to smile in delight.

"And what of the Aurastone?" His voice cut through her thoughts.

A jolt shot through Maeve, and she jerked upright. Water sloshed dangerously close to the edge of the tub. Her Aurastone. She'd been so consumed by recovery, she hadn't even thought about it. "Where is it?"

"It's safe." Tiernan dismissed her with a wave of his hand. "You dropped it during the attack. It's under your pillow."

"Oh." How did he know she kept it there?

"What I'm curious to know," he drawled, "is how you found it."

"I was floating in a lake."

"You were floating," Tiernan repeated. "In a lake." Disbelief tainted his tone.

"Yes. In Kells, there's a place we call the Moors. It's shady, and full of dense trees and..." And all kinds of wonders. Flowers that danced in the sunlight. Cute little woodland creatures that were anything but terrifying. Streams of turquoise where the current sang and hummed. "It was sweltering one day, and I was looking for a place to cool off. The Moors always offered respite. I came across a lake. The Aurastone was at the bottom of it, covered beneath some layers of sand and stone."

"The Aurastone is quite magnificent, as I'm sure you're aware. I doubt you understand the greatness of its power, or the significance of its existence, since you're merely a mortal." Tiernan rinsed the fragrant oil from her hair and Maeve ignored the subtle jab at her mortality. "But answer me one more thing. What do you remember about last week?"

Last week. Last week she was in Kells, traipsing through the city with Saoirse, and working on improving her sword fighting skills with Casimir. The dark fae didn't exist. There was no Scathing, or Hagla, or creatures of night. Her city was safe and protected. "Last week, everything was as it should be."

"No." There was a slight shake of his head. "You were here. The attack against my Court was last week."

"What? That's impossible." Maeve stood up and bubbles slid down her arms and abdomen. From his kneeling position on the floor, Tiernan dragged his gaze lazily across her naked body. By all rights, she should've been furious. Or mortified. Maybe even scared. But she was beginning to understand the High King, and she wouldn't be a pawn in any of his games. She gripped the curved, pearl railing and refused to acknowledge the mischievous glint in his eye. The more she gave in to his arrogant, self-righteous bullshit, the more insufferable he became. She planted her hands on her hips, while water dripped from her hair, and stared him down. "How was I unconscious for a week?"

In her head, it was merely hours. No wonder she smelled so foul and felt like she hadn't eaten in days.

"You were very sick. And your *cursed* magic struggled to keep you alive, to cure you of poison, to mend your pathetically broken bones." He almost sounded bored, like her near-death experience was the last thing he wanted to discuss. He shoved up from the tile, grabbed a towel off one of the hooks, and tossed it to her. "Whatever is inside of you, its full strength is diminished by the cuffs you're wearing."

Maeve dried herself off, enjoying the soft fragrance lingering in her hair and on her body. "What do you mean?"

"I mean, your cuffs aren't protecting everyone like you so foolishly believe. They're hindering your magic. They weaken you. It's why my world feels muted to you." He raked a hand through his hair, then leaned against the door to the bathroom.

"But that doesn't make any sense." Maeve wrapped the towel around her by folding the fabric into itself. "My blood is cursed. It's dangerous. I'm dangerous—to myself, and to everyone else."

"No, Maeve." He spoke her name and it rolled off his tongue with the sweetness of summer. "Your cuffs are dangerous. Eventually, they will suffocate your blood. They will destroy your magic. And then, they will destroy you."

Chapter Nineteen

Maeve pulled the towel a little tighter around her. "What are you suggesting?"

Tiernan crossed his arms and let the door bear the brunt of his weight. "That you let me remove your cuffs."

A terrifying but curious thought. If Tiernan removed the cuffs, there was no telling what would happen to her. There was no way to know how she would react. Or worse, what she would become. She understood it was a painful process, Rowan had confirmed as much, but other than suffering through more pain, she couldn't see a clear advantage. She wasn't entirely sure she wanted to release the monster lurking beneath her skin anymore. And it *was* a monster. Fae magic or not, it was a curse placed upon her, not a blessing. And those two things were not the same.

*But...*a tiny voice in the back of her mind whispered.

But what?

But what if the magic inside her was enough to defeat Carman? What if it was enough to empower her with the strength she needed to overthrow her mother and take her crown? To save her kingdom and her people? To defeat Parisa?

"If I were to agree," Maeve spoke slowly, keeping mindful of her words. "What would you want in return?"

"That depends," Tiernan mused, then sauntered toward her. He captured her chin and tilted her face up towards his own. "What are you willing to give?"

Maeve jerked away from his touch. "That's not the same thing."

"You're right. It's not." He walked out of the bathroom, back into her quarters. He glanced out the large glass doors leading to her balcony, then back to the bed. The linens were still soiled, and the room reeked of sweat and sickness. His jaw hardened. He flicked his hand toward the bed and the sullied bedsheets and pillows vanished, instantly replaced with fresh sets. The air was also purified, the lingering stench of disease gone. "I'll send for Deirdre and have her bring you up some hot breakfast."

"Okay, well then—" She caught herself. It wasn't wise to offer her gratitude to a fae. Especially an Archfae like Tiernan. "I appreciate the clean sheets. And the bath."

"Do you require anything else?"

"Ah, no."

He nodded curtly and left her bedroom exactly how he'd entered—seething with anger. Maeve stared after him once he'd closed the door. What in the stars was that about? For a High King, he really needed to get his mood swings in check.

"Psycho fae," she mumbled under her breath and discarded the towel on a bedpost. She pilfered through the wardrobe, looking for anything besides another excessive gown. Seriously, how was she supposed to breathe in these? Beautiful flowing dresses made of chiffon and other sheer materials were the last thing she wanted to wear when war was on the horizon.

Perhaps she should've asked Tiernan for some clothing other than pretty gowns with pockets.

She was going to settle for a white chiffon dress with a lavender satin bow at the back, but a dull ache took form at the base of her neck and gradually reached her temples. Her shoulders were heavy, the right one worse than the left, and her eyelids began to throb. Exhaustion settled into her bones, and even though she was physically clean and looked well enough, she was not yet to her full strength. Weakness from poison was often intense, and sometimes it could take days to recover fully.

Maeve rummaged through a drawer at the bottom of the wardrobe and pulled out another nightshirt. She tugged it on over her head, then crawled back into bed, just as Deirdre opened the door.

The older woman gasped. "You look..."

"Normal?" Maeve suggested.

"Almost," Deirdre said on a laugh and set a tray before her on the bed. It was filled with fresh fruit, warm biscuits with butter, and bacon. "Not there yet, love. But the room doesn't smell like death anymore, which is always a sign of healing."

"Yeah," Maeve grumbled and shoved a piece of biscuit into her mouth. "The High King gave me a bath."

"He w-what?" Deirdre startled, and the teacup she was holding clattered against its saucer. "He *bathed* you?"

"Don't romanticize it." Maeve reached for a piece of bacon next, reminding herself to take small bites and chew slowly to keep from vomiting again. "He was just as smug and rude as ever."

Deirdre snorted. "Let's hope so. The day he's in a good mood is the day he falls in love."

Maeve imagined most creatures, human or fae, would be in a good mood if they were in love. "Is that such a bad thing?"

"It is for him."

"Why?"

"Once the High King falls in love, he'll lose everything."

Maeve choked on a piece of bacon and Deirdre handed her a glass of water. The cold liquid forced the bit of food down, and she swallowed hard. "Is he cursed?"

"Cursed? Oh heavens, no, child. The High King isn't cursed. It's just some ancient legend from years ago. Nothing for you to worry yourself over." She poured hot tea into the cup, but Maeve left it untouched. "Now, eat your breakfast. I hope to never see another poisoning case as long as I live."

"You can't really expect me to not be curious about an ancient legend, Deirdre." She spread some of the softened butter onto a biscuit. "Isn't there anything you tell me about that? Even just a little bit?"

The older woman cast an anxious glance to the bedroom door, then wandered closer, keeping her voice low. "Now, if anyone asks, you didn't hear this from me. But it's said that the High King of Summer entered into a terrible contract with the god of death."

Aed. If speaking the god of death's name summoned him to the caller, Maeve would've been no less surprised. The balmy air of her bedroom cooled, and the sun slipped behind a thin blanket of clouds. "How terrible of a contract?"

"I've never been privy to the specifics, but I do know the High King was once consumed with so much grief and despair, he was willing to do anything to destroy those who wronged him." Deirdre patted the bun on the back of her head, like she'd been caught speaking poorly of her king. "And rumor has it, it was when he was at his lowest of low, the god Aed chose then to answer his pleas."

A cold, sinking sensation gripped Maeve's chest. She couldn't imagine being so desperate as to enter into a bargain with a god. The god of death, no less.

"Come now." The sweet woman corralled her toward the bed. "You're not yet yourself and will still need a bit of healing time."

Maeve climbed onto the bed and buried herself beneath the satin covers, when a thought occurred to her. Tiernan said a week had passed while she was unconscious, and she had no idea of anything that transpired since. "Deirdre?"

"Hmm?"

"Is everyone okay? Did we...I mean, did Niahvess suffer much loss or damage?"

Deirdre tucked a wisp of gray hair behind her ear, and the lightness of her face dimmed. "Structurally, most of Niahvess is sound. Whatever is broken can always be fixed. We lost a number of soldiers, but the dark fae suffered greater casualties. They retreated not long after you..." She hesitated. "After you were injured."

After you almost died, she meant.

"I'll let you get your rest." Deirdre plucked the towel off of the bed and slung it over her shoulder. "Besides, you have some friends who are anxious to see you."

Deirdre left her and a few moments later, Saoirse came barreling through the door with Casimir right behind her.

"Maeve!" Saoirse rushed to her side and grabbed her hand. Her sapphire eyes were wild with emotions. Panic. Fear. Relief. Bluish smudges from lack of sleep harbored under her eyes, and her beautiful face was drawn with fatigue. The flower pinned behind her ear was a vibrant yellow rose, a bright contrast to her blanched pallor. "I thought you were going to die."

"So did I," Maeve admitted.

"You gave us one hell of a scare, Maeve." Casimir shoved his dark brown hair from his face. He sat down on the opposite side of her bed, and his dark gaze searched her face. "You okay?"

"I think so. Are you?"

He nodded and Maeve looked at both of them. With the exception of obvious lines of worry, they were in perfect health. No marks or bruises. No signs of being harmed in any way. It was strange how they weren't at the battle. Surely Casimir's skill with a sword could've come in handy when battling the dark fae...unless Tiernan thought he might use it against him, which was also probably likely.

"Is it true you were attacked in your room?" Saoirse's gaze shifted from her to the double glass doors leading to her balcony, and back again.

"It's true." Maeve didn't want to remember the spiders pouring from the mouth and eyes of the creature that came for her. "Two dark fae were in my room."

Casimir shoved up from the bed and headed straight to the balcony doors. He ran his hands along the frame of the wood and Maeve noticed the slight shimmer in the space between. The tremor of magic. "How did they get past the wards?"

"I don't know." Maeve didn't even know wards had been placed around her bedroom, or anywhere else for that matter. The thought hadn't even occurred to her.

"It doesn't matter." Saoirse's tone was sharp. Dismissive. "The fact is they did. And we must be prepared if it happens again."

"You know it will. I have no desire to be shuffled into a safer area. I'm a warrior; we all are. And I would rather stand and fight." Casimir's fist clenched, then relaxed. "Especially now that Rowan is gone."

"I can't believe that bastard left us here." Saoirse's face pinched with tempered wrath. "I swear, the next time I see him, I'll kill him."

"You and me both," Maeve added, though she wasn't sure if she really meant it. Movement flashed from the corner of her eye. Startled, she looked over to see Ceridwen standing by her door. She was ethereal. A goddess of sunshine and summer. Her gown of turquoise fell in tiny waterfalls down to the floor. Ribbons the shade of the sky were plaited into her golden hair, and her ruby lips curved into a kind smile. Maeve watched her, and as she did, a resonating warmth filled her from the inside out. It eased the tension from her bones, soothed away the discomfort and soreness from her tired body.

"It was you," Maeve croaked in disbelief, and when she struggled to sit up fully, Casimir slipped an arm behind her back to offer support. But she didn't look away from the Arch-fae. "You...you helped me. Just now. And again when Rowan left, when I was..."

A wreck.

Ceridwen's smile widened.

"How did you do it?" The obvious answer was magic, but it was more profound. Her power was unsettling. It was unique. Remarkable.

Ceridwen glided into the room, her movements fluid like spun silk. "I can control emotions," she said simply, like it was easy. "And make people feel a certain way."

Saoirse edged back, affronted. "That sounds somewhat intrusive."

"Only when wielded for the wrong reasons." Ceridwen tilted her head and clasped her hands in front of her, showing off her gold-dusted floral tattoos. "I can also read auras. I can discern a fae's magical abilities, if they have any at all, and I do...other things."

"Aura readings?" The mere idea of it immediately put Maeve on edge. It brought back a rush of horrid memories from the attack on Kells, from the fortune teller's tent. Another swift pulse of calmness spread through her.

Ceridwen. She was doing it again. Whatever "it" was.

"How?" Saoirse asked, now intrigued, already forgetting Ceridwen could literally control their emotions during any situation. "What do these auras tell you?"

"I suppose it's similar to knowing a person's soul." Her words were lyrical, with a kind of musical quality. Soft and pretty, like a love song.

"Fascinating," Casimir murmured. But Maeve wasn't sure if he was being sarcastic or not.

"Saoirse, your aura is royal blue with streaks of silver." Ceridwen's turquoise gaze locked onto her. "Representing strength, valor, love, and beauty."

Saoirse flipped her braid of moonlight over one shoulder. "So, basically I'm a badass."

Casimir laughed. He actually *laughed*. The sound was so shocking, and so unexpected, everyone stared at him. His dimple winked.

Maeve shifted and Casimir stuck a pillow behind her to keep her propped up. "What about me?"

Ceridwen didn't even blink. "I can't read your aura."

Casimir sobered, his wide smile and booming humor gone as though it had never existed in the first place.

A flare of concern shot through Maeve. "Is that a bad thing?"

"Not bad." The High Princess studied her. "Just unusual. It's like there's a haze over your aura. A filter that blocks the trueness of it from my view."

"Oh. Well, that's disappointing." The cuffs. They had to be the reason Ceridwen couldn't read her aura. There was no other explanation.

"What about Casimir?" Saoirse asked, drawing the uncomfortable attention away from Maeve.

Casimir's head snapped up at the sound of his name.

Ceridwen's perfect smile faltered. A slight, almost imperceptible shift. "Casimir doesn't have an aura." She lowered her lashes. "Because he does not have a soul."

CASIMIR GAVE Maeve three more days of recovery and then she met him in one of the courtyards to train.

It was the last thing she wanted to do. Already too much time had passed since they left Kells and ventured to Faeven in hopes of finding the *anam ó Danua*. There was no way of knowing how badly the Scathing had spread across Kells, if there was anything left, or if anything could be salvaged. Saoirse was concerned the Scathing would spread through the Cascadian Mountains to the south, and then down into the neighboring kingdom of Cantata. The threat was very real. And though they'd already been gone for over a week, it felt as though they'd gotten nothing accomplished and weren't any closer to saving the human lands.

Thus far, the entire trip had been nothing more than a death trap from which they'd narrowly escaped. A harrowing journey that seemingly dumped them in the Summer Court and left them there with no way out.

The glint of Casimir's sword cut through the air above her head, jarring her from her thoughts.

"You're distracted," he mocked, twirling the hilt with one hand.

"No," she snapped. "I'm thinking."

"Same thing." He lunged toward her and their swords clashed, the rattling clang of metal echoing in the courtyard. "Thinking can get you killed. There's only action and reaction when it comes to war."

Maeve blocked his next strike. "You're wrong. Preparation before battle is key."

She whirled away from him, but he matched her step for step. Hand-to-hand combat was second nature to her, especially when she sparred off against Casimir. She moved with him, relied on muscle memory to lead her, depended upon the knowledge he drilled into her over and over. It was like a dance when she trained with him, an intimate study of one's partner. Though it hadn't always been that way. There were many times he sent her back to her quarters in Kells bloodied, broken, and bruised. Today, however, the sun was blazing down upon them and even their shadows seemed to lag with the heat of the day. Sweat slid down her legs, and the cotton dress she wore clung to her skin, so every motion, every jab, was sluggish and leaden.

Casimir struck again, but she dodged the blow. She ducked low, rolled against the soft ground, and popped up behind him. Tangled wisps of messy hair fell from her ponytail and stuck to her dampened skin. She shoved them back from her face and stole a breath of the sticky air.

"Tell me what's on your mind, Your Highness." He stalked closer. Predator to prey. "What's gotten you so distracted that you're out of breath and panting?"

His taunt made her simmer with fury.

"I am not *panting*." She swung hard and the clattering sound caused a few Summer fae guards to stop and stare. Even Saoirse, who was paired off with Brynn, paused to watch them. "The only thing on my mind is getting out of here, finding the soul, and saving Kells."

She ground the last word out, braced herself against his attack, and kicked her leg up high. The snaring of fabric caught in her ears, but her foot collided soundly with his chest and sent them both stumbling back.

"And how do we do that, now that Rowan abandoned us?" There was an edge in Casimir's voice, and he barely gave her a chance to catch her breath before he pounced on her again.

"I've been thinking about what Ceridwen said." Maeve spun away and switched hands. Her right arm was on fire from the weight of the sword. She was far from competent with her left hand, but at least she was proficient enough to give her dominant arm a break. When she was young, Casimir worried her slight frame would make her an easy target. He insisted she learn how to use a sword as well as daggers, so she obliged. And she was grateful to him for it. "Parisa is ruled out because the soul was torn from the Spring bloodline after she murdered her mother. From what I've read, that happened after the Evernight War, but before the plague of darkness. And we know Ceridwen doesn't have it."

"Do you think she would admit it if she did?" Casimir asked and he swung low, forcing Maeve to jump out of the way.

"I do." She left herself open, and her ripped skirts tangled around her ankles.

"So, that leaves Autumn and Winter," he mused, casually slicing his sword through the open air between them. "And if the *anam ó Danua* is only blessed through a maternal bloodline, then all we have to do is find a female Archfae in either Autumn or Winter, and hope the gift was given to one of them."

"Exactly." Maeve kept her eyes focused on the slash of his blade. They paced one another in a slow, cautious circle.

"Easier said than done." Casimir watched her, and their eyes met in a silent contest. "And do you have any suggestions on how we do that?"

"Oh!" Maeve stood straight. "I found a book in the library, and it traces the lineage of all—"

Fire cut across her left shoulder when his sword met its mark. It was just a nick, but sharp enough to shred the cotton sleeve of her dress and slice through to her skin. "Damn it, Cas. That hurt."

He tapped her sword with his own. "*Always* pay attention."

She launched herself at him, but Casimir snared her by the wrist and twisted her arm behind her back. "Anger leads to foolish mistakes, Your Highness."

Maeve grunted and tried to wrangle herself free from his hold, but then she froze. Tiernan was there, leaning against one of the palm trees, watching her struggle with a smile plastered across his infuriatingly handsome face. Behind him stood Merrick and Lir. Since they were no longer required to babysit the mortals, it looked like they were allowed to resume their normal duties; which, she assumed, were respected positions within the Summer Court. She looked past Tiernan and caught Lir's silver gaze.

She gave a small wave. After all, he did burst into her room and save her from those terrifying fae. And he'd let her fight, instead of locking her away in a room somewhere, even if it almost got her killed.

Lir lifted his head in acknowledgment, and she couldn't be certain, but she thought he may have smiled at her. Another small win. Maybe she could befriend him yet. In Faeven, it was always good to have at least one faerie on your side.

Tiernan's brows lifted when he looked between them, but then he strolled forward, and Casimir released her at once. She didn't move, just watched him approach, though she was silently grateful when Saoirse and Brynn appeared within her line of sight. They noticed the High King as well and stalled their own training when the stifling air trapped inside the high walls of the courtyard became ripe with tension.

Tiernan stood before her, looking as though he'd just returned from holding court. He was decadent. Crisp and polished. And there was a ring on his pinky she'd never noticed before. It was made from a shimmering gold and shaped like the sun. The stone cradled inside of it was a perfect match to the color of his eyes. He lifted the ripped piece of fabric hanging off her shoulder.

The corner of his mouth lifted. "You ruined your dress."

"Well." Maeve planted her hands on her hips. "Maybe if I had something more practical to wear, I wouldn't have this problem."

Merrick coughed—loudly—his eyes wide with shock. Lir hit him on the back.

The High King inclined his head. "I assumed as a princess, you would want fitting attire."

"You assumed wrong." She'd never been treated like a princess, even though she was one by birth. She'd never been given pretty dresses, or jewels, or a crown. Sure, the gowns Deirdre brought her were the most decadent things to ever touch her skin. But they were useless when it came to fighting, even if they did have pockets. She needed leggings, corsets, blouses, and boots. They let her move. Defend. Attack.

She pointed to Saoirse. "Why can't I wear something like that?"

Tiernan glanced over to where Saoirse stood in sleek leggings, a cropped purple top with heavy beading, and shiny black boots. "You want to wear something more comfortable so you can fight?"

"Yes." Belatedly, Maeve prayed to the goddess, hoping it wasn't a trick question.

"Fair enough." When he turned back to face her, everything shimmered. The heady scent of orange blossom and cedarwood filled her senses, and she sucked in a breath.

Her tattered cotton dress was gone. Instead, she wore black leggings and a pair of boots laced up to her knees. A strapless corset cinched her waist, cut low across her breasts, and was the color of the sea. Layers of iridescent beading swirled around the corset like a wave, and her Aurastone was strapped to her thigh.

"Better?" Tiernan asked, sliding one of his twin swords from its sheath.

Hesitancy curdled in Maeve's gut. There was a slight chance she may have misunderstood the High King's intent. "Y-yes."

"Good." He nodded to Casimir. "May I cut in?"

Casimir bowed and stepped back without question.

"Well, Princess Maeve of Kells. Let's see what you've got." When Tiernan smiled, it was absolutely sinister.

Maeve had definitely made a mistake.

She barely had time to react before he lunged, his sword cutting through the air right above her head. She ducked and rolled, then jumped up to face him, her own weapon at the ready. But fighting an Archfae was nothing like fighting Casimir. For one, his speed was unrivaled. For every step, every motion, every strike and attack, Maeve was two seconds too late. The tip of his sword nicked her arm, her shoulder. Sliced her cheek. Her curse heated her skin, rushing to tend the wounds he inflicted with ease. Again and again, he attacked, giving her no time to dodge or parry. No time to counterattack, or think.

Tiernan was overpowering her. He was faster. Stronger. And worse, the magic inside her roared. It pulsed against her cuffs, caused her entire body to hum and vibrate with a kind of sporadic energy she couldn't control. Her grip faltered. Her vision blurred. Beads of sweat dripped from her forehead into her eyes. Exhaustion tore at her muscles. The burning sensation of the healing, and the pounding heat of the sun was too much. She weakened. Desperate to defend herself, Maeve lifted her arm high to strike, forced herself to do something, anything to give her some kind of advantage. But Tiernan was too much.

He knocked her sword from her hand and she stumbled back, so he pinned her between himself and the edge of one of the fountains. Sprays of cool water splattered against her backside. He snagged her waist and hauled her close to him.

"You're cheating," she gasped.

"Or perhaps you're just not good enough," he crooned, his voice laced with malice. He raised the tip of his sword so its sharp blade pressed firmly against the base of her throat.

"Maeve!" Saoirse called her name, and there was a commotion of shouts behind them.

"Tell them I won't hurt you, *astora*." Tiernan's harsh whisper scraped across her flushed skin.

She glared up at him. "He...he won't hurt me."

He was too close. The tempting scent of him, of palm trees, and sandalwood, and florals, overwhelmed her. Every inch of her tired body was pressed against every solid inch of him. He ran his teeth along his bottom lip, and her gaze betrayed her, darting down to his mouth.

"You think I'm attractive." He almost sounded surprised, and lowered his weapon.

"No," Maeve ground the word out. "No, I don't."

"You do. You're just afraid to admit it." He leaned in even closer, until the tips of their noses almost touched. "I rather like it when you lie to me."

Then he released her completely and she toppled backward into the fountain. Ice cold water soaked clear through to her bones, and she shoved upward, sputtering and spitting. Her gaze cut to him.

"Bastard," she hissed.

"Dreamer," he whispered. Then he straightened, sheathed his sword, and dusted off his shoulder. Like she was nothing.

"Cool down, darling. I already told you once, I never dapple with mortals."

Fury ignited inside her, but he turned on his heel and left her there, sitting on her butt in a fountain, drenched with water. "Fucking fae," she muttered, and shoved her wet hair back from her face.

"Maeve!" Saoirse rushed over, grabbed her hand, and hauled her to her feet. "Are you alright?"

"Fine." Maeve stared at Tiernan's back, watched him walk away with Lir and Merrick by his side. She couldn't handle his constant humiliation, the way he incessantly shamed her and left her feeling completely worthless. Even in her most vulnerable form, naked and feverish, he'd insulted her, taunted her. Tiernan was the worst sort of fae. He wasn't nightmarish. Or monstrous. Those she could handle. Those she could fight. No, the High King of the Summer Court was a complete asshole.

And she hated him.

He had no intention of helping them find the soul of a goddess. He didn't care what happened to a kingdom of humans. His only concern was his Court, was keeping the Crown City of Niahvess safe from the dark fae. Everyone else be damned. As much as she didn't want to admit it, with Rowan gone now, it only meant one thing. They were truly on their own in Faeven.

Maeve leaned in close to Saoirse. "I'm going to trace back the lineage of the Autumn and Winter Courts tonight. We're going to find the *anam ó Danua*. We're going to find a way to slay Parisa. And then we're going to go home."

It sounded like a solid plan.

She had no idea if it would actually work. If it did, then they would save Kells. Possibly even Cantata. And if not, then she would die trying.

Chapter Twenty

Afternoon sunlight spilled in through the windows of the library. Maeve sat at a large, round table with Saoirse and Casimir, surrounded by volumes of tomes, with leather-bound spines and velvety smooth pages. Spread before her was Aran's book of painted fairytales, though with each chapter she read, the stories grew darker and more sinister. There were paintings of creatures that fed on the living, snatched souls in the night, and hunted the sound of heartbeats. There were water-dwellers, the ones who drowned their victims without mercy, or who kept them imprisoned in the watery depths of lakes and rivers. Then there were the terrifying creatures belonging to the Sluagh. Saoirse was studying the book of bloodlines, tracing the ancestral lineage of the fae back as far as possible to when they were first created by the goddess of life, Danua, and the god of death, Aed.

She shifted, uneasy, aware of the perpetually shifting mural above them. Today it portrayed a battle of some kind. There were swaths of glittering darkness and bursts of blinding light.

There were shadows and sunlight, both of them clashed in an almost sensual manner.

"Maeve." Saoirse's voice dragged her back to the task at hand, and she looked down at the words Saoirse underlined with her finger. "Ceridwen said the *anam ó Danua* was torn from the Spring Court, right?"

"Torn from Parisa," Maeve corrected, and glanced over at Casimir, whose clenched fists paled at the mention of her name.

"According to this diagram, there is a High King of Autumn who reigns, and his wife birthed only sons. A male bloodline is a dead end for us." Saoirse spun the book around so both Maeve and Casimir could see. The drawing of a silver tree was sketched over two unfolded pages. "But in Winter, it looks as though there is a High Queen who could be in possession of the soul. If we don't think it's Ceridwen, then it has to be her."

"And if it's not?" Casimir countered, a twinge of frustration in his tone.

"Then our chance to save Kells, and the rest of the human lands, is lost." Maeve hated speaking the words out loud. She hated thinking there was a chance they would fail, that this entire journey could all be for nothing.

"Okay then, so we go to the Winter Court." Saoirse tapped her fingers along the table. "What's the Crown City?"

"Ashdara," Casimir answered automatically. "It's the northernmost city in Faeven. And the coldest. The only way to get there is through Spring or Autumn."

"Then we go through Spring." Saoirse crossed her arms. "We'll find Parisa first, and make her pay for what she's done to Kells, then move forward to the Winter Court. There's no use in backtracking."

Casimir sat up. "You're talking about murdering an Archfae."

"So?"

"So, we don't even know how to do it. They're immortal, Saoirse." Maeve glanced behind them, assuring the double doors to the library were closed. "You saw how horribly Tiernan defeated me in the courtyard, and that was *without* magic. I don't know about the rest of you, but I'm beginning to think that everything we believed to be true about the fae has been nothing but a lie."

Casimir nodded. "It certainly seems that way."

"But we're surrounded by a library of knowledge." Saoirse let her hands rise and fall. "There has to be something within these walls to give us at least a hint of how a fae might meet their demise."

"I'll do some research." Maeve stole another glance at the closed door, then looked up to the ceiling one last time.

"Just to be clear." Casimir shoved his hood back from his head, and his eyes glinted in the sunlight. "Ashdara is a few days' travel for us. Maybe further. Especially if we route through the Spring Court."

Another thing to consider, Maeve realized, when Casimir drove the unspoken point home. Traveling through Faeven would take time. Energy. Supplies. All of which was dwindling. They came prepared for a week's worth of travel, and already, two had passed. Were it not for Tiernan's generosity when it came to food and clothing, they would have nothing.

Maeve grabbed a pen and a blank piece of paper. "I'll ask the High King for some provisions." It was the least he could do.

"What makes you so sure he'll give us anything?" Casimir leaned back from the table, his face a mask of subdued fury. "He owes us nothing. He could turn us out at any moment."

"But he hasn't." Maeve didn't want to argue; they were supposed to be working together. But lack of progress and

Rowan's abandonment left a damp mood festering between them.

"And why is that, Your Highness?" Casimir didn't yell, but his voice was cold. "Did you ever stop to wonder why an Archfae would so graciously agree to keep three mortals within his walls? Under the careful watch of his henchmen?"

Maeve opened her mouth, then quickly closed it. She hadn't. She hadn't thought about why Tiernan continued to let them stay, even after Rowan was sent back to his Court. "There has to be a reason."

"Yes, and I bet it has nothing to do with helping us find the lost soul of a goddess."

Saoirse's head whipped toward Casimir. "What are you suggesting?"

"Look at us." He gestured around the table. "A princess and two esteemed warriors from one of the human kingdoms."

Maeve's heart sank with dread.

Casimir leaned forward. "Do you really think he intends to just let us waltz out of his Court any time we please?"

"Of course he would," said an airy, feminine voice from behind them.

All three of them turned to see Ceridwen standing by the table, though no one had heard her approach. She smiled softly, and her golden waves cascaded around her like sunlight. "You may leave whenever you like."

"But?" Casimir prompted.

"But I would wait."

"Wait? There is no time to wait, my lady." Casimir was fuming. "I've seen what Parisa can do, what she does to fae who don't bend to her will. Can you imagine what she'd do to a human? I've witnessed her spell another fae, so that for every word the female spoke, for every cry and scream, a vine twisted and grew inside her. Until she was nothing more than a rotting stump with flesh wrapped around it."

Ceridwen paled.

Saoirse winced.

Maeve's jaw clenched but she couldn't speak. She didn't dare open her mouth. Not now. What a terrible, gruesome way to die. Maeve would be full of the same wrath if she'd witness something so atrocious happen to another soul. She blinked away the images of Casimir and Saoirse suffering such a fate.

When Ceridwen spoke, her voice was lush and lulling, like a song. "Your time for vengeance is coming. But it is not now."

"And how do you know?" Casimir stood and planted both of his hands on the table. "Why should we believe you? You're just like the rest of them, are you not? What makes you so different?"

Something like hurt flashed across Ceridwen's face, but it was swallowed quickly by remorse. "I see things. Visions."

"Visions," Saoirse murmured, her complexion deathly pale. "What, like premonitions?"

Ceridwen lifted one elegant shoulder, then let it fall. "Of a sort."

Casimir's body stiffened. "What does that mean?"

"Did you see us coming here?" Maeve asked, overriding his irritation with a question of her own.

Ceridwen's ruby lips pursed. "I saw some things, yes."

"Why so vague, High Princess?" Casimir studied her, much like one would an opponent. Calculating. Cautious. "If we are allowed to come and go as we please, then we must be allies. And there are no secrets among allies, am I right?"

She smiled, but it didn't reach her eyes. "My visions are my own until an opportunity arises to share them."

Casimir scowled. "You mean until you get something in return."

When she failed to answer him right away, Saoirse cut in. She tapped the book in front of her. "So your magic then, your gift, is one of sight. And auras, and emotions. It sounds rather personal, to be so intimate with someone you barely know."

Ceridwen didn't even blink. She didn't appear to be affronted by their accusations, or even angered by their blithe assumptions. Rather, she looked perfectly calm. "Or perhaps it gives me greater knowledge of them, that which I can use to my benefit."

Saoirse inclined her head. "Touché."

"What about the High King?" Maeve blurted out. "What sort of magic does he possess? Other than reading minds?"

Saoirse balked. "He can read minds?"

Maeve's mouth fell open. She hadn't intended to say it, but there was no going back, now that it was out in the open.

"Has he read yours?" Casimir demanded.

"Once or twice," Maeve admitted.

A low, guttural sort of growl escaped him. And for a brief moment, Maeve worried he might do something drastic, like go after Tiernan, or attempt to kill him. Something that would jeopardize their position within the Summer Court.

"It was nothing." The lie left a bitter taste in her mouth.

Ceridwen did not meet Maeve's eyes. She adjusted the bangles on her wrist and pretended to smooth away wrinkles from the front of her silk gown. "Tiernan's magic is his own."

Casimir rapped his knuckles on the table. "He's capable of far worse."

Saoirse's head snapped up. "What could possibly be worse than sneaking into someone's mind and hearing their innermost thoughts?"

"It doesn't exactly work that way—" Ceridwen started, but Casimir gave her no time to finish.

"Do you want to tell them?" His voice was quiet, like the sound of death on the battlefield. "Or shall I?"

Ceridwen straightened and a second later, Tiernan appeared right beside her in a crack of thunder that caused the bookshelves to tremble. Maeve jumped up, and Casimir shot in front of her, one hand already on the hilt of his sword.

"Nice trick," he muttered, refusing to remove his hand from his weapon.

"I've been known to make an entrance a time or two." Tiernan's lips curved into a cruel smile.

It would've been much easier to take him seriously, or at least feel mildly threatened, if he wasn't dressed like some sort of ridiculous woodland creature. His golden chest was bare and broad, save for a band of burgundy that fell from his shoulder to his hip. Sinewy, corded muscle defined his arms and abdomen, and Maeve was pleased to discover she'd been correct about his tattoos. The shimmery swirls crawled along his neck, across his chest, and down part of his bicep in a distinctive pattern of suns, moons, and stars. A cape of dark red fur was pinned around his shoulders, and black feathers were stuck in his wild and messy hair. His brown leather pants were etched in faint golden suns, and a belt displayed both of his swords.

Her brow quirked. "Do you have a date with a rabid raccoon tonight, my lord?"

"I have somewhere to be," he answered calmly, ignoring her jab.

Saoirse looked to Ceridwen. "You weren't invited?"

She lowered her lashes and looked away. "I prefer not to participate in such...festivities."

"What is it?" Maeve asked, now intrigued that Tiernan would be attending, but his twin would remain behind. "Like a giant party?"

Casimir laughed but it was hard. "More like a giant orgy."

"And how would you know?" Maeve asked, her curiosity piqued.

He ignored her assumption with a roll of his shoulders. "I've heard things."

Saoirse snorted and Maeve debated on pestering him for more information when Tiernan cut in. "It's a little classier than that."

Casimir's lip curled. "Not by much."

Tiernan ignored his insolence. "I'm sending two of my best scouts to the human lands to determine the situation in Kells. If the Scathing is as bad as you are suggesting, then we may need to act sooner rather than later."

"You..." Maeve sat back in disbelief. "You're sending scouts?"

The High King inclined his head. "Is there a problem with that, Your Highness?"

Maeve opened her mouth, a retort on the tip of her tongue, but Saoirse jumped up instead. "I want to go, too."

"What?" Maeve swallowed her shock. "Why?"

"Because it's as you said. *He* is sending scouts, which means any report could be skewed to their advantage. I don't think we should take any more risks." She glanced to Casimir. "Captain? Your thoughts?"

"Saoirse returning to Kells would serve us well, and it could be a benefit having one of our own on the ground with them." Casimir's warm brown gaze slid to Maeve. "But I'll leave the decision up to you."

Oh sure, now he wanted to act like she was in charge. "You truly want to return, Saoirse?"

She nodded. "I think it's for the best."

Maeve stood and faced Tiernan, in all of his absurd—if not slightly and unfortunately attractive—garb. "Saoirse will accompany your scouts to Kells. When do they leave?"

"Tonight."

Maeve's mouth fell open. "Tonight?"

But Saoirse didn't hesitate. "I'll be ready." Without a backward glance or a farewell, she shoved up from the table and left

Casimir's head dropped and Maeve could only watch the back of her friend as she walked out of the library. She knew Saoirse was never a fan of saying goodbye, she despised the sentimentality of such things. But still...it stung.

Deciding she didn't want to stay and learn anymore about primitive fae orgies, or think about her closest ally returning to Kells without her, Maeve made the trek back to her room. But even then, her thoughts were distracted by images of Tiernan in sumptuous fur and supple leather, all easily displaying his chiseled god-like body. She knew the ways of males and females. She knew all about arousal, and orgasms, and passion. But they were all just things she'd read about in her books. She had zero firsthand knowledge, save for her most recent education in the library with Rowan.

Which was fine, she decided as she slipped into her bedroom and shut the door. She didn't need to experience any of those...sensations. They were nothing more than a distraction, a diversion of her thoughts, a betrayal of her emotions. They would separate her from a rational mindset, and she never wanted to worry about what it would feel like to have to choose between duty and love, because certainly those two paths usually ended up at war with one another.

No, she was perfectly fine being alone.

Except when Maeve turned around, her eyes widened and panic sliced through her. She wasn't alone.

A PAIR of lavender eyes was all she saw before Rowan crushed her scream with a kiss.

His hands cupped the sides of her face and his fingers tangled in her hair. She wanted to refuse him, to shove him away as punishment for leaving her. For abandoning her. But his mouth was hot, fused to hers, and her lips parted for him. His tongue swept in, furious and demanding. She clutched his biceps and dragged him closer, desperate to be as near to him as possible. He nudged his knee between her legs, and the friction he created left her mind whirling and her body shaking with an unfulfilled need. A crucial desire.

"Rowan," she gasped.

"Ssh." He trailed his kisses across her eyelids, featherlight. The path dipped down to her jaw, then her neck. "Ssh, Princess. It's okay. I'm here."

Her arms latched around his neck and she pressed her forehead to his. "You're back."

The slightest of nods. "I heard...I heard about the attack. I had to see you. To make sure you were okay."

His hands captured her face again, and this time he tilted her chin up, so she could look him in the eyes. "Tell me you're alright."

"Y-yes. I mean, I am. I am now." *Now that you're here.* The words she didn't say lingered in the space between them.

He let his palms coast over her shoulders, to her arms. Then he snared her wrists and dragged her arms up over her head. He guided her backward until she bumped into the wall, and he held her in place with one hand, while the other slid down her in a tender caress. His fingertips danced across her breasts and she arced into him, felt his erection press into her stomach. He hooked one finger into the waistband of her leather pants, and her breath hitched.

"Traded in your gowns, I see." He leaned close, planted slow and tantalizing kisses along her neck. "I like it."

And she liked him. More than that, she *wanted* him. There was a pull when he was with her, an undeniable attraction. She wouldn't be foolish enough to call it love. She wasn't even sure such a thing existed anymore. But she could understand lust. Desire. Mutual attraction. Rowan filled all those empty places in her soul. And he was not so cruel. He'd kept her company when she was alone in the cage. He'd made an effort to know her, to understand her. Even if he was fae, and she was human, and she knew beyond all measure it would be impossible to claim him as her own, at least she could have these stolen moments with him. These glimpses of time when it was only the two of them, and no one else.

"Though I must say, I miss the easy access of your skirts." Rowan gripped her ass and hoisted her up, so she locked her legs around his waist. The hardened length of him ground against her, and a breathy sort of noise escaped her. "These leggings are incredibly...tight. Are you wearing any—"

"I'm not," she breathed, and swallowed his groan with her mouth. He nipped at her bottom lip, and the muscles of her thighs seized and burned, wanting him to touch her. She reached for him, ready to grip him through his pants, and her hand enclosed around his...fur.

Maeve broke their kiss and leaned back, away from him. She absorbed his appearance. He was wearing something similar in style to what Tiernan had been wearing. Fur draped over one shoulder, and his rippling abdomen and chest were dusted in shimmering bronze. Mahogany feathers hung from his pointed ears. Kohl lined his beautiful eyes, and his teal hair swept over one half of his face. His pants were smooth and supple, with another swatch of fur draped at his waist. It was there he strained for her.

"You look...nice." Her eyes lingered over every inch of him and she didn't miss the way he smiled when she finally lifted her gaze to his face. "Are you going to the party thing, too?"

He eased her back down to the ground. "The Autumn Ceilie? Yes, I'm going."

"What's the Autumn Ceilie?"

"It's an annual event the Autumn Court hosts after Midsummer. The seasons never change in the Courts, but the years continue to pass." He gestured to his outfit. "The Ceilie is more or less a celebration of the upcoming autumn season, after the longest day of the year."

"Oh. I see." Maeve dropped onto the bed. The Autumn Ceilie sounded terribly exciting; back in Kells, the fall had always been her favorite season. She loved nothing more than feeling the crisp change in the air, the jewel-toned coloring of leaves, and the delicious scents of apple cider, pumpkin tarts, and other treats that wafted up from the city's center below the Ridge.

A twinge of jealousy spiked through her.

"Do you want to come with me?" Rowan asked.

"Yes." She was nearly breathless.

Yes, she wanted to go with him to the Autumn Court. It didn't matter if it was wild, and full of trooping and solitary fae whose allegiances varied given their mood. It got her out of Niahvess. And it would give her an opportunity to search for the will ó wisp, the rarest of all fae, instead of sitting around and waiting to be attacked again.

"Mm," Rowan murmured and pressed a kiss to her cheek. "Not even an ounce of hesitation. How incredibly attractive."

She looked up at him. "You don't mind taking me with you?"

He grinned. "Never. It would be my pleasure."

Magic settled upon her, soft and silky. His glamour draped

itself around her, and her clothing transformed. A crimson skirt of velvet fell from her waist, and a slit ran up one side to her upper thigh. A tufted cape of soft fur fell down her back. The top was soft black lace, and though it disguised her cuffs well, it left absolutely nothing to the imagination. Her nipples popped through the intricately sheer fabric. Rubies dripped from her ears, like droplets of blood. The low and steady thrum of her blood helped the tension flee from her body.

But it evaporated when Rowan's expression grew grim. "There are a few things you need to understand before you come with me."

"Okay." Unease slithered down her spine.

"The Autumn Court is dangerous. Its Crown City, Kyol, has been in turmoil since...well, since Aran's exile. Once their High Prince was relegated to live the remainder of his life as a Dorai, his other brother took over." An eerie shadow fell across Rowan's features. "And things haven't been the same since."

Maeve sucked in a sharp inhale. She knew Aran had been banished for some unthinkable crime, but she didn't realize he'd been the High Prince of the Autumn Court.

"You didn't tell me he was a High Prince." Maeve shoved her curls from her face. "I didn't think...I mean, I didn't realize he..."

Rowan simply lifted his shoulders, then let them fall. "It's not my story to tell."

Right. She should've known as much. "So, is there anything else I should know?"

"Yes." He reached out, ran his thumb along her bottom lip, and she leaned into his touch. "Don't eat or drink *anything*. Stay close to me. And keep your mask on, no matter what."

"What mask?"

"This one." His fingers coasted across her face, and a mask the same color as her skirt molded to her face. The decadent whorls felt like ink. Soft and subtle. "Are you sure you're ready for this?"

"I think so." She hoped so. She had no idea what she was getting herself into, but it was a chance, a possibility, to save Kells. She would have to rely on everything she'd learned, everything she'd read, to keep herself safe.

"Don't worry, Princess." Rowan offered his hand and she took it. Then he bent down and planted a kiss on her forehead. The action was gentle. Intimate. And it sent her stomach fluttering. "I'll have you home before midnight."

Chapter Twenty-One

Maeve didn't think to ask how they would get to Kyol for the Autumn Ceilie.

"Hold tight, Princess," Rowan whispered, and he pulled her against him. She wrapped her arms around him, and her surroundings slipped away as she was engulfed in a wave of spiraling magic. All the air pulled from her lungs in one sharp, crushing breath. The sensation squeezed her body, nausea rolled in her stomach, and she closed her eyes shut to stop the world from spinning.

It was the same sensation that overtook her when Lir brought her from her room to the courtyard the night Summer was attacked.

When her feet landed upon solid ground, her body continued to vibrate with the potent rush of passion pulsing through her veins. She melted into Rowan, then gasped with relief when her lungs could once again fill with the sweet taste of oxygen.

He glanced down at her, and absently brushed a strand of hair from her face. "Are you alright?"

She nodded. "What was that?"

"It's called *fading*." He offered her his arm and she slipped her hand into the crook of his elbow. "A way of traveling from one location to another, when we need to get somewhere quickly."

Fading. She remembered reading about the term. That was how Lir had gotten her out of her room so quickly when the dark fae attacked. She peered up at Rowan. "Can all faeries *fade*?"

"No, only the more powerful ones." He winked, then swept into a low bow. "Welcome to the Autumn Court, Princess."

Maeve was looking through a kaleidoscope.

Twilight sprinkled in through the overhead canopy of trees. A brisk autumn breeze picked up leaves from the forest floor and swirled them around in a whirlwind of crimson, amber, and goldenrod. The woods were alive with small creatures scampering about to hide in the hollow of a nearby tree, burrow into a pile of fallen leaves, or take shelter in an abandoned moss-covered log. Some of the animals Maeve recognized—foxes, squirrels, and rabbits. Others were not so *natural*. They kept to the shadows with their glowing eyes and beating wings. Every so often bushes would rustle, or she would catch something dart into the sky from the corner of her eye, but she made it a point not to look too long or too hard.

It was an autumn wonderland, filled with the kind of magic that caused her heart to flutter and her blood to hum. It danced along her skin. Shifted through the trees. It was so much like the world of summer, and yet not.

The air was different.

It was fresh. Crisp. Wild. Wonderful. She was drawn, pulled to the smell of bonfires and cinnamon, of sodden earth and decay.

A chill crept down Maeve's spine. An aura of unease lingered over the Court, tinged with tension and hostility.

"We walk from here." Rowan guided her down a trail of logs and planks. It was a staircase of wooden steps embedded into the ground.

Maeve edged closer to him as the forest seemed to swallow them whole. The trees grew thicker and the hollow of leaves above them stretched into a canopy of autumnal colors, nearly blinking out the setting sun. "So, other than Aran, who are the Archfae of Autumn?"

"It used to be Dorian and Fianna, the High King and High Queen. But now it's Aran's younger brothers, Garvan and Shay." Rowan lifted a branch of gilded leaves and allowed Maeve to pass under it first. "A long time ago, the Autumn Court was decadent. They hosted lavish parties. Masquerades. They were a glittering Court of rubies and gold. Of excess and splendor."

"Sounds marvelous," Maeve murmured.

"It was. Their magic was even grander. Dorian could shape shift into any creature of the forest, most notably a fox. He could bring death and decay with a touch." Rowan dipped under an archway of blood red dahlias. Maeve followed, and the forest opened into a clearing. She stood at the edge of a black lake, whose surface was as smooth as glass. It was so still, she could see the reflection of the surrounding trees perfectly. It was a mirror image of every branch, every leaf, cast upon an endless pool of inky water. A memory tugged at the back of her mind, like it was something she'd seen before. A dream, maybe. Or a vision. "Fianna controlled fire. She, too, could bring death. Though her magic in that sense was more subdued, more subtle."

Maeve looked up at the darkening sky, and wondered about the magic from before. "So their magic could kill?"

"If they so chose it, yes. But only in the rarest of cases did they ever use it upon another living creature." He scooped up a pebble from the damp shoreline and launched it across the lake. It skipped four times before exploding into a cascade of ripples and disappearing into the dark waters. "Garvan is not so kind."

Maeve kept her eyes on the surface of the lake. She wasn't sure whether or not a monster would surge up from its black depths, or if vexed merrows would appear and drag him down to a watery death, but she was certain Rowan's skipping stone disturbed *something*.

His hand casually reached for hers, and Maeve's blood warmed, gave her the courage to ask the lingering question in the back of her mind. "What happened to them?"

"After the purge of the dark fae from Faeven, after the Evernight War, the Autumn Court was one of the first among us to begin recovery. At least, until..." Rowan's voice trailed off and he glanced down at her. His expression was torn, and he looked at war with himself on what to say next. "Until a new sort of scourge began. A plague, some call it. Others just refer to it as the darkness."

Maeve remembered hearing about this, about the horrors that ravaged all of Faeven. It was the same story Casimir told her, and there had been mentions of the spreading darkness in some of her books, though never in much detail. "You're talking about when the goddess Danua came from Maghmell and purged the Courts of the evil?"

Rowan nodded and led her away from the lake. "Yes. But the darkness controlled us for another thirty years. We weren't prepared for that sort of attack after the Evernight War, and our realm suffered for it. Despite being one of the strongest Courts to rebound after the war, Autumn was the first to fall. It wasn't long until the rest of the Courts followed, and Faeven was left in a shroud of darkness, destruction, and death."

Leaves crunched beneath their feet, and the sun sank even further until the sky was painted with shades of orange, pink, and plum; the brushstrokes of an autumn sunset. "Fianna disappeared two years before Danua saved Faeven. There was no trace of her anywhere, even after the purge. Dorian searched for his wife for years, but she was never found. Eventually, her loss drove him into a state of madness and despair."

"How awful." She curled her fingers into the crook of his elbow, and tugged her fur around her to keep the chill at bay. "Is Aran the High King of Autumn then? Or is it his brother, Garvan?"

"Neither." Rowan's hand covered hers. "Fianna vanished, and no one knows what became of her or her powers. And well, even though Dorian was driven to madness, his power never transferred to Aran or Garvan, so..."

"So, you think he might still be alive?"

"It's a possibility." They came across a path of stepping stones dotting a stream whose waters sparkled like crushed garnets and citrine. Rowan didn't even pause. He braced one arm around Maeve's back and hooked the other under her knees, lifting her up to carry her across the slippery stones. "But no one has seen him in years."

No wonder the Autumn Court was full of trooping fae, of solitary fae, of fae that decided to live a life of their own choosing. They suffered great loss. They were ravaged by plague, their queen had disappeared, and from what she could gather, Garvan was a shitty ruler. Kells would soon endure a similar fate under the swarm of the Scathing if she didn't do something, and soon.

He set her down on the opposite side of the bank. Dusk was settling throughout the woods and the scent of smoke and the sounds of revelry were drawing closer. They were almost there. He took her hand once more, leading her down a worn and winding path, and the distinctive beating of a drum echoed through the trees. If she didn't ask now, she may not get the opportunity to do so again.

"Rowan?" She stole a glance up at him and tried to be as casual as possible. "Have you heard of the will ó wisp?"

He jerked to a stop beside her, snatched both of her shoulders, and hauled her against him. Her breath hitched in her chest, as he crushed his body against hers, but his gaze darted around the forest's edge, to where any manner of fae or creatures lurked and laid in wait.

"Do not speak of her," he whispered. His breath was hot against her skin, and his words were laced with warning. "It is far too dangerous to search out such a particular fae, even for you, Princess."

"But, Lir said she was an option since..." She pressed her lips together and looked up at him from beneath her lashes. "Since you left us."

His palms coasted up and down her lace sleeves. "I'm here now, aren't I?"

"Yes, but we're no closer to finding the goddess's soul. And you said you could track it. It's why we were sent here in the first place." Frustration was getting the better of her. She sucked in a breath, and Rowan caught her by the chin.

"I can track it." His reassurance did nothing for her. He'd yet to prove anything to her, with the exception of being a marvelous kisser. "And I will."

Maeve stared at him. Expectant.

"There are other things that take precedence."

"Like Parisa?" Maeve countered. "And your loyalty to the Spring Court?"

Rowan's face shuttered, the hurt palpable. "Yes. Like Parisa. Finding the soul was never meant to be a quick and easy process. It requires...things."

"What kinds of things?" she countered.

"Things like asking specific questions without raising suspicions. Things like calling in favors I've held onto for years." He rolled up his sleeve and put his bicep on display. Wrapping around the tanned muscle were three Strands; one navy blue, one silver, one black. "And I'll do it. I'll call them in, for you. But if some other fae finds out it is the soul you seek, there is no guarantee they'll be as generous as Tiernan."

Maeve's nose crinkled. "I'd hardly call Tiernan generous."

Rowan's face darkened. "Then you have not met many fae."

Maeve wasn't so sure she believed him anymore. She wanted to believe all of his promises, all of his whispers, all of his truths. But in her heart, she knew it was impossible. He was fae. Gifted in the art of deceit. Talented. Skillful. And only looked out for himself. But damn it, she enjoyed his company far too much to think such awful things of him. Either way, he'd brought her to the Autumn Court, and she had every intention of using her time there wisely. She would hunt the will ó wisp on her own. She would figure out if the blessing of the *anam ó Danua* had been snatched from the bloodline of Spring and presented to the bloodline of Winter. And she would do whatever necessary to save Kells.

"Okay." She would let him believe she was submitting. But she would not be so easily deterred.

"Okay," he agreed, and planted an absentminded kiss on her temple. Her toes curled and her heart leapt. "Now, remember the rules?"

"Yes." Maeve blew an errant curl out of her face. "No food. No drinks. No fun."

His dark brows arched in amusement. "I didn't say that."

"You may as well have." She entwined her fingers with his own.

"I swear it, Princess. You'll be the death of me." Another kiss, this time on the corner of her mouth. "Just keep your mask on. *Always.*"

"Of course."

They were only a few yards away and already Maeve could hear the call of music, a melody which pounded in the depths of her soul. It caused stirring. Longing. Laughter and voices carried on around them, and as soon as they got closer to the rise of smoke and flames, the thick, musty scent of sex slammed into her. Moans of pleasure echoed in her ears. Casimir had been right. It was absolutely a giant orgy.

MAEVE CLUNG to Rowan's side, wanting nothing more than to take interest in the sodden leaves at her feet, but finding she couldn't tear her gaze away from the provocative activities encircling them. Everywhere she looked there were beautiful, albeit nearly naked fae, dancing, laughing, and celebrating. The males were all tall with broad shoulders and muscular chests that glistened with a healthy sheen of sweat. Loose pants hung on their narrow waists and they wore necklaces of autumn leaves, wooden beads, and knotted leather. They donned detailed headdresses made of feathers, sticks, furs, and even stones. Some were wrapped in cloaks and capes, and every one of them wore a mask of some nature.

The females were just as breathtaking and Maeve's chest burned with envy. They were all blessed with slender bodies and perfect curves. Such painstaking beauty wasn't even fair to witness. But Maeve supposed those were the perks to being immortal. Beads and tiny ribbons of silk barely covered their skin and much of their flesh was streaked with glittering paints. They danced in short skirts made of fur, and streamers of cloth twirled around them. Their arms were jeweled and their masks were far more ornate and embellished than those of the male fae.

Blood heated her cheeks as she watched a female ride a male in a thatch of leaves while other fae danced around them —feral and attune to the music, and completely ignoring the mating occurring on the ground. Two males pleasured a female while she writhed beneath them both. One of them took her from behind, his hips jutting into her over and over, while the other filled her mouth with the hardened length of his cock. Maeve gaped, fascinated, if not slightly intrigued. Rowan instantly filled her mind as she imagined him gripping her hips, pounding himself into her. Delicious heat spread between her legs.

Flames ignited around another bonfire, illuminating two males locked in a passionate kiss, and sun and sky, Maeve couldn't tear her gaze away from any of them. They were mesmerizing. The way they moved with reckless abandon. The way they danced as though they cared nothing for anyone who might watch. Or in Maeve's case, stare. The outward display of sexual desire, of primitive mating, of freeing provocation spread low in her belly and pooled in her core, causing ripe arousal.

Rowan bent down close to her, his mouth near her ear. "Is that you?"

She shuddered into him, her hand clutched in his grasp. "Is...is what me?"

"That...*scent*." His finger tilted her chin up, forced her to meet his hungry gaze, and his nostrils flared. "I can smell your arousal, and it's the sweetest, most tempting thing."

Maeve swallowed and he watched her throat work. "I might be feeling...somewhat hot and bothered at the moment."

And it was true. Oh stars, was it true. Her skin was heated and each movement, each brush of his touch against her, made her want to peel off every layer of clothing until she was flush and naked against him.

Rowan hauled her to him, and his mouth met hers in a clash of lust. Their tongues lashed one another, ravenous and starving. Sucking and nibbling. His palms skimmed up her hips, to her waist, before settling right beneath her breasts. Teeth scraped her bottom lip, and her head lolled back, granting him access to her neck. To anything he wanted. Calloused thumbs brushed over her peaked nipples, back and forth, and the rub of lace left her quivering. She memorized the press of his lips against the column of her throat.

He twirled her away from him, pressed her backside into every solid inch of him. The length of his stiff cock burrowed into the small of her back, and she melted against him. One possessive hand slid across her abdomen, and the other gently cupped her throat. His fingers danced along her jittery pulse while he stroked the underside of her jaw with his thumb. The movement was slow and gentle, and Maeve sucked her bottom lip between her teeth, unable to keep herself from grinding against him.

"Tell me," he purred, allowing his hand to dip lower, beneath the layered velvet of her skirt.

Maeve held her breath.

"Do you like to watch?"

Rowan's voice was a tremor in her soul. But the darkest part of her was ready and willing to admit how much she enjoyed the show. Not only did the sexual appetite swelling to a crescendo within the Autumn Court captivate her, but the way none of the fae seemed to *care* fascinated her. Here, where the heartbeat of magic was its most primal, most passionate, was where hundreds of fae could deign masks for a night and live with heedless inhibitions.

"It's...not what I expected." With painstaking slowness, his warm fingers crept closer, sliding along her thigh to where she pulsed for him. And the moment they swept across her damp heat, she strained against his hand in a silent plea for more. He rubbed the bundle of nerves at her center, teasing and taunting, and her entire body clenched, ready to burst.

"Rowan," she gasped, his name nothing more than a panting whisper to be absorbed by the rhythm of music engulfing them. "What if someone sees?"

His tongue flicked along her ear. "Then let them see. What have you to hide?"

"My decency as a mortal?" Shivers cooled her hot skin as a chilly autumn breeze swept through the Autumn Ceilie. She angled her head back and turned her face to his neck. "The mere fact that I'm still innocent seems reason enough."

"Indeed." Rowan snared her wrist and lured her behind a crumbling stone wall covered with cool moss and pale yellow flowers. Locked in the shadows of the night, with the faint flicker of bonfire flames, he tucked her away from prying eyes.

Music filled her ears and overwhelmed her pounding heart. Coldness seeped through the lace of her top as he pressed her up against the wall and reached for her legs.

"Wait." She grabbed his shoulders and he froze.

"What?" His voice was rough and thick. "What is it? Did I hurt you?"

"No." Maeve shook her head and pressed her lips together, struggled to find her courage. "No, I'm not hurt. But last time..."

"Last time, what?"

She forced herself to meet his consuming gaze. She wouldn't blink. She wouldn't look away. She wanted to know, and more importantly, she wanted to learn. "Last time, I found pleasure and you didn't."

"Well." His grin was positively wicked. "I wouldn't say that—"

"You know what I mean." Her hands slid from his shoulders, to his biceps, down to his forearms. There, the muscles flexed and bunched. Strong. Capable. "I want you to show me."

"What?" Rowan choked on the word, and his eyes widened.

"Show me," she pleaded. She gestured to his cock protruding against the swath of fur draped around his waist. "Teach me how to pleasure you. Please."

An emotion passed over his face and then it was gone. "You're serious."

"Yes." Maeve looked up at him from underneath her fluttering lashes. "I am."

She didn't wait for his response. She just reached down between them, and slipped her hand under the tuft of decorative fur. He sprang free and she tried terribly to hold back her surprise, because he was far larger than any of the diagrams or pictures in the books she'd read. Fascinated, her fingers coiled around the silky length of him and then she squeezed. Once.

Rowan groaned. His hands slammed against the wall, causing her stomach to clench, and bits of rock tumbled down on either side of her head. Her breath echoed in the emptiness of her chest, and his forehead came to rest against hers. "Watch yourself, Princess." His voice was deep. Cavernous. "You know not what you do."

"Then show me." Maeve rose up on her toes and let her hand move up and down his shaft. She planted a kiss on the underside of his jaw, at the base of his throat. His answering growl made her toes curl, and she squeezed again.

"*Fuck.*"

"Is that what you like to call it?" she asked, delighting in his apparent torment.

"That's what everyone calls it," he ground the words out

and snagged her wrist. "I will show you, but there's something we need first."

"What's that?"

His mouth twisted into a mischievous smile. "Lubricant."

"What?"

Rowan shoved her skirt out of the way, and then he lifted her up, pinning her to the wall. With her legs locked around his waist, and her arms circling his neck, she couldn't look away from the intensity of his stare. He bent down and sucked her bottom lip into his mouth, bit gently, then nestled his cock directly at the apex of her thighs. Maeve stilled.

"Don't worry." He whispered the words around each of her eager kisses. "I won't take you here."

The solid press of him between her legs left her gasping. Back and forth, he rubbed himself against her swollen folds, guiding her hips with every stroke. Need spiked, hot and fast. It was all-consuming, a raging fire she couldn't control. Flames licked and spread, danced over her skin, and engulfed her in a blaze of mindless lust. Music drowned out her yelps and cries. She wanted him closer, she wanted to strip off every piece of clothing separating them so they were skin to skin, so he could bury himself deep inside her. Their mouths clashed and he slid her over his shaft, soaking him with her wetness. If she just arced a bit more, if she angled herself the right way...

Fingers dug into her bottom and his rough whisper coasted past her cheek. "Not. Here."

"*Rowan.*" His name was a breathless pant on her lips.

"I know." He smothered her moan with his mouth while he drove her higher and higher, grinding her throbbing, sensitive flesh against his thickened length.

Release sparked through her like a shooting star burning through the night sky. Dazzling and wondrous. Shudders ricocheted throughout her, cool autumn air chilled her flushed skin, and she collapsed in Rowan's arms. With the ease of a practiced lover, he set her down, and when her feet touched the ground, she couldn't stop the trembling of her knees. She braced her palms against his chest to keep herself upright.

"All better?" he crooned and pressed a kiss to the top of her head.

She could only nod, then glanced down to where he gently nudged her belly. In the dim glow and flash of bonfires beyond the wall, she could see the entire length of him coated in her wetness. His cock twitched and pulsed, and seemed to vibrate with demand, so she reached for it again. Wrapping her fingers around his fullness, she watched as Rowan's hand covered her own.

"Gods, just seeing your hand there is enough to get me off." He jumped in her hold and another pool of warmth slid down her legs. Then he helped glide her palm up and down his smooth shaft, again and again. The motion was constant, almost reverent, and she relished in the control she had over him in that moment. Rowan propped one hand on the stone wall behind her head and his biceps flexed. His jaw clenched. "Don't be afraid to grip it harder, Princess."

He tightened his hold on her hand, urging her to squeeze, and to take him with more authority. Ready to learn, she did as she was instructed. Grip firm, she jerked him, mesmerized by the beads of liquid forming at his tip. Curiosity got the better of her, as it often did, and she bent down to swipe her tongue over him, wanting just a taste.

"Fuck." Rowan released her hand and his fingers curled into her hair, dragging her face up to him. "Don't stop," he growled, then crushed his mouth against hers.

Maeve didn't stop. She continued working him, hard and fast, just the way he requested. His breathing grew ragged; his kiss, more punishing. Now he was helping her, thrusting his hips, forcing himself in and out of her fist. His mouth tore away from hers and he roared. Warm liquid slid through her fingers and over the back of her hand as he emptied himself of his seed. A wicked sort of power filled her veins; having that kind of control, and knowing she could bring him to his knees if she asked...it was better than holding a blade to someone's throat.

"You..." He sucked in a harsh breath. "Are entirely too tempting for your own good."

She offered him a simpering smile. "I'll take that as a compliment."

"As you should."

Rowan traced Maeve's bottom lip with his thumb, then helped her clean up and adjust her skirt before returning to the festivities. He tucked her hand into the crook of his elbow and led her out from behind the stone wall to where the Autumn Ceilie was still in full force. Fire scorched the moonlit sky. All around her, the air hummed with musical vibrancy, and the familiar scent of magic mingled with that of all the tempting trays of food she'd promised not to eat. Laughter exploded from across the forest as partygoers sang, danced, and reveled through the night.

"Stay here. I'll be right back." Rowan gave her hand a gentle pat.

Dread pooled low in her belly and she clutched his arm. And just as quickly, the warmth that filled her fled her body, and her blood cooled. "Where are you going?"

His gaze drifted across the sea of faeries. "To make some inquiries."

"You're just going to leave me here?" Maeve knew it sounded pitiful to her own ears, but she would never have agreed to come along with him if she'd known he was going to leave her side.

"Do you want to find the soul?" he countered.

"Of course, but—"

"Then stay put." He kissed her firmly, but when he pulled away, alarm gripped her once more.

"What if..." She glanced around at the swaying and grinding bodies. "What if someone talks to me?"

"Talk back." He gave her hand a squeeze. "I know there's a fae here who can help us, but if they catch any trace of you, or of what we're looking for, it will only be a matter of time until all Four Courts find out." He paused, then kissed her soundly once more. "I promise I won't be long."

Maeve nodded, unable to form anymore words as Rowan disappeared into the fray. Her nerves skittered wildly, and every sound, every noise nearly made her jump out of her skin. But she couldn't draw her gaze away from the hypnotic visions around her. She was spellbound. Bewitched. She absently reached up to touch her cheek, just below her eye, ensuring her mask was still in place. The last thing she wanted was to draw attention to herself. Heading for the safety of the stone wall, she let her hips sway a little, like she too, was lost in a dance.

Suddenly, the tempting scent of cinnamon woods and sex was replaced with something else. Her senses heightened; she breathed in, deeply. And summer surrounded her.

Chapter Twenty-Two

T iernan.

Maeve couldn't move as his voice coasted over her like a ribbon of dark silk.

"You shouldn't be here."

She sucked in a staggered breath, told herself to stay calm. She could play his game. She'd come to understand it rather well. She wouldn't let him win through intimidation, and she wouldn't show him any fear. He was just another fae, albeit one who was intentionally cruel, but she'd held her ground against him before, and she would do it again. Slowly, Maeve turned to face him. She looked up, giving him her most threatening smile. "What are you going to do about it, Your Highness? Take me back to your Court and put me in chains?"

His twilight gaze devoured her, lingering on the slit at her thighs and the expanse of her rather indecently exposed breasts. "I can think of plenty I'd do to you with chains involved."

Maeve paled.

Hells, he was vicious.

"So," he drawled and lumbered toward her, as though he had all the time in the world. "Rowan left you defenseless in a throng of trooping fae. How thoughtful of him."

She jutted her chin up in defiance. "I am *never* defenseless."

His low laugh drowned out the thrum of music. He stepped closer, crowding her, overwhelming her. But she refused to cower and step back. "It's dangerous here."

"Your palace isn't much safer."

Storms clouded his face. "Then I suggest you dance with me."

Maeve drew back and crossed her arms. "Why would I do something like that?"

"To avoid being snatched by the fae over there who is watching you like..." Tiernan cracked his knuckles. "Like he wants to eat you whole."

She glanced over to the fae in question, and a shudder snaked down her spine. For once, Tiernan was not taunting her. Sure enough, a solitary male fae sat upon a hollowed-out log. Curved horns protruded above his pointed ears, and his body was rippled with corded veins of black. His elbows rested upon his knees, his fingers were steepled, and his fierce, other-worldly gaze was focused on her every move.

A tremor of trepidation had her stepping closer to Tiernan.

"Fine." She gave him her hand. "But I'm not a very good dancer."

"Don't worry," he purred, and his whisper caressed her cheek. "I'll make you look like you're the only one who knows what you're doing."

Cocky prick.

Tiernan chuckled. "You have no idea."

Maeve snapped her head up and glared at him. "Get out of my head."

Another smile. "But it's so amusing."

Before she could respond, he whisked her away toward a bonfire. Sparks crackled and threads of smoke curled up into the air. The low beating of drums sounded, a rhythmic melody that sent her blood racing. She watched the other females around her, the ones who seemed to understand the dance was sensual in nature, and it was then she foolishly realized she wasn't dancing *with* Tiernan.

She was dancing *for* him.

The tempo began and Maeve stumbled once, unsure of the movements. Then her hips began to sway of their own accord. Startled, she looked up at Tiernan. He stared back, his hands tucked behind his back, his mask of gold giving nothing away. There was no smirk. No smile. But she could *feel* him. His magic overtook her, overwhelmed her, and suddenly she was dancing. She moved around the fire, following the other female fae, mimicking their motions with perfect accuracy. Her mind tried to fight, to battle against the strength of his power, but she was lost to him. At that moment, he owned her. And it was terrifying. She twirled, alight with the rush of heat coursing through her. Her arms reached over her head, her fingers played the air like a musical instrument. Each step was light and graceful. Every spin was like being wrapped in ribbons of silk. Decadent and sultry. The drumming pounded, and when Maeve whipped around, she was in front of Tiernan again. Her heart thundered and mortification burned her cheeks while she dragged her hands over her thighs, hips, and breasts before him.

He said nothing. But his hand captured her waist and he guided her closer, so she was flush against him. She drew in a ragged breath, and tiny beads of sweat slid down her back. His magic carried her up on her toes, and she stepped back. Once. Twice. And when her body whirled away, shame dug its claws along her back when she was forced to rub herself upon him like a cat in heat. It was brief, but she felt him then. The hard press of his erection nudged against her backside. Anger clogged her throat. She couldn't think. She couldn't breathe. She could only dance around the fiery flames once more. Except now the air was pungent and the curls of smoke caused her eyes to water.

Or maybe it was tears.

Maeve swallowed, choked on a sob. But she wouldn't cry in front of him. She couldn't. She couldn't be weak. She couldn't be vulnerable. She was a princess. A *warrior*. And she had to act like one. Her life depended on it.

The drumming slowed and Maeve sauntered over to Tiernan for what she hoped would be the final time. He held one hand to her lower back, while the other slid to cup the back of her knee. Gradually, he lifted her leg to his hip. She held her breath when his palm moved along her thigh for a better grip, and her body unwillingly arched back, granting him full access to her. Her muscles were aching, shivers overtook her, and she hastily stole a glance at the couple to her left.

They were basically mating. The female's legs were wrapped around her male's waist, and he was thrusting without a care, taking her in the firelight for all to see. Inwardly, she cringed. This is not what she wanted. She didn't want Tiernan. He was awful. Cruel. Punishing.

Maeve squeezed her eyes shut. The warmth of Tiernan's breath lingered on her breasts, on her neck. Her blood curse surged, and her wrists pulsed against the binding of her cuffs. His presence coasted along her skin like the kiss of a summer storm. Cool and pressing. Foreboding and dangerous. Then he planted the lightest of kisses just below her ear, and the drumming stopped. His magic released her on a rush, causing her head to spin. Her knees gave out, softening beneath the weight of her entranced body, and she crumpled against him. She clung to him, not trusting herself to stand on her own.

Tiernan kept his grip around her waist firm and steady. He glanced down at her, studied her, and his eyes sparkled like endless pools of blue and purple. The golden flecks within them glowed like stars in the night sky. He reached up, and gently brushed away a single tear from her cheek.

Proof of her own betrayal.

He cupped her elbow and steered her away from the bonfire blazing around them.

"What was that?" Maeve hissed, even though her chest ached.

He didn't even look at her. "A mating dance."

She staggered back. "A *what?*"

Tiernan adjusted the red fur cape at his neck so it fell around his bare shoulders. Away from the fires, the air held a distinctive chill, and Maeve burrowed into the fur cape Rowan had glamoured for her. "Don't worry. Like I said, I don't enjoy fucking mortals. They're too...easy."

Maeve snorted. "Your erection said otherwise."

His brows shot up and the look of surprise, perhaps even intrigue, vanished a moment later. "Either way, my scent is on you now. So no other males will bother you."

Maeve didn't know if she was supposed to be grateful or disgusted. It seemed like a terribly primitive and barbaric way to establish...a relationship.

"Not a relationship," Tiernan corrected.

"Would you get out of my—" The words died on her lips as the full reality of what just transpired slammed into her. It stole her breath, left her body cold with dread. She took another, deliberate step away from him. "You...you were controlling my body."

It wasn't a question. And they both knew it.

Tiernan dipped his head in acknowledgement. "I was."

"How?"

He spread his muscled arms wide and Maeve struggled not to stare at the sight of him. Then he winked. "Magic."

"You can control others." Her tone was accusatory, but she couldn't help it. "It's not just the mind reading."

"I can't read your mind," he interrupted smoothly. "It's more like I can hear your thoughts, and interject my own when I feel like it."

She threw her hands up. "That is *beside* the point. You can make other people do what you want by controlling them."

"I can."

He grabbed two brown wooden cups off a passing fae with a tray in her hands and handed one to Maeve. She hesitated.

His eyes rolled to the star-filled sky. "It's just water."

She accepted the drink and swallowed it down. Her throat and her body were completely parched. The cool rush of water soothed her, but she didn't dare take her eyes off the High King. She didn't trust him.

"Sometimes, I make it so they have no idea I've taken control of their bodies. Usually they're merely a pawn. A tool, if you will." He walked toward the edge of the celebration, where the music was a low hum that resonated in her soul, and where the sounds of pleasure were no longer so blatantly obvious. A breeze siphoned through the trees, cold and brisk, and Maeve shuddered in spite of herself. "Sometimes, though, I prefer my victims know exactly who controls them. The battle between body and mind is a marvelous thing."

That was what he'd done to her. He'd left her fully aware of everything he made her do. He'd taken complete control of her. He'd made her suffer at his hands, like the dancing strings of a marionette.

"You bastard."

He bowed regally. "At your service."

She launched her wooden cup at him, but he *faded* before the projectile even made impact. She was on her own again, like he'd never even existed. Except this time, she was on the outskirts of a savage social event, completely alone, and with no sign of Rowan anywhere.

Maeve debated on returning to the party, hoping she could find the exact spot where Rowan left her. But she knew if she wandered any closer, she would only draw attention to herself. Even if she was glamoured, it was painfully obvious she wasn't fae. And a mortal female, all alone in the wilds of the Autumn Court, well, she'd heard stories about what happened to them.

But from the corner of her eye, she saw the palest glow along the ground. Leading away from the foray, was a sequence of dancing lights. Soft, iridescent orbs seemed to move and bounce further into the forest.

Faerie lights.

Maeve recognized them at once. And only one fae—one solitary, rare fae—had ever left a trail of faerie lights in their wake.

The will ó wisp.

MAEVE WASN'T sure how long she followed the faerie lights before they vanished. But one moment they were there, and the next they were gone, leaving her alone in the autumn woods. The sounds of merriment and music were far behind her, shrouded beyond the dense expanse of trees. Ribbons of silver mist crawled along the forest floor, and though she tried to walk quietly, every footfall landed upon something startlingly loud.

The crunch of leaves.

The snap of a twig.

She tucked a loose strand of hair behind her ear and drew in a shallow breath. The forest pulsed around her, alive with wild magic. Its song beckoned her, urged her deeper into the woods, but she turned away from the pull. Away from the draw of its mystique. She couldn't risk losing herself here. There were too many unknowns. Too many dangers. More than anything, she needed to make her way back to the party. At least once she got there, she could find a place to hide and wait for Rowan to find her.

But the sounds from the celebration were muffled, and they echoed everywhere at once. The path she followed was barren. There were no markings signaling direction and no way to tell where she was going. Hoping she wasn't venturing further into the woods, she turned back the way she came and prayed to the goddess she chose correctly.

She heard them before she sensed them. The cut of feathers through the wind, the beating of strong, majestic wings. Instinctively, her hand went to her thigh for her dagger. But she came up empty. Rowan glamoured her, but doing so had left her without a weapon.

"Hello, little wild one." A soft, masculine voice cut through the air around her.

Maeve turned, dug her heels into the soft earth, and came face to face with two fae. Both were exceptionally tall, excruciatingly handsome, and bore an eerie resemblance to Aran, but with one major difference. These fae had wings.

Beautiful, feathered, crimson and gold wings. They were grand and majestic, and the expanse was wider than any bird she'd ever seen. One fae had hair the color of burnt gold, and the other's was a deep, rich mahogany. Their faces were similar —hard jawlines, high cheekbones, aristocratic noses, and shining, green eyes. Everything they wore was jewel-toned. Topaz pants. Onyx boots. Ruby shirts. Jade coats. They were well-dressed and reeked of class and elegance. They weren't at all similar to the trooping fae she watched earlier, the ones that partook in particular activities. No, these were not the same fae she'd left dancing around a bonfire in wild abandon.

They were well bred. They were excess. They were Archfae. They *had* to be. Which could only mean one thing... they were Aran's brothers.

She pretended to ignore the scimitars strapped at their waists and the way tendrils of shadows curled from the tips of their fingers.

"Look at what we have here, Shay." The one with the mahogany hair sauntered forward. "A pretty faerie."

"You seem to have lost your way, little wild one." Shay, Aran's youngest brother, chuckled. "What do you suppose a faerie like this is doing all the way out here, Garvan? Lost deep in the woods of autumn and with no one around to help her?"

Garvan. Her throat worked. He was the one blamed for Autumn's fall. He utilized his magic in unjust ways. Rowan told her as much. And without saying so, she knew she should be afraid of him.

"I'm not lost." Maeve lifted her chin and blamed the chattering of her teeth on the autumn chill. It shivered over her skin like a blanket of frost.

"Aren't you though?" Garvan circled her. Stalked her.

"No." She pressed her lips together and locked her spine into place. She wouldn't show weakness. She wouldn't show fear. "I'm here with someone."

In her heart, she meant Rowan. After all, he was the one who'd brought her to the Autumn Court. But he was not a High King, and as much as Maeve hated to even associate herself with him, Tiernan was possibly her only saving throw. And she was desperate.

"Hm." Garvan sniffed the air, then coiled his finger through one of her curls and gave it a little tug. Not harsh. But a warning. "Shay, she has Tiernan's scent all over her."

"And where is your High King, little wild one?" Shay eyed her with disgust, his green gaze glinting in the night. A snarl curled along his upper lip. "It's not like him to be so careless with one of his conquests."

The insult burned through Maeve's core. "I am *not* a conquest."

She would rather die.

"No?" Garvan crooned. "What are you then? A puppet?"

Maeve snapped her mouth shut, remembering the way Tiernan wielded his magic against her, how he'd taken complete control of her body while leaving her mind untouched.

"A plaything, then?" Shay suggested.

Garvan stretched his wings and they flickered like flames doused with starlight. He rolled his shoulders back and Maeve winced. "What sort of games do you like to play?"

Maeve took a cautious step back and unsuccessfully tried to disguise it as a shifting of her weight. "I don't play games."

Shay sighed, a hint of boredom to his tone. "They never do."

Garvan's dark green gaze coasted over her. Studied her. A line formed across his brow. "She's not a *sirra* either, otherwise she would bear his mark."

Sirra? She recognized it as an Old Laic term, but didn't have the time to decipher the meaning. Perhaps once she was back in Niahvess, she would go to the library and look it up. Assuming she ever returned to Summer. Assuming she survived the night.

Garvan's wings flexed once more, and Maeve's gaze betrayed her. They were rapturous. Glorious. And she imagined they'd be as soft as velvet.

"They are pretty magnificent, aren't they?" Garvan smiled at her, but it was off. Crooked, almost. Like it wasn't a natural thing for him to do. A sinking sensation poisoned the pit of her stomach. "Can you fly, pretty faerie?"

She didn't dare open her mouth. Garvan's vicious grin stretched across his face. "Let's find out."

Even if she tried to run, she wouldn't have been able to escape. He was too strong, too fast. She was too weak, too panicked. She stumbled back, tripping over her own feet, when Garvan shot forward. His rough arm captured her waist, dragged her to him like a sack of grain, and he shot straight into the air. Branches clawed at her skin and ripped her cloak from her shoulders, leaves clung to her hair, and the curse sifting through her blood exploded in a frenzy.

Her scream pierced through the thread of clouds.

Shattered the full moon.

She clutched Garvan's silk shirt and wrapped her arm around his neck. She hated herself for it, but sun and sky, the ground was so, so far away. The treetops were a dizzying kaleidoscope of colors and her heart skittered. Her mind raced. Her blood roared. She squeezed her eyes shut. Anxiety crawled along her skin and her throat closed. Her breathing grew hollow. Empty. She had to focus. Had to find a way *out* of this mess. This would not be her end.

"I'm not a toy." Maeve forced the words out through gritted teeth and opened her eyes.

"But you're so fun," Garvan countered and he soared higher into the air.

Her knees buckled. Beyond the Autumn Court, she could barely make out the twin mountain peaks of Summer in the distance. She could just see the massive, carved faerie guardian, protecting the Crown City. She imagined the heat of Niahvess, wished it encompassed her now. He dove, and swooped, and

Maeve's scream was lost on the call of the wind. Over the expanse of treetops stood another mountain range. These were further in the distance, and covered in snowy white.

Winter.

Garvan's gilded wings coasted through the sky. They swept against the dark of night like brushstrokes, a blur of gold and red against a canvas of navy blue. All the while, he kept one arm around her waist, his hold on her looser than anything.

She had to find a way to escape.

"Put me down." Her voice was steady, but her heart hammered like the beating of a song drum. It vibrated against the wall of her chest, causing her blood to pump and her stomach to churn.

There was a rumble in Garvan's chest, a low, guttural sound. "If you insist."

And he dropped her.

Her scream chilled her own blood. Not even in her nightmares had she heard one more terrifying. She fell from his arms through the wisps of clouds, plummeting toward the stretch of crushed orange and burnt yellow trees below. Their branches reached up for her like spindles, ready to snap and break every bone in her body. There was nothing to grab, nothing to save her. Only air. Swift, cold air. Her arms flailed, her legs kicked fiercely through the night as though somehow, through some desperate measure, she could slow down the speed of her fall. Shameful tears burned in her eyes and she cried out once more, the second before she knew her back would break—only to be silenced by Shay.

He caught her, cradled her like one might comfort a crying child.

"Ready to play, little wild one?" he crooned.

"No." The word was a rasp. Her chest squeezed. Her lungs were too tight. She couldn't force the air in, couldn't breathe to save her own life. Tremors wrecked her body and forced the High Prince to hold onto her more tightly. She'd failed herself, shamed herself. Each thud of her heart was a slam in her throat. Uncontrollable. Unstoppable. Wet tears slid down her heated cheeks. "I want to be put back on the ground."

Her voice cracked. "Please."

Maeve looked up into his eyes and begged, silently, for her life.

The pretty green eyes staring back at her shifted from cold and callous to something she didn't recognize—an emotion of some kind. It was raw. Unrecognizable. But there was a distinctive shift. Then he blinked and it was gone.

Shay swooped to the ground, set her down. Her legs failed and she dropped onto her knees, clutched the damp, cool earth in her fists.

"Who are you?" he demanded.

Maeve staggered to her feet, swiped at the fresh prick of tears threatening to spill down her face. "No one." She shook her head, stumbled backward. "I'm no one."

Then she turned and ran as fast as her mortal legs could carry her. She swatted at branches and ignored the overgrowth as it tugged at her skirt, ripping it to shreds. She ran until sweat slid down her back, until it burned her eyes, until her lungs seized like they'd been caught on fire and filled with smoke. She ran back into the forest. Into autumn. Into the wild.

Chapter Twenty-Three

When Maeve's body finally quit on her, she dropped onto a bed of dank leaves. She curled into herself, relishing in the wetness against her heated cheek. Shrubs of evergreen bursting with dark purple berries hid her exhausted body from view, and she released a shuddering sigh. Each inhale scalded her chest. Her knees trembled, but she couldn't move. The misty ground cooled her skin, and she found her breath floated before her, then evaporated into the brisk night.

She pressed her palm to the solid earth, and a faint, whispering hum spread from her flesh to her heart. Magic throbbed in the air around her. Its wondrous scent of cedarwood and orange blossom was more exotic within the Autumn Court. She was filled with the rich scent of cinnamon, of a hearth, of a home. She was safe here. She could stay here. The Autumn forest would protect her.

She laid there, staring up at the towering trees above her, where moonlight flickered through the canopy of branches like spider silk. Minutes ticked by into what she could only assume had become hours. But the woods were blessedly silent, and their stillness brought her a comfort she thought she'd never feel again. Gradually, the beating of her heart slowed, and she could breathe. But she wasn't alone. All around her, encircling her like a ring of illuminated flowers, were the faerie lights.

The same ones she'd been chasing before she ran into Garvan and Shay.

Maeve heaved herself up into a sitting position, careful not to disturb anything around her. She peered into the woods but saw nothing, only the shadows of the plants and trees that had stood watch over her. On a grunt, she eased herself up and stood, then dusted her hands against the tattered remains of her skirt. Her legs were tight and tense from being curled into a ball, and her back was sore from the hard bedding of the ground. In the darkness of night, her vision failed her and she couldn't see, though she could hear a faint sort of humming, almost like a song. When she tried to step out of the ring of dancing lights, it was like an invisible forcefield rooted her in place.

She was trapped.

Apprehension lodged in the back of her throat. Strangled her. But she swallowed it down, and called out to the unknown.

"Hello?"

A flash of light burst through the endless darkness. Maeve threw her hands up to shield her eyes, and a shooting star exploded overhead, leaving a trail of shimmering dust in its wake. Except the star took on a shape of its own, an elegant bird with glowing wings of violet and teal. It had sapphires for eyes, its beak was translucent silver, and every feather was sleek and glossy, alight with rich hues of purple and blue. It resembled the fabled bird Maeve read about as a child, the one also in the tales from the book Aran had given her. Its tail was a mass of stars. It swooped and swirled, then perched on a branch. Its eyes sparkled with curiosity. Then it tilted its head and shimmied its feathers with presumptuous superiority. Entranced, Maeve reached out to the bird. She just wanted to touch her, to run her finger along one feather and ensure something of such beauty was real and not crafted from the finest jewels.

But the bird shattered into a spectacular display of constellations and stardust before transforming into a fae whose beauty caused Maeve's heart to ache and a twinge of tears to temporarily blind her.

She was petite, no taller than a tree stump. Wings of gossamer stretched out with the delicacy of a butterfly. They glimmered like a thousand broken rainbows kissed by the rain. Tendrils of silver hair fell to her waist. Pale, crystalized, blue eyes were framed with dark lashes and brows. Frosty pink painted her lips. Her skin was opalescent, and she wore a gown of crushed stardust.

Maeve blinked, and the will ó wisp stared back at her.

"Well." Her voice was like a whispered song. Light and airy. Musical. "Imagine Lianan's surprise when she finds a... thing. Tell me, what are you?"

"I'm not a thing. I'm a princess. A human from the kingdom of Kells. My name is Maeve." Wide-eyed, Maeve clamped her hand over her mouth. The words simply poured from her, like they'd been siphoned.

The wisp tilted her small head. "No. There's something strange about you. Lianan knows it. She can *sense* it."

Maeve kept her mouth shut. The fae had not asked a question, so she wasn't required to answer. And she worried that if she did, she would tell the will ó wisp her entire life story.

Lianan—at least, Maeve assumed that was her name, considering she addressed herself as such—plucked a muddied red leaf from the branch she sat upon. It was larger than her delicate hand. She twirled it once, poked her finger through it, then discarded the leaf. "What is it you want, Maeve of Kells?"

"I have questions." Maeve bit the words out, careful not to give away too much.

"Don't we all?" Her laughter tinkled through the hushed forest. "Continue."

The will ó wisp pulled the answer from her.

"I want to know about the *anam ó Danua*. I need to know if it can help me. If it can help my people." Maeve clenched her jaw to keep from speaking again. It must be a trick, a strange kind of magic. She was trapped in the ring of faerie lights, so every word she spoke was solid truth. Blunt. Honest. She couldn't lie. She couldn't deceive. It was a terrible position for a human. But then she remembered the book, and what Lir had mentioned to her in the library. When in the presence of the will ó wisp, everything must be spoken in *truth*.

"Lianan knows all there is to know of the goddess Danua's soul. She was there when it was given, when it blessed the Spring Court." Her blue eyes darkened to coals. "And she was there when it was taken away."

"Has it been destroyed?" Maeve asked, surprised she was allowed questions of her own.

"Lianan did not say such a thing." The will ó wisp crossed her legs, placed her hands on her knees. When she looked at Maeve, it was with an air of disappointment, as though she expected more from a mortal. "Listening is an art, Maeve of Kells. Now, pay careful attention. Lianan will give you three answers to three questions."

Maeve stayed quiet. They were going to bargain, and she would have to keep all of her wits about her if she wanted to succeed. This might be her only chance to save her kingdom. To return to Saoirse. To rescue her people from the Scathing and prove she was worthy of the crown.

"Very good." Lianan leaned forward, and stardust fell around her to the wet ground below. "And in exchange for these three answers, I want something from you in return."

"What do you want?" Maeve blurted the question out before she could stop herself.

A flicker of annoyance flashed across Lianan's face, and she made a sort of tsk-ing noise. "A pity you would waste a question on such a foolish mistake. And without yet knowing the terms of our bargain."

Horrified, Maeve started to open her mouth, then quickly covered it with both of her hands. How could she have made such a dreadful error? She'd lost a question. If she'd just waited, Lianan would've freely given her the terms.

"But since you asked," she drew the word out, "Lianan wants what is owed to her. She wants the blood of the one who decimated her family. The one who eliminated all but herself." Malice laced the pretty fae's words, and the starlight dimmed to near dark.

In all the books she'd ever read, there had only been mention of *one* will ó wisp. A solitary fae. One of the rarest. Nowhere was it written that a group of wisps existed. Multiple fae with the depth of knowledge and power of the wisp would have been an extreme weapon to any Court of their choosing. But the fact that someone, or something, had slaughtered them all didn't sit well with Maeve. It seemed like an atrocious crime. An unforgivable offense. And now, she had a choice to make.

"Do we have an agreement?" Lianan asked, and she thrummed her tiny fingers along the edge of a tree branch. "Lianan sees your mind working, Maeve of Kells. She will come to you when she is ready to call in her favor. And then you will know whose blood she seeks."

Seek the one responsible for the annihilation of the will ó

wisps, or leave the fate of her kingdom in the hands of the Scathing?

Lianan stuck out her small hand. "Agreed?"

"Agreed." Maeve accepted, and the fae's grip tightened. A tiny Strand of glowing black burst between the two of them. It swirled around her thumb and took the shape of dozens of scattered stars.

"When the stars align, Lianan will come for you." Lianan released her grip on Maeve's hand and fluttered up into the air. She floated right above Maeve's head, just out of reach. "Now, what are your questions? You've only two left. Do not squander them."

Maeve stared down at the Strand marking her thumb. She needed answers, and the will ó wisp could give them to her. First things first. "Does the *anam ó Danua* continue to exist within a faerie bloodline?"

Lianan smiled, and for a brief moment, it glimmered with approval. "Yes."

Maeve expelled a harsh breath. Her mind raced to keep track of what she already knew. With Lianan confirming the soul's existence, Maeve could already narrow down the bloodline. She knew Ceridwen didn't possess it, and it had been taken from Parisa right before Danua purged the darkness from Faeven. If Autumn's bloodlines were all male, then the Winter Court was the only other possibility. She knew what she had to ask next. It was all that mattered.

She glanced up to where Lianan flitted through the air above her, a sparkling display of purple and blue. "Can the *anam ó Danua* save my kingdom?"

The fae's smile fell away. "It cannot."

Shock tore through Maeve. It ripped through her heart and left her gasping. No. It couldn't happen like this. She shook her head, tried to focus on what Lianan said. The soul of the goddess was the entire reason she'd come to Faeven. Without it, there was no way to defeat the Scathing. There was no way to save her people. If the *anam* couldn't help her, then she was helpless.

"But, then what am I supposed to do?" The truth of her panic expelled from her in a vomit of words. "How can I save my kingdom? The *anam ó Danua* was the only way! He told me it was the only way! I can't leave them to die! I can't!"

Lianan fluttered down so their faces were mere inches from one another. The pixie edged back, then blew a puff of air in Maeve's face.

She stumbled back. "What was that for?"

"For being one who loves books, you do not ask yourself the right questions." Lianan rolled her eyes and shook her head so her hair fell around her like a curtain of moonlight. "I am sorry, but the Scathing that plagues your land is a form of dark magic. It is not dark *fae*. Not even the life source of a goddess is strong enough to destroy it."

Maeve sank to her knees. The crushing weight of defeat pinned her to the ground. In that moment, her heart shattered. The shard of verity struck true and every splinter of hope, every fragment of her resilience broke into tiny, worthless pieces. Everything, all she'd done so far, was for nothing. All the time she'd wasted. All the pain she'd endured. None of it had been worthwhile if she couldn't return to Kells victorious. If she couldn't protect her homeland. If she went back empty handed, it would be the end. The end of her people. The end of her.

Lianan tilted her head and peered up at her, having returned to her seated position on the broken log. "This is not the answer you were hoping for."

"No. It's not." Maeve shook her head. She pulled herself up from the forest floor and scrubbed her hands over her face. "Not at all."

"Lianan will make a deal with you."

Maeve groaned.

"Tell Lianan a truth, Maeve from Kells. A secret. A dark one." She shimmied her wings. "And Lianan will give you some advice to assist you on your journey."

She didn't want to do it. She shouldn't. Making another deal with the same fae was tempting fate. But she was out of choices. And she was out of time.

"A truth…" Maeve met the fae's frosty, sapphire gaze.

"A secret," she urged.

Maeve locked her spine into place. Saying it out loud would seal it as a truth. It would taint her soul. It would mark her. But she would do it. She would do anything for Kells. "When I return to my kingdom, to Kells, I will kill my mother. My people are better without her. I am better without her. And I will take what is rightfully mine. I will take my crown."

"Ooh!" Lianan squealed and bounced off of the hollow log. "How utterly delightful." She floated close, lit by moonlight and stars. "The only way to save your kingdom…is by destroying the magic source of the Scathing."

The magic source.

Parisa.

She had to destroy Parisa. She'd been the key to undoing The Scathing all along. The brutal High Queen of the Spring Court. The one who'd murdered her own mother because she craved more power, more magic. Rowan was wrong. So wrong. The *anam ó Danua* was nothing. It was useless. Parisa was the one. She'd always been the one.

"I have to go." Maeve glanced down at the faerie lights dancing around her ankles. "Will you release me?"

Lianan stuck out her bottom lip. "So soon?"

Maeve lifted her chin. "I'll see you again."

A small, almost friendly smile. "Lianan knows."

The will ó wisp swirled, taking the form of a gloriously jeweled bird with dazzling feathers and sapphires for eyes. Then she vanished in a shock of purple light, leaving Maeve alone in the dark autumn woods. The scent of cedarwood and orange blossom lingered in the air, and she looked down at the Strand wrapping around her thumb. It glittered like starlight.

AGAIN, Maeve was running through the woods. But this time it wasn't fear that pushed her forward, back toward the feral celebration of the Autumn Ceilie, but revelation. Lianan had gifted her knowledge. And with it came a glimmer of hope she thought was lost forever. A glimpse of ambition. The possibility of a plan. She veered onto the darkened path, ignoring the way her shredded skirt snagged on every fallen branch and twig. She didn't care if there was mud caked to the side of her face or if leaves were tangled in her hair. All she cared about was getting back to the Summer Court. Back to Niahvess. There, she and Casimir could form a plan. There, they could find a way to take out the High Queen of Spring.

Music sounded all around her, louder and louder. It seemed the party had grown since she'd run away from Garvan and Shay. Plumes of smoke curled into the air, and the sparks from multiple bonfires shot high into the sky, crackling and bursting with orange flames. Drums and flutes echoed in her ears, in a melody she didn't recognize, and when she finally burst through a bramble bush, she was in awe of the sight before her. No longer was it an exhibition of sexual exploits. Now, it was a full-blown revelry. Fae danced and twirled, their smiles wide, their eyes bright. They sang, they laughed, and they moved with the rhythm filling the air, their bodies naturally in tune with the music carrying them.

A hand fell upon Maeve's shoulder and she looked up to find a female fae frowning down at her. She was lovely. Brilliant and beautiful. Pale, creamy skin. Fox-like eyes. And hair that was a burnished gold, then bright red at the tips. Two huge rubies studded her ears. But when she looked at Maeve, her nose wrinkled in distaste.

"Ooh, what happened to *you*?" The fae stared at her skirts, then looked back up at her face. "You're filthy."

Maeve gave her best attempt at a lighthearted shrug. "I tripped."

"Happens to the best of us." The fae laughed, and Maeve had never heard such a sweet sound. "Lucky for you, we don't judge here. At least, not always."

Before Maeve could respond, the faerie winked and held up a thin red stick that glowed at the tip. Then she blew, and Maeve was encompassed in a cloud of pink smoke. It smelled of crushed leaves, sandalwood, and something else. Patchouli. Or...or...

The faerie appeared blurry, like a painting. Like she was made of watercolors. Maeve could see her, but she couldn't exactly *focus* on her.

"What's..." Her mind wouldn't work. She knew what she wanted to say, but she couldn't get the words out. Tingles cruised along her skin, her muscles softened, and her entire body was warm. Warnings tried to fire inside her brain, tried to send jolts to her system to remind her of something, to tell her this was wrong. But the beating drum sank deep into her bones, and when the female faerie looked over at her, Maeve smiled.

"Come on!" She grabbed Maeve's hand and led her toward one of the bonfires. "Let's dance!"

Maeve couldn't help it. Her mind was barely rational with thought and part of her wanted to object, but her insides were alive with a kind of electric energy. She was reckless and an uninhibited desire to move swept her up with other fae cavorting around the fire. The rhythm took over and suddenly, she was flowing freely. There was no one there to tell her what to do, or to warn her away from the possibilities of danger. All she wanted was to dance. To live, breathe, and *dance*. She spun and twirled, her legs light, her arms carefree. It was like walking on a cloud, like moving through water. She was fluid. Weightless. Magic enveloped her, wrapped around her like midnight velvet. It sang through her veins, euphoric and passionate. Maeve tossed her head back as the enchantment caused her hips to sway and her body to reverberate with the cadence singing in and around her.

She whipped around, and around, and slammed right into a wall. A strong hand clamped down on her elbow. Not a wall, then. She looked up into a set of raging eyes, so dark, they were furious like a storm. She knew that face. It haunted her dreams, made them more like nightmares.

Tiernan.

She grinned up at him, dazed and nearly delirious. "Let's...dance."

The words sounded funny on her tongue, like she wasn't saying them properly.

"No." He snarled and caught her by the wrist, dragging her away from the bonfire. "No more dancing."

Chapter Twenty-Four

Maeve glanced back over her shoulder, to where shadows thrived and bodies glowed. There, she caught sight of her new friend, the one with hair like fire. She threw one arm out and waved, but the movement was sluggish. Like slogging through sand.

"I have...to go," Maeve called out to her faerie friend. "I think...I think I'm...in trouble." The words slid from her mouth just as her toe caught an overturned rock and sent her tumbling forward.

Tiernan's arm wrapped swiftly around her waist and he dragged her against him. He grabbed her chin and tried to make her look up, but her body was no longer cooperating. Her head lolled to the side, and the world tipped on its axis. Colors blurred together in a dizzying mix and Maeve slumped against Tiernan's chest. Wrong. All of this was wrong. The pink dust, the cloud, it must have...she couldn't think clearly. Her mind was fogged, empty and devoid of rational thought.

"Maeve?"

She squinted, stared up at him, sagged against him. "I like..." Her mouth felt like a wad of sandpaper had been shoved down her throat. She tried again, with one eye open and one eye closed. "I like...these."

Her finger landed on his nose.

His brow furrowed. "I've only got one." Concern deepened the line of worry marring his forehead. "Do you see two?"

"No." She opened her mouth slowly. Now it was like paste. Sticky. Yucky. "Eyes."

Now those same dark brows arched. "You like my eyes?"

"Mm."

She thought she heard him mutter something when he scooped her up into his arms. Cold air rushed over her, and it was like flying. No, she *was* flying. Illustrious wings of midnight, cobalt, and aubergine spread out behind Tiernan, and the wingspan was wider than any she'd seen before. Not that she'd been privy to many fae with wings, but as of late, she'd seen more than ever. His wings appeared from nowhere and moved like silk through the air around them. Silent and beautiful. They reminded her of a summer evening, just after sunset, when shades of dusk stole through the sky just before the fall of night.

Without warning, they stopped moving. It was darker here. Not as loud. There was no music and the forest was eerily still. She thought she should be scared.

"Where are..." Maeve struggled to get the last word out from between her lips. "We?"

"Here." Tiernan's voice was cold, and then she was flying through the air without him. Before her scream could pierce the night, before she realized what was happening, she plunged into a black, icy abyss.

Panic seized her, and she swallowed down a gulp of slimy

water. Alarm slammed into her as the freezing water pulled her down, down. She kicked violently, and her arms flailed, desperate to find an anchor, anything to pull her from the water. But there was nothing to grab, nothing to hold, nothing to save her. Swim. She needed to swim. But her arms wouldn't work and it was so dark, and so cold, and she didn't know which way was up. Her lungs screamed for oxygen, and every nerve in her body was wrecked with terror. She was going to drown. For some awful reason, Tiernan had thrown her into a body of water, and now she was going to drown.

A muscled arm wrapped around her, and Tiernan pulled her to him, crashing through the surface. He flew her over to the bank of the lake and set her down where the ground was soft, where her nails clawed into the mud in an effort to secure herself against the solid earth. She clambered away from him, crawled on her hands and knees through the damp leaves and grass. She choked and coughed, gasping every second for another breath of air, until she heaved up all the lake water she'd swallowed.

Shivers stole through her and she convulsed uncontrollably.

"What the fuck, Maeve?" His voice boomed from some-where above her, but she couldn't look up at him. Her teeth chattered until a pounding ache throbbed between her temples. "You can't swim?"

She wrapped her arms around herself tightly, and brought her knees to her chest. She rocked back and forth. Back and forth. Her bottom lip quivered. "N-no. I h-hate...h-hate..."

Maeve didn't know if she was stuttering because her body was succumbing to a state of hypothermia, or if she was having a full-blown panic attack. Neither was pleasant.

"*You bastard!*" Another masculine voice cracked through

the night and Maeve jumped out of her skin. Rowan appeared out of nowhere, his face etched into severe lines of savagery, his muscles flexed with fury. Wild shadows exploded around him and charged the night air with furious energy. He whipped off the cloak of fur he wore and draped it around Maeve's shoulders. Then he stormed toward Tiernan, blocking Maeve with his wide frame. Rage radiated from him, and the magic was so thick, it was nearly suffocating. "You could've *killed* her!"

"Me?" Tiernan's wrath cut through the night, swift like a blade. "You're the one who left her alone with a bunch of wild fae."

"*I* told her to stay put." There was a tremor in Rowan's voice and it lowered an octave. The deep baritone caused goosebumps to pebble along her flesh and another tremor overtook her. "Someone else convinced her to partake in a *mating* dance."

Tiernan lifted his chin, his dark gaze set. He crossed his arms, and every muscle bunched, prepped for battle. "I was protecting her."

Rowan's hands curled into fists. "From who?"

"From Fearghal."

Maeve pushed herself up from the ground, buried herself further into Rowan's cloak. She stepped toward both males. The spark and snap of their magic and tempers was enough to chill her to her bones. But she had to stop them. She had to stop whatever brawl was about to erupt between the two, and a distraction seemed to be the only way. "Who's Fearghal?"

"A very dangerous faerie." Tiernan held out his hand to her without taking his eyes off Rowan.

"Maeve." Rowan stepped up beside her, offered his hand instead.

"You really think you can protect her?" Tiernan sneered

and arrogance dripped from him. "The way you glamoured her like a common whore nearly got her snatched. Don't pretend you don't have any idea what he would've done if he'd gotten his hands on her."

Rowan made a guttural noise, and it resonated deep within his chest. He drew his sword. Tiernan bared his teeth, and violet lightning exploded above them.

"Stop it!" Maeve shoved herself between both of them. "Stop it now." Tiernan glared down at her. His gaze seared her skin. But she refused to let him phase her. "I found the will ó wisp."

Rowan's mouth fell open, and Tiernan reared back like she'd slapped him.

"You what?" he asked.

"When?" Rowan demanded.

"Before..." Her gaze betrayed her and she looked up at Tiernan. "Right before you found me. The second time."

Rowan was by her side in an instant. He took her hand and held it close to his heart—so close, she could feel the steady beat of it. "What did she say?"

"She said the *anam ó Danua* couldn't save Kells. The only way to rid my kingdom of the Scathing is to kill Parisa." It physically ached to say it, to even admit it out loud.

Rowan paled.

"That doesn't make sense. The *anam ó Danua* is strong enough. It has to be." He shook his head, and his teal hair fell across his forehead. "Did the will ó wisp say why?"

"Yes." Maeve shifted and angled herself away from him, then pulled her hand from his hold. "The Scathing is dark magic. Not dark fae. Killing Parisa is the only way to stop it."

His shoulders dropped and he ducked his head, shielding his face from view. "That won't be easy."

"No," she agreed. "It won't."

Her own power rose up then. Not her fae-cursed blood or the warrior lifestyle Casimir had instilled in her. No, this was different. This was her own worth. Her own purpose. "And I'm done standing by, listening to two faeries whose only devotion is to their own Courts. My loyalty is to Kells. Not to Faeven."

Maeve stepped away from Rowan, putting distance between them. She met his confused gaze and though it hurt, she didn't look away. "I will stop at nothing to save my people."

He moved closer to her. Just a step. But uncertainty clouded his features, and when he reached for her again, it took every ounce of her willpower to avoid his hold. She couldn't be swayed. Not by his kisses. Not by his promises. Not by him.

"Maeve," he pleaded, and something in her heart cracked. "I told you I was going to help."

"Yes, I know." She swallowed down the bubble of sorrow beginning to build. "But so far, you haven't."

"It takes time, Princess."

She shook her head, willing herself not to listen. Not to be bribed. "I don't have time, Rowan. My kingdom is under attack. My home is *dying*. I can't wait. The longer I'm here, the longer I do nothing, the faster my world will fall."

Silence occupied the space between them, strained and heavy.

Her shoulders rolled back and she stole a glance at the High King of Summer, the one who stood by quietly without scorning or shaming. And she held out her hand. Tiernan grasped the tips of her fingers and brought her to his side.

"Maeve." Her name falling from Rowan's lips was scarcely a whisper. But it was sharp enough to shred through her soul.

She lowered her chin and dipped her head, refusing to look at either one of them. "My lord, I wish to return to Niahvess. I need to come up with a plan to kill Parisa, the High Queen of the Spring Court."

Tiernan bowed, just slightly. "As you wish, Your Highness."

It was pure torture, but Maeve lifted her eyes just enough to find Rowan. To memorize everything about him. His handsome features. His beautiful lavender eyes. The way she often made the corner of his mouth quirk. "If indeed your loyalty is to the Spring Court, always, then I shall see you there."

It was a promise. One they both knew she would keep.

Tiernan's grip on her tightened, thunder cracked around them, and in a splinter of lightning, they *faded* back to the Summer Court.

THE GLORIOUS WARMTH of Summer and dawn cocooned Maeve like a blanket. She stood in her bedroom, muddy, covered in bits of leaves, with damp hair that frizzed like a pillow of moss. She peeled her mask off her face and Rowan's glamour fell away. Tiernan, on the other hand, stood her opposite, in his usual attire of a crisp shirt with an unbuttoned collar, and pants. He watched her carefully, with his hands tucked in his pockets, like if he moved, she might break.

She didn't care if he watched; it was nothing he hadn't seen before. She stripped out of what remained of her clothing and stalked into the bathroom. She grabbed a washcloth, used the delicate scented soap to scrub the grime from her body, then washed the lake water muck from her hair in the sink. When she reemerged, Tiernan was still there, her night shirt in his hands. He didn't seem at all phased by the fact that she was, yet again, naked in front of him, so she accepted the shirt and tugged it on over her head.

"What?" she asked, annoyed by his calm demeanor. "Why are you staring at me like that?"

He leaned against her wardrobe and watched with interest when she checked to ensure her Aurastone was back under her pillow. Next time she wouldn't be glamoured without it. He inclined his head. "Do you have a plan?"

Maeve spun on him.

"Does it look like I have a plan? I have no idea what the fuck I'm doing." She raked her hands through her wet hair and sent droplets of water flying across the hardwood floor. "I thought I was prepared. I read so many books. I spent hours researching and learning about the fae because I found this world so fascinating. Because I wanted to understand more about my curse."

She dropped onto the edge of her bed, exasperated. Exhausted. Slightly defeated. "But it's nothing like I imagined. And now I've been tasked with killing an Archfae to save my kingdom and my people, and I have no idea how to do it. There aren't any *books* on assassinations and murder plots. At least not any I've found."

Tiernan strolled toward her in his casual way, effortless and uncaring. "Parisa has taken much from me. She's taken from all of us." He bent down, plucked a brown leaf from her hair, then replaced it with a warm summer rose. "You won't have to fight this battle alone. All you have to do is ask."

"Oh, sure. Let me just ask a High King for help and not expect him to want anything in return." She rolled her eyes to the glass ceiling above. "Why would you want to help me anyway? You hate me. You have since the day I arrived."

He shrugged, an indifferent rise and fall of the shoulders. "I hate her more."

A bubble of fresh annoyance rose up inside her. "That can be debated, my lord."

He tilted his head toward her, the barest of inches. "Indeed."

She tucked an errant strand of hair behind her ear. "Just... just leave me alone. I need to think. Or sleep. Or something."

Tiernan's dark brow quirked. "Are you dismissing me in my own palace?"

Maeve challenged him with a hard stare. "Would you listen if I was?"

He chuckled. It was a low, rumbling sound. "Absolutely not."

"I thought as much." She was trying to consider another, less polite way to tell him to piss off, when a thought occurred to her. It'd been at the back of her mind, waiting patiently to be considered. "What's a *sirra*?"

He eyed her coolly. "Why?"

She pressed her lips together. "Just curious." That much was true.

"It's an Old Laic term, most often used to mean soul mate." He idly toyed with the rolled sleeve of his shirt. "Where did you hear it?"

"In Autumn. When Gar—" She snapped her mouth shut, but it was too late. Tiernan went eerily still.

"When *who*?" His voice was menacing. Deep and primal. And slightly terrifying.

She scooted back further, onto her bed. "Nothing."

"Do not lie to me, *astora*." He stalked over and gripped her chin between his thumb and forefinger, jerking her face up to his. "What happened in the autumn woods?"

"I...there was..."

"Be very careful about what you say next."

"After our *dance*," she spat the word out, "I followed faerie lights into the woods. But they vanished before I found Lianan."

292

A curious expression passed over Tiernan's face and he eased his grip.

"The will ó wisp," Maeve clarified.

"She gave you her name?"

Maeve shrugged. "She spoke about herself in the third person, so I assumed..."

He nodded once. "Continue."

"Anyway, before I found her...I ran into the Archfae of the Autumn Court. Garvan and Shay."

Tiernan expelled a breath, but it hissed out through his teeth. "What did they do to you?"

She told him everything, from the way they called her "little wild one," to how Garvan let her free fall, to Shay's demand to know her true identity.

Tiernan was rigid. Unflinching. Unmoving. She wasn't even sure if he was breathing.

"And then?" His low words reverberated through the room.

"And then I ran. I found Lianan, or more so, she found me." Maeve pulled her legs up under her. "I made a deal with her, something that seems to happen to me fairly often now, and she gave me the information I needed. Then I went back to the party. That faerie blew pink smoke in my face and then you tried to drown me."

"The Black Lake washes away all enchantment." He grit his teeth, then leaned back. "Besides, I assumed you knew how to swim."

"Well, I can't."

"Why not?"

She folded into herself. "I hate the water." She meant for it to sound firm. Confident, even. But he saw right through her false conviction.

"Why?"

"Why do you care?" she countered.

His hands returned to his pockets and he lifted one shoulder, then let it fall. "I don't. I'm merely curious."

"It's a...thing."

Tiernan ran his teeth over his bottom lip. "I like things."

"I'm sure you do." She had no intention of revealing any sort of weakness in front of him. She didn't want to give him any ammunition to use against her. But water was water, and she was on a fucking faerie island. He already knew she was incapable of swimming. What did it truly matter if he knew the reason behind it?

"My mother knew I was cursed since the day I was born." She pointed to her ears, where they pointed just enough to not be human, but not long enough to be considered a full fae. "But it was a few years before any signs of magic showed. I think she was hoping it was a fluke. That maybe I just had these fae-like ears and nothing else."

Maeve crossed her legs under her while she told him her story. "I used my magic for the first time when I was five years old. She put the cuffs on me then—to control the magic, to control me. And as a punishment, she put me in a giant metal cage."

She could remember it, all of it, so clearly. Carman swooped into the courtyard on that bitterly cold day and she'd dragged her to some room on the east end of the castle. She'd deposited her in a space far enough away from everyone else so that the servants, and handmaidens, and soldiers wouldn't hear her cries. She created the cuffs from molten liquid she crafted them with her sorcery, then imbued them with magic from the virdis lepatite, and clamped them upon Maeve's wrists to keep the power of her curse restrained. She was crying, scared, and hungry. But Carman had taken her to the Cliffs of Morrigan, to where the old cage groaned and creaked in the wind. To where the angry waves thrashed the coast, and where the jagged rocks below shot up from the frothy sea like the teeth of a raging monster.

Maeve locked the memory away, knowing the fear would continue to linger. "The cage hangs between two branches from an old oak tree. Or it used to, one of them broke the last time I was in it. The wind keeps the metal cold, so cold it burns my skin every time it rocks through the air. And the ocean is below. The waves there are always violent, and their roar haunted my dreams for years. Sometimes they still do. She put me there and left me overnight. The cage was my punishment from then on."

"I see."

There was no sympathy. No pity. No understanding.

She wouldn't expect anything less.

She yawned and tugged the plush comforter back, then crawled under the blankets. The soft silk curled around her skin, wrapped around her like a dream. The mattress cushioned her weary bones. Her eyes were heavy, and fatigue pulled her under. She tucked the comforter under her chin, and snuggled down deeper, and prayed to any god or goddess in the sky for a dreamless sleep.

"One more thing." Tiernan spoke like a whisper and it tickled the damp hair draped across her neck.

She hadn't realized he'd moved so close. "Hm?"

His touch sent the faintest charge through her, when his finger brushed over the tattooed skin of her thumb. The mark of the Strand. "What did you give her? The will ó wisp? In exchange for the information you sought?"

She stifled another yawn and peered up at him. His twilight eyes were inches from her face. She blinked again. Slowly. "I agreed to a favor, one she'll call in later. And I gave her a secret."

Her eyes drifted shut once more.

"What sort of secret?" Tiernan crooned.

"One that will die with me."

The deep timber of his chuckle rumbled across her like thunder, and then Maeve was alone, and she succumbed to the sweet desire of sleep.

Chapter Twenty-Five

"Wait." Casimir knocked back his hood and planted his hands on the table. "What?"

After Maeve slept for a few hours, she crawled out of bed in search of food. She'd found Casimir on the balcony, staring at a bowl of biscuits covered in some kind of gravy. Tiernan, Ceridwen, Lir, Brynn, and Merrick were all enjoying various types of sandwiches, sugared fruit, and sparkling juice. Brynn looked up, and her elbow jabbed into Casimir's side. He'd been none too happy to find out she'd been whisked away to Autumn without his knowledge. She couldn't blame him. She'd be furious if the tables were turned. But his anger and frustration had only mounted to a boiling point when she confessed to learning that the *anam ó Danua* would be absolutely useless in protecting Kells against the Scathing.

Casimir rapped his knuckles twice on the wooden surface of the table, and Ceridwen slipped both hands around her tea cup to keep it from spilling over. "So, you're saying we have to go to the Spring Court anyway? That killing Parisa is the only way to save Kells?"

"That's right." Maeve smiled up at Lir when he poured her a cup of coffee, then added two cubes of sugar. "All this time, we could've been planning for that instead. Which is what we wanted to do from the start."

At least, she'd wanted to go straight to the Spring Court and attempt to murder Parisa. But her plan had been shot down by the promise of the soul of a goddess.

Merrick rocked back in his chair, balancing it on two legs, and tucked his hands behind his head. "How do you figure?"

Maeve told herself if they asked, she'd tell the truth. She wouldn't hold anything back. "I found the will ó wisp."

Lir stumbled on his way to his seat. Merrick's perfect balance bobbled. And Ceridwen spilled her precious cup of tea. The porcelain clattered against the saucer, and she rose in a decadent swirl of gold, blush, and violet—a summer sunrise. Her gaze cut to Tiernan, who was busy stirring his own coffee. "You let her go to the Autumn Court."

It wasn't so much of a question as it was an accusation. But the High King denied his twin either way. "First off, I didn't *let* her do anything. The Princess of Kells does what she wants."

He stole a glance at her and she offered him the slightest incline of her head. Maeve met the Archfae's pointed gaze over the rim of her cup. "Rowan took me."

Ceridwen's perfect lips pinched, and a shadow fell across her lustrous face. "Why am I just now hearing of this?"

"*We*, High Princess," Merrick corrected politely. "Why are *we* just now hearing of this?"

Maeve blew on her coffee, refusing to be put off by their apparent concern. "What was I supposed to do? Wake all of you up in the middle of the night and tell you I planned to frolic through the Autumn Court?"

Merrick leaned forward, his curiosity piqued. "You frolicked?"

Brynn snorted, then thumped him on the back of the head. "Shut up, Mer."

"Obviously," Casimir drawled. "That is exactly what you should've done. How would you have felt if I disappeared in the middle of the night, then returned the next day like nothing happened? Nothing except the fact that our entire reason for being here has completely been tossed aside?"

It was a fair point. "Fine. The next time I do something rash, I'll be sure to let you know."

Ceridwen coughed. Lightly.

"*All* of you," Maeve amended, with a glance at the cloudless sky.

"You made a bargain with her." Lir sat at the opposite end of the table, his silver eyes zoned in on the constellation around her thumb. "You made a bargain with the will ó wisp."

Maeve sipped her coffee. The sweet, rich liquid was like a balm to the distinct throbbing at the base of her neck. "I did."

"This keeps getting better and better." Merrick reached across the table and snatched one of Brynn's sandwiches. "What sort of bargain?"

"That's between myself and the wisp." Maeve winced when Merrick's eyes widened. She hadn't intended to sound so rude. "Mostly because I don't have all the details yet."

Merrick groaned, and even Brynn pinched the bridge of her nose in disappointment. "Mortals," she muttered. "When will you learn?"

"None of that matters anyway." Maeve waved off their displeasure of her agreement with Lianan. "We need to focus on slaying the High Queen of Spring."

"*So ruthless.*" Tiernan's silky voice caressed her thoughts and she cut him down with a glare.

"Not only to save Kells...but to save the Four Courts as well." Her loyalty was to Kells. To Veterra and the rest of the human lands. But if she could save other innocent lives in the process, then she would do it, no questions asked. "As long as Parisa lives, the dark fae will continue to attack Faeven."

Moments of measured, weighted silence passed between the group. The air was thick, and the humidity settled between them. It clung to Maeve's skin, and a trickle of sweat slid down her neck. The cool breeze, as there so often was one, had suddenly died.

Ceridwen shook her head, and her golden waves tumbled. "I don't have a good feeling about this."

Brynn plucked a toothpick from a glass jar on the table and stuck it between her teeth. "None of us do, High Princess."

Maeve looked up at her. "What other choice do we have?"

"We don't know what she's planning." Brynn rolled the toothpick between her lips. Her burgundy curls looked like crushed velvet in the sunlight. "There has to be a reason for all of these attacks. In both realms."

"Power?" Lir suggested.

Casimir's dark brown gaze landed on Brynn. "Revenge?"

A line of worry creased her brow. "Against who?"

"Against us." Lir stood. His towering frame blocked the sunshine like a solid wall. "Every one of us knew the goodness of her mother, the former High Queen Brigid. Parisa knows she will never have our respect."

"Or our trust," Tiernan interjected.

Ceridwen rubbed her ruby lips together. "We can't endure another Evernight War. The Courts won't survive it. Our people won't survive it."

"Then it's settled." Tiernan took a sip of his coffee, but his knuckles were white. "We agree she must be stopped."

Maeve eyed him, eyed the fae whose wrath seemed barely contained beneath the surface of his sun-touched skin. "Can we ask the other Courts for help?"

Harsh laughter erupted around her, and it scraped against her ears like nails on a stone wall.

"Garvan and the rest of Autumn would rather watch us die," Ceridwen said as she stirred what was left of her tea.

"And Winter?" Maeve tossed out, hopeful.

"The Winter Court can be..." Merrick hesitated. He sought the High King, and a silent look passed between them. "Difficult."

"So, it's just us then?" Maeve was met with solemn nods. She had to admit, she didn't really expect any sort of assistance from the other two Courts, but she did have a glimmer of hope that maybe, just maybe, Winter would be willing to assist. It hardly seemed fair. They were the ones risking their lives to venture into the Spring Court and take out its High Queen. They were the only ones willing to fight, to stand up for what was right. Yet if they succeeded, both Autumn and Winter would reap the benefits of never being attacked by dark fae again. Unless, of course, it was only Summer that was under attack.

Casimir reached into the pocket of his vest and pulled out the map he received from Aran. Faeven was painted in a world of shifting and moving watercolors. All Four Courts were depicted. All four Crown Cities were rightfully displayed. Then there were dozens of other smaller landscapes, roads, rivers, and...what looked to be fae.

Maeve examined the map. She followed the lines and traced them with her mind. The fastest route to Spring was through the mountains bordering the Summer Court. But the Crown City, Suvarese, was set upon what looked to be a rugged mountainside, located beyond a river and through a wide valley. If they wanted to cross the border unannounced, then it would be best if they circled around the mountains first.

"Alright. We need to decide if we want to launch an all-out attack or take her by surprise."

Lir shifted, adjusted the studded band across his chest. "The less casualties, the better."

"Agreed." Merrick raked a hand through his hot pink hair. "I'm always down for a sneak attack."

Brynn pulled the toothpick from her mouth and pointed at the map. "It does seem to be the best option."

Tiernan, Maeve realized, had been painfully silent. Again. She looked up at him. "Since this is your realm, and we're in your Court, I think it's obvious you should be in charge of logistics."

He ran his tongue along his teeth and brushed an invisible fleck of dust from his sky blue shirt. "How kind of you to grant me permission."

"Oooh." Merrick's gaze shot back and forth between both of them. Lir sat up straighter, and Brynn stared, wide-eyed.

Maeve stood, ensuring the grinding sound of the chair against the smooth stone patio grated into everyone's ears. Then she faced Tiernan, head on. She was done with his quips. With his snarky remarks. With his blatant cruelty. Everything about him was so hot and cold. His mood flared, his temper raged. He was Summer to the extreme. Reckless. Unforgiving. His mood fluctuated with the weather, brutal and deadly. And she was done with it.

"Oh, I'm sorry, my lord." She lifted her chin, refusing to back down from his harsh stare. "Did you have another plan you wished to share with us?"

Tiernan opened his mouth to speak, but Maeve barreled ahead, silencing him. She jabbed her finger into the solid wall of his chest. "I know you find it *so* amusing to belittle me in front of your friends. But why don't we take it a step further, shall we, and tell them how you *made* me perform a mating dance against my will?"

There were a few smothered gasps, but Maeve didn't spare them a glance.

"Your Highness." Tiernan ground her title out between gritted teeth, and his eyes darkened like storm clouds.

She didn't care. It was time all of them knew how poorly he treated her. How awful he truly was to her. Both Casimir and Ceridwen stood, guarded. "Or how you're constantly sneaking into my mind with your snide remarks?" Maeve added.

"Tiernan," Ceridwen admonished. One hand flew to her mouth. "You didn't."

"Or how you nearly left me to drown in the Black Lake?" Anger toiled through her. Fresh and hot. Her blood burned. The curse throbbed against her cuffs. Stifling. Causing her to sweat, and flinch, and shake.

"Maeve." Tiernan spoke her name like a warning. An omen.

"Is that not what you wanted, *moh Ri*?" She curtseyed dramatically, and spat out his title. "To shame me? To flaunt your power over me?"

In the far recesses of her mind, Maeve became fully aware everyone, save for Casimir, had backed away from them. No doubt they feared their High King's wrath.

"Either stand beside me, stand behind me, or get out of my fucking way." She shoved past him toward the doors leading back inside the palace.

"He'd kill me on the spot if I did that," Merrick muttered.

"You're not her." Lir covered his response with a cough.

Maeve whipped back around and the two fae froze. She ignored them. "Cas, please figure this out." She gestured vaguely to the map spread out on the table. "I need to go...hit something."

MAEVE STORMED THROUGH THE PALACE, past the glittering blush walls and turquoise pools, to the courtyard where she trained with Casimir and Saoirse. The sun blared overhead, its sweltering rays no longer a balm but a menace. She plucked a sword from the table of weapons Lir brought to them for practice and attacked the closest palm tree. She swung, rejoicing in the tension against her biceps. With every strike, she extended her efforts. Again and again, so that her arms ached. So that her joints clenched then begged for release. So that her fingers throbbed from gripping the hilt of the sword so tightly, she swore it would snap in half. The poor palm tree put up no fight, but she hacked at its bark, unyielding. Unrelenting. Sweat slid down her bodice, her hair curled and frizzed, and when she could barely lift her arms, when they sagged with agony, there was nothing left but the shredded, peeling flesh of the tree.

Her muscles burned but it wasn't enough. Another swing, but her usually swift movements were sloppy, and she fumbled her sword. She was fuming, furious with herself. With Tiernan. With the entire situation. Every stress, every worry, every fear continued to pile, to mount, to crush her beneath its tremendous weight. Her blood curse pulsed with a life of its own. It fired against her cuffs, frenzied. Wrought with the need to be released. Anger melded with the darkness looming inside her. Vexation churned and bubbled, boiling over so all she wanted was to explode. To expose the world to the monster within.

Maeve tossed the sword aside and tore through the courtyard, ignoring the random faeries within the palace who plastered themselves to the wall in an effort to get out of her way. Her heartbeat hammered, pumped to life with the blood of her enemy. She ran under one of the flowering archways to where the walkway came to an end, to where there was only a ridge of stone about waist-high separating her from the sea. The vast expanse of the Lismore Marin, with its vivid turquoise waters, spread out before her. Endless. Eternal. Below her was a rocky coast, sandy beaches, and the statue of the warrior fae determined to protect his city.

Summer was beautiful. Dazzling. Dramatic.

And it was her own personal hell.

Maeve gripped the edge of the barrier wall, inhaled sharply, and screamed. Unbidden tears streamed down her cheeks, and she screamed again. And when there was nothing left, when her throat was raw and her shoulders drooped from defeat, Maeve dropped to her knees.

Doubt needled its way through her. It pinpricked along her neck, along her spine, sinking its way in, deeper and deeper. She had no idea how to save Kells. There were no books to teach her the art of killing an Archfae. There was no time to learn or study. This was a mistake. Coming to Faeven was a mistake. A complete and utter waste of time. She should've stayed in Kells. At least there she would've been useful. She could've gotten her people to safety. She could've helped to salvage whatever remained. In the distance, she heard the faint call of thunder. For a moment, she thought nothing of it...until she smelled the tantalizing scent of *him*.

Maeve didn't even turn around. She shoved her sweaty, sticky hair back from her face and sucked in another painful breath. "Go away."

"I'm getting a little tired of you telling me what to do."

Maeve stood up, turned around, and ignored the pain that seemed to keep her paralyzed before him. "And I'm getting a little tired of you being a self-righteous dick."

Tiernan closed the distance between them, and his teeth scraped over his bottom lip. "You know nothing about me, Your Highness."

"And you know nothing about me, my lord." Her fists clenched, and her nails bit into the skin of her palm. "I didn't *want* to come here. This wasn't my choice. I didn't ask for the Scathing to ruin my kingdom. I didn't know there were dark fae under the guise of glamour going about their everyday lives within my city walls. And I sure as hell didn't ask to be cursed. But here I am, okay? Here I am, doing the best I can to save my world. I wasn't given an option. Either I went to Faeven in search of this mysterious soul, or my mother was going to kill me. So there you have it. Possible death or inevitable death, and neither of them had very good odds."

She spread her arms wide. "Is that not enough for you?"

Tiernan grabbed her hips and he hauled her against him. The pressing sensation of *fading* slammed into her. Thunder roared, a deafening crack, and the heady scent of magic filled her lungs. She squeezed her eyes shut.

When she opened them, she found herself in what could only be described as an office. If it hadn't been for the sunbeams coating the wooden floor in a golden glow, she would've sworn they'd left the Summer Court completely. The walls were navy blue but completely bare. No artwork. No nothing. A mahogany desk was positioned to overlook the city of Niahvess, there was a small sofa along one wall, and a hearth surrounded by brick on the other. Two leather chairs the color of tobacco sat in front of it, and there was a plush, sandy rug, though she didn't understand why the High King would want a fireplace in his office.

Her legs quaked only slightly, and she trusted herself enough to step forward. Tiernan stood before a small gold pushcart. One shelf was filled with crystal glasses, and the other was stacked with bottles of various liquors. He poured three fingers' worth of amber liquid into two of the glasses.

"Is this your office?"

He ignored her.

"You didn't have to *fade*. We could've just walked here."

Tiernan spun around so fast, Maeve was shocked he didn't spill any alcohol on the wooden floor.

"Shut up." He shoved one of the drinks into her hand.

Maeve took a large gulp and instantly regretted it. The warm rum burned down the back of her throat and unbidden tears sprang to her eyes, but she refused to cough. She wouldn't choke, but the next time she inhaled, it felt like she was breathing fire.

Tiernan paced, keeping his back to her. He propped his elbow up on the window frame and stared down at the city—his city—below. Absently, he swirled the rum in his glass. Once. Twice. When he spoke, his voice wrapped around her like lush silk. "I owe you no explanations."

It was the last thing she expected him to say. If he didn't want to talk about the obvious tension and fury between them, then fine. But if that was the case, he should've just left her alone so she could scream her heart out in peace.

"I wouldn't expect anything less. We've already established that you only care about your Court, and when it comes to anyone else suffering, you're just a heartless bastard." She took another, albeit smaller, sip of the rum, then set the glass down on his desk. "I appreciate the beverage, but I'm going to go and—"

He was on her with dizzying speed. She didn't even have time to react. Her back slammed into the wall, her heart lodged in her throat, and he splayed his hands on either side of her head. His face was inches from her own. Chiseled. Beautiful, but painfully so. And his eyes, endless blue and purple with the gold of the sun, held her in place. "You're not going anywhere."

Dark power radiated off of him and his magic crackled through the air around them, sparking and spitting in rage. She didn't dare cross him, even though there were any number of insults she could toss back at him. But right now, it was just the two of them. It would be too easy for him to kill her. He was quick. Powerful. Deadly. She was in possession of the same attributes, but with one startling difference. He was magical and immortal. She was human and cursed.

"Do you want to know why I have all of these tattoos?" His warm breath coasted over her lips and she detected the pungent smell of alcohol. Apparently, the nearly full glass of rum he poured wasn't his only libation of the day. "I have them because I was tortured."

The sound of ripping fabric filled her ears, and Tiernan tore his shirt off, tossed it aside like garbage.

Maeve tried to push herself further into the wall, away from him, but there was nowhere to go. No way to escape. He stood before her, pinning her body, wearing nothing but boots and a pair of gray pants that hung low on his waist. Golden tattoos crawled all over his sun-kissed skin in shimmering lines of waves, suns, and swirls. He looked crafted from the hands of a god with his broad shoulders, solid abdomen, and narrow waist. His muscles jumped with each ragged breath he took, and he raked a hand through his messy, windswept hair.

"During the Evernight War, my mother, father, and I were captured by trooping fae. They held no allegiance to any Court and to them, we were fair game. I was held captive, while my parents were tortured. I will never forget the sound of my mother's screams." He was so close, his forehead nearly pressed against hers. "They bound my parents to a tree, and dragged me out in front of them. My mother and father had to watch as they sliced my skin with blades dipped in nightshade. Over and over."

Maeve gasped and clamped one hand over her mouth. She knew from one of her books that nightshade was a poisonous flower. On humans, it guaranteed a slow and painful death. And on fae, it was just as lethal. If not cured, it would drain them of their magic. Steal their life force. Over time, they would waste away to nothing, leaving their souls to rot.

"And Ceridwen?" When she spoke, it was a harsh whisper that barely filled the space between them.

"Spared. Her tattoos are of her own choosing, nothing more." Tiernan squeezed his eyes shut. When he opened them, they were aflame with raging fire. "The trooping fae thought I was dead. There's rumor it was my supposed demise that killed my mother. Some say she died of a broken heart and her magic passed to Ceridwen. My father, however, I think he knew better. They left me in the woods to die. But when they killed my father, his magic passed to me. It was his death that ultimately saved my life."

Maeve opened her mouth, but Tiernan jerked his head.

"Don't you dare. Don't you *dare* apologize to me." He eased back, away from her. He grabbed his glass of rum from off of the desk and downed it in one gulp. "So you see, every tattoo covers a hideous scar. Every tattoo serves as a constant reminder of my Court's suffering, of my greatest loss."

She tried to swallow, but guilt coated her tongue like sand. Dry and gritty.

"Now tell me, Your Highness," Tiernan spoke so softly, it reminded her of a lover's caress against her cheek, "who deserves pity more?"

Maeve couldn't think. She couldn't speak. She couldn't fathom such loss, to have to experience such horror. She didn't ask how old he was, because age was merely a number when you were an immortal Archfae. All her life, she'd read that faeries didn't experience emotions the same way as mortals. They had no concept of grief, love, or fear. They were simply beings existing in a separate realm, mindful only of their personal wants, needs, and desires. Yet here was Tiernan, his torment unmistakable, and his suffering caused her gut to clench with sympathy.

"You'll forgive me, Your Highness, for being so...*heartless.*" He looked upon her with cold disdain. With disgust. With repulsion. "My heart was carved out long ago."

A crack of thunder exploded in the study. Maeve flinched and a moment later, Tiernan was gone, leaving her completely alone.

Chapter Twenty-Six

Dawn simmered along the horizon of Niahvess. Pinks and corals set fire to the sky, burning back the fading plum of night. Humidity clung to Maeve's hair and skin, already relentless with the rising sun. Beyond, the sea rolled lazily against the shore, and she could just make out some children running on the sandy beach. Fae children, she noted, were exceptionally fast, despite their lack of powerful magic. She leaned further out over the balcony, watched a few wisps of clouds unravel across the blue sky, and listened to the hushed murmurs behind her.

At the table where they usually dined, Casimir was speaking in low tones with Lir and Brynn. They were talking about possible routes north to Spring, and the inevitable details that would either make or break their journey. Like the fact that the mountains dividing both Courts were rumored to be exceptionally treacherous. The weather was unpredictable, sometimes the roads were impassable, and there was always the threat of dark fae lurking in caves, among other places. Ceridwen was in attendance as well, and

Maeve noticed she looked none too pleased to be awake at such an hour. Her hair was a rumpled mess, her lips were lacking their signature ruby shade, and she stared blankly into a steaming cup of tea.

But Casimir was in agreement with Maeve. They needed to act, and quickly, otherwise Kells and the other Courts would continue to suffer. Tiernan's scouts had returned, but when they arrived in Niahvess, Saoirse wasn't with them. She'd asked to stay behind in Kells, and when Maeve heard the report, she understood why. The Scathing had spread, families and businesses were displaced, and her people were suffering. Already it had demolished the Gaelsong Port, and its decay was slowly devouring areas to the west of the sea as well, inching closer to the Moors. So, Casimir called a meeting early to discuss a necessary plan of attack. Their time was running out, as Maeve knew it would.

"Finally." Ceridwen's usually pleasant voice held a bite, and Maeve turned to see Tiernan stalk out onto the balcony with Merrick right behind him.

He wore black pants, a shirt the color of the darkest part of the sea, and the collar was popped, giving him the look of someone who blatantly did not give a fuck.

"Apologies, Cer." Tiernan inclined his head. "I had more pressing matters I needed to see to first."

"Not sure what could possibly be more pressing at this hour," Maeve muttered, loud enough for him to hear. His gaze cut to her and she held it, daring him to look away first. Tension filled the space between them, enhanced only by their absolute loathing for one another. She leaned back against the railing, kicked one ankle over the other, and crossed her arms. The movement distracted him, just enough for his icy glare to drop to where her bodice displayed her ample cleavage.

All males are the same.

Rolling her eyes to the glow of dawn, she walked over to the table, knowing he watched her every move.

Merrick pulled out a chair for her, then dropped into his own. "You two should just have sex and get it over with." He grabbed a cup of coffee and yawned. "Save us all the trouble."

A blush bled into Maeve's cheeks, but she refused to acknowledge the way every pair of eyes at the table zeroed in on her.

"Merrick." Tiernan's voice dropped an octave, and when the summer breeze whispered through the balcony, it held a distinctive chill.

Merrick looked up, cup of coffee halfway to his lips. "My lord?"

"Do you want to die today?"

"I...uh, no. Right. Sorry. Not my place." Merrick ducked his head and took a hasty gulp of coffee. He winced, no doubt scalding his tongue. He eyed Maeve from over the rim, then winked. "But seriously. You'd be doing us all a favor."

Brynn thumped him in the back of the head. "Shut up, you idiot."

"I have no desire to ever give myself to the High King of Summer." Maeve tossed her chaotic waves over one shoulder, dismissive. "He doesn't fuck mortals. He already made that point quite clear."

Merrick spit out a mouthful of coffee, and Brynn attempted to smother her laugh with a coughing fit.

"Right." Lir blew out a breath, his silver eyes lit with surprise and something that could've been mistaken for admiration. "So, anyway. Let's get this started."

"The weather in Spring is erratic. Volatile. Just like it's High Queen. There's rarely any sunshine anymore, and that will work in our favor." Tiernan paced. His movements were slow and methodical. His boots clicked against the smooth stone floor. "It's mostly damp, wet, and cloudy. Moody, if you will. The Spring Court lost its luster after the demise of the High King and High Queen. It is my belief that with Parisa in power, against the will of the fates, she is gradually destroying her Court. Crossing the boundary into Spring should be done under the guise of a thunderstorm."

Lir nodded. "What of the giants, my lord?"

Maeve balked. "Giants?"

"Don't worry about them." Brynn dismissed her concern with a wave of her hand. "They're mostly legend."

"Yeah," Maeve muttered. "And so were the dark fae."

"There are other ways." Casimir's molten gaze latched onto Maeve and she knew he was about to make an admission. Pain etched the hardened lines of his face, and shadows crowded the beautiful amber of his eyes. Whatever he was about to say, it was a secret. Something he'd never told her. Something he'd never told anyone. Something he'd carried within himself for a long time. "There are passages beneath the mountains. A series of tunnels. They lead straight to the dungeon of Suvarese."

"How..." Ceridwen shook her head. "How do you know this?"

"I was held there once," he revealed. "Against my will."

Maeve covered her hand with his. "You never told me."

"It never seemed like anything worth telling. Worth remembering." He squeezed her fingers. "Until now."

Casimir stared at her, and she stared back, and it was as though an unspoken bond sealed their fate. Together, they would go to the Spring Court. Together, they would slay the High Queen. She'd known Cas her entire life. He'd been her rock when she thought she would crumble. He was her life-saver when she thought she would drown. He taught her to read, and then he taught her to fight. She'd grown from a floundering girl following his shadow, to a woman who knew his every subtlety, his every thought, his every tell, as though it was a mirrored extension of her own.

She thought she knew everything about him. She was certain he knew everything about her. And yet she'd never known the full extent of his past. She didn't know he'd been held in the Spring Court against his will. She knew he was without a soul, that Carman held the strings of his destiny in her hands, but she never thought—never imagined—a portion of his existence had been in captivity within the boundaries of Faeven.

"So." Brynn traced the edge of her dagger with her finger. "Say we make it through these underground tunnels. Say we actually corner Parisa. How do we kill her?"

Lir leaned forward and propped his arms on the table. "Killing her isn't exactly the problem. She's been stripped of her magic. The god of death, Aed, saw to it as punishment for killing the High Queen. But with her controlling the dark fae somehow, it seems she's found an alternate means to maintain power. And that is where the real issue lies."

"The Princess of Kells can do it." Tiernan didn't even so much as blink.

Maeve stared at him. "What?"

"You have the Aurastone. It's imbued with old magic, and has been since the before. Since our creation." He nodded to her thigh, where her dagger was strapped in its sheath. "And it just so happens, I have this."

Tiernan pulled a dagger from one of the five strapped across his chest. Its handle was wrapped in gray leather, and upon first inspection, the blade appeared black as night. But then sunlight reflected off its surface, and a surge of colors broke free. Like a rainbow piercing midnight.

"You didn't tell me you had the Astralstone." Ceridwen's

lips pursed, and a fissure of displeasure left her sullen, if not slightly miffed.

"You didn't ask." Tiernan spared his twin a hasty glance and dropped into the chair beside her. "Besides, Rowan had it for longer than necessary. It most recently made it's way back into my possession."

"Aww." Merrick grinned, and his dimples appeared with a hint of mischief. "It's like you and Maeve are twinsies."

Brynn's hand curled around the sleeve of his shirt, and in one swift move, she jerked him closer to her. "Merrick." She ground his name out between clenched teeth. "Do you have a death wish?"

"Sheesh. Matching is cool." He shrugged out of her grasp, and brushed his shirt where her fingers crumpled the fabric. "That's all."

No wonder the High King was curious about where Maeve found the Aurastone. He was the owner of its other half. Later, if he wasn't tormenting her or inciting her will to kill him, maybe she would ask the same of him. As much as she hated to admit it, she'd be interested in learning the history of both daggers, especially since she'd found hers within the human lands, and it was obviously a fae weapon. Of course, she could always go to the library instead. Surely there would be a book, or some archive she could read. Anything to avoid actually having to have a conversation with him.

"We need to decide when," Lir said, drawing her from her wandering thoughts. "The timing must be perfect."

"We could send a scout." Brynn flashed a ruthless smile in Merrick's direction. "Surely, Parisa has patterns. A weakness, even. She'll fall to complacency at some point. We all do."

"Perhaps the Princess of Kells could ask her new boyfriend." Tiernan sat back, and smugness settled into his painfully beautiful face. "Rowan must have information about the Spring Court and its High Queen. He is in her confidence, after all."

The intentional jab struck true and Maeve's confidence faltered. She despised how smoothly he could get under her skin.

"Yes." Ceridwen nodded. The tea she sipped had seemingly done its job. Her eyes were as bright and compassionate as her demeanor. "I think that's a rather splendid idea."

Maeve opened her mouth to disagree, but Merrick spoke first.

"That's right." He lifted his cup in her general direction. "You can use your feminine wiles against him."

"That's not fair," Maeve countered.

Lir admired the stonework of the balcony. "No one plays by the rules in Faeven, Your Highness."

Casimir gave her hand a reassuring squeeze, then released her. "Didn't he say he wanted to help us?"

"Yes, but—"

"But what?" Tiernan taunted. "You don't want to use him the same way he used you to get back to Faeven? Did you really think he'd help you? That he had any interest at all in saving a human kingdom when his own Court was responsible for its demise?"

Each word he spoke was a barb. A stab at her conviction. A wound to her hope. "I thought he...I mean, he acted like—"

"Like he was in *love* with you?" Tiernan snarled. He jerked himself upright, sent his chair crashing to the ground. "Is that what you truly think? That he *loves* you? Are you worried about breaking his heart?"

"*He is a fae, astora.*" Tiernan's voice filled her mind, callous and wicked at once. "*You are nothing to him.*"

Maeve sucked in a ragged breath and stood. She refused to cower beneath Tiernan's cold-hearted gaze. She didn't care if he suffered loss. His past was no better or worse than her own. He lost family. She lost herself. As far as she was concerned, they were one and the same.

"My feelings are my own," she snapped and kicked back her own chair out of spite. "I'll do it. But not under false pretenses. I'll make sure Rowan knows exactly what I want from him." And then, because she was feeling particularly spiteful, "And I'll ensure he understands *exactly* what I'll give him in return."

Fury ravaged the High King's face. In a flurry of wind, thunder, and heat, he spun around and walked away.

Merrick's brow arched. "I still think you two should do it," he mumbled.

"*Merrick!*" Tiernan's baritone cracked through the sky, and every glass on the table shattered into pieces.

Maeve didn't wait for anyone else. She left the balcony, in the opposite direction of Tiernan. She wanted to be as far away from him as possible, just in case she had the sudden desire to puncture his heart with her Aurastone. Oh, but he was a bastard of the worst sort. Untrustworthy. Irrational. He was moody. Violent. Ill-tempered. He was all the things she hated in a male. And she would be thrilled when she never had to see him again.

Which would hopefully be sooner rather than later.

Maeve wound through the soothing corridors of the palace, and every step past swaying palms, blooming flowers, and trickling streams brought her a sense of peace. A breath of calm. The more distance she put between herself and the High King, the better. All she had to do was survive a few more days. Once she spoke to Rowan, once she uncovered when Parisa was her most vulnerable, then she would be free of the torment that was the fae realm.

Rowan.

She didn't want to think about him. She didn't want to think of the hurtful, antagonistic things Tiernan had said. And she certainly didn't want to believe there was any truth in them. Of course she wasn't foolish enough to think Rowan loved her. Those were the dreams and fantasies of a child. When she was a girl, she would've loved to have been carried off by a fae prince. But now, she knew better. She knew the faerie realm was far more dangerous than she ever imagined. And yet...and yet, she felt certain there was a flicker of affection between them. He protected her. He saved her life. Were those truly the actions of someone who thought nothing of her?

Who deemed her as less than worthy?

Unwelcome emotions seeped into her, leaving her reeling with doubt. Confusion. Uncertainty. And most importantly, trepidation.

Maeve walked into her bedchamber and shut the door soundly behind her, determined to block out all the noise, all the racket and chaos of what she was about to undertake. Her palms slid against the solid wood, and the intricate carvings pressed into her skin. A shuddering sigh escaped her, and she let her forehead come to rest on the door.

What everyone failed to see, what none of them understood, was the entirety of their plan fell upon Maeve's shoulders. She had to be the one to seduce answers from Rowan. Her blade had to deliver the killing blow to Parisa.

All of it fell to her.

All of it, for her people.

And after what she'd said to Rowan in the Autumn woods, she wasn't even sure if she'd ever see him again. There was a good chance he would hate her for giving up on him, for hurting him with nothing more than harsh words. She didn't even know how to find him.

"You look like you've got the weight of the world on your shoulders, Princess."

Maeve's heart lurched, and when she spun away from her door, there was Rowan, with the uptick of a smirk on his devilishly handsome face.

"Rowan."

"Did you miss me?" He spread his arms wide, but she kept her body planted against the closed door.

"You're here." She eyed him coolly. "I didn't think you'd come back."

"Neither did I," he admitted.

Her mouth fell open but he recovered quickly. "That is, I didn't plan on it. I know you think I'm a bastard, and that I've made no efforts to help you find the *anam ó Danua*."

"You're not wrong." She crossed her arms, and focused on his every move. On the way he kept the movements of his body easy and light. How he carefully tucked his hands behind his back as he approached her. "Why are you here?"

"I found something."

"Oh?" She wasn't sure how useful anything he had to offer could be, unless it was a manual on assassinations.

"This." He brandished a book and held it out to her. The leather binding was worn, a mottled brown shade, and the lettering had long ago faded with age. Embossed on the top were two daggers, crossed over one another, and they looked painfully familiar.

"What is it?" she asked, hesitant to reach for it.

"A book I found. In Parisa's library." He shifted on his feet, looking uncomfortable in his skin. "It contains information on your Aurastone. And...the High King's Astralstone."

Her fingers itched to snatch it from his grasp, to devour every word the book had to offer. There'd been no mention of the Aurastone in any of her books, and she didn't even know the Astralstone existed until recently. But a vision of something flashed through her memory. It was foggy, and when she reached for it, the images gradually cleared. It was when they were in the Fieann Forest, when Rowan pulled her from the clutches of the Hagla. There'd been a gleam of something. Like twilight. Or moonlight.

"You had the Astralstone in the forest." Her gaze darted from the book in his hands, to his eyes. "You used it to save me. Against the Hagla."

He nodded once. "I did."

"And it belongs to Tiernan?"

"It does."

Maeve considered this, even as more questions burned in the back of her mind. There was so much she wanted to know, so many things she wanted to ask. Who made the daggers, where were they from? Why does Tiernan have one, and how did Rowan get it? Did Tiernan find his in a lake as well? Those last few questions, however, could only be answered in person. The book wouldn't give her such information. She reached out and he placed the book in her hands. The old tome vibrated in her grasp, reverberated with an ancient kind of magic.

"Thank you."

"Maeve," he warned, but there was no malice.

"I know, I know." She waved him off in dismissal. "You don't want my gratitude. But in exchange for this book...I can think of something to give you in return."

He took another slow, purposeful step toward her. "Is that so?"

"Yes." She held his gaze and refused to lose her nerve. If she wanted to get information from him, it was only fair of her to give him something, too. At least this way, they were both benefiting from the bargain.

Rowan slid the book from her hands and tossed it lightly onto the bed behind him without even looking back. He cupped her face like she was a treasure, something he'd waited for his entire life "And what, dear Princess, did you have a mind?"

"A kiss." She deliberately rubbed herself against him, ensured he felt the swell of her breasts against his solid abdomen.

He slammed both hands on the wall above her head, still refusing to touch her. "Only a kiss?"

She shrugged, a pointed display meant to rouse him. "And maybe other things."

There was no response, and no time to think. His mouth covered hers and he tasted like fresh rain and misty mountains. Tempting and alluring all at once. His fingers threaded through her hair, angling her, deepening their kiss. His tongue traced the seam of her lips, and she opened for him, loving the slight graze of his teeth while he nipped and sucked on her tongue and lips. She arced into him, guiding his roughened palms down to the sides of her breasts, to her waist, then hips. She dragged her ankle up the back of his leg, and hooked it around his waist. Her body was on fire, everywhere he touched was electric, and sent spasms of desire rocketing through her system. Every inch of her wanted him. Every inch of her wanted to be touched. Tasted. She squirmed in his arms, urging herself closer to him, grinding her hips against the hardened length of him.

Rowan groaned and her muscles bunched and clenched. They were wound so tightly, she thought for sure she'd combust. Nerves she didn't even know existed screamed with the need for release. Her breasts ached, and her blood thrummed, wrapping her in a blanket of sexual desire. He gripped her ass, then hoisted her other leg around him so she was anchored against him. He pinned her against the wall. A gasp, and a cry of pleasure, tore from her throat when he wedged his erection snugly between her thighs. Anytime he rocked his hips, he rubbed her budding bundle of nerves, and it was all she could do to keep from whimpering. Between the solid build of his body, and the friction from her leggings, Maeve nearly toppled over the edge.

"Rowan."

"Yes, Princess?" He smiled, and his lavender eyes flashed. He nuzzled her neck, flicked his tongue along the bottom of her ear. Her nails scoured his flesh. "Do you need something?"

She relished in the way his hair moved through her fingers like satin, then she dragged his mouth to her own. Their noses touched, and he inhaled. Expectant. Waiting. Carefully, she ran her teeth along his bottom lip, then sucked it into her mouth. "Do not make me beg."

He swore, briefly. "This is why you shouldn't wear these damned leggings. It makes it far too difficult to get to you when I want."

"I'll keep that in mind for next time."

Rowan looked down at her, and his gaze skimmed every inch of her body. "There's so many laces, and bindings, and buttons."

"Wait." She closed her hand over his when he reached for the leather knot holding her bodice in place. "Not here."

She didn't want Tiernan to know, or hear, or smell. She didn't want him to mock her, or ridicule her for feeling lust for a fae. For a creature she'd been bred to despise. But Rowan wasn't like the rest of them. He saved her. He came back for her. She told herself not to be stupid. She'd spoken with enough fae to know the rules and understand the implications.

There would be no love here, no adoration. It was merely consensual. A basic, carnal instinct. She knew better than to get wrapped up in the vices of Faeven, in believing, in trusting he would always have her best interests at heart. Just as she knew it was a dangerous game, but one she was willing to play. Because for a slice of time, for a moment of her miserable existence, he showed her what it was to be wanted.

"I know a place." He leaned down, threaded his fingers through hers, then grazed kisses along her knuckles. "Do you trust me?"

"Yes."

Rowan pulled her into him, and the rise of magic overwhelmed her. Filled her. The world fell away, blurred out of sight as they *faded*. The colors of Summer whirled around her, a spiral of such intense beauty, her heart started to race. Adrenaline pumped through her veins, fast but fleeting. And when at last she touched back down on the ground, her feet were bare and the whisper of cotton played along her ankles.

Rowan had glamoured her. Gone were her leggings and bodice, with all its straps and laces, and in its place was a silvery blue dress. The fabric was light and soft, a cloud upon her skin. It dipped low in the front, and draped off her shoulders, the sleeves just long enough to cover her cuffs. The gown billowed around her, alive with a magic of its own.

Cool, damp grass tickled her toes, and towering trees stretched up overhead, their full and lush branches an umbrella of shade. Sunlight sprinkled in, dappling the leaves, and a rainbow of flowers unfurled in splendid blooms, soaking up every ray. A river ran along the tall, grassy banks, leading to a waterfall where the pool was such a brilliant shade of blue, it reminded her of crushed sapphires. Her skin sizzled with the kiss of Summer, and when she looked over to Rowan, he was already stripping off his shirt. She drank him in, and a splinter fractured her heart when she saw the depth of his torture. Raised scars twisted along corded muscle. They lashed in ugly lines around his abdomen, cut up to his shoulders, and across his torso. Wounds her mother inflicted.

He caught her watching him.

"I'm sorry." The words fell from her lips like a croak. Apologies would never be enough. There wouldn't ever be anything she could do to remedy him, to erase the memory of what he'd been forced to endure under Carman's hand.

"You," he snatched her hand and pulled her close, "have nothing to apologize for. This is the work of your mother. Not of you."

Her nose stung a bit, a little tingling burn. The promise of tears.

"Ssh, Princess." He wiped away a fallen tear with his thumb, then brushed her cheek. Her lips. "Don't cry for me."

Maeve jerked her head away. Even looking at him felt like an admission of guilt. "I wish I had known, I could've stopped her."

"You and I both know there is only one way to stop her."

One way. Death.

"Want to go for a swim?" Rowan asked, pulling her from her regret. He nudged her toward the shallow pool, but she dug her heels into the soft earth.

"No." It didn't matter if the waterfall looked magnificent, if she could imagine the cool water coasting over her heated body. She didn't care if the air was fragrant with...plumeria, and other bursting blooms. And it wasn't at all appealing to imagine Rowan drenched, with rivulets of water sliding down his chest and back, and the sun glistening off his tanned skin while he hovered over top of her.

Maeve clenched her legs together, but the motion wasn't lost on Rowan. His brow arched in amusement.

"We'll stay where it's shallow, I promise. It'll be just you and me. It's safe here." He smoothed her hair back from her face, and his lavender eyes left her melting against him. "I'll protect you. I'll be right beside you the whole time, and I won't let you drown."

He bent down and planted a kiss where her neck and shoulder met, then trailed the spot with his tongue. "You're safe with me."

Uncertainty kept her rooted in place. She wanted to go into the water with him. She wanted her feet to move. She wanted to be carefree. Wild and reckless. She didn't want to be consumed with doubt, worry, and fear. But it was hard. It was hard to let go of who she'd always been, in order to find the person she wanted to become.

"If you're going to survive in Faeven, you're going to need to know how to swim, right?" He offered his hand again, waited patiently for her to decide.

"I suppose you're right." She wished he wasn't.

"Will you let me teach you?"

Maeve's mind warred with wanting to overcome one of her greatest fears, and worrying she would drown from sheer panic. Dread was the only thing holding her back. Apprehension would keep her rooted on the soft, grassy bank. She'd faced down dark fae, monsters and terrors; she could conquer the water, and she would do it for herself. With one stiff nod, she allowed him to lead her to the dazzling waters of the faerie pool.

Chapter Twenty-Seven

Maeve froze at the edge of the bank and looked down at the pool. Her toes curled into the grass, clutching its emerald blades like they were strong enough to hold her in place. The bed of the pool was made of smooth stones in varying shades of gray, and up close, the flowing water shimmered beneath the shifting rays of the sun. She itched to submerge herself, to sink below its glittering surface. But her boldness was lacking.

Rowan, however, looked completely at home. He kicked off his boots, and when he stripped off his pants, Maeve swore her entire body turned scarlet.

He was *beautiful*.

His scarred upper body remained perfect despite his wounds, and his lower half...well, Maeve had to clamp her jaw shut to keep from gaping. Sinewy thighs gave way to lean calves, and sun and sky, even his backside looked carved from granite. Delicious warmth spread through her once more, and though she'd yet to see the front of him in daylight, she was certain every inch of him would be just as impressive.

Her nipples hardened into tiny little buds out of spite.

One minute he was on the grassy knoll beside her and the next, he was jumping into the faerie pool. His entire body went under and Maeve held her breath, counting the seconds until he reemerged.

Rowan burst through the surface, a smile stretched across his face, and he swam toward her. "Take off your dress, Princess."

Maeve reached for the hem, then paused. "Wait a minute. Isn't this a glamour? Couldn't you just...poof it out of existence?"

His grin widened. "Poof, you say?"

She tossed him a look. "You know what I meant."

"I could, but it's much more fun to watch you undress for me." He moved his arms through the water, treading it around him like ribbons of sapphire, and Maeve found herself stealing a glance below his waist, wanting just a peek.

"If you want to see," his voice drew her closer to the water's edge, "you have to get in."

Lips pressed together, she bunched the fabric in both of her fists, then lifted her arms up overhead. She pulled the dress off slowly, intentionally, pleased to find his eyes had darkened to a lovely shade of blackened purple at the sight of her naked.

Subconsciously, her hand drifted to her thigh. Smooth leather wrapped around her, and her Aurastone was safely tucked inside. He hadn't left her without a weapon this time. Rowan nodded encouragingly. Clinging to the shreds of fear that bound her, Maeve stepped into the pool and the cool water rushed over her ankles and calves, sifting higher to her thighs as she moved closer to Rowan's side. She gasped when it rose over her abdomen, then to the underside of her breasts. The pebbles shifted beneath her feet, and with every step she took, Rowan's smile faded. He moved through the pool, and his hands gripped her waist, pulling her against him.

"You are exquisite." He kissed her lightly on the nose. "And now, we work."

Maeve reared back. "Work?"

"Yes." He gestured behind him, to the wide expanse of the pool. "I'm going to erase your fear of the water."

Panic sluiced over her, but he held her hands inside both of his larger ones. "No harm will come to you. Hold your breath."

"What?"

"Hold your breath."

Maeve squeezed her eyes shut and sucked in a deep breath. Rowan's arm slid around her and then they went under the water together. Immeasurable fear sunk its claws into Maeve, and her arms flailed. She cut through the pool, begging for the surface. And then, as quickly as they submerged, Rowan lifted her up.

Maeve gasped and shoved her wet hair back from her face.

"There. How was that?" Rowan asked.

"Terrifying."

He inclined his head. "It shouldn't be. You moved through the water like you've done it before."

"I have," she admitted.

"So, you *can* swim?"

"Yes." Maeve nodded, then stopped herself. "I mean, no. It's complicated. I know how to swim. I know the basics. I've studied it. And for awhile, I was teaching myself." Like when she found the Aurastone in the hidden lake within the Moors. "But when the water is used against me, when I see it as a threat, I just...freeze up. I panic. It's like I forget everything I've learned, everything I've practiced."

"We need to break past that barrier." Rowan led her out further, to where the water rose up over her chest, and her breathing grew labored. "It's okay, Maeve. I'm right here. Why don't you show me what you do know?"

"O-okay." She inhaled through her nose, blew out through her mouth. It was like moving through sand, but she leaned back and allowed her legs and arms to coast on the surface of the faerie pool. She floated, and the warmth of sprinkling sunlight washed over her, bringing her a sense of calm. Of peace.

"Very good." Rowan's hand slid to the small of her back, beneath her. The pads of his fingers drifted lazily, back and forth, across her butt.

Maeve quaked with tension. It was wrapped tightly, coiled inside her, ready to spring free.

"Can you tread?" he asked.

"I've never been very good at it. I usually sink." Maeve eased herself up from a floating position, and furiously kicked her legs. Her arms moved through the water like lead, heavy and sluggish. The water came up to her chin, then nose, and she sputtered.

Rowan captured her waist, and hefted her up. "You're trying too hard. You don't have to expend so much energy when you kick your legs. Make your movements more languid."

He demonstrated, moving through the water the way a blade sliced through silk. "And for your arms," he continued, "cup your hands like this, so you push the water down and away. It helps to keep your head above the water."

Maeve nodded and tried again. And again, and again. Rowan worked with her on her stroke, so she could cut through the water with more speed. She practiced jumping into his arms at first, and eventually he moved further and further from her reach until she was forced to jump in and swim to him. Her arms were sore, her legs were like putty, and when she grew tired, he shifted her to a back float. She wasn't sure how many hours passed, but eventually, the sun sank into the western horizon and painted the sky in crimson, fiery pink, and soft orange. At one point, Rowan chased her along the spongy bank, and she would be the first to admit that she didn't try very hard to escape him. Her feet slid over the soft grass, and his clever grin set her heart racing.

She barely made it back to the tree before he reached her. His muscled arms encircled her, and swept her up off her feet. A shriek peeled from her lips and then he was running and jumping into the water with her in his arms. They surfaced together.

Maeve lifted her face to the fading sunshine, reveled in its beauty, and her laughter filled the air around them. "Never in my wildest dreams did I imagine I'd be swimming naked and playing in a faerie pool."

Maeve laughed again, and her cheeks started to ache. She couldn't remember the last time she'd laughed so hard. She wasn't sure she ever had, as the sound was almost foreign to her. When she looked back to Rowan, her heart lodged itself in the back of her throat. His lavender eyes blazed with an emotion she couldn't place. Beads of water dripped from his teal hair, slid down his tanned chest. He stood still, completely unmoving, with his broad shoulders set and his arms locked into place beside him.

She shoved her wet curls from her face and dared to speak, worried she'd break the spell around them. Worried she'd shatter the moment. But Rowan's expression was so solemn, so...intense, she couldn't let silence dictate their fate. "What is it?"

His jaw ticked. "You laughed."

"I did." A blush bled into her cheeks. It heated her skin, expanded across her chest.

The water seemed to move *for* him, to bring him closer to her. "I've never heard you laugh before."

"Not many have." Maeve held the heat of his stare. "I almost forgot what it sounded like."

"I'll never forget it."

"Rowan..."

He snared her waist and crushed her against him. His mouth slid over hers in a wet, succulent kiss. Their tongues clashed, exploring and tasting, wanting all of what the other had to offer. His hands roamed freely over her, and every touch was like fire and ice. Heat from his skin. The cool sensation of the water. Cupping her breasts, his thumbs drew lazy circles around her nipples. A whimper escaped her, and she entwined her arms around his neck dragging him closer to her. It was then she felt him. The full, pulsing flesh of him. His erection pressed against her belly, rigid and firm. She wanted to look. To touch.

"I can hear your mind working," he murmured, his voice a balm. "What are you thinking about?"

Maeve shook her head. "I just...I don't want to think anymore."

"That can be arranged."

His hands captured her wrists, lifting them up over her head. Droplets of water rained down on them like diamonds. He maneuvered her into a twirl, a dance, spinning her just enough so she faced away from him. Anticipation stole through her in the form of ragged breaths and clenched thighs. In one motion, Rowan lowered their arms and tugged her back toward him, so her backside was pressed firmly against his chest. His fingers found their way to her neck, tilting her head just slightly to gain access to her throat. Hot lips scorched her skin, searing her with kisses from her ear to her shoulder, and her head fell back against him. Rowan held her there. Marking her. Branding her with his mouth.

But the need between her legs was unbearable. The most basic part of her, the wanton desire, overwhelmed her, left her trembling. She snared Rowan's hand, guided it to her stomach, and lower still. His fingers played across her skin, rubbing, and taunting the bundle of nerves that so desperately sought release.

He chuckled softly, and a rumble in his chest resonated all the way down her spine. "Do you want something?"

"Yes," Maeve gasped, and writhed in his hold. She wanted him. All of him. She wriggled her butt against his erection, urging herself closer, wanting to feel every thickened inch of him. Rowan groaned. Chills broke out over her flesh and her nipples hardened, turning to pink peaks.

"You will be the death of me." He ground the words out, then sank two fingers deep into her core.

Maeve bucked, but Rowan held her in place against him. It was like the reprieve she didn't know she needed. His sure fingers glided in and out of her, over and over, pumping, pleasuring, until she thrashed in his arms. All the while, his thumb toyed with the bundle of nerves begging for attention.

"Rowan!" His name exploded from her like a whisper. An anguished prayer.

"Tell me what you want, Princess." He peppered kisses along her jaw and neck.

"You." The word tore from her lips. "I want you."

"Then it's me you shall have." He slipped his fingers out of her, scooped her into his arms, and carried her out of the faerie pool.

She was grateful for him, for the pure and raw strength of him. She wasn't sure she'd be able to walk. Her legs were like sand, soft and pliable. And her body, every part of her wanted to be marked by his lips. With every touch, every taste, every lick, she wanted to scream his name until her voice was lost to the wilds.

ROWAN LAID her down on the ground, beneath the shadow of the tree. There, the grass flattened for her, and the flowers laid down their petals like a bed of velvet. He hovered above her, his hands planted on either side of her head. She reached for him, tangled her fingers in his damp hair, and pulled his mouth to hers.

He tasted like dreams and darkness. Like magic and fate.

He broke their kiss with haste, leaned down, and sucked her breast into the hot confines of his mouth.

A cry broke from somewhere deep inside her as his tongue swirled over her nipple. Maeve arched up, and she dragged her nails over his shoulders, down his corded biceps, where she held onto him. Her hands sought purchase on any part of him that would keep her grounded, that would keep her from toppling over the edge before he even slid inside of her. His tongue left a trail of liquid heat between the valley of her breasts up to her neck, and this time, he settled himself between her legs. The head of his cock nudged the wetness pooling at her center, and every fold, every nerve, throbbed for him.

"Shit." Rowan dropped low, pressed his forehead to hers. "This is your first time."

It wasn't a question. They both knew the answer already. He'd learned of her innocence in the library. But she nodded anyway, breathless, then squeezed her eyes shut in preparation for what was about to happen.

He wiped her damp hair back, smoothed it from her face. His words were a gentle caress across her cheek. "I can't."

Her eyes flew open. "What?"

Rowan shook his head and droplets of water rained down upon her. "You're pure. And perfect. And..."

The pause was heavy, full of whatever he didn't want to say. Whatever he wasn't willing to tell her.

Maeve propped herself onto her elbows and he lifted himself off her. "So, after all that build up, you're just going to leave me unfulfilled."

He groaned and nudged the hardened length of him in between her legs. "You're not the only one."

"But I'm ready, believe me, I've *been* ready." She rolled her eyes to where the sky was bleeding into dusk, filling the sky with shades of amber and navy blue. "My fingers only take me so far, Rowan."

The sound that peeled from his lips was feral.

"I want to, believe me, I want to take you. I want to pump myself into you over and over, until my seed is spilling down your thighs. Until you scream my name so even the gods and goddesses are raging with jealousy." He kissed her cheek. Her nose. Her temple. Her jaw. "But I can't. I simply can't."

"Fine." Fresh annoyance fired through her, and she flopped back down onto the soft bed of grass and rolled over, away from him.

"What are these little scars here on your back? The ones that look like crescent moons?"

Of course he would change the subject, how typically male. Then she shivered, and he pulled her close to him, keeping her backside flush against his rock-hard abdomen. It took every ounce of effort not to grind her ass against his cock that was so cozily nestled against her.

"I'm not sure." Maeve snuggled closer, relishing in the rise and fall of his chest, in the warmth he offered. "I've had them for as long as I can remember. I think Casimir mentioned an accident of some sort. Something that happened to me when I was younger."

She couldn't really recall and she supposed it didn't really matter. At least, not anymore.

"Hm."

Rowan didn't say anything else and she wondered if he could hear the erratic beating of her heart. With him beside her, she could sleep. She could breathe. She didn't feel the need to be on guard, or sleep with a dagger under her pillow. Because she knew then, within the disquieted depths of her soul, that he would protect her.

Maybe not forever. Maybe for only so long as he chose. But for now, he would keep her safe. Which was why the leaden weight of guilt settled upon her heart, and caused her chest to cave, she roused up her courage to get what she needed from him. "Rowan, I have to ask you something."

"You do love your questions," he mused, and she could hear the smile in his voice.

"I need to know when Parisa is most vulnerable." Behind her, he stiffened. Barely, but it was enough for her to notice. "I need to know when she's weakest."

"You plan to attack her."

Again, it was a statement and not a question.

"Yes."

"When?" he asked.

"Soon." It wasn't a lie, but in truth, the day they chose to undermine the Spring Court would very much depend on his answer.

"As with almost all fae, Parisa is most vulnerable when she bathes."

Maeve started in his arms and he locked them tighter around her. "What? Is that a thing?"

"For most of us. For many, it's a luxury." Rowan moved her curls to the side and nuzzled her neck. "No weapons. No fighting. No thought-provoking, ground-breaking discoveries or realizations."

"I see." She supposed it made sense, but when she washed, she spent most of it in solitude. Thinking. Analyzing. Or worrying. Doing all of the things Rowan said Parisa didn't do. "And um, when is that? I mean, how often does she bathe?"

"Often enough." Rowan tucked her closer, so she was satiated with warmth. "But the best time would be right when the rain starts."

Despite the urge to ask more questions, Maeve felt her eyes grow heavy with sleep. Maybe it was from all the swimming. Or maybe, it was simply because she'd spent an entire day with a fae who offered her comfort, respect, and...

No, she warned herself. Don't even think it.

Love was *off* the table.

"Stop thinking, Princess." Rowan stretched behind her and even though his still-hard erection prodded into her back, a yawn broke apart his words. "Go ahead and sleep. I'll be here when you wake."

His voice was groggy, tinged by exhaustion. Perhaps he was tired, too.

"Promise?" Maeve asked, and let her lashes flutter shut.

"I promise." His hand slid over her belly to find hers, and he laced their fingers together.

Her foolish heart wanted to believe him. To trust him. But everything she read, everything she learned, warned her against it. Seven hells, even Rowan told her not to trust him. When his soft, even breathing settled in the air around them, and the arm and leg that covered hers grew heavy from the weight of sleep,

Maeve stayed silent, and stared out into the darkening forest beyond.

It seemed Rowan made the right decision by refusing to take her innocence. Yes, it made him honorable. But it also made her wary. Because any male, mortal or immortal, who denied the pleasures of sex when it was offered up to him on a silver platter, was never one to be trusted.

Chapter Twenty-Eight

Cool air swept over Maeve's bare skin. It coasted down her spine, across her shoulders, leaving her chilled with pinpricks of goosebumps pebbling all over. She curled closer to Rowan, sought the warmth of his body in her sleep, but when her arm stretched out, it collided with solid ground.

Maeve startled awake, and a jarring spike of adrenaline forced her upright. Instinctively, her hands went to cover herself, but she was alone. The forest was eerily still, and it seemed as though even the waterfall had quieted in the solitude of night. A gentle breeze sifted through the trees, rustled the leaves, and lifted the fallen flower petals around her in a swirl of muted color. Stars littered the sky, some twinkling, some shooting, and with the exception of an occasional flap of wings, Maeve heard nothing but the increasing beat of her heart.

Rowan had left her. Alone. Naked. In a forest.

What the fuck?

Had he seriously abandoned her again, and this time left without saying anything? The fucking fae. A tiny part of her supposed there was a chance he might come back, but the loud voice of doubt within her knew she was wrong. He'd left her. Again. Except this time she was in an unfamiliar forest without clothing and the High King of Summer would not be coming to rescue her. She jumped up and scrambled to the edge of the banks, her fingers clawing through the wettish grass in search of the dress he'd glamoured for her. But there was nothing, and that could only mean one thing. Either Rowan removed the glamour from her, or he was no longer close enough to keep it in place.

She was utterly alone.

She forced herself to breathe. In and out. She allowed the calm of the night to soothe the rapid-fire racing of her heart. It didn't matter if she was by herself, or if he'd left her. Sure, it was a bit of an awkward predicament that she was without clothing, but she wasn't completely defenseless. She had her Aurastone, and it would be enough.

The deafening crack of a twig snapping from behind her zapped all of her feigned confidence, and she pulled her dagger from its sheath. She crouched low along the bank, hating that a slickness seeped from between her legs. A memory of their time together. But her fingers coiled around the hilt of the Aurastone and she narrowed her gaze on the tree line, refusing to be caught off guard. Refusing to show weakness or fear. No matter what, she would *not* die naked.

She held herself to a much higher standard.

Another branch snapped and a shadowy figure bolted out from between two trees, heading right for her.

Maeve did the only thing she knew to protect herself.

A battle cry peeled from her lips and she charged forward.

"Maeve!" A familiar, masculine voice caused her to stumble. She lowered her weapon.

"Cas?"

"Maeve, sun and sky, you're alive." Casimir shoved his hood back and rushed for her. He grabbed her shoulders and held her back, scanning her for injury. "Goddess, I've been looking everywhere for you. What happened? Are you hurt? And you're naked...why are you..." In the moonless sky, in the faint glimmer of starlight, his amber eyes darkened to molten gold. "Rowan," he seethed. "I swear, if he—"

"He didn't." Maeve shook her head, and another spine-tingling chill shuddered through her. She lifted her chin, refusing to be ashamed at having been caught in such a state. Casimir was silent, for longer than he should've been, but then he nodded sharply. "As long as he didn't hurt you."

"He did not."

He slung a pack from over his shoulder. "Here." He pulled out a bundle and handed it to her. "I brought you some extra clothing, but you must dress quickly."

"Clothing?" Maeve reared back. "How did you know I... that we...?"

"Consider it a lucky guess. I'm not blind, Your Highness." He looked away while she unraveled a blouse, a pair of leggings, and some black slippers. "Everyone in Niahvess knows that you and Rowan have a mutual interest in one another."

Despite it all, the heat of a flush burned across her chest. "Yeah, well, I wouldn't call it mutual anymore, considering my current situation." She tugged on the leggings and slippers, then pulled the blouse over her head. "But why am I hurrying? Is something wrong? And where is Rowan?"

Without a bodice or corset, she knotted the blouse at her waist, and when she looked up at Casimir, hard lines etched his face.

"Rowan has returned to Suvarese."

Suvarese. The Crown City of Spring. So, the terrible pit of

341

dread in her stomach was correct. He'd left her to return to his Court. To his *duty*. The amount of crude swear words that spewed from her mouth were so foul, even Casimir blushed.

"Parisa has gotten wind of our plans, and she's attacked the Summer Court again," Casimir continued, unbothered by the sheen of sweat coating her skin. He offered her his hand. "We must leave. At once."

"What? No. If Summer is under attack, we need to stay and fight."

He leveled her with a glare. "Do you remember what happened the last time you tried to stay and fight?"

Right. She'd been poisoned and had nearly died.

"Yes, but if she's in Summer, we need to kill her. To save Kells." Maeve took his hand but tugged him south, in the direction she assumed would return them to Niahvess.

"She is not in Niahvess, Your Highness." Casimir led her in the opposite direction. West. Toward the coast. "All of her forces are on alert. She's raised an entire army of dark fae to do her bidding, and it is no longer safe for you here."

"Casimir, no." Maeve tried to stop but Casimir was stronger. He pulled her along with him. "My duty is to Kells."

He whipped around on her. "And my duty is *to you*. I am here so that you do not die."

"Returning to Kells without Parisa's blood on my hands is a death sentence unto itself! Carman wants me dead—don't you understand that? My own *mother* wants to kill me!"

"Not if you kill her first."

Maeve froze. "What?"

His voice was calm. Collected. "I said, not if you kill her first."

"But even if I do, even if I were to try, it wouldn't be enough to save Kells. To save my people." She wanted to stall, to stop and ask what was happening, to figure out how to fix everything, but Casimir urged her further through the woods. Away from Niahvess.

"I need you to listen to me very carefully, Your Highness." There was coldness in his voice, and a trigger of alarm blared in the back of her mind.

"Okay..." she drew the word out.

He spared her a glance, but continued to barge onward, until the trees thinned to reveal an expanse of rounded gray rocks that rose up from the earth between patches of seagrass and stretches of sand. When he spoke again, she could barely hear him over the call of the sea. "There is no saving Kells."

This time she did stumble, but Casimir was there. He caught her arm and held onto her, looked her right in the eyes, and she thought he ventured further. Into her soul.

"What do you mean?" She tried to swallow the bubbling rise of terror, but the grip of it was maddening. Strangling.

"When Saoirse chose to stay in Kells, Tiernan sent Merrick and another scout back to find out just how far the Scathing had spread since our departure." He paused, and the ache in her heart swelled. "It's overwhelming the city, Maeve. They're in the process of evacuating people to Cantata, south of the Cascadian Mountains."

"Wait, what?" Tiernan sent scouts? Again? It almost seemed unreal. So much so, she didn't believe Casimir. "No. Impossible. It couldn't have destroyed that much of the city so quickly."

"But it *has*. Almost all that remains is the castle, and that's only because the Scathing is having to move upward, along the Ridge." He closed his eyes, and when he opened them again, they were colored with loss. "We will return to whatever is left of Kells. *You* will kill Carman. They will have a rightful queen, and not a sorceress. And then once she is dead, we will return to Faeven...and do what we must."

"Cas, it doesn't make sense. I don't understand." She shook her head, cleared her mind of the ruthless images of her beautiful city plagued with decay and death. "We're in Faeven now, why should we leave when we can just destroy Parisa now?"

"Because." He took her hand, gently encircled it with both of his. "Once Carman is destroyed, my soul will be released back to me. If my soul is released, my full strength will be restored."

"Your full strength?" Maeve stared at the man she'd known her entire life. The one who never aged, who never changed. "What are you talking about?"

"It was the one thing I refused to talk about with you, because I worried you would view me differently because of it." Casimir continued to aim for the edge, where the cliffs jutted out over the calm sea. "When I sold my soul to Carman, my reasons were my own. I was foolish and desperate, and I thought my actions would be enough to save myself. And the woman I loved."

Maeve nearly tripped over one of the protruding rocks, but she caught herself, and stared up at him. "You were in love once?"

He rolled his eyes, ever the annoyed mentor. "Don't act so surprised."

"Sorry, I just—"

"It doesn't matter." He shook his head sharply, swiftly ending that part of the conversation. "What matters is that I'm..."

Casimir hesitated.

"You're what, Cas?"

"I'm a Drakon."

This time Maeve did fall. Her hands hit the soft ground and a laugh bubbled up from her chest. She shoved up from the rocky beach, dusted the sand off on her pants, but when she glanced up, Casimir wasn't smiling. "Seven hells, you're serious."

"Yeah." He shoved his dark, windswept hair back from his face. "I'm serious."

"Oh." She wasn't even sure what to say to him. A Drakon. They were legendary, magnificent creatures with the ability to shift between their dragon and human forms at will. She remembered being fascinated by Drakons as a child, reading all she could about the mythical beasts of wonder who once ruled the skies, seas, and underworlds. They were exceptionally powerful, full of magic, and often lethal. "You never told me."

"Very few know."

"Why didn't you tell me?" She wasn't mad at him for keeping such an extraordinary secret, but the abrupt revelation stung. "Do you not trust me?"

"No." He turned on her then, and took her by the shoulders. Gently. "No, Maeve. It's nothing like that."

She looked up the warrior she thought she knew. Only half of his face was visible, the rest was hidden away beneath the shroud of his hood. "Then what is it like?"

"Drakon aren't always accepted in the human lands, much like fae. To humans, we're seen as the enemy. We're monsters who fly through the night, burning down cities, stealing treasure, and leaving nothing but ash in our wake." His hands fell away from her, and he straightened, never one to show defeat. "Carman hates everything with more power than her. It's why when I traded her my soul for the ability to remain in a mortal form for eternity, she took my power to shift as well. I thought, that is, I assumed, if you knew the truth about me...you'd hate me as much as she does."

"What? Cas, no. That's ridiculous." She grabbed his hand and squeezed. "I could never hate you."

"We'll see." He ducked his head. "You may change your mind when you realize what I am."

"It doesn't matter. But you're right, we need to return to Kells so I can...do what must be done to Carman. So you can have your power restored." She pulled her shoulders back, determined, and ensured her Aurastone was at the ready for when the time came. Her gaze drifted out over the endless horizon, where it was so dark, there was no way to determine sky from sea. "How will we get back to Kells?"

He shifted and lifted his face up to the inky night sky. "I called in a favor."

Maeve followed his gaze, and though her eyes could see nothing but charcoal clouds and a sprinkling of stars, it was from over the crashing waves she heard the cut of a solid mass through thin air. Wings. *Big* wings. Diving down toward her through a swirl of silvery mist was the most incredible winged beast. It possessed the body of a dragon, and its scales were glossy and black. Three heads protruded from its massive form, each one of them reminiscent of an eagle with golden beaks and curved horns. Its fiery wings flapped, then coasted closer, while its tail thrashed soundlessly through the cool breeze. It turned and swooped lower, hovering just above the rocks and sea, and it was then Maeve noticed a rider sitting atop of the creature.

She stepped closer, moving through the densely packed sand. The three eagle heads spun as one, keeping a sharp eye on her every movement. Maeve didn't even dare to breathe, lest she startle them. The shadow of night fell away with a wave of the rider's hand, and he was suddenly illuminated in a crackling glow of crimson. A pair of emerald green eyes focused on her.

"Aran?"

He nodded curtly. "At your service, Maeve of Kells."

"What are you doing here?"

"I told you." Casimir gently took her by the elbow and steered her to where the sand met the sea, where Aran sat upon the beast whose three sets of eyes focused solely on her. "I called in a favor."

"Indeed, you did," Aran agreed. But when he said it, the words sounded wrong. They were laced with spite. "We must go. It will be dawn by the time we arrive in the human lands."

He held out his hand, and Maeve accepted, letting him pull her up onto the winged creature in one fell swoop. Casimir hoisted himself up behind her. In three beating bursts, the beast pitched skyward, and Maeve locked her arms around Aran's waist. They soared in a sea of mist, and the scent of magic—of orange blossom and cedarwood—permeated the air around them, intensifying with every swoop. Midnight clouds drifted past them, and Maeve swore if she reached out, she could touch the stars.

"Aran?" Maeve leaned forward so he could hear her over the breeze rushing past them. "What is this thing?"

He turned his head, and the outline of his handsome face was illuminated by starlight. "This is Effie. She's a *trechen*."

"She's, um..." Maeve's fingers coiled into the soft fabric of his cape when Effie dipped downward. Her scaly body prodded against Maeve's leggings like cold metal discs, sharp and distinct. "She's lovely."

Effie squawked and shook one of her three heads. The pale feathers of her eagle heads glinted and ruffled, poking up like daggers along the length of her necks. Aran tossed another look at Maeve from over his shoulder. "She thinks the same of you."

Maeve opened her mouth to ask where he found her, or where she came from, but a glow of brilliant orange sparked from the coastline of Faeven, like little balls of light. "What's going on down there?"

"That's Niahvess," Casimir said from behind her, his voice devoid of any emotion.

Aran stiffened. "It burns."

Maeve smothered her gasp. Ceridwen was down there. Ceridwen, and Lir. And Brynn and Merrick. And fine, even Tiernan. She couldn't just abandon them, just leave them. She had to *do* something. But Casimir sensed her growing alarm, and his hand came down firmly upon her shoulder.

"Kells and Carman first." His whisper skated past her cheek. "Then we return."

She nodded, but an uneasy lump settled between her chest and heart. Guilt. Kells, she reminded herself. And Carman. She had to take care of her home first. And then she'd come back. Then she'd return to help Faeven. Or at the very least, to help the Summer Court. But as they headed south, toward the human lands, Maeve couldn't tear her gaze away from the beautiful Crown City of Summer, alight with fire and smoke.

THE SCENT of burning wood slowly faded, and was replaced with the stench of decay. Maeve could smell the rot, pungent and acrid, even though Kells had not yet come into view. In the east, the sky was already beginning to lighten, the deep purples and midnight blues of night gradually giving way to the soft, pink rise of dawn. But there was a heavy bank of gray clouds forming over the Gaelsong Sea, and though she kept quiet, her mind screamed. It was a horrible sign. An omen of things to come.

Effie soared downwind and finally, Kells came into view.

At least, what was left of it.

Her heart shattered at the sight, and a thousand shards cut

through her. Pierced her soul. Her city. Her home. There was nothing left, save for the castle atop the Cliffs of Morrigan.

"Cas." She inhaled sharply and behind her, his entire body tensed. She knew he saw it, too. The absolute destruction of everything they loved, succumbed to a plague greater than them both. The Scathing had wrecked all of Kells. The scenic city center, with its brightly colored shops and gurgling fountain, was now nothing more than a crumbling black ruin. Every building was corroded; the plants and flowers were shriveled up and leached of color. It covered the docks, leaving a trail of perishing life in its wake. The Moors were already falling victim as well. The outer barrier of trees surrounding the forest was withered, their branches bare, their trunks bowed over to the breaking point.

Aran guided Effie down, closer toward the balustrade that jutted out over the sea. The entire castle looked dark and devoid of life. There were no guards on outer battlements, and none in the adjoining courtyards within the mighty walls. There was no laughter or music. No steady thrum of voices rising up from the city and carrying on the wind. An eerie hush wound its way through the grotesque remains of the streets, save for the scampering of vermin and other unfavorable creatures. It was as though the hand of death had left its mark throughout Kells.

Effie circled lower, and her fiery wings cut through the early morning like ribbons of fire. She swept down to the balustrade, to where the stone banister curved into miniature arches. Roughened granite pavers spiraled out from ivory pillars to Carman's empty throne room, but when Effie swooped lower and hovered above the terrace, Maeve noticed a figure dressed all in black approaching them. A silver braid tossed over her shoulder.

Saoirse.

"Saoirse!" Maeve waved frantically, and nearly toppled off Effie.

Casimir hopped down from the *trechen*, landing soundly on the balustrade. He reached up, took Maeve by the waist, and plucked her off Effie's back.

"Fair winds, Maeve of Kells." Aran tugged on Effie's corded reins and she lifted higher, away from them.

"Wait, you're leaving?" Maeve spun around. An unnaturally cold wind picked up from off of the sea and barreled into them.

"I must." Aran inclined his head, and a rush of shimmery auburn hair fell forward. He swept it back from his face, and when his brilliant eyes found her, they softened. "Perhaps we'll see each other again soon."

"Yes. Perhaps."

Effie lurched into the sky, taking Aran with her, and Maeve waved. But he didn't look back. And she watched as they disappeared in a mist of silver and magic.

"Maeve!" Saoirse called out, and the loud clacking of her boots echoed across the granite. "Maeve!"

She turned to see Saoirse running toward her. Her summer blue eyes were wide, and there was a slash of red along the side of her beautiful friend's face. The wound looked fresh, barely healed, and the skin surrounding it was angry with red splotches. The slice ran from the outer edge of her eyebrow, down to her jaw. There was some slight discoloration under her eyes, a bluish-green shade, the remnants of a bruise. Exhaustion tugged at the lines of her face, and the closer she got, the more Maeve realized it wasn't surprise that reflected in Saoirse's eyes.

It was fear.

"Saoirse, what happened to you?"

"Carman happened to me." Pain clouded her friend's face, like a memory she didn't want to relive. But then her arm shot out, and she pulled Maeve closer to her, away from Casimir. She ducked her head low, and her harsh whisper scoured Maeve's skin. "Maeve, what are you doing here?"

"What do you mean?" Maeve searched the warrior's face for something, anything that would explain why Saoirse was acting like she was committing treason. "I came back for Kells. And for...other things."

Other things she wouldn't mention out loud, because all walls within the city had ears.

"You shouldn't be here." Pieces of Saoirse's braid fell loose, and it was then Maeve noticed her flower. Instead of the usual bright bloom tucked behind her ear, she was wearing a half-wilted black rose. "It's not safe."

"Nowhere is safe." Maeve tossed a look over at Casimir, who turned away from them. He faced the horizon, where the sun seemed to halt its rise mid-air. "I've come to help."

"No. No, no." Saoirse shook her head violently. "You should go now. You need to leave. Before she finds out."

"Saoirse." Maeve pulled back, away from the paranoia oozing off of Saoirse in heavy waves. "What is going on?"

A low, familiar laugh echoed across the terrace. It was a petrifying sound Maeve knew all too well. It was Carman, and the noise she made was not one of amusement. It was that of victory.

"It's a trap, Maeve." Saoirse's voice cracked. Dread sank deep into her features. And when she took Maeve's hand, her skin was slicked with cool sweat. "A trap."

Chapter Twenty-Nine

"**A** trap?" Maeve shook her head. Such a thing was impossible. No one knew they were coming back. "What are you talking about?"

"She's talking about you, wretched girl." Carman stalked across the terrace, flanked by ten soldiers on each side. Her raven hair was twisted high into a tightly coiled bun, her strapless gown draped around her like graying clouds, and a black cloak tumbled to the ground around her. The virdis lepatite pinned to her chest burned bright, in a sickening shade of green. "How dare you return here without the soul."

Maeve stepped back as the guards circled around her, separating her from Casimir and Saoirse, a lethal wall of silver and night. Each of them approached her with swords drawn, the tips of their blades aimed true. Distrust and anger shaded their faces. Faces she recognized. Names she knew. All of them now turned against her.

"I searched for the *anam ó Danua* as you requested. But it won't save Kells." Maeve longed to reach for her Aurastone, but didn't dare. One slip, one wrong move, and she'd meet her death. "Rowan was mistaken."

"Don't lie to me!" Carman shrieked. Distorted veins bulged along her neck; they wrinkled her hands and aged her hideously. "Three weeks you were gone! Three! And with nothing to show for it. You abandoned your city. You left your people to die. Tell me, Maeve, how many innocent lives do you think were stolen, while the Scathing ravaged Kells, while you wasted time in Faeven?"

Maeve inched away from the soldier with the tip of his blade nestled at her spine. "I didn't think—"

"Enough!"

Carman's hand shot out and an invisible grip tightened around Maeve's throat. She gasped, but the pressure only increased. She clawed at her neck, thrashed violently against Carman's dark magic. But the sorceress only smiled, closing her hand into a white-knuckled fist. Maeve's knees slammed into the solid granite of the balustrade. Her chest was too tight. The air wouldn't come. Her vision blurred, a warped convulsion of shapes and darkness. Above her, the sky roiled with anger. Cold wind bit her cheeks, harsh pelts of rain slashed across her face. Death had finally come for her and yet...

Vaguely, she made out Casimir's form coming closer. His hood was pulled down low and she could barely see the bow of his lips. When he spoke, his voice was hushed and quiet, words meant only for Carman. Whatever he said, whatever he promised must have convinced Carman to spare Maeve's life. She relented her power, slamming Maeve's oxygen-deprived body onto the hard stone. Pain spasmed through her, ripped through her back and neck. It tore into her shoulders and head. Delirious stars danced in front of Maeve's eyes, and when she rolled onto her side, a coppery, metallic tang filled her mouth. Blood. It's sticky, wetness trickled out from the corner of her mouth, and slid down to her chin. Drops of freezing rain pelted her. Ruthless and unforgiving.

Above her, Carman's lips peeled back into a wide sneer.

"I don't..." Maeve wanted to speak. She wanted to defend herself. But her tongue was too thick, and the words wouldn't form.

"Tell me, Maeve. Do you know what happened after the Evernight War? After the dark fae attacked and caused the Four Courts to turn against one another?" Carman paced in a slow circle, ensuring every click of her heels echoed off the stone and reverberated in Maeve's head. The storm assaulted them, but Carman didn't falter. She seemed to revel in the malicious weather, marveling in its fury. "Do you know of the plague that ravished Faeven once they finally realized the dark fae were the source of all their problems?"

Maeve dragged herself onto her hands and knees, and stared at the vile woman who was her mother. She spat, and bloodied saliva coated the granite. Rain drops smeared it away in a river of water and blood. She wouldn't give up. She would never give up for Kells. She would fight, if it meant every bone in her body would break, if it meant she took a thousand blades to the heart. A tremble threatened to take her knees out from under her, but she pulled herself upright and stood before the sorceress. The wind barraged her, gust after stinging gust, and a chill took hold deep in her bones. Her soaked clothing clung to her skin, but she lifted her chin and kept her head held high.

She held her mother's wicked gaze. "What of it?"

"It was me. It was *all* me." Carman threw her arms out, and wind barreled across the balustrade. She tilted her face to the sky, and a maniacal laugh ripped from inside her. Her hair came unbound, whipping around her like gnarled, tangled vines. The rain grew sharper, hammering against them. Drenching them. And the virdis lepatite blared a hideous green. "I invaded Faeven when they were broken, and bloodied, and still collecting their dead from the battlefield of war among their own kind. It was my realm to conquer. To defeat. Ruling Faeven was to be my legacy."

Maeve's mind whirred like a clock spinning out of control. *Her* mother was the plague? Carman was the reason for all of the suffering, for the darkness, and despair? But it was impossible. Such a task would require an unmatched force of strength, and Maeve knew the exact number of soldiers who fought to defend Kells. It was nowhere near the necessary number to overthrow an entire realm...unless she had help. Unless there was a dangerous, more powerful, underlying force offering her assistance.

Carman strode to the center of the human barricade surrounding Maeve. A soldier stepped forward, carrying a small brown bowl in his hands. Every so often, ducking between the stiff shoulders of the armed guards, Maeve caught a glimpse of Saoirse's silver hair, but she couldn't see any more than the top of her head. The soldier with the bowl stood beside Carman, his face expressionless, devoid of any emotion. But there was the faintest tick in his jaw. A tell. He was... displeased? Angry?

"Such an odd turn of events." Carman drew a slim blade from the folds of her cloak. Her cold gaze skimmed the cloth-bound hilt, admiring it. "All this time, I wanted you dead. And as it turns out, I need to keep you alive."

A bizarre sensation cut through Maeve, and she wasn't sure if she should be relieved or afraid.

Carman held her hand over the proffered bowl, the blade placed directly above her palm. "Now, to bring them back."

Maeve startled. "Bring who back?"

Her mother cut her down with an obsidian gaze loaded with malice. "My *sons*."

Sons? She had *brothers*? Siblings? And not once had Carman ever thought to grace her with such knowledge? Maeve's gaze sought that of any soldier who would meet her eye, anyone who would confirm such a claim, but not one dared to look in her direction.

Carman gripped the edge of her blade, and with a hiss, she sliced it down the center of her palm. Scarlet blood oozed down her alabaster wrist and dripped into the waiting bowl, mixing with the steadfast drizzle of rain. Thunderclouds tormented the skies, building layer after layer, swallowing the atmosphere like a mass of impending doom. The soldiers banded together, tightening their ranks, ensuring Maeve's capture. Over the roaring wind, Maeve heard someone yell her name in the distance. She sought a silver-haired girl from beyond the human barricade, but Saoirse was nowhere in sight. Casimir stood along the outer edge with his hands tucked behind his back. She couldn't see his eyes, they were shrouded beneath the thick fabric of his hood—but she felt them upon her. She knew he watched her every move.

Carman pointed one sharpened nail at Maeve. "Bring the girl."

She didn't even have time to fight back. Two soldiers grabbed her, clamped down on her shoulders and pinned her arms to her sides, restricting her. She struggled against them, but their fingers only sank further into her skin, clenching and digging, tightening their grip. Carman snatched her wrist and pried open Maeve's clenched fingers one by one.

"What are you doing?" She watched in horror as Carman cut the blade into the flesh of her hand. Maeve yelped as the serrated edge ripped through her skin like it was tanned leather.

"What I should've done years ago. Best to move quickly before the fae blood closes your wound." She squeezed and

Maeve's blood dripped from the tips of her fingers into the bowl. In one swift movement, Carman ripped the virdis lepatite from her cloak and dropped it into the swirling red mixture. The concoction of blood and dark magic gurgled. It bubbled, foamed, and hissed. "Set the bowl down quickly, you fool!"

The soldier holding it immediately lowered it to the ground, placing it right in front of Carman. He backed away, stumbling for a position within the ranks that was furthest from the spewing bowl. The guards who held her dragged her away from Carman, tugged her to the other side of the circle. The fear among them was palpable. No one seemed to know her intent, but her onyx gaze was now rimmed in red, and tears of blood were streaking down her pale cheeks, only to be washed away by the rain.

"Blood of my blood, life of my life. Bring back the darkness, the pain, and the strife." Carman lifted her voice and started reciting the verses of a spell. "Blood of my blood, sons of my soul. Take from me, whatever the toll."

At those words, her hair turned snowy white, streaked with messy threads of gray. Her shoulders hunched forward as the years of her life slipped away. She withered before them all, becoming a shell of her former self. Bulging black veins marred her arms and crawled up her neck. Wrinkles scoured her face, settling around her eyes, hollowing her cheekbones. Within seconds, Carman was no longer an eternally youthful sorceress, but a haggard old crow. Near her feet, shadows rose up from the blood bowl, large and imposing masses that gradually took shape. The shape of three men. All of them possessed midnight hair, so dark it was nearly blue, and obsidian eyes like their mother. They were clothed in the shadows of night. Their bodies jerked and spasmed to life, their anguished cries ripped through the storm, and a frightening alarm sounded in the back of Maeve's mind.

She'd seen these men before. These *brothers*. She'd seen the harrowing darkness that shrouded their every move. The destruction they left in their wake. The trail of death behind them. *Darkness. Destruction. Death.* These men were in the paintings in the castle's library. Their demolition of worlds, their massacre of lives, was forever entombed and displayed as a reminder of the terror they brought upon Faeven under Carman's rule. For her, it was an oath. A promise of her selfish vengeance.

Saoirse shouldered her way through the blockade of soldiers, her sword drawn. But then her gaze landed on the three males swirling up like shadows before them. Her blue eyes widened, and her mouth fell open in shock. Maeve stumbled back into the guards restraining her. One of them faltered, and loosened his grip. The other sucked in a sharp breath, muttering a stream of foul words and prayers to the goddess for mercy. It seemed as though none of them knew what Carman had planned. No one, save for Casimir.

He stood off to the side. Unbothered. Untroubled. As though spirits were brought back from the dead every day.

"Balor. Tethra. Dian." Carman's papery lips stretched into a smile, cracked and bleeding. "Blood of my blood, behold the magic for thee. Rise now and breathe, pledge your lives unto me."

The brothers took full form now. They towered over every soldier, even Casimir, and black, bulging veins protruded from their bodies. Their eyes were cold and empty, bereft of emotion or feeling. Only one of them drifted forward toward Carman, and his feet never touched the ground. It was as though he was caught between two worlds, that of the living and of the dead. Restless. Frightening and furious all at once.

"No." The one named Dian spoke first, and his gravelly voice was coarser then the rugged Cliffs of Morrigan.

Carman's smile thinned, and she craned her neck forward. "What did you say?"

"I said *no*." Dian's vast frame overcrowded her, and the sorceress shrank back. "We will not pledge our lives to you. We did so once before, and look where it got us."

The other two brothers, Balor and Tethra, growled their assent.

"You will obey me," Carman snarled, and the handful of soldiers closest to her stepped back, retreating away from her. "Together, we will invade Faeven once more. Together, we will take back what I am owed. I brought you back. I gave you life!"

Dian laughed, and it caused the granite beneath Maeve's feet to shudder and crack.

"Foolish woman," he scoffed, and he shook his head in mockery. "*You* did not give us life. *She* did." He inclined his head to Maeve. "And therefore, we answer to *her*."

"*No!*" Carman shrieked. She coiled her bone-thin fingers into fists. "I will not have my sons answer to a *faerie*!"

"I'm not fae!" But Maeve's voice was lost in the collective disturbance that rushed through the soldiers. Their suspecting gazes slid from one another before latching onto her. The one holding onto her arm threw her down and the loud crack of bone meeting granite echoed in her ears. Someone cried out in agony as she slid against the wet balustrade. She thought the horrible sound might've come from her. The burning sensation of the healing fae magic was almost too much. Her shoulder was on fire. Throbbing pain blinded her, her vision swam, and darkness crept in from the outskirts of her line of sight. It threatened to drag her under, to take her into the oblivion of her subconscious.

"Maeve!" Saoirse's scream ripped through the fury and she charged forward. One soldier reached to stop her, but she cut him down without a second thought. Two more attacked. She swung and parried in a devastating display of stealth and grace. Blood colored the ground a murky shade of rust. But she was far outnumbered.

"Saoirse, no!" Maeve sought purchase on the slippery stone, but her stomach heaved when the nauseating crack of metal and bone sounded in her ears.

The beautiful warrior crumpled to the ground; it took four of them to bring her down.

"Saoirse!" Maeve tried to crawl to her, to see if she was still alive, if she was still breathing, but the toe of Carman's boot met her cheek. Maeve's head snapped to the side and hot blood poured from her mouth.

"Wretched girl." Carman grabbed a handful of Maeve's hair, and her dagger-like nails tore into her scalp. She dragged her up off the ground and angled Maeve's head back. Cold drops of rain cleared her eyes, washed away the wave of dizziness. Icy metal chilled her flesh, and the bite of a blade's edge pressed to the base of her throat cleared her mind. "I should kill you for what you've done."

"I haven't done anything!" Maeve protested, knowing this moment, when Carman was filled with rage, would be her only opportunity.

Maeve didn't waste another second. In one fluid movement, her fingers curled around the hilt of her Aurastone and she tugged it free. Her elbow jerked back with purpose and she plunged the dagger into Carman's heart. Her mother clenched, her frail husk of skin and bones trembled. The blade poised at Maeve's neck fell away, clattering to the ground. Rancid fumes poured from Carman. Curls of fetid green vapors exited through her nose, her mouth and ears, and from the gouge in her chest. She shriveled to the ground, writhing like a snake, until her garbled breaths ceased, and what was left of her decaying body turned to ash.

"She murdered the queen!" someone shouted, as Maeve watched the rain rinse away the stains of blood from her Aurastone.

"Seize her!" cried another voice.

"You," a fearsome snarl cut through the increasing fray of soldiers, "will never touch her."

There was an audible snap, and the accompanying bellow was almost inhuman. Maeve whipped around and clamped one hand over her mouth, but nothing could hide the horrific scene in play before her. Dian ripped both arms off one of the guards, leaving gaping holes filled with shredded cartilage and tendons seeping from either side of the man. Acidic bile surged in her stomach and clawed at her throat. She heaved once. Twice. She fought the urge to vomit, but the scent of blood clogged her nostrils, and then the screaming started.

She stumbled back, away from the carnage and chaos, until her back met the balustrade railing behind her. She gripped the frozen metal, held on while her fingers burned. Saoirse's body had yet to move, and blood pooled beneath her fallen form.

Her mind was a wreck of irrational thoughts, torn into a million illogical explanations. Her gaze shot from the bowl of blood to the three brothers murdering soldiers like they were rag dolls, to the jagged slash across her palm. The same wound her blood curse had already healed. But it didn't make sense, none of it made sense. In all of the books she read...there was never even a discussion of necromancy. It was thought to be folklore, myths from the days of before. She stared down at her open hands, to where the gash from Carman had healed, revealing no injury at all. It was impossible. Something was wrong. She shouldn't hold that kind of power. Her fae blood was not a blessing. It was a curse.

She was a monster. A danger to all around her. Yet somehow, she'd brought three grown men back from the dead. Her blood was the key to giving them life. Carman hadn't been strong enough to do it on her own. All along, she'd *needed* Maeve, but she hadn't known it at the time. Carman had wanted to kill her. But how...

Rowan's voice drifted through her thoughts—something he said before they started the journey to Faeven, when they were standing within the walls of the throne room.

"The anam ó Danua is unrivaled. It is the one true source. The lifeblood of fae magic."

No.

"Time to go," a familiar voice whispered in her ear.

Casimir.

"Go," she repeated, numb to the notion that she'd just slaughtered her own mother in cold blood. That her best friend lay on the ground, dying. "Where are we going?"

"Away."

Away. Yes. She needed to get away from here. Far away. She was a murderer. Treasonous in every aspect of the word. It didn't matter if Carman was going to kill her first. The soldiers of Kells would never bow to her now. They would never respect her. She'd slain their queen in cold blood, and considering she used the magic coursing through her to bring three fearsome warriors back from the Ether—the land of lost souls— she would never trust them enough to ensure they wouldn't assassinate her in her sleep.

"Come, Maeve." Casimir took her hand. "Before it's too late."

"But...Saoirse."

"Leave her."

No. She didn't want to leave her friend behind. It was no longer safe in Kells. She had to get to her. They could bring her with them, back to Faeven.

"Cas, wait." Maeve tried to pull her hand from his grasp. "Saoirse. I can't leave her here. We can still save her. We can—"

But a spark flashed before her eyes. There was a puff of pink smoke, and then she was encompassed in crushed leaves. Sandalwood. And...and...patchouli.

Faintly, she thought she heard Casimir apologize before she lost herself to delirium.

Chapter Thirty

Voices hovered above Maeve, a mix of indistinct words and hushed whispers. They floated down to her, drifted around her like an early morning fog rolling in from off of the Gaelsong Sea. Dense. Mysterious. Untouchable. Muttered responses were met with soft laughter, but the sound of it was off. It was brittle and unpleasant. Her temples pulsed at the noise, a nauseating ache that stretched around to the base of her skull. Heaviness pulled her, and her head lolled from one side to the other. Cautiously, she blinked her eyes open. Darkness consumed her, and her vision strained in the dim light. She was seated upright in a chair, but her ankles were bound together with rope, and her arms were tied behind her back. She was a captive. A prisoner.

But where?

And why?

Floor-to-ceiling metal bars proved she was locked in a cell. Stone walls lined the other three sides of the room, and there was a distinctively musty, earthy smell, which could only mean she was far underground. A steady *plop plop plop* dripped from somewhere nearby, but other than the thatch of old hay against the far wall, she couldn't make out much of anything else. Faint amber light glowed from a hanging lantern and reflected off the puddle of an unknown substance on the uneven floor.

Maeve forced her gaze up, and caught sight of movement by the cell's door.

"She's awake," a gruff voice called out.

Footsteps approached, timely and powerful. The harsh scraping of boots and stone. Two other figures appeared, while a third fiddled with a key. Clanging and grinding metal filled the empty dungeon, and with a sudden click, the door to her cell groaned open.

"Well, well." A feminine voice slid through the stillness and the tiny hairs along the back of Maeve's neck stood on end. "I've been looking for you for a long time, Maeve of Kells."

She snapped her head up and instantly regretted it. Pain splintered down her neck and her vision blurred, like a dingy, smeared watercolor. "Who are you?"

A hysterical sort of giggle erupted from the female, who lurked under the guise of shadow and the trick of muted light. "Did you hear that, boys? She doesn't know who I am."

Dread curdled like spoiled milk in Maeve's stomach, and when the woman stepped into the haze of amber, she immediately knew why. *She* wasn't a woman at all. She was fae. Slender and pale with ashen skin, she glided over to Maeve with the practice of purebred royalty. Her long and pointy ears were decorated with tiny silver diamonds that mimicked raindrops, and her dark brown hair was cut into a severely angled bob, with longer pieces framing her sharp features. Glowering eyes of honey were lined with kohl, but it did nothing to hide the folds of exhaustion sagging at her flesh. She wore a gown of plain, emerald green velvet that outlined her svelte figure. The neckline dipped low and silver beads studded the shoulder straps.

A trigger of warning burrowed into Maeve's subconscious. "Parisa," she breathed.

"Oh, good!" Parisa clapped her hands twice. "You *do* recognize me. How wonderful." She lifted one shoulder and gestured vaguely behind her. "But where are my manners? Allow me to introduce you to Kane and Fearghal, two of my very close, and *very* personal friends."

Fearghal...she'd heard that name before, but whenever her mind reached for it, whenever she tried to recall the memory, it slipped further away.

Her gaze cut to Kane and Fearghal, the two male fae Parisa had just introduced. One of them watched her with a sternly arched brow of disbelief. The other stared at her like she was a piece of sweetened summer fruit, prime for picking. Her skin crawled, uncomfortable with the way his eyes lingered over every inch of her. She adjusted her wrists, maneuvering them against the secured rope, and her cuffs clanged together.

"Welcome to Suvarese, darling. Crown City of the Spring Court." Parisa's close-lipped smile looked steeped in poison. "Though I am sorry about your current arrangements. I know dungeons aren't the most ideal accommodations, but it's only temporary. Just until we get you...situated."

"Situated?" Maeve straightened in the wooden chair. "What are you talking about?"

Parisa blinked. "My, for a princess, you certainly lack decorum. Tell me, were you not raised to address other nobility of a realm by their proper rank?"

Shit. She couldn't afford to piss off the High Queen of Spring. "Forgive me, my lady. The pink powder left me in a bit of a trance."

Pink powder. Casimir. Where was he? And what had

happened to him? To them? She tried to search her memories, but everything from before she woke up was indiscernible. The images were there, but they were murky and out of order. Thinking on it too much caused splitting pain to pound into the side of her temples once more.

"Yes, *spraedagh* can have that effect on those whose magic is stifled." Parisa clasped her hands together in front of her, prim and proper. The perfect image of a princess. "Now, back to your previous question. First, Fearghal is going to remove your cuffs, and then—"

"What?" Maeve's voice pitched with panic, but Parisa's brows lifted. A quiet reminder to remember her place. "I mean, I'm sorry, Your Highness. But I don't know if taking my cuffs off is a good idea. My blood is cursed."

"Is that what she told you? How absurd." The Archfae's perky little nose wrinkled in disgust and she circled Maeve. "You, my darling, have everything I want and need. And all of it has been kept suppressed by these." She tapped her nails against Maeve's cuffs.

"I'm afraid I don't know what you're talking about."

"Of course you do." Each step brought Parisa closer to the cell door while Fearghal inched closer to Maeve. "Don't you want to be free now that Carman is dead? Don't you want to know what kind of power truly lurks beneath the magical cuffs bound to your wrists?"

She did, with all of her heart and soul, but she didn't want Parisa and her minions to be the ones to do it. She would have to defer and find a way to stall this madness. "What if I can't control it?"

"That's where I come in." Parisa dragged her fingers along the cell's metal bars and her nails clinked in warning. "I have been hunting for you since I first felt that which was taken from me breathe again. It was why I sent Rowan in search of you. It was why I would stop at nothing to find you."

Maeve's heart quit on her.

"You...you sent Rowan to hunt me down?" Rowan. Rowan had been sent to find her. To capture her. To bring her back to Faeven. Cold sweat beaded along her forehead, and she struggled for air within the dank walls of the cell. No. He wouldn't... it was too much. Too awful. He wouldn't stoop so low. All the things he'd said, all the things he'd done. The crushing weight of despair lodged itself somewhere between her heart and lungs. But Casimir...When Cas found her in the summer woods, he told her Rowan returned to Spring. What if he intended to turn her over to Parisa? And perhaps he would have done so, if Casimir hadn't found her first.

"Where is Casimir?" Maeve demanded.

"Now, don't you fret." She pulled the key from the lock and tossed it to Fearghal. "We've got a special room just for him."

Fear gripped her, an icy-cold vise that slicked her skin with frost. "If you hurt him, I swear it, I'll kill you."

Parisa tossed her head back and laughed, then pretended to wipe away a fallen tear. "You're simply too much, you know that? No wonder so many adore you." Her honeyed gaze landed on Fearghal. "Take them off."

Maeve struggled against her bindings but there was no give, and the ragged threads of rope rubbed her flesh raw while her attempt at escape failed.

"Oh, don't worry, darling. I have no intent on keeping you hostage. You're only down here in the dungeon so no one can hear you scream." Parisa's head tilted, considering her. Then she smiled, and it was terrifying. "We're going to be the best of friends, just wait and see."

"Let me go!" Maeve jerked back and forth, but she couldn't

break free. Something hot and wet slid down her hand, and the rope dug deeper into her skin, burning it.

Parisa gathered up the hem of her dress and swept out of the cell, with Kane following in her wake. "Send for me once it's done."

Fearghal nodded.

"You can't do this!" Wrath ripped through Maeve, and darkness bloomed in her chest. She would set the Spring Court ablaze. "You'll never get away with this! You'll watch your beloved city burn, and I'll be the one to set it on fire!"

Tinkling laughter answered her.

"We'll see," Parisa hummed as she disappeared into the pitch black of the cavernous dungeon.

The rush of turbulent anger melted into bitter fear when Fearghal stood before her. In the dismal shred of light, corded black veins ran up and down his arms. A set of curved horns protruded from his head, curling away form his long ears. His eyes flickered over her, and he pulled a dagger from the band at his waist. It glowed like iron burning over a molten core. "I think I liked you better when you were dancing."

Dancing?

Maeve's heart plummeted into the acidic ball of fire burning in her stomach. Oh no. Dancing. That's where she'd heard his name before. He was the fae Tiernan protected her from when she'd been by herself at the Autumn Ceilie. He was the one who'd been watching her, waiting to pounce. She paled.

"So, you do remember me? How nice." He smiled, displaying a set of pointy teeth. "Let's see what the sorceress has been keeping from us, shall we?"

There were few moments in Maeve's life where she humbled herself enough to beg, and seeing Fearghal with malevolence enhancing his every move, stooped her to such a level. "Please don't do this."

He spread his hands wide and the blade banked like embers. "A shame you ask so nicely, but orders are orders."

"You don't have to follow them." If she could just keep him talking, maybe she could convince him not to follow through. "You can free me. You can let me go. You could come with me."

He gathered up Maeve's hair and she stilled, holding her breath until he draped all of it over one shoulder. "Wouldn't want to ruin your pretty hair."

"Please, Fearghal. Please don't do this."

"But I enjoy it." He grinned and flashed his fangs once more.

Maeve reared back. "Anything," she blurted out. "I'll do anything. I'll make you a deal, anything you ask."

He bent down and peered up at her. "That's a rather dangerous ask, don't you think? Entering into a pact with a fae you've never met, and offering him anything in return."

Her chin jutted up. "I always stay true to my word."

Fearghal stood abruptly. "Then you're a fool."

Maeve's breath hitched when he rounded the cell and came up behind her. She could sense him standing there, debating on how best to torture her.

"It'll only hurt for a minute." His low, mocking laugh whispered along her neck and she recoiled. "And then, you won't feel anything at all."

There was no time to react. White-hot heat seared her tethered hands and a scream ripped free from the barest part of her soul. Her skin was on fire. Burning. Melting. The stench of charred flesh, singed hair, and dissolving metal left her gagging, choking, as scream after harrowing scream scalded her throat. Broken sobs erupted from a place inside her she didn't even know existed. Her mind begged for death, for this to be her end. Curls of black smoke filled the cell, and nausea swept through her. The pain was too much, the agony was too insufferable. Shadows crashed across her vision, slammed into her, and ate away at her consciousness, until the torment became more than she could endure.

With one fitful, fleeting cry, Maeve went under. Everything around her gave way to the darkness and she felt nothing.

MAEVE GROANED.

A thousand needles were prodding at her skin, their uncomfortable poking urging her awake. She rolled onto her back and dragged her eyes open, seeing nothing but rocky walls lurching up on both sides and above her. The cell.

She jolted upright and her senses exploded. Her movements were too quick and she lurched to one side, nearly face-planting on the thatch of hay she'd slept on. Her hands slid against the ground and she caught herself before her chin hit the floor. Then she noticed her wrists. Her cuffs were gone, but her skin was flawless. There was no sign of burned flesh or melted silver. The skin beneath her cuffs was perfectly normal. A little pink near her wrists, but normal. Her blood rushed freely, and the magic she'd come to know that was once so dull and distant, now thrived inside her. The vibrancy of it stole her breath. She was wild. And pure.

And fae.

"You're awake."

Maeve's gaze darted to the door of her cell, and there stood Casimir. "You're alive."

"I'm alive." His hood was pulled back, revealing his crop of rich brown hair, and his dark amber eyes skimmed her, hovering over every inch of her. He held a silver cup in his hands, and every so often he'd look down into the contents, then back to her. He tilted his head. "How are you feeling?"

"Exposed." It seemed like the only logical explanation. The magic flowing through her was unencumbered, and every sensation, every thought and feeling, seemed heightened by it. She glanced at the cup in his hand. "Thirsty."

"Here, drink this." The corner of his mouth quirked, but it wasn't a full smile. He reached through the bars and handed the cup to her. "It should help a little."

"Thank you." She took a sip and grimaced. It was bitter and smelled faintly of an overly steeped tea. Taste-wise it wasn't bad, but it wasn't good. Turmeric and ginger melded together on her tongue, and she downed the rest of the lukewarm liquid quickly, then passed the cup back to him. "It doesn't taste the best."

"No, it's nothing like your favorite coffee." Casimir dropped down onto the damp stone floor and stretched his legs out. "But it'll help keep you calm, if you start feeling like you might spiral out of control."

Spiral out of control? "Why would I do that?"

He sighed, and it was the sound of a man who'd been broken so many times, he no longer knew what it felt like to be whole. "Because of what I'm about to tell you."

"Cas, what are you talking about?" Her fingers curled around the metal bars and she searched his face, looking for any tell, any fracture that would help her understand what was happening. "Aren't you here to rescue me?"

His head dropped back against the wall outside her cell and he folded his hands in his lap. "I was afraid you'd ask me that."

"I don't...I don't understand." A bubble of paranoia rose up inside her, and her magic stirred. Sparkling and vivid. But the herbal tea he'd given her, whatever was in it, had already started working. Her blood calmed, her mind ceased its endless barrage of questions, and she simply plopped down onto the cold stone next to him. The bars supported most of her weight and she found her gaze drawn to the puddle of the same unrecognizable substance from before.

"Let me tell you a story, Maeve. A story about a warrior who'd seen too much in his youth. Who wanted to end his life... until a beautiful faerie princess found him and saved him." Casimir's voice was steady and even, a methodic lullaby, rising to meet every cadence. And Maeve found herself enthralled with the tale he wove. "This faerie princess took him to the safety of her home, and soon enough, they fell in love."

Maeve nodded, and her body relaxed into itself. "That sounds terribly romantic."

Casimir scoffed, but it wasn't unkind. "So you would think. But then one day war came to the fae realm, and this warrior, he fought endlessly for his princess. But her father was greedy, and craved power, and so the greed spread like a disease and it claimed the warrior's true love as well."

Maeve rubbed her hands along her leggings. An invisible ridge covered part of her thigh, a slight glimmer and shifting play of the light. It was her Aurastone, but it was glamoured. She stared down at it, her curiosity piqued. When had her Aurastone been glamoured? "How unfortunate."

"Indeed." Cas turned to the side and when the faint glow of amber faerie lights fell across him, she could finally see his face. It was drawn, pulled down with exhaustion. A kind of sadness haunted his eyes, and the coldness, the deadly accuracy from before, was gone. "But the warrior didn't give up on her. He fought her battles, all of them. He used the fullest extent of his power, shape-shifting into that of a dragon to wreck worlds for her. Then one day he realized, maybe it was his own magic the princess desired. He convinced himself she would come around, that she would overcome this desperate craving for more, if he could simply get her to see the truth of his heart. And then a plague spread across the realm."

She was tracing one finger over the glamoured Aurastone when her body went entirely still. While the tea kept her emotions and reactions calm, it was no match for her mind. Something about this story was painfully familiar, a memory she didn't want to relive, from a time she'd forgotten. "Cas..."

But he continued on like she hadn't spoken. "The sorceress who ruled the spreading darkness claimed love always conquered. If the warrior chose to remain in his mortal form for eternity, it would remove the temptation of his endless power, and his princess would be saved from that which would eventually destroy her. The sorceress would bind his soul to her and in return, she would bind him in his mortal, human form. It sounded too good to be true, because it was. You see, the faerie princess was too far gone for redemption."

"No." The whisper scraped through the air between them and Maeve's mouth ran as dry as a stream without rain. This couldn't be happening. He couldn't be saying what she was hearing. Not Casimir. Not him. She'd known him all of her life. She'd trusted him since the day she was born. For years, he'd been her friend, her constant ally. Her protector and guardian. "Tell me it's not true, Casimir. Tell me it's not her."

His eyes were lost, focused on a memory she couldn't see. "One day, the faerie princess became so obsessed with enhancing her abilities and magic, that she killed her own mother. And as punishment, the gift of the *anam ó Danua* was ripped from her. Her power was seized by force. The goddess Danua graced all of Faeven with her presence, and she rid the realm of the horrors brought on by the wicked sorceress Carman. And when Danua banished Carman to the mortal realm, the warrior—soul-bound by an oath—went with her, leaving his true love behind."

It wasn't possible. It couldn't be...she would've known. Wouldn't she? She sank into the bars supporting her, while her mind tried desperately to piece together the puzzle pieces Casimir tossed her way. He was the warrior, the one who'd traded his soul in exchange for the ability to remain in his mortal form for eternity, in an effort to save Parisa from her power-crazed madness. But he'd failed, because he wasn't enough. He was in love with her, but his love wasn't enough to save her, to help her see past the thirst for more control. Maeve sucked in a breath but it was mildewy, and tinged with lingering smoke. Casimir and Parisa. Parisa and Casimir. All this time, all these years. She'd placed her trust in him. Fully and completely. He'd taught her, molded her into a formidable weapon, albeit one who loved books. But she *knew* him. Though now, it seemed, she knew nothing about him at all.

A tiny, insignificant detail flared to life from the darkest corners of her mind. From the place she didn't want to go, from the truth she feared most.

Maeve shoved up from the ground and her accelerated movement sent her careening across the cell. She lurched forward and grabbed onto one of the bars in an attempt to hold herself into place. On the other side, Casimir stood and faced her. He didn't move. He didn't speak. He just watched her watch him, and she hoped he burned under the heat of her gaze.

"Are you free from Carman's soul bond?"

Casimir shoved his hands into the pockets of his loose black pants. Silence emanated from him.

Maeve's grip on the bars tightened. The cold metal burned into her skin and she rattled them until she ground her teeth against the clanking racket. Bits of stone and pebble shook from the ceiling.

"Answer me, you bastard!" Her arm shot out between the

bars, and her fingers snared into the collar of his shirt. She dragged him, crushed him to the bars, so their faces were less than an inch apart. His hands flew up and captured her wrists, but it was all for show. He wasn't applying any pressure. He didn't fear for his life. He wasn't even threatened by her.

"Yes." He nodded sharply. "I am."

Maeve released him and pulled back, recoiled away like he was diseased. Blemished. A hammering noise echoed in her head, and she realized it was probably her heart. "So, my mother, is—"

"Is not Carman."

There it was, out in the open between them. The bewildering truth of her darkest hope. She was not Carman's daughter. For years she'd wondered, maybe even imagined...but now the confirmation was almost just as terrifying.

Maeve looked up at him. "If not Carman, then who?"

Casimir straightened, and when he spoke, he sounded eerily detached. The emotion from before now gone, leaving him empty. "You are the youngest child, and only daughter of Dorian and Fianna, the former High King and High Queen of the Autumn Court."

"*What?*" Maeve blanched. She searched his face again, but now he wasn't looking at her. He was looking through her. Like she was nothing. Like she was the enemy. Maeve shook her head. She didn't believe him. "No. You're lying. I would *know* if I was fae. I'm cursed. You know that, Cas. You know it. You were there, remember? You told me—"

"What I told you was a lie." He pointed to the murky puddle on the ground. "See for yourself."

She rubbed her lips together and peeked over. The reflection gazing up at her was not the same woman from before. Her ears were long and pointy, her hair fell in pink, strawberry blonde curls, and her face was without blemish. The curve of her body was more defined, more voluptuous. She was different, yet the same—a quandary to her kind, though she wasn't too keen on calling herself a fae just yet. Her eyes however, were the most discerning change. An endless sea of gray-green, speckled with fiery gold.

"Look at you," Casimir murmured. "You are fae incarnate. Sunshine and moonlight. The fire of Autumn, the lifeblood of magic. There is no denying your birthright."

The lifeblood of magic.

Her heart sank and seized, and that feeling, that drowning sensation of angst clenched around her. The beat of her heart quickened and jumped, pulsed with vengeance. Her chest was tight, like she'd been wedged between two brick walls, and with every breath, her lungs squeezed even more. It was the gut-check feeling, the one that slammed into her with such force, she wasn't sure she would ever recover. If Casimir plunged a blade into her chest, she would've been no less surprised.

He stepped closer, but the lines of his face were hard. There was no trace of remorse or regret. "You were still in your mother's womb when Carman ruled Faeven. So new, such a fresh beginning of life, that not even Dorian knew his wife was with child. So Fianna, wonderful as she was, glamoured herself as a human. She told no one. She abandoned her husband, her sons, and her throne, all to save you."

Hot tears welled in Maeve's eyes and she furiously blinked them away. Her heart. Oh, stars, but her heart was ravaged with uncontrollable despair. The truth *hurt*, it physically pained her. She'd been flayed open, left raw and defenseless, her entire world flipped upside down. Everything she thought she knew, everything she thought to be true, was a lie.

"Fianna made a human king fall in love with her," Casimir continued, oblivious to her inner torment. "And then she safely birthed you."

"How?" The word ruptured from somewhere deep inside her. "How do you know all this?

His face remained impassive, his warm eyes, now cold. "Because I'm the one who slayed them. I killed the human king. I killed the Autumn queen. And I conquered what is now Kells, under Carman's order."

Maeve gasped.

"I didn't have the heart to slaughter an infant, so, I brought you to Carman." His gaze dropped to the floor. "And she raised you as her own...you were barely a year old when we overtook Kells. "

"You sentenced me to a life of suffering!" The effects of the tea were fading and her fury was rising. But her magic, no matter how many times she called to it, no matter how many times it moved inside her, ready to burn down the world, it remained just out of reach. "How could you have kept this from me?" she snarled.

Casimir shrugged. Careless. "I didn't realize you were anyone special. I knew you were fae, or at least partially, because of your pointy little ears. The strength of your magic didn't show right away, and for awhile, I believed you to be a halfling. You were young and harmless, I thought nothing of it. Then that one winter the snow fell for so long, and you were so small, and so tired of it. You created a crown of roses out of thin air and I knew you were powerful. I convinced Carman to put you in cuffs, claimed she could wield you as a weapon once you fully came into your power."

"You should've let her kill me." Maeve stormed to the opposite side of the cell, away from him.

"I could have, I suppose. But I'd grown fond of you. At the age of five, you were already wielding a dagger while most little girls your age played with dolls." He slumped, and leaned against the bars. "The cuffs were never meant to be permanent.

But I believe the older you got, the more Carman feared who you would become. Especially when Rowan arrived."

She reeled back. Parisa hadn't been lying. She had sent Rowan to hunt her down like an animal.

"But I found him first." Casimir kicked a small, stone pebble and it skittered down the hall outside the dungeon. "I didn't realize Rowan was sent to Kells by Parisa. I didn't know he'd come looking for you. His cuffs were a means to an end. For information and nothing more."

"And did he give any?" Maeve snapped.

"No. He took his torture without a word and gave Carman nothing." Casimir refused to look at her. He kept his gaze focused on the stone floor at their feet. "When we arrived in Faeven, I wasn't sure we could trust him. Obviously, we can't—"

"You're one to talk."

He ignored the slight and continued speaking. "I didn't put it together right away. Not at first. But small pieces of the puzzle slowly clicked into place." He rubbed his hand over his face, like he was trying to wipe away the knowledge of it. Of her. "But when the dark fae attacked Summer that first night, when you were poisoned, I thought maybe I knew why. And then the second time...when I found you in the summer woods, I knew for certain."

"And how did you know?"

"Rowan told me."

Maeve reared back. His admission was a slap across her face. Goddess above. Knots of pain twisted violently in her stomach and she planted her hands on her knees. She sucked in gulps of the damp, stagnant air to keep from throwing up. Rowan. Fucking Rowan. Her mind whirred, but she couldn't focus on a single thought. She couldn't breathe. "Are you fucking serious? He knew? All this time he knew it was me?"

Casimir took to pacing. His boots clicked almost sound-lessly against the roughened floor. "He knew. He knew the reason he was sent to Kells was to find the *anam ó Danua;* Parisa recognized the burst of power as soon as you took your first breath, but it was faint. When you created your crown of roses, she sent him to find you and bring you back to her."

"Then why didn't he just turn me over to her as soon as we got to Faeven?" Maeve demanded. She charged across the cell, kicking up hay, and grabbed the bars. Hands clenched around the cold metal, she rattled them, wishing for a brief second it was Casimir's neck instead. The reverberations left her teeth aching. "Why didn't he just throw me at her feet? Why drag me along, why torment me, why make me suffer?"

Casimir stilled. "Only he knows the answer to that."

Maeve screamed. She screamed until her throat ached and her chest burned. Power flowed inside of her, bursting, nearly breaking her. "I hate this place! I hate all of the stupid riddles, and all the dangerous games. I hate that not a single soul in this goddess forsaken land can even speak one fucking truth!"

Silence descended upon them. It was heavy, weighted with tension and heartache. She slumped down to the ground, let her head fall back against the cell door, let the bars hold up the weight of her body.

"So it's me." Her voice sounded like a half-dead frog. "I'm the *anam ó Danua.*"

"You are."

She was an Archfae, daughter to Dorian and Fianna. A High Princess of the Autumn Court. Which meant Aran, Garvan, and Shay were her brothers. Siblings. She had a family. A slightly dysfunctional one, but that was beside the point. A new kind of betrayal sliced through her. "Casimir."

He flinched when she used his full name.

"Why have you brought me here?"

"Don't ask me that question." His lips grew thin, and he paled. "You already know the answer."

"You asshole." She jumped up from the slimy ground and slammed her weight into the bars with as much driving force as she could muster. The clattering pained her ears, but they didn't budge. "How could you side with her? You know what she is and what she does. You've seen her kill and destroy, wreck and ruin, yet still you choose her?"

"Parisa doesn't want you dead." He shifted his weight back, away from her, and flipped up his hood. "If you simply do as she asks, she'll keep you alive."

"Well, then." Maeve crossed her arms and let the resentment flow from her. "That explains why you're still here."

Casimir's gaze darkened, but he didn't correct her. "You'll be her greatest weapon, Maeve."

She spat at his feet when he turned away. "I'd rather die."

"I'm sure you would," he muttered, and started walking away.

"Fuck you, Casimir!" It wasn't enough. It would never be enough. But all she could think of, all she could focus on, was her intensely passionate fury for the man who'd once been her friend. "I hate you."

He stopped, frozen in place, then turned just enough for her to hear his whisper. "I thought you might."

Chapter Thirty-One

Maeve paced the tiny cube of the cell for what felt like hours. Maybe more. With every step, she grew more aware of the magic vibrating within her. It was the same awareness that helped her understand the cell was charmed, that there was some kind of magical ward surrounding it which kept her power at bay. She could feel the magic flowing through her, but she couldn't touch it. She couldn't access it. Parisa was no better than Carman. She was the same. Vile. Cruel. And foolish. Maeve stalked from one side to the other, listening for voices, forming a plan. She couldn't sit, she couldn't remain still. Images from pages of books she'd read flashed in her mind as she tried to recreate the truth of her past. Unbidden knowledge overcrowded her mind, bits of memories that were stolen from her, innate abilities gifted to her from her birth parents, the High King and High Queen of Autumn.

No wonder she'd experienced those wild images when she forged a Strand with Aran. No wonder Shay demanded her identity; he must have been able to sense something between them. A bond of some kind. Perhaps that was why the Autumn forest protected her, and kept her hidden from trooping fae when she fled from Garvan and Shay. Autumn recognized her. It knew her blood, it knew her magic. It was home, and like always called to like.

Maeve stared down at her hands. The Strand forged between herself and Tiernan was still there. The golden sun inside in her palm.

She wasn't sure of her magic yet, of what she could and could not control. From some of her studies, she knew she would automatically inherit her mother's magic. Fianna's magic. Unfortunately, that was a blank spot, an emptiness she wouldn't be able to fill on her own. Except...Rowan mentioned Fianna controlled fire, which would supposedly pass to Maeve. She also knew the *anam ó Danua* transformed her into a magic source. Not only could she give life and create, she could also bestow magic. At least, she remembered as much from what Rowan told her.

A nagging voice pilfered through the jumble of thoughts in her mind.

What if Rowan was lying?

Her heart shattered. There was no reason for him to be honest and she supposed it all made sense now. Another rule of the fae had been broken. Years and years of written word said fae were bound to the truth, that they were unable to speak a lie. This never stopped them from bending statements with riddles and twists; it enabled them to fabricate their own honesty. Or lack thereof. But she was fae. And she'd been able to lie, easily and often. Which only proved the original theory to be wrong. Fae *could* deceive. And Rowan had done as much to her. Deceived her. Mortified her. Her past had been stolen from her. Her loyalty, betrayed. Everyone, *everyone*, had lied to her. Everyone had tried to break her, to weaken her, to kill her.

Everyone except Saoirse. But Maeve was fae now, perhaps even her best friend would turn away from her. If she was even still alive.

Another wrench twisted through her. She would not go down so easily.

She would not be made to suffer and endure, to tremble and fear. She was the hidden dawn come to destroy the night. The cliffs that withstood the thrashing of the storm. Nothing, and no one, would ever break her again.

"Maeve," a sing-song voice called her name. "Are you awake?"

Her body went on full alert. Her muscles clenched and her joints stiffened. Ready to attack. To fight. One hand slid to her thigh, and though she could feel the hilt of the Aurastone rub against her palm, she couldn't grab it. Not even her weapon would respond to her.

Her throat worked, and she blew out a slow, even breath. She would face whatever Parisa brought to her without fear.

"Oh good, you're up." Parisa floated around the corner. This time she was in a dress of pale pink, and it tightly cinched her waist and thighs, then spread out like a fan near her calves. Jewels dotted her fingers and the same raindrop diamonds sparkled along her ears. She no longer looked mythical and lethal. Now, she looked like a spoiled princess who always got her way.

Not anymore. The thought reverberated through Maeve's mind like a mantra.

Casimir stood beside Parisa, but gone were his loose-fitting pants and vest with a hood. Instead, he'd been decorated in a uniform of emerald green and silver, with serpent coils running along the hem. His hair was smoothed and combed. And he donned a ribbon of regalia displaying various medals and awards. He looked ridiculous, like an overstuffed peacock.

Maeve wondered if Parisa made him dress like that as a means of humiliation, or a demonstration of power.

Next to him, however, was Fearghal. And all the empowering, vengeance-seeking blood drained from Maeve's face at the sight of him. His lip curled in response, fully aware of the effect he had on her. Fearghal opened the door to her cell and stepped back, allowing Parisa and Casimir entry first.

Maeve held her ground.

I will not yield. I will not break.

"Now, don't you feel better without those terrible cuffs holding you back?" Parisa offered a half-hearted smile.

"Not really." Maeve's gaze flicked around the cell, then back to the three of them. "You had someone ward the cell to stifle my magic. You're clearly no better than Carman."

"Mm." Parisa's honeyed eyes deepened to the color of burnt oak. She nodded to Fearghal who eyes flashed white, and the charm encasing the cell vanished. The second it happened, magic flooded through Maeve, pure and vital. It filled her with a fiery passion, determination, and power. The blood magic of her mother, and the soul of the goddess Danua, imbued her. She felt alive. Her magic wove a song of melody and only she knew the words.

"There." Parisa crossed her arms, her lips pulled into a tight smirk. "Come now, let's see what you can do."

Desire to release the full brunt of her power swirled inside her. Hate shredded through her, and she thought only of burning the entire Spring Court down.

"Ooh, she's smoking. How lovely." Parisa nodded, clearly impressed. "She obviously received all of Fianna's power, maternal lines and such."

"It's her scent as well." Fearghal crossed his arms and Casimir's head whipped toward him. "Smoke. Death. Life. She's quite the misfit, that one."

"Agreed. Positively problematic." Parisa clicked her tongue. "Don't be shy, Maeve. Use your magic. Show me how absolutely glorious and dangerous you are."

It was tempting—*so* tempting—to do something. She knew she could defend herself against them to some extent, she was an Archfae damn it. But she had no idea what she was capable of, no clue how to control herself, and if she attacked and blew it, they'd have her restrained before she could even figure out how to retaliate.

She opted for stubborn pride instead and remained silent.

To her right, Casimir shifted a fraction of an inch closer. "Do what she asks, Maeve."

"Fuck you, Cas." Maeve refused to even look at him again. She would never forgive him for what he did to her. For how long he made her suffer. For murdering her true mother.

"My, my. Such language." Parisa crossed her arms. It was clear her patience was waning. "I'm only going to ask nicely one more time. Show me what you can do. *Now.*"

"No." Maeve snapped her spine into place, and from the corner of her eye, Casimir dropped his head.

Fearghal was on her without so much as an order. He twisted his meaty palm into her hair and yanked her head back. Fire sparked from the tips of Maeve's fingers and her magic pulsed to life. But Fearghal was faster. He slammed his dagger into her shoulder, just below her collar bone, and dragged it across her flesh. A torturous scream erupted from Maeve. She'd been cut before, but this...this was different. Whatever weapon he wielded against her, it was not standard. It was spelled. Or charmed. Blood seeped from the wound, soaking her blouse, splattering the floor.

"Now look what you've done. You spilled blood on the stone, you spoiled little bitch." Parisa swept toward her and jerked her chin up with the tip of her claw-like nail. "And I just had it cleaned."

"Bullshit."

Parisa's hand collided with the side of Maeve's face, and the thick, metallic taste of blood filled her mouth. "Don't you dare disrespect me, you filthy halfling."

"Halfling?" Maeve smiled and blood leaked out through her teeth. Fearghal jerked her backward. "I'm not a halfling."

Parisa faltered and cut a look to Casimir. "What is she talking about?"

"Oh, he didn't tell you? My father is *not* a human king." Maeve spat and the disgusting mix of saliva and blood stained the murky floor. "My father is Dorian, High King of the Autumn Court. And my mother is Fianna, High Queen. Which makes me a *High Princess*, you spoiled little bitch."

"Casimir!" Parisa's furious cry shattered part of the walls and the faerie light lanterns swung violently. Her piercing gaze shot to Fearghal. "Again."

Maeve sucked in a breath but it was too late. His dagger lanced her hip, and curved upward toward the underside of her breast. It cut through her blouse, shredding it. Glaring pain scorched her skin, ripped through her muscle, and a swell of dizziness took her knees out from under her. He tightened his hold on her hair, pulling her upward, and a pathetic whimper escaped through her lips.

"Do you want to know why it hurts so much? It's been dipped in nightshade." Parisa did a slow turn about the cell, her voice a callous whisper in the somber space. "Do you know what nightshade does to a body, Maeve? It's lethal to a mortal. But you? Well, your magic is stronger than the poison it emits, so you will bleed and bleed, until the healing starts. Then you'll be left with lovely, mutilated scars to show the world just how well you obeyed me."

Maeve clenched her jaw. She would not submit. Not to Parisa. Not to Fearghal. And Casimir, the prick, didn't even have the balls to look her in the eye while his *beloved* tortured her. No, she would stay strong. She would die before she ever became one of Parisa's pets.

"Still nothing?" Parisa nodded to Fearghal and this time he hit her thigh, ripping her leggings and scouring her skin in a long, winding slice up her leg.

Maeve screamed again. The pain was too much. And though it weakened her resolve, and her cries echoed off the walls, she refused to give Parisa what she wanted.

"Can I let you in on a little secret, Maeve?" She gripped her chin again and squeezed until the prints from her fingertips bruised Maeve's face. "I know how desperate you are to watch the Spring Court burn, and do you know what? I plan to set fire to it myself."

Fearghal ripped into her again, a nasty curl along her back. Maeve was panting now. It was excruciating. Nightshade ravaged her skin, left it bloody and blistered. And the burning. Sun and sky, the burning from the healing was more than she could handle.

"You see," Parisa continued, unsympathetic to Maeve's stifled cries, "I've created a Dark Court. One comprised of nightmares and terrors. Of dark fae and the poorly neglected, terrifying creatures who skulk, and stalk, and prey. My own personal Sluagh. It's exciting, really. And I plan on utilizing you, and your significant *power*, against everyone. Especially that prick, Tiernan."

Tiernan.

And to think, at one point Maeve thought *he* was cruel.

"I *will* break you, Maeve. Just wait."

Maeve offered her nothing but a bloody smile in return. "That's 'Your Highness' to you."

Casimir stormed forward. "Damn it, Maeve!"

"Don't touch her," Parisa commanded and he shrank back into place beside the Spring High Queen. But Maeve didn't miss the way his eyes pleaded with her, a silent solicitation to obey. "Fearghal?"

He lifted his dagger, admired the streaks of blood running down its blade. "My lady?"

"Do your worst."

"Parisa, I don't think—" Casimir started but Parisa silenced him with a look.

"You're right. Sometimes, you don't think at all."

"Take a good look, Cas." Maeve lifted her chin, dared him to glance her way. "I want you to remember me like this. I want the guilt of what you've done to me to haunt your dreams for the rest of your miserable eternity."

He swallowed, but said nothing.

"Come along." Parisa looped her arm through his, and he led her out of the cell and into the tunnel. "Have fun, darlings."

Fearghal waited until they vanished from sight before he tossed her to the sticky, wet ground. "You've got quite a mouth on you."

Maeve snarled. "Piss off."

There was a flash in his eyes, perhaps a warning. Then there was nothing but endless suffering as he carved her body up like a piece of meat. Maeve's screams were futile. No one could hear her, Parisa had made sure of it. His dagger was everywhere at once. The back of her calves. Her stomach. And when the tip of it scoured her nipple, Maeve begged the goddess to bring her death. To send the god Aed to take her away from this place. She didn't want to live in this world. She never asked for this life. Her magic was supposed to have been a curse. She was supposed to have been a monster. Yet now, with her head lolling back and forth on the stone, and her body convulsing beyond her control, she knew she was none of those things.

She was a warrior once. A princess. Smart and knowledge-able. Quick with a blade. All those things were stripped away from her as Fearghal sculpted her with measured brutality. Eventually, the savage sounds coming from her were lost to the blinding pain. Her tears dried up, and the salt of them burned the slice along her cheek. And when he finally ceased creating the horrific swirls and whorls on her flesh with his blade, and he strode out of her cell without a backwards glance, Maeve softly sang a lullaby to keep herself from shattering.

"Beyond the shores, o'er the sea,
There's a land where magic blooms and grows.
But n'er will be, the power of the thee,
Until comes back, the one whom she chose."

AT SOME POINT, Maeve managed to roll from the repulsive floor to the thatch of hay. It offered her little comfort, a slight warmth, but it was far better than the solid ground. There was scarcely anything left of her clothing, save for a piece of her blouse hanging off one shoulder and a swath of fabric around her waist. Cold seeped into her bones, and it numbed the fire ravaging her as the healing property of her magic sought to save what was left of her lacerated body.

Blood continued to drip from a number of her wounds, and the ones her magic healed were ugly and red, rigid and hideous. They reminded her of the scars across Rowan's chest and she wondered if he, too, suffered this same kind of abuse. Then again, his scars were not so...detailed. The ones littering Maeve were precise, intricate, and done with convoluted care.

She gazed up at the worn ceiling and let her eyes drift close.

She would live another day, and in the morning, she would refuse to aid Parisa again.

I will not yield. I will not break.

A shuddering breath heaved from her and she was already drifting off into what she prayed would be a dreamless oblivion when a very distinct clanging noise startled her awake.

She bolted upright and scampered to the far back of the cell. "Who's there?"

A shadowy figure stepped inside with a bundle wrapped in his arms. "It's me."

Her heart sank, but her determination swelled. "Go away, Casimir. You've done enough already."

His low voice coasted over her. "I'm here to help you."

She opened her mouth to object when he wrapped a soft, thick blanket around her shoulders. "What are you doing?"

"I told you." He scooped her up off the ground, swaddled her like a babe. "I'm getting you out of here."

Maeve didn't relax in his arms. She couldn't. That trust was forever broken. "Why?"

"Because it wasn't supposed to be like this."

"Oh, really? Please, tell me how you thought this was going to work out, Cas." She bounced lightly against his solid frame while he ran down what seemed like an endlessly pitch-black tunnel. "Did you honestly think I was just going to sit back and agree to let Parisa use me however she saw fit? Did you think I wouldn't fight? Did you think I'd just give up?"

He turned sharply and she sucked in a breath when his hand put too much pressure against one of the cuts on her leg. He instantly loosened his hold but kept her in his arms, and continued to sprint down winding corridors.

"I don't know what I thought, Maeve."

There wasn't enough light to read his face, and she was still in too much pain to try and understand the inflection in his tone.

She opted to remain silent. Suddenly, cold droplets of water began to fall on her lashes and cheeks. She gazed up to what she assumed, or hoped, was the sky. But there was no moon. And no stars.

"Are we outside?"

"Yes." He was quiet. Too quiet.

There was another sound, a rustling of leaves, and Maeve's breath hitched. They weren't alone.

"Here." Casimir shifted her into someone else's arm like he was smuggling a package.

"Let me go." She hissed and wriggled inside the confines of the blanket, trying to break free.

"Be still," Casimir commanded. Then his voice changed, and when he next spoke, it was lit with a panic Maeve had never heard before. "Go. Go now." And then, "Don't think I never cared for you."

Without warning, a massive gust slammed into her. Wind and rain sluiced over her like she was nothing more than a passing cloud and she realized she was...flying? Her gaze snapped to the face of who she hoped was a rescuer and not someone else who wanted her dead.

A set of lavender eyes met hers.

"Rowan," she breathed.

"Surprise, Princess."

"You're here." A knot of unchecked emotion lodged somewhere in her chest. In her heart. "You came back for me, but... you were sent to hunt me down. To find me. You knew what I was and you *lied* to me."

He shifted her in his arms, and pressed a faint kiss on the top of her head. "Yes, I knew what you were and I had no intention of ever handing you over to Parisa. I was trying to save you from *this* fate, to protect you from her wrath." He dove downward, away from the moonlight that was beginning to emerge from behind a curtain of clouds. "I know what you *are,* and said nothing to keep you safe. The Spring Court will forever be my home, but my High Queen is ruthless. She's vile and cruel. And her allegiance to her own Court of birth has all but vanished."

Maeve curled into the blanket and he bundled her closer against his chest. She tilted her head back and looked up at him, at the hard line of his jaw, at the fierce determination in his eyes. "But you left me, Rowan. You abandoned me in the summer woods. Alone. *Naked.*"

"No. That night I heard something not far from where we slept. And when I went to investigate, dark fae were waiting for me. Casimir had sent them." His arms tightened around her. "I would never have left you willingly. I hope you know that."

She wanted to believe him. But there were more questions, like if he'd actually found her when she was a child, would he have turned her over to Parisa then? And what about the favor he called in when they were at the Autumn Ceilie? But more importantly, how was he flying?

"You've got wings," she blurted out when she caught sight of the long, silky black feathers protruding from his back.

He grinned. "I do."

"But, how? You never told me—"

"Another time, Princess. Right now, let's focus on getting you out of—" He jerked, stuttered in the air. His lips pulled back over his teeth and he groaned as they started to tumble from the sky. "Hang on!"

He wrapped her close to him and a glint of silver streaked by, right over top of their heads. For the briefest of moments, Maeve thought it could be lightning.

Rain splattered her face and the wind whipped around

them like a cyclone while Rowan struggled to maintain control of their downward descent. But the trees were moving too quickly, and colors and shapes careened by them without recognition. They were all blurs. Blobs of muddled colors that were worthless in terms of gauging the distance they had left in their free-fall until they ultimately crashed and burned.

Rowan flipped over at the last minute, holding her against him and cradling her head. Together they slammed into the ground and rolled once, then Rowan was already back on his feet and hauling her up alongside him.

"Keep moving." He grabbed her hand and took off at a sprint, and she witnessed the fleeting look of shock when he realized she could actually keep up with him. He chuckled. "I forgot you're a fae now."

"Funny story about that..."

Another flash of lighting streaked overhead and Rowan ducked, then pulled her along. "Some other time. Right now, we run."

He darted forward once more, taking her with him, hand in hand. He pointed up ahead. "We just have to get to that tree line."

"Why can't we just *fade*?"

"I can't *fade* anymore."

Her gaze snapped to his face. "What? Why?"

"Let's just call it a shitty bargain." He nodded toward the rise of stoic evergreens up ahead. "If we can get to that point, you'll be safe."

Maeve stared to where he was pointing and though she knew her eyesight had vastly improved since the removal of her cuffs, she still couldn't see much of anything, save for the outline of the forest. There was no light. No play of shadows. Only rain and low-lying clouds. Her bare feet hit the soft, spongy earth, sinking into a mist that wound its way like a ribbon of the palest blue over the rolling hills of Suvarese.

More splinters of lightning shot past them, and it was then Maeve saw the crimson soaking some of Rowan's feathers.

"You're bleeding."

He didn't even look. "It's nothing."

But then he was hit again and a muffled grunt erupted from him. He stretched his wings wide, a barrier of protection, and the revelation of what was truly happening caused Maeve to stumble. The glints of silver cutting through the air weren't bolts of lightning at all. They were *swords*. Dozens of them. A rain of swords.

"Rowan..."

"Fucking bitch," Rowan ground out as the tip of a passing blade clipped his ear. "Over here!"

He dragged her over to where a small mound protruded up from the earth. It was covered in bundles of colorful wildflowers. A faerie hill. But there was no mysterious entrance and no path to the fae realm. Another lie ripped from the pages of her books.

Rowan grabbed her wrist and shoved her back against the hill. He slammed both hands on either side of her head, and lengthened his wings around her like a blockade. He was her shield. Her armor.

"Rowan!"

Maeve clamped both hands over her mouth, horrified. She shrank back against the rounded earth and hot, unexpected tears sprang to her eyes. Blade after blade sank into him, piercing him from behind. They hit his back and came clear through the front of his chest. They tattered his wings and weakened his legs.

"No." Maeve shook her head and reached up, wanting nothing more than to cup his cheek and tell him everything would be alright—even though she knew it was a lie. Her heart cracked. Fractured. "Rowan...no."

"Stay down, Princess." His words were clipped, and his breathing was ragged. Tiny drops of blood escaped from the corner of his mouth and slid down his chin. But it was nothing compared to the blood leaving his body in terrifying amounts. It soaked his shirt and pants, drenched his feathers, and drained his face of color. "I never betrayed you. I would've died before I let her have you."

The faerie hill was the only thing left to keep her upright and she sagged into the soft, wet grass. Her sobs broke free. "No. Please, no."

"You'll go on to do great things in this world." His raspy words ripped through her. "You have a heart like no other, Maeve."

"Rowan, please." She shuddered and her tears fell freely. They slid down her face, hot and fast, cooled only by the rain that continued to fall.

He cracked a broken smile. "Don't cry for me, Princess."

In the distance there was a shout, and a burst of voices sounded close by.

"Look!" A male called.

"Over there!" A female.

There was more noise now, like running. Rowan didn't budge. He just steeled himself against the onslaught of swords. "Get her out of here." He ground the words out. "Now."

Maeve's head snapped up, and there stood Lir, Merrick, and Brynn.

"On it." Lir ducked under Rowan's outstretched wing and scooped Maeve into his arms.

"No! No, we can't leave him here! He'll die!" Hysteria bubbled up in the back of Maeve's throat. Her mind wanted to stay, to fight and save him. But her body was too fragile. Too ruined from Fearghal's work. "Lir, please. *Please.*"

She struggled in his grasp but Lir's arms locked around her, iron-tight.

"Now," Rowan growled. Then those beautiful lavender eyes locked onto hers. "Go, Princess. Rise and rule. Take your crown."

"Rowan," her voice cracked, split open by the thousands of wounds she'd carried over her brief lifetime.

"I'll find you, Maeve. In another lifetime. In another realm." He sucked in a garbled breath and winked. "I'll find you."

"ROWAN!"

But Lir held her close, crushed her against him. "I've got you, little bird."

The amplified scent of orange blossom and cedarwood smothered her, and without giving her a chance to say goodbye, they *faded.*

Chapter Thirty-Two

A soothing balm floated over Maeve, and all the torment, all the anguish and grief, melted away. Warm, gentle waves of compassion drifted over her. They rose and fell like the tide, sweeping up to collect her hurt and trauma, pulling back to restore her with peace and calm. Magic tingled inside her. Shifting. Awakening. The tranquil scent of the ocean breeze, sweetened coconut, and eternal sunshine surrounded her. A familiar breeze kissed her skin, and Maeve's eyes fluttered open.

The first thing she saw was the glass ceiling above her and wisps of feathery white clouds as they lingered in a sky of blue. The glow of the sun poured in from a set of glass double doors. She was in a room. But not just any room. *Her* room. In the Summer Court. She slid one hand under her pillow and felt the security of her Aurastone. Someone knew where she kept it, and someone had put it back where it belonged.

Easing herself up from the bed, a slight movement flickered out of the corner of her eye.

"Ceridwen?"

The High Princess sat in a plush teal chair, with her legs curled up under her. From the looks of it, she'd been in that position for hours.

"I'm here." She reached over and took Maeve's hand.

The tender, affectionate act cracked something inside her heart. Tears spilled down her cheeks, swift and silent. She reached out. "Ceridwen."

The faerie was by her side in a second. She wrapped her arms tightly around her and held on while Maeve's fractured soul bared itself.

"Rowan," she gasped. "He saved me, but there were...there were so many swords." Sobs wrecked her shoulders and she trembled in Ceridwen's embrace. "And he was bleeding. Everywhere. And I couldn't save him. I couldn't do it, I was too weak."

She stared down at her hands, marred with her own guilt.

A chilling wail escaped when she realized what she'd done. Or more so, what she hadn't done. She could have saved Rowan. She could have saved his life. She was enough, more than enough. Her magic was blessed by the goddess. She was the lifeblood. The source. But she let him die, she let him give his life for her, instead of trying to save him. She was rocking now, back and forth, unable to keep the tremors from wrecking her. Ceridwen ran a hand down her hair, smoothed away the unruly curls.

"It's okay, Maeve. It's going to be okay."

She held her closer. Tighter. The High Princess nurtured her and cared for her, she wiped away her tears, and let her unleash all of her heartache.

"And I lost Saoirse. They struck her down in Kells, right before I killed my mother. I couldn't save her either. There were too many of them. And Cas..." Maeve shook her head and buried her face in Ceridwen's shoulder. The depth of his deception left her breathless. "Casimir betrayed me."

"The best ones do." Ceridwen's voice was a salve to her crestfallen heart, as though it was an experience she shared. She rose from the bedside and carefully brought Maeve to her feet. "Come on, let's get you cleaned up."

She looped Maeve's arm around her shoulders and held her steady by the waist. One slow, shuddering step at a time, she maneuvered her to the bathroom, careful to block Maeve's view of the mirrors. She was pretty sure she knew why. She'd been carved up like she was on a butcher's block. Tears burned but she blinked them away. Ceridwen turned on the water, added a few drops of some purple liquid from a vial, and before long, steam filled the tiled space and the soothing scent of rose and soft florals wafted over her. Maeve stepped into the shower, allowed the hot water to shock and scald the swirling of scars covering her. The ridges had smoothed away—apparently her magic was stronger than most—but horrendous red marks remained as a constant reminder of her suffering.

Maeve stood in the stream and let it engulf her. The searing water soaked her hair, ran over her shoulders and belly, down to her toes. She grabbed a bar of soap and lathered it up, then scrubbed at every inch of herself. She washed away Fearghal's touch, the feel of his breath on her neck. She scrubbed away the image of Carman crumpling onto her blade, of raising furious beings from the dead. Down the drain, with dried blood and clumps of dirt, Maeve watched her memories of the past few days swirl around and around. Tilting her head back, she shampooed her hair next, and squeezed her eyes shut. But she couldn't rid herself of Rowan. She couldn't cleanse herself of his memory. He was harbored there in her mind and she wasn't strong enough to cut the rope.

"Are you alright?" Ceridwen asked.

She would never be alright. Not anymore. Not ever again.

"I don't know." Bubbles skimmed down her back and legs, and met with the grime by the drain before being swallowed down, out of sight.

"Will you be okay if I go? I'm just going to grab you some clothes."

"Okay." It wasn't really an answer. She planned on standing under the stream of water until it ran cold. Until it left her numb. Until she could no longer function.

"I'll be right back."

There was one more rise of magic, of warmth, of Ceridwen's silent emotional support. And then she was gone. Maeve stood under the spray of water a few moments longer, then switched it off and stepped out, relishing in a blanket of steam. She was grateful the mirrors were fogged, that she couldn't visibly see what had been done to her. Sure, she could look down and take inventory, but she didn't. She couldn't. At least, not yet. A gentle knock sounded outside the door of the bathroom, drawing her attention.

"Maeve." A rumbling baritone reverberated through the door separating them.

"Tiernan." She didn't want to deal with him. Not today.

"May I come in?"

She hesitated. "You're going to either way."

"You're right." The door creaked open, sucking out the partition of steam. He didn't look at her right away. In fact, he respectfully kept his gaze averted. But in his outstretched hand, he held a crisp blue towel.

"Thanks." Maeve reached for it and froze.

The steam of the shower had evaporated, leaving all of her reflection on full display in the gilded mirrors. She was unrecognizable. She was absolutely fae, but instead of being gorgeous like every other female she met, she was ruined. A gruesome example of Parisa's punishment. Scars curved and twisted all over her in ribbons of angry red lines. The one on her cheek was the worst. It started near her ear, rose up over her cheekbone, and curled into a rose.

Sick.

Fearghal was a demented asshole who took pleasure in torturing others. In leaving his mark, like he was an artist of the flesh. She would kill him, too.

A strangled gasp escaped her and Tiernan's head snapped up.

The look on his face was nothing short of tempered rage. His eyes flashed, a menacing summer thunderstorm. His fingers closed into fists, leaching all the color from his knuckles. Every muscle flinched, pulled taut with restraint. His anger, or resentment, or whatever it was, made her shrink into herself.

Her knees quaked, unable to withstand the horror of her own reflection. "Now I really am a monster."

The glittering tile rose up to meet her, but Tiernan was faster. In one swift movement, he caught her up in the towel and lifted her into his arms. "I will kill her for what she's done to you."

Tiernan carried her like she weighed less than air. He stalked out of her bedroom and into the passageway of white arches, bursting florals, and sparkling streams. Maeve peered over his shoulder at dumbstruck fae and servants alike who either averted their gaze or shoved themselves against a wall to get out of his way. He wound his way through a maze of palms and stopped in front of a wooden door before kicking it open.

Maeve glanced around the room. "Where are we?"

Soft, sage green colored the walls and glass doors were shoved open so their white chiffon curtains shifted and moved in the breeze. A large plumeria tree with bright pink and yellow star-shaped blooms stretched over the balcony, its intoxicating scent sweetly floral, yet oddly familiar. The plumeria. That was the tempting, flowery scent she detected whenever Tiernan was around. Palm trees. Warm sand. And *plumeria.*

A large and sumptuous bed with all white sheets and bedding stood in the middle of the room. A long desk was positioned against the opposite wall, and shoved to the side were pots of shimmering ink and a jar of paintbrushes. A guitar was in the far corner, propped up on a stand, and a black, floor-to-ceiling mirror stood opposite. Like hers, his ceiling was open to the skies.

"Is this your room?" Maeve tried again. She much preferred their banter over the unstable silence between them.

Tiernan set her down on the edge of the desk, and the towel slid to her hips. Mortified, she snatched at it, but his hand clamped down over hers. "Leave it."

She watched as he grabbed two pots of shimmering ink. One was gold and the other was a shade of crimson flecked with magenta. He picked out three paintbrushes, a slender one with tiny bristles, and two others that seemed to be made for thick, precise lines. Tucking one behind his ear, he glanced over at her.

"Do you remember when I told you about my tattoos? How they cover my scars?" He grabbed an empty pot and began stirring the two colors together, mixing them to create an illustrious rosy gold.

"Yes."

Tiernan set one brush down beside her on the desk, along with the pot of newly mixed paint. Then he started to roll up the sleeves of his shirt, cuffing them to just below his elbow, exposing the swath of tattoos crawling up his arms. "I'm going to cover yours as well. If you'll let me."

MAEVE NODDED, her voice lost to such a simple kindness.

Tiernan reached over and grabbed a rolling stool, then sat down before her. "Just...try and relax."

"Okay." It was slightly disconcerting having him positioned between her legs in such a manner, but he didn't seem at all bothered, and she attributed his lack of nerves to having done this sort of thing before. It wouldn't surprise her at all if he'd painted numerous females, and the thought left her wondering about all fae's tattoos.

"No." His voice was soft. "I don't make a habit of painting females."

He dipped one of the brushes into the ink and carefully set to work. He started on her legs first, and the rose-gold ink slid onto her skin like satin. Around each calf he followed the swirls, tracing them up over her knees, and then to her thighs. Gradually, Maeve eased back and braced both of her palms on the surface of the desk behind her. Tiernan switched brushes then, clamping one between his teeth, and dipping the new one in paint. Focused and intent on his work, he mirrored the slashed swirls along her hip and abdomen. She bent over as instructed, and he copied the long, and winding marks on her back.

"You have two scars on your back." He lifted the brush from her flesh. "They look like crescent moons."

"I've had them since I was little."

"Do you know what they're from?"

Maeve glanced over her shoulder at him. "No." Whatever story she'd been told about them was probably another lie. The thought made her stomach turn.

"Hm. Go ahead and sit back for me." Tiernan set both brushes aside, looking for the third one. "Support yourself with your hands, just like before."

She did as she was told, and this time he grabbed a paintbrush with velvet bristles.

"The..." He cleared his throat and didn't meet her eyes. "The scars here are more severe, so I need to work with a larger brush."

"I understand."

Maeve squeezed her eyes shut, and the unexpected shock of the soft brush against the underside of her breast set her eyes on fire with the threat of tears. Her cries were silent, and for herself, because she knew beyond a shadow of a doubt that Fearghal had ruined her on purpose. He'd been considerably more vicious when sculpting her breasts with his blade.

The brush slid over both of her breasts, under and around, and when the tip of it skimmed her nipple, a single tear slid down her cheek.

Tiernan hissed, then painted what felt like a small circle over her heart, with tiny lines spiraling out on all sides. She didn't remember getting cut there, but then again, she'd barely been conscious. He dropped the paintbrush and stood abruptly. Maeve pressed her lips together, biting down to keep the tears from falling. Tiernan reached out, cupped her cheek with one hand, and gently wiped away the fallen tear. Dark, midnight hair fell into his face, and his stormy eyes hovered over every inch of her.

"I swear to the goddess, I will make Parisa beg for her life beneath my blade."

Maeve carefully sat up and peeked at the rosy gold ink shimmering all over her naked body.

I will not yield. I will not break.

"I'd rather kill her myself." Resolved burned bright inside her.

Tiernan met her fierce gaze with one of his own.

"Then we'll do it together." He picked up one of the finer

brushes and collected some more ink. "Don't move. Just a few more to go."

Maeve took slow, steady breaths and tried to remain still while he applied the ink to her throat, and then finally, to her ear and cheek. But it was difficult to find something else to focus on when she was so naked and he was far too close for comfort. He gently gripped her chin and tilted her head to the right, then angled the brush along her cheekbone. He was so intent. So serious. Golden flecks of captured sunlight surrounded by the stormy swirls of twilight reflected in his eyes, and they were so lovely, she had to hold back her sigh. His lips were full and parted while he worked, and up close, she could see the faint hint of scruff along his jaw, like he'd forgotten to shave. Sun and sky, he was so pretty. It almost hurt to look at him.

The corner of Tiernan's mouth ticked up in a smile. "You're not so bad yourself."

Her mouth fell open. She'd all but forgotten he was capable of hearing her thoughts. Her eyes rolled to the dark wooden beams outlining the glass ceiling above them. "I'm too exhausted to fight you."

His smile faded. "I know."

Then he leaned back. "There. All done."

"Does it have to dry?"

"No." He lifted her up off the desk and cautiously lowered her to her feet. He snapped his fingers and a gown of aubergine appeared, draped over his arm.

"Magic," he said with a wink at her stunned silence. "Don't worry, I'll teach you all of my tricks." Then he held out the gown. "I know it's a dress, but I figured it would be more comfortable while you heal, as opposed to leggings and a corset."

Maeve accepted the beautiful gown. It was softly spun

cotton, loose-fitting, with thicker straps instead of sleeves. "It's lovely."

He shrugged and stepped back. "It has pockets."

Three simple words, but they released all the tears she thought she'd already cried. "Thank you."

Tiernan draped his arm around her shoulder. Carefully. Mindful. "Don't cry, *astora*. Please."

Astora. It was one Old Laic term she couldn't figure out. The way he said it with an accent made it difficult to discern the meaning and she was too drained, too lost, to try and figure it out. She didn't want to cry. She was tired of it, exhausted from expelling all of the emotions she'd drowned inside of herself for so long. "She wrecked me."

"She freed you." He smoothed an errant strand of hair back from her face. He turned her so she faced the floor-length mirror propped in the corner of the room. "Look beyond the scars, Maeve. What do you see?"

She stared at herself. Long ears were accentuated by defiant curls. Now that her hair had dried, she could see it was a beautiful strawberry blonde, an almost pink shade. Pale, green-gray eyes gazed back at her, and tattoos of ink covered her scars, hiding them in plain sight. "I see someone who learned the hard way that nothing is ever as it seems. A princess who lost her kingdom, her mother, her best friend, and..." She didn't know what to call Rowan. "And the shell of a soul who once believed a great many things, but who no longer knows where to put her trust, because her entire life has been a lie."

"I never lied to you."

"You've said some pretty awful things." Maeve met his gaze in the reflection. "So, I'm not entirely sure that's the kind of thing you should readily admit."

"Fair enough." A flare of amusement flickered in his eyes. "Do you want to know what I see?"

"I don't know," Maeve muttered.

"I see an Archfae, a High Princess of the Autumn Court, whose mother was stolen away from her. Who was held captive in the human lands, who was brainwashed into thinking she was cursed. I see a warrior who is willing to stop at nothing to save her kingdom, and who would show her new realm the same loyalty and devotion, no matter the cost." He gave her cheek a gentle pat. "Get it together, my lady. You're a fucking fae."

Maeve almost smiled. Almost. She was fae. A faerie. An immortal. And she would ultimately have an entire lifetime to suffer a hundred more mistakes and a thousand more opportunities. And maybe later, when she was alone in her room, she would wallow in her grief once more. She would mourn her losses, and then she would move on. "What do we do now?"

Shadows fell across his face. "There's someone who wants to see you."

"No." Maeve threw her hands up. "No, I don't want to see anyone. Not now. And not for awhile."

"I'm afraid this one can't wait."

"Tiernan, please. I'm not ready, I—"

"You're going to be fine." He reached into his pocket and pulled out a necklace. Hanging from a thin gold chain was a round amethyst, and a dazzling opal that held the sparkle of a thousand rainbows, all wrapped in golden wire. "This is for you."

She blanked. The High King of Summer was giving her jewelry?

"Um..." She stepped back. "Thanks, but we're not on that level yet."

"That mouth of yours is going to get you into some serious trouble one day." Tiernan rolled his eyes to the ceiling. "Ceridwen charmed the necklace and imbued it with her magic. It will allow us to sense whatever you're feeling, so long as the feeling is strong, no matter where you are."

Her brows lifted and Tiernan shook his head.

"Get your mind out of the gutter, Your Highness. I mean fear. Terror. Pain. Rage. Grief. *Those* kinds of feelings." He draped it around her neck. "Just take the fucking necklace."

"Okay." She pulled her hair to one side. "Fine."

He fastened the clasp and stepped back. "You're missing one more thing."

Maeve groaned. "Now what?"

"A crown."

"Why do I need a crown?" She crossed her arms. "You don't wear one."

"That doesn't mean I don't have one," he countered.

She stared up at him. "Well, I *don't* have one."

"Then make one."

"I don't know how."

Now it was Tiernan's turn to lift his brow. "Is that so? I've heard otherwise."

"I was like five."

He spread his arms wide. "So?" But then he glanced down at her chest, where the necklace nestled against the curve of her cleavage, and a line formed across his brow. "You're afraid."

"I—" She opened her mouth to argue, then closed it abruptly. Apparently, the charmed necklace worked. "I am. Yes."

Tiernan grabbed her hands and cupped them with his own. She hesitated but he held firm. "You are the High Princess of Autumn. You are the *anam ó Danua*. You are the life source of all magic, the beginning of its creation. Imagine your crown, and take it."

Maeve stared down at her hands. She knew what she wanted it to look like, the same as it had been all those years ago when the snow never seemed to stop. Her magic flowed through her, easily and freely, like calling upon an old friend. Every nerve inside her tingled, and she gasped in wonder as roses the color of summer pink and autumn gold blossomed into the shape of a crown. Eternal blooms, she would call them, for they would never wilt. Never die. Golden whorls rose up from the top and took the shape of a crescent moon. In its center sat the sun, flanked on either side by two stars.

Tiernan lifted it from the air and placed it on her head. "Fearless dreamer."

It was as much of a compliment as she'd ever received from him.

He offered his arm and Maeve accepted. Together they strode through one of the sun-drenched courtyards, passing under swaying palms, and avoiding the spray of water fountains. The Summer Court was exactly the same, except for one distinct difference. The fae they passed no longer laughed at her with mocking eyes or bemused smiles. They'd stopped whispering loud enough for her to hear, talking about the foolish mortal girl who thought she could find the soul of a goddess and save her kingdom. Instead, they bowed and curtseyed the moment they saw her, and mumbled a varying array of titles in which to address her. Their eyes darted between her and Tiernan, like it was some kind of game to see who would look away first.

Tiernan always won.

They rounded a corner and she spotted a balcony filled with gold vases bursting with hibiscus and roses. Out on the balcony, basking in the glorious sunshine, stood Ceridwen. She lifted her hand in a small wave and opened her arms.

Maeve rushed into them.

"Rose gold suits you." Ceridwen squeezed her tightly, then stepped back in awe. "And your aura..."

Maeve's breath hitched. "What of it?"

"It's something else...something wonderful." Her gaze slid to her twin, then back to Maeve. "How are you feeling?"

"Better, thanks to you." She grabbed Ceridwen's hand, and without thinking, took Tiernan's as well. "Thanks to both of you."

Tiernan stood there, motionless, but Ceridwen laughed. "Offering up your gratitude so quickly, Your Highness?"

Maeve's eyes widened and Ceridwen's laughter exploded. "I'm only teasing. We'll let this one slide." She winked.

Maeve released them both, but when Tiernan stepped back to put distance between them, he flexed his hand. It was a barely imperceptible motion, hardly worthy of note. Her gaze flicked up to his face, but he turned around and walked away. She brushed off the strange reaction and returned her attention to Ceridwen instead.

"What are you doing out here?"

Ceridwen's ruby lips curved into a smile. "Waiting for you."

Maeve's brow furrowed. "Why?"

"You'll see." She gestured to the sea beyond.

Maeve peered out over the railing, her eyes locked on the skies. At first, there was nothing but sun and sky. Endless and eternal. Then she spotted it. A glimmer between the clouds and a tug in her heart. A recognition. A calling.

A burst of mist seemed to tear open between the sea and the horizon, and Effie, in her terrifyingly beautiful magnificence, swooped into her line of sight. Atop her back sat Aran. Something swelled up inside her, she squealed, and reached out for Ceridwen. But only air moved between her fingers. When she looked over, the High Princess was gone.

Wind gusted into her, blew her hair back behind her face, and Effie tossed her fiery wings twice before settling onto the railing like the majestic dragon-bird she was. The three eagle heads tilted, eyed her speculatively, then dipped in acknowledgement.

Aran leaned forward and crossed his arms, letting them come to rest on top of one of Effie's overtly alert heads. Then he grinned. "Hello, little sister."

Chapter Thirty-Three

"Aran."

It didn't matter if she'd known him for only a minute or for a hundred years. There was a connection. A link between them, a blood bond, one her magic recognized, and it sent her heart soaring. She hoisted herself up over the railing of the balcony and leapt into his waiting arms. He caught her mid-air and laughter erupted between them. The sound was musical. Magical. He cupped her cheeks with his smooth palms and simply looked at her.

"It's you." Aran crushed her against him. "It's actually you."

She threw her arms around him, and affection colored her world in a swell of unexpected tenderness.

When he finally released her, there was a slight sheen to his emerald eyes.

"How did you know?" The question spilled from her before she could stop it. "How did you know I was your sister?"

He pulled an apple out of the tanned sack hanging from the

side of Effie's scaly body and tossed it to her, then ducked his head. "Casimir told me."

She held the apple with both hands, and the tips of her nails bit into its skin. "So...so, you let him take me?"

His gaze snapped to hers. "Not by choice."

"A bargain then?"

"So many questions," he murmured, then shook his head. "But no, not a bargain. Blackmail."

The apple bobbled in Maeve's grasp. "What? He blackmailed you?"

"He did." Aran pulled another apple from the sack and took a bite. "You probably haven't noticed, but the Strand between us is gone."

She glanced down to where the crimson Strand of a leaf should've marked her forefinger. But it wasn't there anymore.

"I called in my favor with Casimir. In exchange for crossing all of you into Faeven, I asked about you." Aran tossed his apple in the air and caught it with one hand. Then crushed it in his fist. "The bastard tricked me. He told me you were a lost faerie princess."

Aran's harsh laughter startled Effie and he patted one of her heads to soothe her. "When I demanded more information, he agreed to tell me on one condition...that he be granted a favor of his own with no questions asked and no consequences. It was a foolish mistake and one I regret, but at the time, I considered it a harmless request. His favor was that I pick the two of you up and return you both to Kells. And he told me if I gave away any hint at all that I knew who or what you were, he'd kill you right in front of me."

Maeve almost choked. She coughed, eyes burning as she swallowed her bite of apple down. The wound from Casimir's betrayal was ripped open once more, and her heart sank a little bit further into her chest. "I see."

"He swore to me no harm would come to you." He skimmed the tattoos now covering most of her body and traced the one on her cheek. His jaw hardened. "I see now that was a lie."

"Well, that seems to be the way of things around here."

Heavy silence settled between them, interrupted only by the sound of Effie's snorts and an occasional shuffling of wings. Then Aran reached up and twirled one of Maeve's loose curls around his fingers. He gave it a gentle tug and it bounced free.

"You're looking rather fae." The corner of his mouth quirked up. "I like your crown of roses."

"Thanks." Maeve held his gaze. "I made it myself."

"It's beautiful. Much like this other treasure I have here." Aran reached into his pocket and when he opened his hand, a small piece of sea glass was cradled in his palm. It was the exact one Maeve had given him when he brought her to Faeven on the Amshir.

Warmth spread through her. "You still have it."

"I do. It's my small piece of land." He tucked it back into his pocket, but his gaze was drawn to Niahvess, and the Courts beyond. "And I'll keep it, until I can return home."

"What happened? I mean, why were you exiled from Faeven?" Maeve bit into her apple again.

"That, dear sister, is a story for another day."

"Do all Dorai live at sea?"

"Not all. No." He fiddled with the compass around his neck, the one that didn't really point north. "Some choose to live in other realms."

Other realms. She supposed, if her homeland rejected her, then she'd want to be as far away from it as possible. She knew she wanted to return to Kells. Her heart needed to know if Saoirse had lived or died. And one day she would, but there would be nothing left of the city she once called home. It would be full of rot and decay, ruined by the Scathing until she killed Parisa. But even after, assuming she succeeded, her people would never accept her. Not when they'd been born and bred to hate the fae. She was better off not going back at all. Maybe she was a Dorai in her own right. A fae, banished from her home...just like her brother. Her mind drifted to all the maps Aran created, to all the worlds he'd traveled to, to all the places he'd been, and she wondered if perhaps one day he would take her on such adventures.

A thought occurred to her. "I think I'd prefer to live on the sea, with you."

"Don't be foolish. The sea is just as unreasonable as the rest of the world."

"There's nothing for me here."

His hand came to rest on her shoulder. "Faeven needs you, Maeve. Parisa has committed unspeakable crimes against her own kind. She's been corrupted by the lure of dark magic, and the constant desire for more has left her unhinged. War will come. Darkness will come. But you..." He tilted her chin up so their eyes met. "You are the sun, the moon, and the stars. Never setting. Always rising. Eternal."

Maeve shuddered, and a broken sigh escaped her. "No pressure," she muttered.

"I'll be with you every step of the way."

She threw her arms around Aran's neck and hugged him. "I'm glad I have you."

When she finally released him, he nodded toward the balcony. It was time for her to go back...to whatever lied in wait. "You're leaving me here."

It wasn't a question. "The Summer Court has a much stronger defense system than Autumn. You will be safer here under Tiernan's protection."

Lovely.

"When Garvan learns of your existence..." he continued, then trailed off.

She didn't want to think about what Garvan would try and do to get her in his grasp. He'd be furious when he discovered he'd had her once before and let her go.

Carefully, Aran lifted her up and Effie extended one of her long necks toward the balcony. Maeve slid down her smooth feathers and landed barefoot upon the terracotta flooring. She glanced back up at Aran, perched on Effie's back, and memorized everything about him. The cleft in his chin, made more pronounced by a scar. The way his rich auburn hair always looked windswept. The bright green and gold of his eyes. How when he smiled down at her, she felt safe. Secure. She felt like she was home.

She lifted one hand and shielded her eyes from the glare of the sun. "When will I see you again?"

His smile widened. "Trust me, you'll know."

"He saved me." Her nose tingled, like she might cry, but she clenched her jaw tight. "Rowan," she clarified, in case he didn't understand. "You said he wouldn't be the hero of my story...but he was. He saved my life."

"I know." His voice was soft and filled with a sympathy she didn't deserve. "And I'm sorry for it."

"I'll miss you."

"I'll be back before you know it." He winked and Effie spread her magnificent wings, stretching them wide, before lifting off of the railing. "You look like her, you know."

"Who?"

Aran grinned. "Our mother."

Effie soared into a sea of mist, her wings cutting like fire into the late afternoon sky. Magic pulsed, the air shimmered, and then Aran was gone.

MAEVE WAS FAIRLY certain she knew where she was, so she decided to find her way back to her room. Even if Aran insisted she was safer in Summer than in Autumn, she would not be so foolish as to let down her guard. At some point, Garvan would come for her. And she already knew Parisa would stop at nothing to subjugate her; her infatuation with power and magic, and her desire to control all of Faeven made her the largest threat. All of which meant Maeve would trust no one. Ever. Save for Aran. Her Aurastone would remain strapped to her at all times, and she would need to arm herself with a sword as well.

She wandered through the maze of open-air corridors. The summer breeze lifted her hair off her shoulders. The tranquil scent of warm florals and palm leaves brought her a small sense of peace. A shimmer of magic settled over her, easing her thoughts and troubled mind, and though Maeve couldn't see her, she knew Ceridwen must be close. The sparkling ivory stone was soft against her bare feet, and for a split second, Maeve debated on walking through one of the streams winding through the lush courtyard to cool herself. She paused beneath the shadow of a palm tree, the magic inside her suddenly pulsing with acute awareness. She inhaled, and knew someone was following her.

Maeve whipped around to see Lir standing a few yards behind her. He bowed slowly. "Lir, what are you doing out here?"

He didn't smile. Just maintained his stoically calm presence. "The same thing as before, my lady."

She arched a brow. "Following me?"

His head tilted to the side and his shoulders lifted in a feigned sort of shrug. "Protecting you. But also, yes."

"So, you're back on babysitting duty then?"

"I prefer to say I'm ensuring the will of my king." He walked toward her, and she didn't miss the way his sharp, silver eyes absorbed every detail about the space surrounding them. They darted to every tree, past the fountain, up to the terraced rooftops, then back down to her. He'd absolutely been tasked with protecting her.

Maeve sighed and looped her arm through his, liking the way their skin was a clash of color. Warm peach and jeweled umber. Light and dark, and lovely. "I suppose I could make it easy for you."

His lips twitched into what could almost have been mistaken as a smile. "I would appreciate that."

They strolled through the rest of the courtyard together. He told her stories of the different kinds of magic he'd seen throughout his lifetime, the most he'd ever spoken to her in one sitting. He explained the difference between sprites and pixies, merrows and sirens, and promised to take her to the library at least once a day so she could read about them, and all other fae creatures. She'd also be able to learn more about Old Laic, which brought to mind another question entirely.

"Lir?"

He glanced down at her.

"What does *astora*, mean?"

A slow smile spread across his handsome face. "*Astora*. Now, that is a term I haven't heard in a very long time."

"What does it mean?" she asked.

He stopped and grabbed her hand, placing it over his heart.

Her gaze snapped to his. "It means your heartbeat?"

"Almost." Lir tucked her arm back into the crook of his elbow. "It's a revered term of endearment. It means *pulse of my heart.*"

Color drained from Maeve's face. *Pulse of my heart.* All this time, Tiernan addressed her with *that* painfully romantic phrase? Her heart slammed hard against her chest and she tried to keep her breathing calm and even, praying to the goddess the necklace she now wore wouldn't set off any alarms about her emotions.

When they reached her quarters, Brynn and Merrick were lounging in the hall. Brynn dropped into a clumsy curtsy, but Merrick's brows shot up in interest before he bowed before her. Then he let out a low, approving whistle.

"My lady," they said in unison, and a distinctive heat bled into Maeve's cheeks.

"Oh, thank the gods!" Deirdre burst out of her room, clutching a handkerchief while she dabbed at her red-rimmed eyes and pink nose. "You're okay! We were so worried. When we found out what she'd done to you, I...I mean my heart...that is to say—"

Deirdre clutched one hand to her chest and her eyes brimmed with fresh tears when she took note of all the tattoos marking Maeve's body. She rushed forward, pulling Maeve into a fierce hug. "Oh, my sweet child."

Another clutch of emotion strangled Maeve, and she tried to keep the burning sensation of tears in check. Blinking them away only forced them to fall. Deirdre pulled back and wiped them away with her thumbs. "You're home now. You're safe here."

Maeve nodded, unable to find her voice.

"Come along, dear." Deirdre gestured to her room. "Everything is ready. I can run you a hot bath if you want one. I've stocked you with leggings, blouses, and corsets. Though you *are* Archfae, which means you will *have* to wear gowns on certain occasions."

She ducked her head. "Of course, Deirdre."

"Is there anything else you require?" she asked.

Maeve met Lir's gaze over the top of Deirdre's silver-streaked bun of hair. "I'll need a sword."

Lir nodded at once. "That can be arranged."

"Go on in, dear heart, and get some rest." Deirdre edged Lir out the door. "Your books are arranged by subject, and Lir will be just outside your room if you need anything at all."

They filed out of her room and Deirdre quietly closed the door behind her.

Her books. The mere thought of them made her smile. She planned on reading every single one, especially the collection of fairytales filled with Aran's paintings and the tome on interpreting Old Laic. She went straight to her bed and slipped her hand under the pillow. Her fingers instantly found her Aurastone. She tossed the pillow aside, hiked up her dress, and her breath caught. There were rose gold swirls all over her. They shifted and moved, shimmered like pink-dusted diamonds along her skin. Her stomach clenched. She hadn't realized how badly Fearghal had ruined her. With her lips pressed together, she looked away, refusing to stare at them any longer. They were a part of her now, a message of her sacrifice, of her endurance, to all who saw her. She was capable of being tortured, of being betrayed, and her loyalty to those who needed it most would not waver.

And now she was alone.

She would finally be granted a moment of peace and quiet. Except, there was a strumming sound coming from somewhere nearby. The double doors to her balcony were open, the sheer curtains fluttering in the breeze, and she thought maybe the music was coming from outside. From somewhere within the city walls of Niahvess. But the sound didn't appear to be carried on the wind. It seemed to float through the walls.

Maeve glanced around the room, and then she saw the door. The one that had always been locked was now cracked open. She tiptoed over, daring herself not to breathe. At first, there was nothing to see. It looked like an ordinary room. There was a bed just like hers, except bigger, and gauzy pieces of turquoise fabric drifted down from its four posters. There was a wardrobe almost identical to the one in her room. But then she saw him.

Astora. She rolled the pet name over in her mind. *Pulse of my heart.*

She blew out a soft breath and listened.

Tiernan was stretched out on a leather sofa, his ankles crossed and kicked up over the edge, with a guitar in his arms. His eyes were closed, his head tilted back against one of the cushions. And his fingers were strumming a melody, one she recognized in her heart. His lips were barely moving, and over the steady beating of her heart, she heard him sing in a low, rumbling baritone with such a tempting accent, that shivers to ran over her skin.

"O'er the mountain and through the mist
Is the wild, the magic, and unseen
And none will 'er be as bright
Nor the sun, nor starlight
As the once now and forever faerie queen."

Maeve stepped fully into the room, and the door groaned open, announcing her arrival. Tiernan didn't even open his eyes. "Hello, Your Highness."

"My lord."

He stood up then, decked in his usual attire of dark pants, a cuffed shirt, and wild dark hair. Painfully as beautiful as ever. He set his guitar on the bed and walked over to her. Each step was measured in time with her heartbeat. When he stopped before her, he shoved his hands into his pockets. "Can I help you, my lady?"

She glanced into the room he was currently inhabiting, then back to hers, before finally meeting his curious gaze. "Your room is next to mine?"

He shrugged. Nonchalant. "It is now."

"For how long?" She wasn't too sure she wanted the High King of Summer to be sleeping in the room connected to hers.

"For as long as it takes."

She had no idea what that meant, but now wasn't the time to ask. There was a more pressing matter on her mind. She lifted her chin and his brow quirked, just barely. "I have something I need to tell you."

He nodded once. "I'm listening."

"I was raised by Carman. The sorceress who brought darkness and death upon Faeven was the same woman who bound my magic with cuffs and locked me in cage." She swallowed, but her throat was too dry. She shoved an errant curl from her face, entirely conscious of the way he was watching her. "I'm sure you were told I killed her."

His face was a mask of hardened stone. "I'm aware."

"But she...before I was able to kill her, she did something."

Clouds formed in Tiernan's eyes, the calm before the storm. "What did she do?"

"She used my blood, she used me, to bring her sons back from the dead." Thunder cracked around them and Maeve jumped. "Balor, Tethra, and Dian...they're alive. She brought them back. *I* brought them back."

He jerked his head. "No. You did not do this. It was against your will. And *no one* will hold you responsible." But there was no mistaking the way his hands flexed, then coiled into fists. He was *furious*. "Where are they now?"

"I don't know. Kells, maybe. Casimir stole me away to Suvarese before they could stop him."

"Stop him?" The question dripped with a tone she didn't recognize. "Why would they stop him?"

"Because I gave them life." She could see it in his eyes, in the clench of his jaw. The way he was struggling to maintain control of his rage while simultaneously attempting to act as though nothing was wrong. "But it doesn't matter."

"How do you figure that?" he ground out.

"Because they answer *to me*."

Tiernan's gaze drifted over her. Up and down. "I see."

"But, um..." Now her confidence was wavering. "It's actually a bit worse than that."

"I'm not sure how much worse it can get, *astora*." He chuckled softly, shaking his head, and her heart skipped a beat at the use of the affectionate name again. "What could possibly be worse than the three Furies coming back from the dead?"

"Parisa." Maeve winced and blew out a short breath. "She told me what she's done, Tiernan. She's raised an entire Dark Court. The Sluagh...it's hers."

He paled. "She what?"

"When I was being tortured, she told me she established a Dark Court. The dark fae answer to her. All of them do. All the creatures of night, the ones we thought no longer existed once they were banished from Faeven." Maeve's voice dropped to a whisper. "All of them."

"Fuck." He raked a hand through his midnight hair and his eyes darkened to such a shade, the sunlight within them nearly blinked out. "There will be another war."

"Yes."

"We must prepare."

"I agree."

"You should get some rest."

Maeve reared back. "Telling me what to do already?"

He smirked. "Only when you let me."

"I don't want to rest."

He swept his arms wide. "Then what do you want?"

Maeve looked down at her hands, where magic flowed freely and fully inside her. "I want to see what I can do."

Tiernan nodded. "Very well. Let's see what we're working with."

His arm shot out and he hauled her against him. She instantly felt the crush of magic, the overwhelming rush of cedarwood and orange blossom as they *faded*, and when she could finally breathe again, she found herself on an empty beach of pale pink sand with Tiernan standing opposite of her. His pants were rolled and he stood barefoot across from her. He removed his shirt, tediously undoing every button before tossing it aside. With his gilded tattoos caressing his skin, he looked to be carved from the sunlight. An eternal Summer King.

"Alright, High Princess." He outstretched his arms and curled his fingers toward her. "Come at me."

Her magic billowed within her and his nostrils flared.

She hesitated. "Do I smell bad?"

He blinked, stumbled back a step, and a strange look reflected in his eyes. "What?"

Humiliation stung her cheeks. "Do I stink?"

Tiernan said nothing, bewildered.

Maeve strode toward him through the sand and jabbed a finger into his chest. "You hesitated. I do smell bad."

"No. You don't smell bad." He caught her wrist before she could poke him again. "Why would you even think such a thing?"

"Because...because Fearghal said I smelled of smoke and death." She let her shoulders rise and fall. "I can't smell it, but it doesn't sound very appealing."

"Maeve." He gingerly placed both of his hands on her shoulders and inhaled deeply. "You smell of tempting cinnamon woods. Of autumn bonfires and toasted vanilla. You smell of life, of fire, and a sweetened smoky scent lingers whenever you leave a room. It's fucking intoxicating."

His hands fell away.

"Oh." An unexpected blush crawled up her neck and spread across her chest. "Okay."

"Good. Now let's get started." He stepped back to put some space between them on the stretch of beach. "So, when the time comes, you'll be prepared."

Maeve nodded sharply, the command in his voice enough to steer her stubbornness back into place.

"Are you ready?" he asked.

She wasn't, but she damn well wasn't going to tell him that. "Yes."

Maeve would fight for Faeven, and she would fight for Autumn. She would kill Parisa, and she would bring Aran back to their Court. She would purge the Scathing, and she would find Saoirse. She would take her crown, and she would take her throne. She was the breath of life. The touch of death. The source of all magic.

I will not yield.

I will not break.

She was the sun. The moon. And the stars.

Never setting. Always rising. Eternal like the night.

The End

PREORDER your copy of Throne of Dreams, book two in the Faeven Saga, now!

For book boxes, merchandise, and signed editions, shop here:

www.hillaryraymer.com

Acknowledgments

I don't even know where to begin...this book is the book of my heart. I've written and rewritten it over the course of ten years. I edited it and changed the plot, and doubted myself every step of the way. I sent it off to agents and got a few full requests, only to have them respond three months later that they weren't interested. I put it away. I told myself I wasn't good enough. I stopped writing fantasy for three years.

I knew more than anything that I *wanted* to write this book. And Maeve was always there, waiting for me to come back. So, I did. Now, here we are.

I'd like to thank my mom for believing in this book even when I didn't. Also, please tell Dad this book is not for him. Seriously. Please don't let him read this. To Lori McCaa, who first read it years ago when it had some other title and was some other version of this story. Thank you both for waiting so long to read the finished product. Thanks to my family for always supporting me on this journey and for your constant belief in me.

Thank you to my wonderful beta readers, and I owe so much to Angie Alicea and Chelsea Scott for not only being awesome beta readers, but for pointing out the nitty gritty details and not being afraid to hurt my feelings. Thank you to Rietta Boksha for helping me to believe in myself, for always listening, and for coming to my rescue in my state of panic during the book cover design process. To Megan Turner, who so graciously brought my characters to life with her art. To Elayna Maratta for designing such an absolutely beautiful map of Faeven. You're going places darling, and I can't wait to watch you bloom. A dozen thank you's to my ARC readers, who hung in there even though I originally sent them the wrong file. To Angie Olberding, Joella Stern, Jenny Schultz, Katie Faffler, Erin Davis, Joelle Asoau, and Lindsay Brodie—your confidence in me and your love carries a special place in my heart.

To Booktok. To Chaos. To the people I've never met in real life who have offered me more support than I ever thought imaginable. And Jennifer Sebring, your love of my story gives me life. Just know that whatever I write, it's always for readers like you.

And to my forever favorite, Nate. I love you a million. Thanks for always keeping me anchored whenever my head was in the clouds. To Lobug and Breezy, mommy loves you to infinity.

And finally, my readers. I owe you the world and then some. Thank you for being my biggest fans.

About the Author

Hillary Raymer is a fantasy romance author. She's a wanderer, a storyteller, and the founder of BohoSoul Press.

Hillary has always been a dreamer, and lucky for her, she turned those dreams into stories. She has an unfinished Bachelor's Degree in English because she ran off and married a Marine halfway through college. She has an affinity toward plants, loves the mountains, and enjoys scoping out metaphysical markets for crystals. Wanderlust comes to her naturally, and she's doing her best to instill the same wild and free values in her daughters. When not writing, Hillary can be found attempting to do yoga, buying more makeup she doesn't need, or discovering small businesses on Etsy.